Out of
HOURS

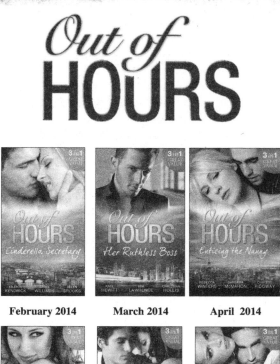

| **February 2014** | **March 2014** | **April 2014** |

| **May 2014** | **June 2014** | **July 2014** |

Out of HOURS

His Feisty Assistant

HEIDI RICE

NATALIE ANDERSON

ANNE OLIVER

MILLS & BOON

Published in Great Britain 2014
by Mills & Boon, an imprint of Harlequin (UK) Limited,
Eton House, 18-24 Paradise Road, Richmond, Surrey, TW9 1SR

OUT OF HOURS…HIS FEISTY ASSISTANT
© 2014 Harlequin Books S.A.

The Tycoon's Very Personal Assistant © 2008 Heidi Rice
Caught on Camera with the CEO © 2010 Natalie Anderson
Her Not-So-Secret Diary © 2011 Anne Oliver

ISBN: 978 0 263 24636 0

027-0514

The Tycoon's Very Personal Assistant

HEIDI RICE

Heidi Rice was born and bred and still lives in London, England. She has two boys who love to bicker, a wonderful husband who, luckily for everyone, has loads of patience, and a supportive and ever-growing British/French/Irish/American family. As much as Heidi adores 'the Big Smoke', she also loves America, and every two years or so she and her best friend leave hubby and kids behind and *Thelma and Louise* it across the States for a couple of weeks (although they always leave out the driving off a cliff bit). She's been a film buff since her early teens, and a romance junkie for almost as long. She indulged her first love by being a film reviewer for ten years. Then she decided to spice up her life by writing romance. Discovering the fantastic sisterhood of romance writers (both published and unpublished) in Britain and America made it a wild and wonderful journey to her first Mills & Boon novel, and she's looking forward to many more to come.

To Chessie Welker, my American dialogue
coach, for telling me that rubbers went out in the
fifties and rich guys don't drink cheap beer!

CHAPTER ONE

'I TOLD YOU I'm not a working girl.' Kate Denton shifted on the stiff leather chair and shot the man sitting on the other side of the mahogany desk her don't-mess-with-me look. Jet-lagged, shaken and as good as naked under the hotel robe she had on, Kate knew the look wasn't one of her best.

He didn't reply. The insistent tap of his pen against the desk blotter seemed deafening in the silence. Bright Vegas sunlight shone through the wall of glass to his right and cast his face into shadow, making it impossible to tell his reaction.

Oh, goody, Kate thought grimly. After the most humiliating experience of my entire life, I get interrogated by a hotel manager with a God complex.

Apprehension slithered around in Kate's stomach like a hyperactive snake. Why on earth had she demanded to see the hotel manager in the first place? It had seemed like a good idea when the concierge had started making noises about calling the police, but once she'd been whisked up to the penthouse suite of offices and ushered in here, she'd started having serious doubts. The guy wasn't behaving like any hotel manager she'd ever met.

She felt more intimidated now than before.

Obviously hotel managers had a much higher profile in the States. This guy's workspace would have made the Oval

Office look tacky. A lake of luxurious blue carpeting flowed to floor-to-ceiling windows, showcasing the hotel's enviable position towering over the Las Vegas Strip. The view wasn't the only thing giving Kate vertigo. The room was so big it accommodated a separate seating area with three deluxe leather sofas, and Kate had recognised the striking canvas on the far wall as that of a modern artist whose work now went for millions. She'd also noticed the guy had not one but three secretaries standing guard outside.

No wonder he had a God complex.

'A working girl? You mean a hooker?' His deep voice rumbled out at last, sending an annoying shiver of awareness up Kate's spine. 'I don't recall saying I thought you were a hooker, honey.'

Kate heard the hint of amusement and her jaw tensed. 'Who gave you permission to call me honey?' she said, grateful for the crisp note of condescension in her voice.

'I don't need permission,' he replied dryly, 'when the lady in question was trying to break down a door in my hotel wearing nothing but a bra and thong.'

Kate swallowed. Okay, there was that.

'It's not a thong. I have proper knickers on,' she blurted out, and then winced.

The memory of getting caught by the bell captain and bundled into a robe flooded back to her. Embarrassment scorched her cheeks. The fact she had something slightly more substantial than a thong covering her bottom suddenly didn't seem all that relevant. That she'd mentioned it to *him* was mortifying. She'd yet to get a proper look at the guy and already he knew far too much about her underwear.

The metronome taps of his pen interrupted her thoughts. 'Proper panties or not, you were causing a disturbance.'

The heat in Kate's cheeks soared. What was this guy's problem? She was the one who'd been manhandled. So she'd raised her voice and kicked the door a little, but wouldn't anyone who got stranded in a hotel corridor practically naked?

'I was trying to get back into the room.'

'Yeah, but it wasn't your room, was it?' He leaned forward, propping his elbows on the desk, and the sunlight illuminated his features at last.

Kate's heart pulsed hard. Hooded green eyes studied her out of a tanned face that was quite simply dazzling in its masculine beauty. Sharp black brows, chiselled cheeks and short dark hair that curled around his ears only added to the firepower. Even with his face carefully devoid of expression, the guy might as well have had a huge neon sign over his head flashing the word 'irresistible' at her.

From the way he was watching her, she wondered if he was waiting for her to swoon. She tightened the tie on the robe, absolutely determined not to start drooling.

Luckily for her, she was currently immune to the alpha male of the species.

'It *was* my room, or at least it was supposed to be,' she said, annoyed by the quake in her voice. She wrapped her arms round her waist, far too aware of the air-conditioned breeze chilling her bare legs.

His gaze swept over her and Kate felt the throb of response. All right, maybe not completely immune.

'You're not registered here.' His emerald eyes shifted back to hers. 'Mr Rocastle, who *is* the registered guest, has made a complaint against you. So, why don't you tell me why I shouldn't just kick you out in your proper panties?'

There it was again, the tell-tale lift in his voice. Kate went rigid. Was he making fun of her?

Andrew Rocastle had duped her, practically assaulted her and then humiliated her into the bargain. And now this guy thought it was funny. When had this become stomp-all-over-Kate day?

'It's not my fault Mr Rocastle didn't put my name on the

registration card when he checked us in this morning. I thought he'd booked us separate rooms,' she ground out, angry all over again at Andrew's underhanded attempt at a seduction. 'And anyway, I don't have to explain myself to you. None of this is any of your business. You're a hotel manager, not my mother.'

Zack Boudreaux's eyebrow winged up. For such a little thing, she sure had a big mouth. He didn't consider himself arrogant, but women were usually a lot nicer to him. He'd certainly never encountered this level of hostility before.

In the normal course of events, he wouldn't even know about this type of minor disturbance, let alone be asked to deal with it. But with The Phoenix's manager on vacation for the day and his deputy on a training programme, the concierge had referred the matter up to Zack's PA. He'd heard the commotion in the outer office and buzzed the woman in out of curiosity. Truth be told, after clearing his calendar for the rest of the week in preparation for his trip to California, he'd found himself with nothing to do for the first time in close to ten years and he was bored.

One thing was for sure, the minute this feisty little firecracker had waltzed into his office wrapped in her bathrobe and a very bad attitude, he hadn't been bored any more.

He knew it was perverse, but for some weird reason he found her sassy comebacks entertaining. Imagining her in the corridor without the bathrobe was doing the rest.

'I don't manage this hotel,' he said. 'I own it, as well as two others in the South West.'

'Bully for you,' she shot back, but the statement lacked impact when he spotted the flicker of panic cross her face.

'And anything that happens in my place is my business.' His gaze remained steady on hers. 'I make a point of it.' He kept his voice firm. He hadn't made a fortune at poker in his youth by showing his cards too early. He didn't want to let her off the hook just yet. She *had* caused a disturbance and he was intrigued enough to want to know why.

'Maybe you could make a point of getting my clothes back for me, then,' she snapped.

Zack's lips twitched as she glared at him. With her blonde hair haloing around her head in haphazard wisps, her full lips puckered in a defiant pout and her round turquoise eyes bright with temper, she looked cute and mad and sexy as hell. Kind of like a pixie with an anger-management problem.

His lips curved before he could stop them.

Her round baby-blues narrowed dangerously. 'Excuse me, but do you think this is funny?' The clear, precise English accent made his pulse spike.

Her voice should have reminded him of weak tea and pompous aristocrats—the two things he'd hated most during the years he'd spent in London as a teenager—but it had a smoky, seductive edge that made him think of rumpled bed sheets and warm fragrant flesh instead.

He cleared his throat, and stifled the grin. 'Funny's not the word I'd use,' he said.

She tugged hard on the lapels of the thick robe, hastily covering the hint of red lace.

His eyes rose as he acknowledged the quick punch of lust. 'Don't worry, you'll get your clothes back,' he said. 'But first I want to know how you and Rocastle are connected and what he did to make you want to cause my hotel criminal damage.'

Kate jerked one stiff shoulder, feeling trapped but trying desperately for nonchalance. 'I'm his PA, or at least I was.' She raised her chin, struggling hard to keep the quiver of nerves out of her voice. 'He wanted to take our association to another level. I didn't. I told him so. End of story,' she said, putting more pomp and circumstance into her accent than a Royal Jubilee.

Maybe if she told this nosy American Adonis that much he'd lose interest and let her leave. The smouldering look he'd given her a moment ago—as if he could see right through the towelling—had not been good for her heart rate. And it wasn't doing a great deal for her peace of mind, either.

How could she possibly find the man attractive? He might look good enough to eat. But, from what she'd seen so far, he was an over-confident, insensitive jerk. Surely she'd dealt with enough of those today to give her indigestion. So he owned the hotel. So what? That hardly gave him the right to have a laugh at her expense.

'I see,' he said in the same wry monotone, as if she were sitting here in her underwear for his personal amusement. 'And you told him this without your clothes on?'

'I was about to take a shower. I didn't know he'd booked us into the same suite.' Tears of frustration stung Kate's eyes, his careless comment bringing the whole sordid experience back in vivid colour. She blinked furiously, determined not to cry.

How could she have been so stupid?

If only she'd figured out Andrew's real reason for employing her sooner she might have been able to salvage a tiny bit of her pride. But she'd been so eager to impress him, to prove she was worthy of the opportunity he was offering her, she'd made a total fool of herself. That she had been idiotic enough to trust Andrew hurt more than anything else, even more than finding herself in the corridor in her bra and knickers when she'd informed Andrew exactly where he could shove his proposition.

She swallowed past the boulder in her throat. 'I still don't see how this is any of your business.' Her fingers clutched the robe, now wrapped so tightly around her she could barely breathe. 'Are you going to press charges or not?'

The two-second wait for his reply felt like two decades. She was sure he knew it.

He dropped his pen on the desk and steepled his fingers. 'I guess not,' he said at last.

Relief coursed through her. 'Thank you,' she said, trying to sound as if she meant it. At least he hadn't made her beg. 'I'll be off, then.' She stood up.

'Hold it, we're not through yet,' he said.

To her dismay, he stood up too and walked round the desk towards her.

Lord, he was tall. Long and lean with a very impressive pair of shoulders filling out his pricey linen shirt. She was a perfectly respectable five feet four herself but had to tilt her head back as he approached. She curled her toes into the soft carpeting and fought the desire to drop into the chair. She wasn't about to give him even more of a height advantage.

'I don't see what else there is to discuss,' she said, despising the tremble in her voice.

'Oh, I don't know,' he said, slowly. 'How about—?' He broke off as the phone rang. 'Stay put,' he said, pointing at her as if she were a trained beagle. He leaned across the desk and grabbed the phone. 'Boudreaux,' he barked into the receiver.

Kate bristled but did as she was told. Infuriatingly enough, it occurred to her she would need Mr Sex God's permission to get back into Andrew's room to get her clothes.

'Uh-huh.' He nodded, obviously engrossed by whatever was being said on the other end of the line. 'Did he say where he was going?' He listened some more, his gaze fixing on her face. His eyes hardened and his beautifully sculpted lips flattened into a thin line. 'What about ID?' he said into the phone, sounding annoyed. He raked his hand through his hair and cursed under his breath. The short dark waves fell back into place perfectly. He must have spent a small fortune on that haircut, Kate thought resentfully.

'Sure. No, don't bother. I'll figure it out.' He slapped the phone back in its cradle, nodded at her chair. 'You better sit down.'

Irritation edged his voice but there was a touch of warmth in those remarkable eyes that hadn't been there before. The knot of anxiety in Kate's stomach tightened. She sat in the chair, heard the leather creak as she pressed her knees together. What now?

Leaning on the corner of the desk, he crossed his long legs at the ankle. He was so close, Kate could smell the intimate scent of soap and man. She concentrated on the perfect crease in his trousers, trying to ignore the way the expensive fabric stretched across powerful thigh muscles.

'Rocastle's checked out,' he said above her.

Kate's chin jerked up. The knowledge she'd never have to see the contemptible worm again had her breath gushing out in an audible puff. Maybe now she could start putting this whole humiliating business behind her. 'If you could give me a key to the room, I'll get dressed and leave, too,' she said.

She'd expected him to look overjoyed at the prospect of her departure. He didn't, he looked pained. 'It's not going to be that easy.' He crossed his arms over his chest, making the rolled up sleeves of his shirt tighten across his biceps. 'He took your luggage.'

'What? *All* of it?'

He rocked back and nodded. 'Everything but your ID.'

'But why?' Kate's mouth hung open.

He uncrossed his arms and braced his hands on the desk behind him, tilting his upper body forwards. 'Rocastle said to tell you you're fired and he's taking your stuff and cashing your ticket home to cover his expenses.'

'But…' Panic clawed up the back of her throat. She gulped it down.

How could Andrew do this? He must know he was leaving her stranded.

'But he can't do that. Those are my things.' Indignation seared her insides, but beneath it was the bitter sting of fear. Surely this couldn't be happening. 'How will I get back to London?'

Zack had expected her to get mad again. In fact he'd been looking forward to seeing her eyes spark with temper. But when he saw confusion and desperation on her face instead, her situation didn't seem all that funny any more. Maybe there was more going on here than a lover's spat.

Her boyfriend or boss or whatever he was sounded like a real piece of work. Maybe the girl was nuttier than a jar of peanut butter, but there was something cold and calculating about the way the guy had cleared out the suite and left his girlfriend in a strange city, in a strange hotel in nothing but her underwear.

She ducked her head and stared down at her lap. Her fingers clutched together, the knuckles whitening as she took an uneven breath. When her head came up, she didn't look mad, she looked devastated. He noticed the rim of purple surrounding the deep blue of her irises. The hint of moisture in her eyes accentuated the unusual colour. She sniffed and straightened in her chair, but no tears fell. He felt an unfamiliar constriction in his chest that he recognised as admiration.

'You want me to call the cops?' he asked, figuring that was the logical next step.

She shook her head, thrust out her pointy little chin. 'Could I ask you a favour?'

His chest loosened. Here it came. She was going to ask him for money. It didn't surprise him. She was in a fix and from her accent and her flaky behaviour so far he figured she must be the rich, pampered daughter of some stuck-up Brit. He doubted she'd ever had to fend for herself in her entire life. Still, he felt oddly disappointed. 'Fire away,' he said.

'Would you give me a job?'

'A job?' Was she serious?

'Yes, I've done some bar-tending and waitressing and I've got lots of experience as a chambermaid.'

'You've scrubbed johns? You're kidding me?' He could see the Queen of England doing it sooner than he could imagine *her* doing it.

'No, I'm not,' she said, sounding affronted.

'Have you got a work visa?' he asked, although he didn't know why. He didn't want her tending bar, or scrubbing johns—it just didn't seem right somehow.

'Yes, I have dual nationality. I was born in New York.'

'Right.' Dumb question. 'Look, we could work something out for you if you want, but you don't need a job. All you need do is get the cops to have a talk with your boyfriend and—'

'He's not my boyfriend,' she interrupted.

'Whatever he is, he can't steal your stuff.'

'I'm not going to go grovelling to the police or anyone else,' she said. 'They're only clothes. As far as I'm concerned Andrew can keep them. And he paid for the plane ticket, so he can keep that too.'

'Aren't you forgetting something?'

Annoyance flashed, but she kept her gaze locked on his. 'What's that?'

'You can't tend bar in your underwear.'

She blinked, then looked away. The slight tremor in her shoulders made his chest constrict again.

He felt as if he'd just kicked a puppy.

Kate twisted her hands in her lap. 'You may have a point there,' she said, trying to sound flippant as she forced her gaze back to his. The fighting spirit seeped out of her, though, as she endured his long, steady stare. Did he still think her situation was funny—or, worse, pathetic?

She couldn't get the police involved. Her pride wouldn't

allow it. She'd rather prance down The Strip stark naked than see Andrew again. But she didn't have more than twenty pounds in her purse. When she'd arrived at work yesterday morning she hadn't expected to be whisked off to Las Vegas on a 'business trip' by her boss. She didn't have a job any more. Her one credit card was maxed out. None of her friends had the sort of money she'd need to get home. And she'd sooner amputate a limb than ask her father for help.

She'd been surviving on her own since she was seventeen years old. Kate squared her shoulders, tried to control the panic making her hands shake. She'd got herself into this predicament. She'd just have to get herself out again.

The knowledge she'd have to throw herself on the mercy of the man in front of her made her stomach hurt. She hated to be indebted to anyone. Especially someone like him. Someone so rich, self-assured and domineering. But her pride had taken so many hits already today, how much damage could one more do?

Kate curled her hands into fists. 'I know it's a bit cheeky, but if I start work tomorrow could you give me an advance on my salary?'

Zack could see the request had cost her. The colour had washed out of her already pale face and she sat so rigidly on the edge of her chair it was a miracle she didn't topple off onto the floor. Even so, the urge to take that defeated look out of her eyes surprised him.

He wasn't the kind of guy who rescued damsels in distress. Especially not damsels in distress with enough attitude to make Joan Rivers look like Snow White.

But try as he might, he couldn't quite shake the desire to help her out.

Maybe it was that combination of guts and vulnerability. Or maybe it was just her honesty. She could have used her looks, could have resorted to the usual feminine wiles, but she hadn't. He had to give her points for that.

'The suite's paid up till the day after tomorrow,' he lied smoothly, knowing Rocastle would have got a refund on the booking. 'I'll get the concierge to let you in and we'll send up some clothes.'

Surprise and relief flittered across her face, but then a wary look came into her eyes. Small white teeth raked over her bottom lip. 'I'm not...' Whatever she was going to say she stopped herself. 'That's very generous of you.' She hesitated again, but only for a moment, before she stood up. 'I'm sorry if I was rude earlier.' She sighed, the little gush of breath making the hairs on the back of his neck stand up. 'It's been a difficult day.'

'No problem.' He shrugged, feeling a slither of guilt for having baited her. 'No harm done.'

She held out her hand. 'My name's Kate, by the way. Kate Denton.'

Kate. Sweet, simple and kind of plain. It didn't suit her one bit he decided as he gripped her fingers.

'Zack Boudreaux. Good to meet you, Kate,' he said, surprised to realise it was true. He felt a slight jolt run through her before she pulled her hand out of his grasp. 'What size are you?' he asked, glancing down at her figure. It was impossible to tell beneath all that terry cloth.

'I'm an American size eight.'

The tint of colour that hit her cheeks amused him. Good to know she wasn't entirely indifferent to him.

'I'll start work first thing tomorrow,' she continued, all businesslike.

He smiled.

'I'll probably be up at the crack of dawn anyway because of the jet lag,' she said, rushing the words.

Yeah, he was definitely making her nervous. The thought

pleased him. 'The personnel manager will be in touch,' he said, with no intention of following through.

No way was he giving her a job. He'd get the concierge to give her a couple hundred bucks, send her up some clothes and organise a plane ticket home. It was the least he could do for the entertainment value.

'Don't forget to take the cost of the clothes out of my salary,' she said over her shoulder as she turned to go. His gaze drifted down her back as she walked to the door. Her bare feet sank into the carpet, making her seem almost childlike. But then he noticed the stiff set of her shoulders and the seductive sway of her hips through the shapeless knee-length garment.

She was quite something, he thought as the door clicked closed behind her. He was going to miss her. Which was dumb, considering he'd only just met her and during that time she hadn't exactly been coming on to him.

He sat at his desk and picked up his pen to begin jotting a 'to-do' list for his trip to California at the end of the week.

Twenty minutes later Zack still sat at the desk, pen in hand, without having put a single solitary item on the list.

'Hell!' He ripped the sheet of paper off the jotter, balled it up and sent it flying into the trash. No wonder he couldn't think—a certain blue-eyed pixie with blonde hair and an attitude problem kept popping into his head.

Why did Kate Denton fascinate him? She was pretty, but she was hardly his type. He liked his women sleek, sophisticated and most of all predictable. On the evidence of their brief encounter, Little Miss Proper Knickers was about as predictable as Lady Luck.

He stood up, dumping the pen on the desk, and rubbed the back of his neck.

Maybe that was it.

Since he'd given up gambling ten years ago, invested all

his time and money into building his hotel empire, the women he'd dated had looked beautiful, behaved impeccably and never once made him work for what he wanted. They'd certainly never talked back to him, challenged him the way Kate Denton had. How many years was it since he'd felt the thrill of the chase?

He'd once thrived on the rush of adrenaline that came with the turn of the cards, and he'd transferred all of that drive, all of that ambition into his quest to change his life—to drag it out of the shadowy world he'd grown up in of gambling dens and back-alley casinos. At thirty-two, after ten long years of hard work, he'd been featured on the cover of *Fortune* magazine, was ranked as one of America's top-ten entrepreneurs by *Newsweek*. He owned a beach house in the Bahamas and a Lear jet. And The Phoenix franchise had evolved from a small casino hotel in Vegas into the most vibrant, sought-after hospitality brand in the South West.

He strolled over to the office's window. Resting his hand on the glass, he looked down. Twenty floors below, the afternoon sunlight laid The Strip bare. Without the cloaking spell of nighttime, the glamour of a million colourful neon lights, the famous street looked jaded, its seedy underbelly plain for everyone to see. This was a town that had been built on the promise of an easy buck, the promise of a quick green-backed fix to life's woes. It was a promise that could destroy lives—it had almost destroyed his—and he'd decided over the last decade that, if he was ever going to truly escape his past, he couldn't be a party to that promise any more. He'd already expanded The Phoenix brand into New Mexico and Arizona with huge success and now, at last, he was ready to sell his flagship hotel and get the hell out of Vegas—and the casino business—for good.

He let his arm drop back to his side. From what Monty, his best friend and business manager, had said in his call from California yesterday, Zack was only a few weeks away from taking that last crucial step into the light. He didn't really need any distractions right now.

But with his dream about to be realised, why did he still feel as jaded as the city he had come to despise?

After his run-in with the feisty, fascinating Kate Denton and her big mouth, it occurred to him that fulfilling his long-term business plans was only going to solve part of the problem. His personal life needed a makeover too. During the last ten years he'd allowed himself to drift through a series of lazy and unfulfilling affairs. What was that old saying about all work and no play? He had a few days off for the first time in, well, for ever. Surely there'd never be a better time to play.

Zack turned to stare at the empty chair opposite his desk. Yeah, Kate Denton would be one heck of a distraction. But she'd also be a challenge. And he always thrived on challenges.

As Zack picked up the phone, he pictured her captivating face, the wild blonde hair, those striking sky-blue eyes, her plump, kissable Cupid's bow mouth, and didn't try to deny the sharp tug of sexual desire.

Volatile or not, she'd be worth the effort, he'd lay odds on it.

As he tapped out the concierge's number Zack let the heady mix of adrenaline and arousal pulse through his veins. Damned if he didn't feel better already. More alive, more excited than he had in years.

They might only have a couple of days to enjoy each other, but he planned to see a whole lot more of Miss Kate Denton and her 'proper knickers'.

CHAPTER TWO

CONTRARY TO POPULAR opinion, Kate didn't believe crying ever made anyone feel better. In her experience, crying made you feel rubbish—and look even worse—and now she had conclusive proof, staring back at her out of the bathroom mirror.

Dabbing at her puffy, red-rimmed eyes with a damp tissue, Kate willed the tears to stop. She'd been at it for over twenty minutes and it was giving her a blistering headache. She wasn't even sure what she was crying about any more.

Yes, Andrew had been a creep, but she should have seen that one coming. She'd convinced herself his interest in her had stemmed from admiration and mutual respect. But she should have known better. Since when did guys admire and respect women like her? Women who had an opinion and voiced it. She should have guessed something was wrong as soon as Andrew said he liked her sassiness. No man ever had before, starting with her father.

Kate watched her brow furrow in the mirror, felt the wave of sadness and inadequacy that always accompanied thoughts of her father.

James Dalton Asquith III had only wanted her mother for one thing—and he'd certainly never wanted a daughter. When he'd been forced to take her in after her mother's death, Kate had tried desperately to please him, to be who he wanted her to be. At seventeen she'd finally accepted the truth—that the fault lay with him, not her—which made it all the more galling that in some small, forgotten corner of her heart his rejection still hurt.

Running away from home all those years ago had been the smartest thing she'd ever done. A liberating experience that had made her realise she didn't need her father's approval, or his charity. She took a slow, calming breath and gave her cheeks one last swipe with a fresh tissue from the vanity unit.

Finally figuring out what a heel Andrew was could well be the next smartest. She breathed out again, glad not to hear a single hitch. She'd cried her last tear over Andrew Rocastle— and her father for that matter.

She screwed the tissue up and shoved it in the pocket of the bathrobe. Flushing the toilet, she walked out into the living area of the suite. Her stomach knotted as she spotted the soft leather sofa where Andrew had been sitting when she'd walked out of the bathroom in her underwear.

Surprise had quickly given way to fury when she'd discovered what Andrew had in mind for their so-called business trip. Didn't she realise where their relationship was leading? he'd said. As if she'd been a party to his ridiculous fantasies. Frankly she'd been more turned on by one look from Zack Boudreaux, the hotel tycoon from planet sexy, than she had by all Andrew's attention in the last few weeks. He'd accused her of sending him mixed messages. Tears of humiliation clogged up her throat as she recalled how he'd shoved her out of the suite while she'd been giving him another message entirely, at top volume.

Kate sniffed the tears back and gave a weary sigh, pushing the aggravating memory to the far reaches of her mind. She had other, more pressing problems to deal with now. She was back at square one, right where she'd been when she'd walked out on her father and his indifference ten years ago—broke and 'scrubbing johns' for a living. Except this time she was doing it thousands of miles from home with a distinct lack of clothing.

She plumped herself down on the sofa.

At least she'd learned something from this situation. Never trust anyone, and don't kid yourself. If something looks too good to be true, it is.

Picking up the TV remote she switched on the huge plasma screen that took up the opposite wall of the suite.

Perma-pressed chat show hosts and adverts for haemorrhoid cream flicked by as she trolled through the channels. Her thumb stopped dead as a raunchy scene in a daytime soap opera flashed onto the screen. A buxom blonde appeared to be Unibonded to a hairless muscle-bound male torso. Kate tilted her head, trying to figure out where the chest ended and the blonde began.

'For Pete's sake, isn't that a bit much for ten in the morning?' she said out loud as the camera lifted and the couple proceeded to suck each other's faces off.

Then the guy came up for air. He droned a series of banal lines but all Kate noticed was the jewel-green tone of his eyes. It reminded her of someone.

She tucked her legs up under her, refusing to acknowledge the tingling sensation between her thighs. Her thumb jerked down on the channel-change button, but not before she'd had the errant thought that Zack Boudreaux's eyes were a much more compelling shade of green and that she'd bet her knickers the hotel tycoon had hair on his chest.

Of course, once she'd conjured up the picture of Boudreaux's naked torso in her mind she couldn't get it out again. No matter how many channels she surfed through.

Eventually she gave up and turned the telly off. Throwing the zapper down on the glass-topped coffee-table, she grasped her ankles and willed herself to calm down. Hadn't she just promised herself she wasn't going to put herself at the mercy of any man again, especially not a man like Zack Boudreaux? The guy had testosterone oozing out of his pores. Not only that, but she'd spent all of twenty minutes in his company and it had taken her about two seconds to realise he was exactly the sort of guy any woman with a single independent thought should stay well away from. A man like him would trample all over you without even realising he was doing it.

Stop thinking about him right this instant, she told herself sharply. Now if she could just get rid of the warm, liquid and completely unprecedented feeling that had settled between her thighs…

Kate's head snapped up at the sharp knock on the door.

'Hi, I'm Michelle.' The pristine young woman standing in the corridor had one of those megawatt sales assistant's smiles pasted on her face. 'I'm from Ella's Boutique downstairs. Mr Boudreaux asked us personally to bring up a selection of clothes for you to look at.'

Kate cursed the guilty flush that spread up her neck at the mention of his name. 'He did?'

'Yeah, he did.' The young woman beamed back and then shuffled into the room wheeling a portable garment rail behind her. A profusion of colours and fabrics hung from it. 'He said for you to pick out as many outfits as you need for your stay with us.'

'Oh.' Kate didn't know what else to say. She'd expected a pair of hotel overalls or something, not a selection of the latest catwalk fashions.

'Would you like me to lay them out for you?'

Kate stared at the rail. 'Um.' She bit her lip. 'No, don't bother.'

Silk dresses vied for position with designer jeans, cashmere sweaters, a Dolce & Gabbana T-shirt. Kate rubbed a satin top between her thumb and forefinger. The cloth was a deep vivid purple, cool and whisper smooth to the touch. Lifting it off the rail, she studied the perfect stitching, the delicately beaded neckline, the way the cloth draped in shimmering waves. She'd never owned a piece of clothing this gorgeous in her life. Or, she imagined, this expensive.

'Why don't they have any price tags?' Kate asked, hooking the purple blouse back onto the rail.

'Oh, well.' The girl's smile faltered as she hesitated. Obviously her customers didn't usually concern themselves with something as mundane as prices. 'You don't need them, ma'am,' she said, brightening again. 'Mr Boudreaux said to charge everything to the hotel.'

Kate gaped at the girl, momentarily struck dumb by Boudreaux's generosity. Then reality intervened. That was ridiculous—he couldn't possibly have intended to give her hundreds of dollars worth of clothing. The boutique staff must have misunderstood. He had probably intended for them to charge the clothes to Kate's hotel room.

'I'd still like to know the prices,' she said, trying not to sound ungracious.

The girl looked confused. 'I guess I could call down to the boutique and get Monica, my supervisor, to itemise them once you've made your selection.'

'All right,' Kate said. Although it wasn't all right. She'd much rather know the prices up front. As beautiful as the clothing was she didn't want to be scrubbing johns in Mr Irresistible's hotel for the rest of her life, which could very well happen if she picked the wrong thing. Most of this stuff would retail in the hundreds, possibly even thousands.

But at the same time Kate didn't want to embarrass herself further by making a big deal of it, and she also didn't want to seem ungrateful. Frankly, she'd been astonished when Boudreaux had offered to help her out in the first place, she didn't want to press her luck.

She opted for the plainest pair of jeans she could find and a simple blue T-shirt with The Phoenix logo on it. At the bottom of the rail was a box with a selection of shoes. Once again, the designs, colours and craftsmanship had her controlling a whimper. She recognised a pair of Fendis and some Manolo Blahniks from the style magazines she loved to paw over at home. She turned to Michelle, who was busy boxing up her selections.

'Do you have any trainers?'

'You don't like the shoes here?' Michelle looked thoroughly crestfallen now.

'Oh, no, it's not that, they're gorgeous. It's just I need something less dressy.'

'Dressy?' The girl glanced at the shoes, her eyebrows lifting. She obviously considered five-hundred-dollar shoes perfectly acceptable for day wear, but to Kate's relief she didn't say it. 'The sportswear store in the hotel forum sells Converse and Nike—is that what you mean?'

'Perfect.' Even with the hotel mark-up, she was sure she could find something for fifty dollars.

The girl's eyes widened, but she nodded. Kate had no doubt at all the shop staff would soon be abuzz with gossip about the dotty English girl in the Sunset Suite with the dress sense of a teenage boy. She forced herself not to care. With the stuff she had she could at least leave the suite—and start work tomorrow—without being indentured for life.

The girl took her shoe size and promised to have a pair sent up to the suite. She wheeled her rail back out the door, but stopped when she got over the threshold. 'Oh, I almost forgot. Mr Boudreaux sent up a package for you.' The girl unclipped a white hotel bag from the end of the rail with an envelope attached to the front. 'I swear, I'd forget my head if it weren't glued to my neck,' she said, giving Kate a nervous smile.

Kate smiled back, or at least she tried to. Why would Boudreaux be sending her packages? Her hand shook ever so slightly as she reached for the bag. 'Thank you.'

'Well…' The girl hesitated. Kate guessed she might be waiting for her to open the package. She wasn't about to oblige. She had no idea what was inside, but the way her luck was going lately she thought it might be bad, like a demand to leave. Maybe he'd changed his mind about helping her out.

'He brought it into the boutique and gave it to me specially,' the girl continued, the awed tone of her voice making it sound as if she thought Boudreaux were the new Messiah.

Kate slung the package under her arm and rubbed her dampening palms on her hotel robe. 'I really appreciate you going to all this trouble. Do tell your supervisor thanks from me, too,' she said, as politely as possible.

Maybe the girl was waiting for a tip? If she was, she was going to be waiting a very long time.

The girl gave a slight hitch of her shoulders. 'No problem, it's all part of the service.' Her eyes flicked to the package one last time. 'Have a nice day.' So saying Michelle took off down the corridor, the clothes-laden rail making a swishing sound on the carpet as she pulled it along behind her.

Kate closed the door and leaned back against it. Why did her knees feel wobbly? She glanced at the flimsy package, which she could have sworn was now throbbing under her arm like a ticking bomb. While she'd been standing in the doorway waiting for the girl to leave it had occurred to her just how dependent she was on Boudreaux's largesse. Sucking in a deep breath, she walked into the room and flung the package on the coffee-table. The white envelope attached to the front had her name written on it in bold black ink. It had to be his handwriting, she thought. The large looping letters and the thick black line slashed under the words seemed to exude confidence, arrogance even—just as he did. She could imagine him writing it with the fountain pen he'd been tapping on his desk, his long tanned fingers moving quickly and efficiently across the paper.

She sighed and sat down. Oh, stop it, you dope. Just open the stupid thing and get it over with. If he'd asked her to leave, she'd leave. He'd honoured the promise about the clothes, which was the main thing. No reason why she couldn't find a job in another hotel now, until she paid him back and earned her airfare home. That the thought of leaving the hotel made her feel a little depressed was simply ridiculous. Why on earth should she care? She wasn't any better off here than she would be anywhere else in Vegas.

She guessed the butterflies jitterbugging in her stomach and the cold fingers of dread flitting up her spine must be the result of exhaustion and her recent emotional trauma, nothing more. She folded her legs and tugged the envelope off the package in one quick, decisive move. Still, as she put her finger into the seam and ripped the envelope open the feeling of dread tightened into an icy fist.

Five crisp new hundred-dollar bills spilled onto her lap. She scooped them up and stared at them. Clutching them in one hand, she unfolded the thick cream paper with the hotel's green and gold letterhead at the top. It took a moment for her eyes to focus on the brief note, scrawled in that same dominant black ink in the middle of the page.

Kate,
Hope you found something to go with those proper knickers.
Meet me for dinner tonight, 8pm in the Rainbow Room.
Z

The signature Z had been slashed across the bottom like the mark of Zorro.

Kate blinked and read the note three more times, but there was still no mention of the five hundred dollars. The feeling of foreboding had gone, but in its place was something much more disturbing. Heat shot into her cheeks and the butterflies in her belly were all burned to a crisp. What was this fixation he seemed to have with her knickers? Why did she find it arousing instead of insulting? And what exactly was the five hundred dollars for?

She didn't want to meet him for dinner tonight. She didn't want to make a fool of herself again, or, worse, come across like someone on the make. But the invitation sounded like an order, and she couldn't afford to annoy him.

She remembered the small package then. The hotel bag had been taped shut. It didn't look as if there was much in it. Undoing the tape she upended the bag and a scrap of lacy crimson satin with a Post-it note stuck to it fell out onto the coffee-table. She picked it up, and pulled the satin thing tight between her fingers.

A thong! Her cheeks blazed and her breath got choppy.

She read the Post-it note: 'These are for you, Kate, in case you want a break from your proper knickers.'

'Why, you cheeky…' Kate was outraged.

But a bubble of something worked its way up her torso. The light and airy feeling fanned out across her chest and a smile she couldn't seem to stop spread across her face.

Then, completely against her will, she began to laugh, for what felt like the first time in a millennium.

CHAPTER THREE

KATE WASN'T LAUGHING when she stepped into the elevator that evening. As the empty car whipped soundlessly up to the nineteenth floor she knew the weightlessness in her stomach had more to do with nerves than gravity.

She studied her reflection in the mirror on the elevator's back wall. At least she didn't look like a vagabond. After a short but fortifying nap, she'd taken one of the hundred-dollar bills Boudreaux had given her and hit The Strip, aware she could hardly wear her Tom Sawyer outfit to the hotel's swankiest restaurant.

She absolutely was not dressing up to impress Boudreaux, but she didn't want to look ridiculous either. Luckily for Kate, she happened to be an expert at styling on a budget. She'd found the vintage blue and gold silk dress in a Salvation Army thrift shop for twenty dollars. It was a little snug around her breasts, showing a bit more cleavage than was probably intended, but otherwise it could have been made for her. The classic hourglass nineteen-fifties styles looked retro, not out of date, she told herself, especially once she added the heeled sandals and clutch purse she'd found on sale at an outlet store on Fremont Street. Kate had never been a shopaholic, she'd never had the finances for it, but she did get a buzz out of co-ordinating the perfect outfit for peanuts. She'd trolled the cosmetics counters at the nearest mall and picked up a sack full of free samples, so even with the headscarf she'd bought to tie up her hair she'd managed to keep her spending under eighty dollars.

Keeping back twenty dollars for emergencies, Kate stuffed the other four hundred dollars Boudreaux had lent her inside her new purse. She pressed it against her belly and peered over her shoulder to get a view of her bum. The tangle of nerves and anticipation eased a little. She looked great. Maybe a bit unusual, but still great. Unfortunately, she didn't feel all that great.

Ever since she'd started getting ready an hour ago, a troop of Morris dancers wearing hobnailed boots had been having a hoedown under her breastbone.

Why did Boudreaux want to have dinner with her?

They hadn't exactly hit it off up to this point. The obvious answer was that he saw in her an opportunity for a quick conquest. While the thong had made her laugh, she knew letting her guard down with Boudreaux could lead to disaster. It wasn't the quick fling he no doubt had in mind that she objected to *per se*. She didn't consider herself a prude. She enjoyed hot, healthy sex as much as the next girl and it was a very long time since she'd had any. Plus, she had a feeling hot, healthy sex would be Boudreaux's forte. But her confidence had taken a huge hit with Andrew and she didn't want to end up feeling used again—however mutual it might be.

She'd worked out her strategy. She would be polite and distant. She must not encourage him. He was a dangerous man, both good-looking and magnetic, and he knew it. From the tone of his note, and the teasing sparkle in his eyes earlier, she suspected he would be well practised at the art of seduction. And, if that wasn't worrying enough, her attraction to him had a heat and intensity she'd never experienced before. She must not rise to the bait, or she could end up getting seriously burned.

The lift doors opened onto a plush lobby area, but Kate barely noticed it, her gaze drawn to the panoramic view of night-time Vegas on the other side of the restaurant. Past the *maître d'*'s lectern and the candlelit tables, a wall of glass showcased The Strip and the darkness of the desert beyond. Boudreaux's hotel wasn't the largest of the huge casino hotels, but it certainly had pole position. Nineteen storeys up, the neon plumage of The Bellagio, The Mirage, Caesars Palace and a host of other famous names lit up the night like a flock of narcissistic peacocks. The city, seen from this lofty angle, glowed with expectant glamour.

Kate drew in a careful breath as she approached the *maître d'* and gave him her name. She was bang on time, but as the waiter led her to a booth at the back of the restaurant she saw Boudreaux had arrived ahead of her. He stood up as she approached, his tall, imposing physique silhouetted against the flickering neon of the cityscape.

He was wearing a conservative, expertly tailored grey suit, one hand tucked into the pocket of his trousers and his white shirt unbuttoned at the neck revealing a few wisps of chest hair. Kate realised he looked relaxed and completely at home in his surroundings. Tall, dark, handsome and devastatingly sexy. As her pulse buzzed in her ears and the Morris dancers went for broke in her stomach she wondered if she had over-estimated her ability to resist the irresistible.

Zack had been sitting at the table for ten minutes, nursing a Scotch and soda and debating whether the thong might have been a tactical error at this stage in the game. He'd bought it on impulse and dashed off the note because the thought of getting Kate all fired up again had amused him. But once he'd been shown to their table, he'd begun to wonder if he might have overplayed his hand.

Did the woman even have a sense of humour?

But as soon as he spotted her walking towards him through the dim lights of the restaurant, Zack found all his misgivings obliterated by an explosive surge of lust.

She looked stunning. The gold threads in her dress caught the candlelight, shimmering over her curves and accentuating the way the material clung to every delicious inch of her. She was taller than he'd first thought, her blonde hair piled up on her head with a flash of blue silk and her smooth bare legs finished off with a pair of glittery gold heels. Whether or not she had a sense of humour, she certainly had a sense of style. The outfit looked like a throwback to the days of Marilyn Monroe, but it worked on her. His eyes drifted down to her cleavage where the pale flesh of her breasts strained against the fabric. His mouth went bone dry.

Marilyn, eat your heart out.

He made a mental note to give the boutique manageress a raise for her inspired product purchasing. Kate gave him a polite smile as the waiter placed the menus on the table and excused himself.

'Hello, Mr Boudreaux,' she said in that snooty, husky voice that made him think of warm flesh and soft sheets. 'I hope I didn't keep you waiting?'

'Call me Zack.' He took the hand she offered. Her fingers trembled and he caught a whiff of the perfume she wore. Sultry but subtle, the provocative scent whispered to him as she let go of his hand. He resisted the urge to bury his face against her neck and breathe it in, but only just. 'You were worth the wait,' he said, letting his gaze wander over her figure. 'That's one hell of a dress.'

'Thank you.' She smoothed her hands over the silk and sat down, the picture of demure, but he caught the spark of mischief in her eyes as they met his. 'Better than a bathrobe, then?'

His lips quirked. So she did have a sense of humour. Damned

if he wasn't going to have fun tonight. 'Depends,' he said, 'on what you've got under it.'

Regrets, he decided, were for wimps.

With his emerald eyes hot on hers and his devastating face relaxed in a challenging grin, Kate felt all her good intentions jump up and shoot straight out of the window. 'Gosh, are we talking about your knicker fetish already?' she said in her haughtiest voice. 'I thought you'd at least let me have a drink first.'

He barked out a laugh, his eyes glittering with appreciation. 'Okay, let's get you a drink.' He snapped his fingers at the waiter. 'But I've got to warn you, this fetish is fast becoming an obsession.'

'Really, Zack?' The corner of her mouth inched up. 'That doesn't sound very healthy.'

The waiter arrived and she ordered herself a glass of Kir, conscious of Zack studying her the whole time. The trickle of awareness became a torrent.

'You're right, it's not healthy,' he said, once the waiter had gone, his voice low and intimate and full of fake concern. 'Maybe I need therapy?'

'Or maybe you should stop sending thongs to women you don't know.'

The glass of cassis-tinted wine arrived and she took a fortifying sip.

'That might work,' he said, the gravity in the words not the least bit convincing. 'Or maybe I should get to know her first.' He reached across the table, stroked his thumb across the back of her hand. 'How does that sound?' The light touch had heat spearing up her arms and across her chest.

Okay, not just practised in the art of seduction, more like world class. And to think she'd thought he was forbidding in his office earlier. He wasn't forbidding, just extremely dangerous. But the perilous urge to play with fire overwhelmed her. Why not? After the day she'd had, a bit of harmless flirtation would do her good.

'As long as you're not talking about getting to know her in the biblical sense—' she took a sip of wine, her mouth suddenly dry '—because that's going to bring us right back to your knicker problem again, isn't it?' she said, her voice tapering off as his eyes flashed hot and a muscle in his jaw tensed.

He arched one black brow, the heat in his gaze undimmed. 'It won't be a problem for long, Kate. I guarantee it.'

Uh-oh, Kate thought as the temperature in the room soared and a blush spread up her chest. This flirtation was nowhere near as harmless as she'd intended. He was looking at her as if he'd stripped her naked already. The fireball of need between her thighs meant he might as well have done. She had to cool things down now, or they'd both go up in smoke. She wasn't playing with fire here. She was playing with an inferno. And she had no idea how to handle it.

Zack knew the instant he'd gone too far. Colour stained her cheeks and her eyes clouded over. He thought it was a shame, but he didn't blame her. He'd never got so hot, so quickly before in his life. Hell, when she'd put her lips on her wine glass, his blood had gone south so fast he got a little light-headed.

She opened the menu, a slight tremor in her hands as she studied the listings in silence. She lifted her head, a nervous smile on her lips. 'Shall we order? I'm really hungry.'

He was hungry too, he thought, hungrier than he'd been in a very long time, and he wasn't thinking about food. But he nodded, picking up his own menu. 'Sounds good to me.'

He allowed her to let the conversation drift to harmless small talk as they ordered.

The quiver in her voice a moment ago had been a big red stop sign. As much as he would have liked to drive right through it and risk the crash, he knew he shouldn't. He'd found out as a young man that patience was more than a virtue. It was a pleasure. It got you what you wanted, but allowed you to savour it first.

He had a feeling that Kate Denton—with her smart mouth, her lush little body and her sassy sense of humour—would be worth savouring.

The food was exquisite, and Kate was starving, but by the time the delicate slice of chocolate pecan torte was placed in front of her she'd barely managed to swallow a bite. She couldn't seem to stop babbling. Maybe it was the intense way he absorbed everything she said. Or the questions he asked, as if he really cared what she had to say.

He knew London well, had lived there for several years in his teens, apparently, and they'd chatted about her home town for most of the meal. It should have been a relaxing, innocuous conversation, but every time she caught his eyes flicking down to her lips, every time she noticed the sexy way his mouth curved when she said something sharp or funny, her blood pressure shot up another notch.

She placed a spoonful of the rich chocolate dessert onto her tongue. It tasted dark, sensual and delicious, despite the jumble of nerves and excitement making whoopee in her tummy.

'How's your pie?' he said, his gaze dropping to her mouth again. Her pulse jumped.

'Fabulous.' She licked her lips, shocked by the reckless thrill when his eyes followed the movement. 'Chocolate should be one of the seven deadly sins, don't you think?'

'I thought it was,' he said, his voice as rich and sinful as the chocolate.

It is now, thought Kate, spooning up another mouthful of chocolate. 'Do you fancy a taste?'

'I thought you'd never ask,' he said, the intensity in his gaze convincing her they weren't talking about her dessert.

She lifted the spoon. Wrapping strong fingers round her hand, he guided it to his lips. As she watched the thick velvety chocolate being devoured the well of desire she'd been holding back geysered up. Her nipples tightened against the smooth silk of her dress and her thighs tensed, unable to hold back the flood of heat. The sensual battle she'd been waging with her body all evening had been well and truly lost.

'Thanks. That was delicious.' He caressed her fingers before releasing her hand. She saw the glow of triumph in his eyes and realised he knew he'd won.

It didn't take him long to claim the spoils.

'Kate,' he said, leaning back against the leather booth, one forearm resting casually on the table. 'You're beautiful, you intrigue me and I'm very attracted to you. I'd like to make love to you tonight. How do you feel about the idea?'

Well, he was certainly direct and to the point, she thought, her breasts throbbing now, her heartbeat pummelling.

She should have said she wasn't attracted to him, that she didn't want to make love. It was sheer madness to encourage something so reckless, so impulsive. But the lie refused to come out of her mouth. It was as if some devastating chemical reaction had taken control of her body and wouldn't let her utter the words.

Maybe it was madness, but it wasn't just that she couldn't say the words—she knew she didn't want to. Zack Boudreaux was every woman's fantasy. And the way he was looking at her right now was giving her heart palpitations. She'd never been this sexually aware of anyone before in her life. This man could make her forget the mess she was in—if only for one night. Didn't she deserve at least one fleeting chance of escape?

Kate concentrated on his face, revelling in the rush of desire as she decided on her reply. 'I feel quite enthusiastic about the idea, actually.'

His eyes widened and she wondered if she'd shocked him

with her forwardness, but then the deep green ignited with passion. He threw his napkin onto the table and stood up. 'We need to go to my penthouse, then' he said, his voice a little hoarse. Towering over her, he took her arm and hauled her out of the booth. 'Before my knicker fetish gets the better of me.'

She laughed, giddy with excitement as he wrapped his arm around her waist and steered her out of the restaurant.

CHAPTER FOUR

KATE WATCHED AS ZACK slid his passkey into the lift panel. Slipping it back into his pocket he turned to her. 'Time to get down to business,' he said.

Kate pressed against the lift wall as he walked towards her. *Okay, woman, you asked for this. Do not pass out.*

He rested one hand against the panelling above her head and leaned over her. He was so close she could see the crinkles at the corner of his eyes, the slight bump marring the perfect line of his nose. The musky scent of him filled her nostrils—a potent mix of soap, aftershave and industrial-strength pheromones.

'What business did you have in mind?' The question came out on a breathy sigh. Goodness, she'd practically melted into a puddle of lust already and he hadn't even touched her.

He cocked his head to one side, his eyes sweeping over her face. She heard the rustle of fabric as he took his other hand out of his trouser pocket. The brush of blunt fingertips on her bare leg made her quiver. 'I'm making it my business to find out what you've got on under that dress.'

She gasped as his fingers stroked under the hem of her dress, bunching the silk as they trailed upwards. 'Do you think that's wise?' she said, although she was already past caring. 'What if someone else gets in the lift?'

'This is my private elevator.' He ducked his head, nuzzled his lips against her ear. 'No one gets in here but me.' He bit into the lobe, sending a riot of chills pulsing across her nerve-endings.

She shivered violently and dropped her purse. She didn't even hear it hit the floor through the throbbing in her ears. Raising her arms, she stretched against him, pressing her breasts into the solid wall of his chest, threading her fingers through the short, silky curls at his nape. She turned her head and his lips were hot on hers. Firm and wet, his tongue thrust deep. She shuddered, tasting chocolate and man and pure, unadulterated lust.

Then his questing fingers found her bare buttock and he stilled. 'Damn!' He pulled back, his breath feathering her cheek. He stroked the naked flesh, and slipped his finger under the satin string. 'You're wearing the thong?'

'In this dress?' The words choked out on a sob. 'Of course I am. I wouldn't want a VPL.'

'A…what?' he rasped as his fingers continued to explore her intimately.

'A visible panty line.' She gasped.

His thumb traced across the core of her and he groaned. 'I'm a dead man.'

She pulled his face back to her, nibbled kisses along his jaw. 'If you die now, Zack, I'm afraid I'll have to kill you.'

He gave a gruff laugh. 'Fair enough,' he murmured, pushing her against the wall, his strong body enveloping her.

Placing hot palms on her bare backside, he lifted her. 'Put your legs round my waist,' he demanded, the teasing gone.

She did as she was told, her centre throbbing at the unyielding pressure straining against his trousers.

She clung on as he walked out of the lift. Strikingly modern, esoteric luxury surrounded her but she saw only glimpses, impressions—all her thoughts and feelings concentrated on the heat and hardness between them—until she caught their reflection in the hall mirror. She was wrapped around him like a wanton, her dress hiked up to her waist, his large hands dark against the pale skin of her bum.

She watched her skin flush red, before he strode into the bedroom. A huge bed dominated the sparsely furnished space, long drapes on the far end of the room were drawn back revealing the same romantic view of Vegas at night. His breathing was harsh against her hair, her body so hot she could barely breathe.

He let her down, slowly. The soft swish of their clothing as their bodies brushed sounded like a force ten gale. The thick wool carpet tickled Kate's bare feet. She must have lost her sandals in the lift.

Putting firm hands on her shoulder, he turned her away from him and stood behind her. She heard the sibilant hiss of her zipper and then his teeth nipped the bare skin of her shoulder. He dragged the dress off with impatient hands, then unclipped her bra. Her breasts swelled as he released them from their lacy confinement.

She looked up, pulled in a jerky breath. The sight of the two of them reflected against the night was unbearably erotic. She, naked and trembling but for the wisp of red satin underwear defining her sex. He, tall and dark and dominant behind her, still fully dressed. His hands cupped her breasts, the rough skin of his thumbs stroking across the stiff, sensitive peaks. Then he captured the nipples in his fingers, tugged. She moaned, her legs shaking as the bolt of heat rocketed down to her core.

Their eyes met in the glass.

'You're exquisite,' he murmured.

She felt exquisite, she realised, for the first time in her life.

She turned, desperate to see him, to feel him too. She pushed at his jacket, her hands clumsy in her haste.

'Hold on. I've got it.' He stepped back, shrugged off the jacket and pulled the shirt over his head, buttons popping.

Her eyes devoured his firm, muscled chest. A sprinkle of dark hair thinned over a taut mouth-watering six-pack and arrowed down to his groin. 'You're not bad yourself,' she whispered.

His trousers did nothing to hide the strength of his arousal.

'I want you inside me,' she whispered.

Good Lord, had she just said that out loud? The blush burned into her cheeks.

He wrapped one arm around her, bringing her flush against him. Strong fingers ploughed through her hair, making the swatch of blue silk flutter to the floor and her curls cascade down. 'I intend to be—and soon,' he said, before his mouth covered hers in another bone-melting kiss.

His chest hair abraded her nipples while his tongue did devilish things inside her mouth. She writhed against the storm of sensations. Trailing unsteady fingers down the smooth, firm skin of his abdomen, she cupped him at last. The heat and length of him pulsed against her palm through the fabric. He groaned and shifted away. 'Let's get into bed before I embarrass myself.'

As he stepped out of his trousers and boxer shorts her eyes devoured the magnificent erection. Her gaze lifted back to his face. 'I hope your condoms are extra large,' she said, only half joking.

He laughed, pulled her against him and tumbled them both onto the bed. 'Don't worry,' he whispered next to her ear, one powerful leg pinning her to the bed. 'I'm practically a boy scout.' His teeth tugged on the lobe. 'I'm always prepared.'

He fastened his lips on hers, his tongue insistent, tangling deliciously with hers as his hand swept down her curves, kneading her breasts, caressing her hip. He moved away for a moment to pull the thong down her legs. As his lips came back to hers insistent fingers slipped into the swollen folds at her core.

She shuddered viciously as he probed, pushing his finger into the liquid heat. His thumb circled the burning nub of her clitoris and then stroked hard. She jerked and cried out, flooding into his hand.

'That was amazing,' he said, his voice thick with urgency. 'You're amazing.' He leaned over her, fumbled in the bedside drawer and held up the foil package. 'You want to do the honours?'

She took the condom from him with trembling fingers. 'It would be my pleasure.' She rolled the latex down the length of him, his penis twitching at her touch.

The intimacy of the gesture and the feel of him, so smooth, so strong, made the heat build again. She'd never felt so aroused, so desirable or so bold before in her life.

He cupped her face in his palms, his sensual smile as devastating as the fire in his eyes. 'Thanks,' he muttered and nudged her legs apart with his knee.

'You're welcome,' she said on a shaky sigh.

His hands held her hips, angling her pelvis and forcing her thighs wider still.

The head of his penis probed gently and then in one long, slow thrust he lodged inside her. She moaned, the fullness bringing a surge of pleasure so overwhelming it was almost pain.

He began to move, the sure solid thrusts taking him even deeper.

She sobbed, gasped, unable to control the waves of ecstasy crashing over her as he touched a place inside she had never known existed.

He stopped. 'Are you okay?' he asked, his voice strained but tender, his whole body shaking with the effort to hold back.

'Yes, it's just it feels so incredible.' She choked the words out. She'd never climaxed so quickly before or with such intensity.

'You're telling me.' He groaned. 'Hang on,' he said. 'It's about to get better.'

She didn't believe that could be true, but as he began to

move in an exquisite, unstoppable rhythm she realised she was wrong. The orgasm gripped her in a fevered fist and hurled her over the edge, only to pull her up and hurl her again.

He stiffened above her and shouted out her name as the final shuddering wave seized her and flung her over into the abyss.

'Kate, are you all right?' Zack's heart stuttered as he watched her eyelids flutter open.

Thank God—he'd thought she'd passed out there for a minute. Hell, he'd almost passed out himself. He'd never felt anything so incredible. He rested his palm against the damp skin of her cheek. 'I'm sorry,' he said, brushing his thumb across the crest of her cheekbone.

He ought to be, he thought, he'd just taken her like a man possessed.

Her small hand came up and covered his. The sweet smile that curled her lips made his heart rate slow. 'What are you apologising for, you dope?'

He rested his forehead against hers. 'That was kind of fast and furious.' He lifted his head, looked down at her. He'd never taken a woman with so little sophistication before in his life, even as a teenager. It was embarrassing. 'You didn't get much in the way of foreplay.'

She pressed a fingertip against his lips, silencing him. 'Well, now, Boudreaux.' Her eyes twinkled and her smile became more than a little smug. 'I like foreplay as much as the next girl. But a guy should never have to apologise for giving a woman her first multiple orgasm.'

He laughed, relief washing over him. 'How many did you have?'

'Honestly?'

He nodded, the surge of pride surprising him.

'I lost count.' She sat up suddenly, holding the sheet to her breasts as she beamed down at him. 'Zack, I think you found my G-spot.' Her voice bubbled with excitement. 'And to think, I always thought that was an urban myth.'

'You did, huh?' He slipped a hand under the sheet, found the soft swell of her butt. 'Well, I nearly blacked out, and that's a first for me, so I guess we're even.'

'No, we're not.' She laughed. 'I'm pretty sure I *did* black out.' She pursed her lips and held her finger against them in a deliberately comical pout. 'Oh, dear, does that mean I owe you one?'

'You know what,' he said, incredulous at the renewed rush of blood to his groin. 'Seeing as you lost count, I figure you owe me more than one.' He whipped the sheet out of her hand, grabbed her wrist and hauled her out of the bed with him. 'And I know a great way to make you pay up,' he said, dragging her giggling and squirming towards the bathroom.

Forget the thrill of the chase, he thought, the thrill of the catch was going to be a whole lot better.

CHAPTER FIVE

'YOU'RE AN EARLY RISER. I guess I didn't tire you out enough last night.'

Kate's fingers slipped on the package of Pop Tarts at the sound of the deep, sleep-roughened voice. She turned slowly to see the man she'd had the wildest night of her life with leaning against the kitchen doorway, a cocky smile on his face. He'd pulled on a pair of sweatpants, but otherwise he was gloriously naked. All tanned, leanly muscled male rumpled from the bedroom, his short hair sticking up in sexy tufts.

Her mouth watered and her stomach clenched at one and the same time.

Kate was no expert in morning-after etiquette. Contrary to her wanton behaviour all through the night, she'd never slept with a guy on a first date. Until now. What exactly did you say to a man who'd brought you to unspeakable pleasure too many times to count but whom you hardly knew? She had no idea.

'It's the jet lag,' she said, brandishing the box of breakfast treats. 'I found these in your cupboard. How do you feel about coffee and a sugar rush for breakfast?'

He yawned and stretched long arms above his head, arching his back. The play of muscles across his torso drew Kate's eyes. His arms dropped to his side. The bottom dropped out of Kate's stomach.

'Those are Joey's.' He nodded at the package as he scraped his fingers through his hair bringing his hand to rest briefly on the back of his neck. 'He'll be mad if we finish them.' He walked towards her, his bare feet padding against the smooth granite tiles of the cavernous and luxuriously appointed kitchen. He smiled, a dimple appearing that Kate hadn't noticed yesterday.

The cold marble work surface pressed into the small of her back as he stopped a few inches from her. His big body radiated heat. He lifted the Pop Tarts out of her hand and leaned across her to put them down on the surface. 'Anyway,' he said, his hands resting on her hips. 'I'm sure we can do better than that.' He pulled her against him, his thumbs stroking the silk of her dress. The light caress sizzled through her, making her toes curl.

'I could cook, or we could call room service,' he murmured, dipping his head to lick the pulse point in her neck. The sizzle flared into her breasts and her nipples hardened. 'They do great maple pecan waffles, if you're in the mood for something sweet.' He wiggled his brows at her lasciviously. 'I sure am.'

She took several shallow breaths, placed her hands on his chest and eased him back, her brain engaging for the first time since she'd spotted him in the doorway. 'Who's Joey?'

Did he have a son? Goodness, he might even have a wife? She'd seen no trace of a woman's presence when she'd done a little tour of the penthouse after waking up, but, still, he could be married. It horrified her to realise she didn't know for sure.

He straightened and let her go, studying her face. 'Don't look so scared.' He rested his butt against the kitchen's central aisle, folded his arms across his chest. 'Joey's my five-year-old godson. He sleeps over sometimes when Stella and Monty, his mom and dad, need a babysitter. Who did you think he was?'

'I just wondered,' she said, looking down at her toes, faint with relief. She forced a smile. 'You don't strike me as the babysitting type.'

'There's not a lot of babysitting involved.' He smiled, the dimple winking at her again. How *had* she missed that yesterday? 'I'm a total pushover. Joey calls all the shots. Hence the Pop Tarts. If Stella knew about those we'd both be toast. She's like the sugar police.' As he spoke his face softened and his voice deepened with affection. He obviously adored the little boy and his parents.

This was a facet of him Kate never would have imagined. It made him seem almost as sweet as the Pop Tarts all of a sudden. Why the discovery should make her stomach tighten and her breathing become even more rapid she couldn't guess.

'So how about I order waffles?' He arched an eyebrow, looking more dangerous than sweet. 'We can get to the deadly sins we missed last night while we wait.'

She laughed, feeling pretty dangerous herself. 'Did we miss any?'

He stepped back to her, his enticing male scent enveloping her as he brushed a knuckle across her cheek. 'I bet I can find a few.'

'Hmm.' She considered him, holding her tongue between her teeth. 'I'd love to take that bet,' she said.

His hand dropped from her face as he grinned. He looked so delicious, it was almost indecent how much she wanted to take him up on his offer. Disappointment covered the fire in her belly like a wet blanket. 'But unfortunately, I've only got fifteen minutes before I have to meet with your housekeeping manager, Mrs Oakley.'

To think she was going to be making beds all morning when she could have been tearing up the sheets with Zack Boudreaux. She'd had her one night of bliss, and now reality was back with a vengeance.

A line formed across his brow. 'Why are you meeting Pat?'

'I think it's just a formality.' She shrugged, turned to pour herself a cup of coffee. Looking at his bare chest was only adding to her misery. 'I filled out the forms yesterday afternoon.' She put the pot down, recalling the brief phone conversation she'd had with Patricia Oakley and the reams of paperwork that had been sent to her suite.

'What forms?'

She pulled a cup out of the cabinet, placed it on the surface with a sharp click. 'I couldn't find any milk—will black do?'

'I said, what forms?'

She looked at him over her shoulder, her eyes widening at his flat tone.

She turned round. 'The employment forms, all two thousand of them.' Cradling the mug of coffee in both hands, she blew on it, inhaled the delicious coffee scent. 'Mrs Oakley's going to sort out my social security number for me. It's a good thing Andrew didn't take my American passport with him. Or I really would have been up the creek.' She took a quick sip. It might smell like coffee, but it tasted like water. She wrinkled her nose. 'No offence,' she said lightly, 'but American coffee is disgusting.'

'Why were you filling out employment forms for Pat?'

She frowned. Why was he behaving as if she were talking in a foreign language?

'Because I'm going to work here—why else?' She narrowly avoided adding a *Duh!* It didn't seem appropriate any more. The teasing mood of a moment before had disappeared.

His brows drew together in a forbidding line.

'We talked about it, yesterday in your office, remember?' Kate prompted. 'You said you were going to ring her about it.'

'Yeah, but I didn't call her.'

'I know you didn't,' Kate said, shifting uncomfortably against the hard marble.

She'd felt pretty foolish the day before when she'd mentioned his name to the housekeeping manager. He owned the hotel, for goodness' sake, of course he didn't concern himself with trifles. Still, she'd been oddly hurt when Mrs Oakley had told her she hadn't been contacted by Mr Boudreaux, especially after getting his dinner invitation.

'It's all right,' she said with a brightness she didn't quite feel. 'I sorted it out myself. Turns out two of the maids quit last week so Mrs Oakley was more than happy when I—'

'You're not working here.' He interrupted her.

'I..? Excuse me?' Had she heard him correctly? She couldn't have.

'Kate…' his voice softened a little '…I've got a strict rule against sleeping with women who work for me.'

'Oh.' The flush working its way up her neck made her feel foolish and more than a little hurt. She hadn't realised how much she'd been looking forward to continuing their fling. She blinked, determined not to let her sadness at the dismissal show. Of course he'd only been looking for a one-night deal. So had she. When had she started thinking it could be anything else?

'I understand,' she said, concentrating on a space above his shoulder. She noticed the clock on the wall behind him and saw her get-out clause. She needed to leave before she embarrassed herself any further. 'Well, it's been fun, Zack,' she said, putting her mug down on the counter. 'But I really should be going. Mrs Oakley will be waiting.' She gave him what she hoped was an unconcerned smile. 'I don't want to be late my first day on the job.'

She went to walk past him, but his fingers closed over her arm, stopping her dead.

'You're not listening to me, Kate. You're not working here.'

She gawped at him. 'Yes, I am,' she said carefully. What was he on about?

'No, you're not,' he said, the definite edge to his voice start-ing to worry her. 'You don't have to now.'

'Of course, I do. I need the money.'

His jaw went rigid. 'I gave you five hundred dollars. If that's not enough, say so.'

'Don't be ridiculous.' She crossed her arms over her chest, trying to hold back her own temper. 'I don't want you to give me any more money. The more I take, the more I'll have to pay back.' Why was he being deliberately dense? 'I left four of the hundreds you gave me in the living room, by the way. Mrs Oakley was nice enough to say she'd sort out a proper advance in a couple of days. When I—'

'What are you talking about?'

She stiffened. Why was he so irritated?

He twisted away, shoving his fingers through his hair and combing it into unruly furrows. Frustration snapped in the air around him before he gave a long-suffering sigh and turned back. 'You say you need money.' He said the words slowly, surely, as if he were talking to a dim-witted child. 'I gave you money. Why are you giving it back to me?'

'Because it's not *my* money,' she shot back, annoyed at having to state the obvious. 'It's yours.'

'So what? It's only five hundred bucks. I don't want it back.'

'But I thought that was the advance we'd talked about.'

'What advance?' he said, holding his palms up in exaspera-tion before slapping them down on the sideboard.

Realisation suddenly dawned on Kate. With it came the grinding feeling of helplessness, of inadequacy, she'd fought throughout her childhood.

'Wait a minute,' she said, carefully. 'You mean you *gave* me five hundred dollars. Why would you do that?'

She'd thought the money was an advance, but if it wasn't…? The events of the previous night came reeling back to her. Without the glow of sexual excitement, the romance of the moment, what she'd done took on a whole different hue.

She pressed her thighs together, felt the lingering tenderness and was suddenly ashamed of all the times he'd been buried deep inside her.

What had he been thinking when she'd flirted with him, when she'd thrown herself at him, when she'd come apart in his arms? She covered her mouth, scared she might throw up.

'I've got to go,' she blurted out, desperate to get away.

Zack couldn't believe his eyes as the colour drained out of her face and she turned and ran out of the room. 'What the…?'

It took him a minute, but he caught up with her in the hallway, snagged her arm. 'What's wrong with you?'

She shot him a disdainful look, but he could feel her shaking. Something had really upset her, but what?

'I thought I told you yesterday,' she said, the tears hovering on her lids. 'I'm not a prostitute.'

'What? Who said you were a prostitute?'

'You don't give someone five hundred dollars for nothing.'

So that was it. They were back to the money again. Damn, the woman had more issues than a daytime chat show. 'You were in a fix. I helped you out. It's not that big a deal.'

'It is to me.' He could see by the stubborn tilt of her chin she wasn't kidding.

She tried to wrestle her arm free. He held firm. No way was she skipping out on him until they got this settled.

'Will you let go of my arm?'

He softened his grip, but kept her in place. 'Not until you tell me what the problem is.'

'It's simple. I don't accept money from men I don't know.'

'First off,' he said, pulling her closer, 'you do know me. After what we did last night you know me pretty damn well.' He felt a stab of satisfaction when she blushed a vivid red.

'Second off, the five hundred wasn't payment for sexual favours.' Now he thought about it, he was pretty damned insulted himself. 'I've never paid for sex and I never will.'

The blush intensified, but her arm relaxed. 'Okay.' Her breath gushed out and the rigid line of her shoulders softened. 'I'm sorry I accused you of that. It's just… It looked… I don't know—it looked funny.'

'It was a gift between friends.'

She nodded. 'All right, but I still can't accept it.'

Now she was just being stubborn. 'Why not?'

'Because I can't,' she said, her voice rising to match his.

Her lips puckered up into the defiant pout he'd admired the day before. He wasn't admiring it so much any more.

'Look, calm down, okay?' He ran his palm down her bare arm, struggling to soothe while his own emotions were in turmoil. He could see the hot flash of temper in her eyes, but beneath it was something else that looked suspiciously like hurt. It bothered him he might have caused it.

He tried to figure out where he'd gone wrong. How things had got messed up so fast.

Everything had been great when he'd woken up, his body still humming from one incredible night of mind-blowing sex. He'd spent the next ten minutes lying in bed, the hazy dawn sunlight streaming over him while he'd breathed in the lingering scent of Kate's perfume overlaid with the smell of freshly percolating coffee and enjoyed some inventive fantasies about what they could do for the rest of the day.

When he'd found Kate in the kitchen, clutching Joey's Pop Tarts, the soft blonde hair he now knew was natural still damp from her shower and that sexy dress stretched across her lush rear end, he'd figured it wouldn't take him long to start making his fantasies reality. The next few days had spread out before him like a smorgasbord of sexual pleasures and he'd had every intention of digging in.

Then she'd started babbling on about Pat and employment paperwork and money and everything had gone to hell in a handbasket. Well, she could forget about working here. He didn't want her working for him, he wanted her with him—in bed as well as out—for the next couple of days, but he could see he was going to have to change tactics to get what he wanted.

'Kate, this is dumb.' He forced reason and logic into his voice. 'We hit it off last night. I've got a couple of days before I have to head out to California.' He stroked his thumb across the inside of her elbow, encouraged by her shiver of response. 'We could have a lot of fun in that time.' She didn't say anything so he pressed on. Surely she could see this was the smart option. 'You can stay here as my guest and then I'll buy you a ticket home to London when I leave. How does that sound?'

Kate didn't think she'd ever been more humiliated in her whole life. This was worse than being turfed out into a hotel corridor in her underwear. She stepped away from Zack, humiliated all over again by the terrible yearning that seized her. That her body was clamouring for her to say yes to his insulting proposal only made the situation that much more unbearable.

'I pay my own way. I always have and I always will.' She tightened her arms across her breasts, willing herself to stop trembling. 'And I'm very sorry, but, as much *fun* as we had last night, I'm not prepared to be your paid plaything for the next few days.'

He cursed softly. 'That's not what I meant and you know it.'

'Mrs Oakley's offered me a job here and I'm taking it,' she continued, grateful when he made no move to touch her. 'If you don't want me working in your hotel you can have me fired, that's certainly your prerogative.' She prayed he wouldn't do that, but she wasn't about to beg. 'But you don't have to worry about sleeping with the staff, because we're not sleeping together any more. How does that sound?'

He swore again, his big body rigid, his hands fisted by his sides. The frustration was coming off him in waves but he didn't say a word.

She walked down the hallway to the elevator with as much dignity as she could muster and stabbed the call button.

'Have it your way, sweetheart,' he said, his voice brittle, before she heard the door slam shut behind her.

Her shoulders slumped in a cruel mixture of relief and regret. The lift pinged its arrival, the sound reverberating round the empty lobby like a mission bell.

As Kate stepped into the private car she spotted her gold sandals where they had fallen the evening before. The lurid memory of being wrapped around Zack, her body quivering with anticipation, made her tense as she bent to pick up the shoes.

The lone teardrop glittered as it splashed onto the golden leather.

CHAPTER SIX

'YOU'VE GOT TO BE KIDDING me.' Zack scrubbed his hands over his face, feeling weary. 'She was coming to California with me. How am I going to get another PA so soon?' And how could a day that had dawned with such promise have turned into this nightmare?

'Seems Jill didn't take too kindly to your attitude this afternoon. She said you shouted at her,' Monty said from the other side of the booth. His friendly cockney accent rubbed Zack's last nerve raw.

'I did not shout at her,' Zack said firmly, pretty sure he hadn't. He could barely remember the incident with his PA. He'd been fixated on a certain blue-eyed temptress most of the day. 'She did a half-baked job on the report I asked for on The Grange's customer profile. All I did was point it out.'

'Yeah, well, maybe next time you could point it out with a few less decibels,' Monty replied amiably, lifting the bottle of beer to his lips.

Zack watched his business manager. 'Fine.' He took a swallow of his own beer, let the chilled amber liquid ease down his throat and forced his shoulders to relax. 'Point taken.'

Jill Hawthorne's resignation wasn't worth getting worked up about. He expected one hundred and ten per cent from his staff and paid them the salaries to match. Jill hadn't been up to the job since the day he'd hired her. It was just bad timing she'd picked today to walk off in a snit. He could have done without the aggravation.

Monty straightened in his chair and leaned forward, resting his forearms on the table. 'What were you doing in the office anyhow? I thought you were taking a couple of days off before you headed out to Cally?'

That had been the original plan, thought Zack, aggravated all over again. Until a certain Kate Denton had walked out on him bright and early this morning. After that, he hadn't been in the mood to hang out in his penthouse. Every place he looked brought back memories of her lush, sexy body and the incredible things they'd been doing to each other most of the night.

'Plans change,' he said dismissively. He wasn't about to get into a blow by blow of what an idiot he'd been with Monty. He still wasn't sure how he'd let Kate get under his skin the way she had. 'I should let you get home to Stella,' he added reluctantly, mentioning Monty's wife. 'She'll give me the look next time I see her if I keep you out drinking on your first night back.'

Monty had returned to Vegas late that afternoon after a week of meetings with Harold Westchester, the owner of the hotel Zack was buying out in California. It had been Zack's idea to meet up in the loud, lively and informal surroundings of the Sports Bar. He and Monty had spent the last half an hour going over the details of the negotiations together before Monty had dropped his bombshell about Zack's PA.

'No worries,' said Monty. 'Stel understands you wanted the low-down on how things went with Westchester.'

Truth be told, the meeting could have waited till tomorrow, but Zack hadn't been in any great hurry to go back to his bed alone tonight. And Monty was always good company. They'd been best buddies ever since their early teens, when Monty had tried to pull a short con on Zack one rainy afternoon on London's Oxford Street.

'I guess we've covered everything for today,' Zack said. 'Why don't you go on home? Tell Stella I said hi,' he finished, not quite sure where the ripple of envy came from as he said it. Sure, Monty had a beautiful wife in Stella and a real little pistol of a kid in Joey, but that kind of wedded bliss had never been what Zack was looking for in life.

'I'm good for another round, yet,' Monty said, glancing at his watch. 'Look, Zack, there is one other thing I wanted to sound you out on with The Grange buyout.'

'What?' Zack asked.

'Why don't you tell Westchester who you really are?'

Zack slapped his beer bottle back on the table with more force than was strictly necessary. 'I told you before. No way.'

'We could get a better deal out of him. I'm sure of it.'

'Don't count on it.' Zack had been after The Grange for two solid years—the fact that Westchester had no knowledge about their prior connection had been paramount to the old guy agreeing to the deal in the first place, Zack was sure of it. 'Westchester and my old man didn't exactly hit it off together. I'm not risking the deal on—'

'How do you know he blames you for what JP did?' Monty butted in.

'Drop it, Mont.' Just thinking about telling Westchester made Zack feel edgy.

'Fine, I tried.' Monty threw up his hands. 'It's your choice.'

'That's right. It is. Now, do you want another beer or not?'

'Just one. Then I better shoot off.'

Zack picked up a handful of mini-pretzels from the bowl of bar snacks, glad to have at least one thing settled. He turned to signal their waitress when something caught his eye across the darkened bar. He stared in the half-light.

Another waitress was dishing out drinks to a group of guys over by the pool tables, her blonde hair shone white in the harsh neon light. He squinted, trying to focus. It couldn't be, could it?

She walked back towards the wait-station, her empty tray dangling from one hand. Her voluptuous figure looked ready to spill right out of the uniform all the female bar staff wore.

'I don't believe it,' he murmured.

He'd recognise the soft, seductive sway of those hips anywhere.

Kate was floating. At least, that was what she tried to tell herself as she pushed through the crowd of people at the bar, her head throbbing in time to the electric guitar whining from the sound system and her heels and toes burning in the shoes she'd borrowed for the evening. She'd gone past exhausted about an hour ago, entering an alternative reality where her many aches and pains were buffered by a sea of numbness—sort of.

She dumped her tray on the wait-station and shouted out her latest order to Matt, the barman. Matt waved, not even attempting to be heard above the din, and went off to fill it.

Pushing an annoying tendril of hair behind her ear, Kate swayed slightly. She gripped the bar, steadied herself, forcing her knees to lock, and took another glimpse at the clock above the bar. The stupid thing had to be broken—the hands had barely moved since the last time she looked. Still over an hour to go till her shift ended.

She groaned, the next couple of weeks spreading out before her in a never-ending kaleidoscope of spilled drinks, over-eager hands, dirty toilets and unmade beds.

Kate forced back the depression settling over her like an impenetrable fog. It could only be tiredness. So the next few weeks were going to be murder while she held down the two jobs she'd talked her way into. She'd worked this hard before. When she'd been seventeen, and newly free of her father's influence, she'd held down three jobs to keep afloat. She could do it again. All she needed was a decent night's sleep.

Thanks to the night flight two days ago, the bedroom Olympics she'd indulged in with the very creative Zack Boudreaux last night, a day spent changing sheets and cleaning toilets and the last four hours spent tottering around on heels that were two sizes too small, Kate reckoned she'd managed about four hours sleep in the last forty-eight.

She glared at the clock again, willing the hands to move faster.

Extreme fatigue was the only reason the picture of Zack and his insatiable body kept popping back into her brain. She didn't regret her decision to turn down his insulting offer one bit. She would never be any man's kept woman, no matter how gorgeous he looked or how fantastic he might be in bed. Her mother had done that and look what had happened to her.

She let go of the bar. When she stayed upright, she pulled a long fortifying breath into her lungs. Only an hour to go, then she could collapse into bed. She vowed she wouldn't so much as twitch her little finger until ten minutes before her housekeeping shift started at six tomorrow morning.

'Katie, Katie.' Marcy, Kate's fellow waitress, elbowed her way towards Kate on ice-pick heels, her chocolate-brown eyes beaming. How *did* she walk in those shoes, Kate wondered, without dislodging a kidney?

'Honey, you hit the jackpot.' Marcy slapped her tray down on the bar and snapped the gum she was chewing.

'Oh really?' Kate said, trying to muster some enthusiasm. She liked Marcy. She was so perky she made Mary Poppins look like a killjoy. But right at the moment Kate could barely string a coherent sentence together, let alone have a conversation with someone as full-on as Marcy.

'Oh, yes, really,' Marcy said, mimicking Kate's accent, her smile so bright it was practically radioactive. 'You'll never guess who's in my Number Four booth and just asked to have you serve him his next beer?'

'Who?' Kate asked, sure she didn't want to know unless the guy was Rip Van Winkle.

'Give me a minute.' Marcy winked and shouted out an order to Matt for two bottles of premium beer. She turned back to Kate, her face still beaming excitement. 'Only the big boss man.' Marcy pointed out one of the booths near the entrance. 'He's over there with Monty Robertson, his business manager.' Marcy touched Kate's arm. 'Mr Zack "Gorgeous Butt" Boudreaux, no less.'

At the mention of his name, Kate felt the headache gnawing at her temples roar into life. Then her stomach rolled over, the burn in her feet flared up and the dull ache in her back shot straight up her spine. So much for numbness.

'Honey, he's taken a real shine to you. He asked for you special.' Marcy nudged her, still talking a mile a minute, but the words barely registered on Kate.

'Here you go, babe, three margaritas.' Matt placed the drinks Kate had ordered on her tray. As Kate thanked Matt Marcy whisked the tray away.

'I'll take care of these for you.' Marcy checked the tab and hefted the tray onto her shoulder. 'You take the beers over to Boudreaux's booth when they get here.' She wiggled her eyebrows suggestively, grinned. 'This could be your lucky night, hon.'

Before Kate could form a protest, Marcy waltzed off, weaving expertly through the crowd as she balanced the tray of margaritas on one hand. Kate stared dumbly at Marcy's back, her jaw clenched so tight it was a miracle she didn't crack a tooth.

'If I get any more lucky, I might as well shoot myself,' she grumbled.

Zack was fuming, but he was keeping a lid on it.

What was she doing working tables in the Sports Bar? If she had set out to torment him she couldn't have done a better job. Just when he was trying to get her off his mind there she was, all hot and luscious in a skimpy skirt that showed her panties every time she moved and a too-tight V-neck sweater that pumped up her breasts. She might as well have been naked, the amount of flesh she was displaying to the whole bar. Watching her walk towards him and Monty, the tray of beers held high, her head down and tantalising little wisps of hair framing her cheeks, Zack had to force his eyes to stay on her face. He guessed he must be the only guy in the place who wasn't staring at her butt.

'Wow, she's built,' Monty murmured, confirming Zack's suspicions.

'Keep your eyes to yourself,' Zack snapped, 'or I'll tell Stella you've been checking out other women.'

'I wasn't checking her out,' Monty said, sounding offended. 'I was just stating the obvious. What's between you two anyway?' Monty wasn't dumb—he'd already asked the question twice since Zack had called their waitress over and asked her to send Kate back with their beers.

'Nothing,' Zack said, determined to prove himself right, even if his mouth was drying up and his muscles tensing the closer she got. The ache in his crotch didn't mean a thing either. It was just residual heat from last night. He stretched his legs out and crossed them at the ankle, making his eyes go blank as she stepped up to the booth and slid the tray onto the table.

'Hello, Kate,' he said, his voice as bland as a slice of white bread.

'Hello.' Kate gave him a brief look before concentrating on putting the bottles on the table without spilling them.

Even in a plain black T-shirt and worn jeans the aura of power pulsed around him, intimidating her. But worse than that was the wet heat that had pooled between her thighs and the parched feeling in her throat brought on by the sight of his lean, solid length relaxed against the leather bench seat.

Her eyes connected with his. She must not show any weakness. He was watching her, the handsome planes of his face defined by the light coming from behind her.

'What are you doing here?' he asked in a slow, measured voice as if he wasn't really all that interested in her reply. 'I thought you were working for Pat today?'

'I did work for Pat today. I'm working here tonight.'

A muscle in his jaw clenched. 'I see,' he said, still in that controlled, indifferent monotone. 'You know, I don't think I want you hanging around my hotel.'

Heat seared Kate's cheeks at the callous words, the assessing, dismissive once-over he gave her.

'In fact, I'm sure of it,' he said, slinging his arm casually across the back of the booth.

He looked confident and in control. Probably because he was. The rat.

Kate slung the tray under her arm. Her fingers fisted on the hard plastic. She'd like nothing better than to pick up his fancy bottle of beer right now and pour it over his head. 'You're the boss,' she said, annoyed beyond belief by the quiver in her voice. 'I'll leave.'

She turned to go, but he snagged her wrist.

'Not so fast,' he said, his fingers clamped tight. 'We need some more pretzels first.'

Kate tugged her arm loose and glared at him. She wanted to tell him where he could shove his pretzels so badly she could taste the words.

She savoured the image for a moment, then let it go. Bone-deep weariness and despair rushed up to replace it. She nodded. 'I'll go get them,' she said.

'Eh-hum.' Monty cleared his throat loudly. 'Now, are you going to tell me what the bleeding heck that was all about? Who is that girl?'

'No one.' Zack ignored his friend, still staring after Kate as she made her way back to the wait-station. Something wasn't right.

The idea had been to goad her, get her to rise to the bait and then slap her down. It was still bugging him that she'd dumped him this morning to do drudge work. But he didn't feel the satisfaction he'd expected. In fact, he felt like a jerk. Her face had been cast into shadow by the overhead light, but she'd sounded resigned, weary even. It wasn't like her to take an insult lying down. He ought to know.

'All right, why don't you pull the other one?'

Zack looked at his friend. 'What?'

'If there's nothing going on between you two, I'm Bugs Bunny. And you know carrots make me hurl.' Monty sipped his beer and skewered Zack with a look.

Zack sighed. He knew that look. It was Monty's only-dynamite-will-make-me-drop-this-now look.

'We slept together last night, okay?' Zack said at last. He took a long swig of his beer, hoping it would ease the dryness in his throat. 'Although there wasn't a whole lot of sleeping going on.' He put the bottle on the table, his throat still dry as a bone. 'Then she decides this morning she'd rather scrub johns than date me. End of story.'

Monty studied Kate's retreating figure, then turned back to Zack. 'She dumped you?' He gave an astonished chuckle. 'You've got to be joking?'

'I'm real glad you find that amusing.'

'Not amusing, mate, more like miraculous.' Monty laughed again, his eyes darting back to the bar. 'Oh, fab, she's coming back. Maybe I'll get to see her give you the kiss-off again.'

Zack jerked his gaze up, not finding Monty's teasing at all funny. As he watched Kate approach the familiar tightening in his crotch only aggravated him more.

Kate concentrated on staying upright and channelling Mahatma Gandhi as she approached Zack's table, the mini-pretzels balanced precariously on her tray. Somehow she had to get him to let her stay till the end of her shift. She hated being a pushover, but she didn't have the energy to fight and she needed her share of tonight's bar tips. If she left an hour early, she might not get them.

'Your pretzels,' she said, putting the small bowl on the table and keeping her eyes down. Maybe if he didn't mention her leaving again she could just carry on.

'Thanks,' Zack said, sounding surly. What did he have to sulk about?

She picked the empty bowl up from the table, intending to make a quick exit, when the man sitting across from him spoke. 'Don't run off, love,' he said, his broad cockney accent surprising Kate. 'It's Kate, right?'

His smile was charming and somehow cheeky at the same time. She hadn't even noticed him when she'd been at the table earlier, but then she'd been wasting her attention on Zack. She took his hand, feeling her anxiety ebb as his grin widened.

'Yes, that's right, Kate Denton,' she said.

'Lovely to meet you, Kate,' he replied chummily. 'I'm Monty Robertson.' He let go of her hand, settled back into his seat. 'Do I detect a touch of the old country in your accent?'

She nodded.

'Londoner, right?' he asked, the warmth in his soft ebony eyes putting her at her ease.

'Chelsea, actually,' she replied, feeling ludicrously grateful to be talking to one of her fellow countrymen.

'Very la-de-dah. I'm honoured,' he said, then his face fell comically. 'You're not a bloody Chelsea supporter, are you?'

Kate laughed. 'Of course I am—best team in London. You're not one of those saddos who—' The thump of a bottle hitting the table made her head whip round.

Zack was staring at them. 'I need another beer,' he said, his voice deadly calm.

Tension knotted at the base of Kate's neck. A snide retort came to the tip of her tongue, but the sudden wave of exhaustion caught her unawares. She stepped back, trying to counterbalance the wobble in her legs and stumbled.

'Hey, love, are you okay?' She could barely hear Monty's urgent question over the buzz saw in her head.

The tray clattered onto the floor. She tried to grab the table, scared of falling, but then Zack was towering over her. His fingers grasped her upper arms, holding her upright.

'What is it? What's wrong?' he asked.

She frowned, confused by the temper in his voice. What had she done now?

The familiar scent of him assailed her, she tried to pull away, but he held firm. He turned her body and the neon light from the bar shone on her face, making her squint.

He cursed. 'You look like hell.' His voice came from miles away. 'When's the last time you slept?'

She tried to lift her hands to shake him off, but someone

had tethered ten ton weights to her wrists. 'I'm fine,' she said feebly, but she couldn't seem to stop shaking.

'The hell you are,' he said, still sounding angry with her.

She wanted to argue with him. Wanted to tell him to get lost, but all that came out of her mouth was a pathetic whimper.

The world tilted and suddenly she was floating for real, her cheek rubbing the soft cotton of his T-shirt, her limbs weightless.

'Mont, tell the bar staff she's taking the rest of the night off. I'll see you tomorrow.'

She heard the words but couldn't quite process them. All she could see was the strong column of his neck, the shadow of stubble under his chin. Embarrassment washed over her as she felt his arms tense under her knees and across her back. For goodness' sake, he was carrying her. The harsh light of the casino hit her as he walked out of the bar. She wriggled, tried to lift her head away from the rock solid shelf of his shoulder blade.

'P-put me down.' Where had that stammer come from? And why was everything whirling around?

'Forget it,' he said, sounding even surlier. 'If you can't look after yourself, someone else is going to have to do it.'

Her mind tried to grasp hold of the indignation, the humiliation she should be feeling. But she couldn't shake the thought that she was in a chilling fog and the only warm, solid thing there was him. She couldn't push him away yet, or she'd be sucked into nothingness. Shivers of exhaustion raked her body.

His arms tightened around her and she heard the reassuring thud of his heartbeat. 'Relax, Kate,' he said, his voice gentle now, coaxing. 'You're okay, I've got you.'

'Don't drop me,' she pleaded, too tired to care if she sounded pathetic.

'I won't,' he said.

She softened into his strength, shut her eyes and let the fog envelop her like a warm, comforting blanket.

Zack felt Kate grow heavy in his arms. The machine-gun shots of his heartbeat finally began to slow as the deep, steady rhythm of her breathing brushed his neck. He tucked her head under his chin, adjusted her weight as he pushed the elevator call button.

He'd just lost ten years off his life.

Shock had propelled him out of the booth when she'd staggered in the bar. But as soon as he'd felt the tremors raking her body, seen the bruised smudges under her eyes, a cruel rush of guilt had replaced it. She looked shattered.

They'd got all of two hours' sleep last night and while he'd been lying in bed most of the morning, feeling put upon, she'd been working in his hotel trying to make up the money she owed. Maybe she was nuts, maybe she drove him nuts, but the woman had guts.

The elevator button pinged and she stirred. 'Shh,' he hummed as if comforting a child. She relaxed against him. She wasn't exactly light, but still she felt fragile. He tightened his hold, stepped into the elevator and nudged the button to the penthouse.

He ought to take her to her own suite, but he couldn't do it. He wanted her with him, and not just for the obvious reason. He wanted to keep an eye on her. The urge to protect her surprised him, but he didn't question it. He'd been right on the money earlier. If she couldn't look after herself, someone else would have to do it. And at the moment, whether she liked it or not, it looked as if that someone was him.

CHAPTER SEVEN

KATE STOOD IN THE DOORWAY of the palatial open-plan kitchen, cinched the tie on the silk kimono she'd found on the end of the bed and studied Zack's back. He seemed surprisingly at home standing over the gleaming steel hob, spatula in hand. The buttery perfume of cooking eggs filled the air. The smell wasn't the only thing making her mouth water. He looked tall and gorgeous as always in a pair of worn jeans and a faded sweatshirt with the sleeves torn off at the elbows.

What was it about watching macho guys cook that made a woman's head spin? The sight wasn't helping Kate's nerves one bit.

'Hi.' Her voice came out on a silly little squeak. She cleared her throat and tried again. 'Um, good morning.'

He stopped stirring, turned slowly and gave her an easy smile. 'Morning.' He nodded towards the breakfast bar and pointed at one of the stools with the spatula. 'Take a seat. Breakfast's done.'

She didn't move. 'What am I doing in your penthouse?' she said blankly, trying hard not to be charmed.

Why was he cooking her breakfast? And what exactly had happened last night? All she remembered was passing out. She'd woken up from a deep, dreamless sleep ten minutes ago to discover herself in his bed with only a few scraps of underwear on, the mid-morning sunshine peeking through the curtains on the huge picture window.

It didn't look good.

'We'll talk after we eat,' he said, dishing the eggs onto plates already loaded with bacon and toasted muffins. 'You want to grab the coffee?'

She didn't want coffee, or breakfast for that matter. Her stomach was tied in greasy knots of apprehension. The only thing she did remember was making a complete fool of herself last night—swooning like the heroine in a bad B-movie. But she had absolutely no clue as to what had happened afterwards.

Had they made love?

If they hadn't, why was he being so friendly now? He'd as good as ordered her off the premises last night in the bar.

If they had, she didn't think her pride would ever recover.

Zack transferred the plates to the breakfast bar, which he'd already laid with cutlery and glasses of orange juice. He frowned when he looked up.

She was still rooted in the doorway.

'Okay, spill it, whatever it is,' he said, sounding exasperated. 'I spent twenty minutes cooking breakfast—I don't want to eat it cold.' He placed the coffee pot and a couple of mugs next to their plates and waited.

Kate had always believed in being direct. Still she had to force the words out. 'Did we sleep together last night?'

His eyebrows shot up and then he laughed. Kate's back stiffened like a board. He slid onto one of the stools, keeping his bare feet on the floor, and poured himself a cup of coffee, still chuckling.

Heat rose in Kate's cheeks. She wrapped her arms round her waist. 'What's so funny?'

He looked at her over the cup, still grinning at the private joke. 'Sweetheart, you've given my ego some major-league hits in the last couple of days.'

The self-deprecating shake of his head and the warmth in his voice made Kate relax a little. 'How so?'

He took a gulp of his coffee, put the cup down and patted the stool beside him. 'Sit down and I'll tell you.'

She hesitated, then walked to him and lifted herself onto the stool. Propping her feet on the foot bar, she tugged the silk over her bare legs.

He put a hand on her knee. She tensed, only too aware of the warm pressure through the cool silk, and the clean, devastatingly familiar scent of him.

'All I'm saying is, when I make love to a woman, the lady usually remembers it in the morning.' He lifted his hand. 'And I don't take advantage of women when they can't say no.' He fixed his eyes on hers. 'You were out cold last night. So I took one of the other bedrooms.'

'Oh, well, that's good.' She should have been relieved, but for some inexplicable reason she wasn't, quite. 'Thanks.'

'You're welcome,' he said, picking up his fork. 'Now, eat up.'

She did as she was told, suddenly at a loss as to what to think. Okay, so they hadn't slept together, but why was he being so nice to her, then? They'd hardly been on good terms the night before.

As soon as she tasted her breakfast, Kate's appetite pushed the doubts to one side in a surge of hunger. She tucked into the light fluffy scrambled eggs, crispy bacon and hot buttered muffins, savouring every delicious bite. She was polishing off her second cup of coffee when she noticed he'd finished his breakfast and was watching her.

She put down her cup.

'I see you found the robe,' he said casually. 'It suits you,'

Kate looked down at the luxurious blue silk kimono embroidered with a flame-breathing dragon down one side. 'It's beautiful,' she murmured, pulling on the lapels. 'Whose is it?'

As soon as she'd asked the question, she wished she could

take it back. No doubt one of his other conquests had left the silk robe behind. She knew she had no claim on him, but somehow the thought of sitting in his kitchen in some other woman's clothes made her lose her appetite.

'I was given it on a business trip to Japan,' he said, refilling his coffee-cup. 'Over there, guys wear those things, too. It's not really my style, though.' His gaze wandered over her figure. 'It looks better on you.'

Kate let out the breath she'd been holding, and then felt annoyed by her reaction. Why should she care who the kimono belonged to?

She wiped her mouth with her napkin. 'Breakfast was delicious, Zack. Thanks, it was nice of you.'

'Not really,' he said, his expression unreadable. 'I owed you an apology.'

'You did?' Why did she feel as if she was missing something vitally important here? 'What for?'

'For behaving like a jerk yesterday morning and last night in the bar.'

She blinked, surprised by the admission. She had assumed apologies weren't his style any more than silk kimonos were. 'Apology accepted, then.'

Time to leave, she decided, before she let that smouldering look get the better of her again. Popping off the stool, she reached for his plate.

He took her wrist, stilled her hand. 'What are you doing?'

'I thought I'd clean up, before I go.'

'No need,' he said, turning her hand over. 'The housekeeping staff'll get it later.' He stroked his thumb across the pulse point, making her shiver. Then he lifted her hand to his lips and bit softly into the pad of flesh at the base of her thumb.

A sharp dart of desire shot straight down to Kate's core.

'Don't,' she said, curling her fingers into a fist. She tugged on her hand.

His eyes locked on hers, making her feel both trapped and needy. 'Why not?' he said, his voice gentle but firm. 'What are you afraid of, Kate?'

You, she thought, the panic making her throat constrict. It had been hard enough walking away from him yesterday morning. Kind and considerate were the last things she would have expected from him. They pulled at a place deep inside her she didn't want pulled at. There was nothing between them except one night of spectacular sex, and it would cost her if she ever forgot it.

'I have to go,' she said, struggling to ignore the jackhammer thumps of her heartbeat. 'I need to check out of my suite today, and then I have to find another job.'

He let her hand go, swore under his breath. 'Why are you so hung up on paying your way?'

'I'm not hung up on it.' She'd rather die than tell him the real reason—it was far too personal. 'It's just, it's important to me, that's all.'

'Yeah, I get that.' Frustration hardened his voice. 'I was the one who stopped you falling on your face after you'd worked yourself into a coma, remember.'

The words came out harsher than Zack had intended. When he saw her flinch he could have kicked himself. Here he was trying to persuade her to stick around and he'd blown it, already. How did the woman get him worked up quicker than a wolf at a rabbit convention? He was famous for being smooth with women, and yet with her he found it all but impossible to keep his cool.

'Yes, I do remember,' she said, her shoulders ramrod straight under the floating silk. 'I also recall you telling me to leave your hotel. Which is what I intend to do, so you won't have to pick me up off the floor again.'

'Kate,' he said, aiming for easygoing. 'I'm not having that

same argument all over again.' Okay, maybe easygoing was going to be a stretch.

'Good, because neither am I.'

She tried to walk past him. He stepped in front of her.

Defiance flashed in her eyes but behind it was something else. Something he'd seen the night before when he'd held her. Something that looked a lot like vulnerability. It gave him the cue he needed to say what he had to say.

'I've got a proposition for you.'

Her eyes flared and he had to suppress a grin.

'Not that kind of proposition.' Well, not quite anyway. 'It'll be worth your while. I swear. If you'll sit down and listen.'

She still looked mutinous.

'Please.' The word made him feel uncomfortable, but when she huffed and sat back on her stool he figured it had been worth it.

'All right, I'm listening,' she said, her chin still thrust out.

She looked stiff as a poker, perched precariously on the edge of the stool, but at least he wasn't watching her cute rear end walking out the door.

Now, how to say what he wanted to without setting her off again?

Luckily for him, he'd spent most of the night giving the problem a whole lot of thought and he had a plan. All he had to do was stick to it.

When he'd got her up to the penthouse the night before, his first concern had been getting her out of her outfit without waking her up.

It had been an exquisite kind of torture, the flowery scent she wore making him instantly hard as he'd recalled just how hot and ready she'd been in his arms the previous evening. He'd had no trouble keeping his thoughts G-rated, though, once he'd eased off her shoes and seen the raw, reddened skin on her heels and toes.

The guilt had swamped him. He'd tried to tell himself it wasn't his fault that she'd worked herself to exhaustion. He wasn't the bastard who'd stranded her in a foreign city with no clothes, no money. But he hadn't quite managed to convince himself. The feeling of responsibility and the urge to keep her safe were as strong, if not stronger, than they had been when he'd carried her out of the bar.

He'd never met a woman as independent, as self-sufficient as she was or as determined to prove it. And he'd certainly never met a woman he wanted to take care of before. That the thought was arousing as well as infuriating was just another one of the contradictions that made his reaction to this woman unique.

He'd spent the previous day sulking, telling himself she could go hang herself for all he cared. But once he'd been sitting on the edge of his bed, watching the gentle rise and fall of her breathing, he'd had to admit that whatever it was that was between them, it wasn't over. Not by a long shot.

While he'd been sitting there in the half-light considering that startling fact, a part of the conversation they'd had during their first meeting had poked at the back of his brain. Had she told him she'd been working as Andrew Rocastle's PA? The possibility had seemed almost too fortuitous to be true so he'd had the concierge pull out Rocastle's registration details and then made a late-night call to Rocastle's company offices in London where it had been already morning. He'd spoken to a very helpful personnel woman who'd pointed out that Kate Denton had indeed worked as Rocastle's PA until an 'unfortunate incident' two days ago. He knew all about the 'unfortunate incident' and it hadn't put him off in the least. Anyhow, he only need offer her a two-week contract. If she wasn't up to the job he was offering her it hardly mattered. Her typing skills weren't the main reason he wanted her at his beck and call.

Kate Denton was a fire in his blood he needed to get out.

A few weeks with her working as his PA ought to cure him of his obsession once and for all—and if she did a halfway decent job, all the better.

Having decided to give the idea a shot, the only remaining obstacle was figuring out how to make Kate go for the deal. He'd stayed up half the night working out his strategy. Cooking her breakfast had been the first part of the plan. He'd stumbled, badly, by letting his frustration show a moment ago. Now he had her back on the stool and marginally willing to listen to what he had to say, he wasn't about to make the same mistake again. Keep calm, he thought, keep cool and give the carrot the hard sell. He could get to the stick later, if he had to—he had the connections to stop her from getting any other jobs in Vegas—but for now, he figured the carrot was his best option.

'The truth is, Kate, I'm in a fix and I need your help.'

'What kind of a fix?'

'My PA quit yesterday and I need someone with me in California for the next couple of weeks. How about it?'

'You want to employ me? As your PA?' Kate was so astonished, it was a miracle she didn't fall off the stool.

'Yeah. I can only offer you a two-week contract,' he said, as if he were discussing the weather, 'but it'll be a lot more dough than you can get doing bar work and I'll cover your expenses during the trip, naturally.'

'You're not serious?' Surely this must be some kind of joke? He didn't say anything, just looked at her, his eyes steady, his lips curving ever so slightly. 'You *are* serious,' she said, completely incredulous.

'I need to close a deal I've been setting up for over two years. I'm selling my holdings in Vegas, buying a resort hotel in Big Sur called The Grange. Great coastal location, established clientele, with loads of potential for expansion and modernisation. I need someone to handle my planner, do the secretarial stuff as I hammer out the final details of the negotiation with the owner.'

'Oh, I see,' Kate murmured, her pulse scrambling into overdrive as her mind whizzed through the possibilities.

This could be the answer to all her prayers. A proper job, a challenging and exciting job that didn't involve wielding a loo brush or toting a tray of margaritas looking like a pornographic sports groupie. She might not have liked Andrew much, but she'd adored being his PA and she'd been good at it too. Just from the lowly jobs she'd done over the last day, she knew The Phoenix franchise had a much higher profile than Andrew's piddling Covent Garden design firm. Of course, it was only for two weeks, but in two weeks she could pay off her debts, get some invaluable experience to add to her CV and prove her...

Whoa, there, girl.

Kate's enthusiastic ramblings slammed to a stop as they ran full tilt into a brick wall. There was one humongous problem with the sparkling career opportunity she was being offered—and it was sitting right in front of her with a sinfully tempting smile on its face.

'So what do you say? You want to be my Girl Friday?' the devil said.

Kate gave her head a quick shake, trying to clear out the burst of stardust that had momentarily short circuited her brain cells.

The problem was, she wouldn't be working for Andrew. She'd be working for Zack. Gorgeous, irresistible, domineering Zack, who insisted on having everything his own way and would be entitled to demand it if he were her boss. As his PA she'd be working closely with him. Handling all those minute details that could feel so personal, so intimate. Hadn't Andrew once joked that Kate was so efficient she was part personal assistant and part wife? Coming from Andrew it had seemed like an innocuous compliment. If she allowed herself to get into that role with Zack she'd be in considerably more danger. Maybe she ought to clarify what it was he was expecting of her. 'Do you mind if I ask you something?'

The corners of his mouth quirked up in a knowing grin and she cursed the blush that worked its way up her neck. 'Sure, ask whatever you want,' he said.

She licked her parched lips. 'What do you expect from me, exactly?'

'What do I expect?' He rolled the question off his tongue as if he were savouring the words. 'Hmm, let me see.'

The blush scorched Kate's cheeks as she waited for his answer and she clutched the silk tighter. She wondered if the penthouse's air conditioning had suddenly gone on the fritz, because she could have sworn the temperature in the kitchen had just shot up by a good ten degrees.

'Apart from typing, shorthand, that kind of stuff, I expect you to be available twenty-four-seven. I'll be honest—I'm not always the easiest guy in the world to work for.' His gaze flicked to her cleavage. 'At times I can be real demanding.' His eyes moved back to her face, the dimple winking in his cheek. 'But then you already know that.'

Kate felt the melting sensation between her thighs and squeezed the muscles tight. How infuriating that she was unable to deny her instinctive response to him even though she knew he was being deliberately provocative.

'Stop teasing me,' she said firmly. 'It's not remotely funny.' The very last thing she wanted to do was look this gift horse in the mouth. She wanted this job, desperately, and probably not just for the career opportunity it offered if she was being completely honest with herself. But she wasn't about to serve herself up on a platter, job or no job.

He laughed easily, held up his hands in surrender. 'Okay, Kate, I'm sorry. But the look on your face. It was irresistible.'

'Answer the question. Why are you offering me this job?'

He skimmed his thumb across her cheekbone, his eyes bright with appreciation. 'We were pretty spectacular together our first night out. You're smart, you're beautiful and you're desirable and I had a hard time forgetting about what we got up to after you walked out on me yesterday morning. So I'll admit, one of the reasons I want you with me in California is so we can get up to a lot more of the same.'

It was just as she had suspected. Kate sighed. He was only offering her this job so he could jump back into bed with her. The fact that she didn't feel nearly as indignant about it as she should made her feel like a besotted fool. 'I can't accept the job under those circumstances and you know it.'

Zack leaned against the breakfast bar, but he didn't look disappointed—just the opposite, in fact. 'Hear me out here. I'd like to make love to you again. I'm not going to pretend otherwise. We were good at it. But I don't pay for sex. While we're in California, you'll be working your butt off as my PA, and while you're doing that I'll be calling the shots, because I'm the boss. But what happens in the bedroom is private and between us. It's not part of your job description. And I sure as hell don't intend for it to be a chore,' he finished, sounding exasperated.

She let out an unsteady breath. At least he'd been totally honest with her. But could she even consider such a proposal? 'What if I said I won't sleep with you?'

He shrugged. 'If you wanted to say that you could and it wouldn't affect your employment.' A sensual smile spread across his face. 'But I've gotta warn you now, I'll do my best to change your mind.'

Fabulous, Kate thought weakly, feeling the familiar inferno flare to life in her belly. What she had here was essentially a frying-pan-or-fire situation, then. Whatever way you looked at it she was liable to get burned. Because she knew she wasn't going to say no to what he was offering. Unfortunately, she had a bad feeling that the real temptation wasn't just the promise of a fulfilling day job or the night-time fun and frolics that were going to be even harder to resist. The simple pleasure of spending time with him, working side by side with him, getting to know what made him tick, was by far the most tempting possibility of all. And that was the reason why she should say no. If she let her guard down, if she allowed him to insinuate his way into her heart, she could get badly hurt.

But somehow she couldn't bring herself to do the sensible thing and say no. He was looking at her expectantly, the intensity in his face playing havoc with her pulse rate.

Surely, if she was careful, if she knew the risks going in, she could take what he offered, enjoy it and survive with her heart intact. Men did that sort of thing all the time. Why shouldn't she? Independence was the key. She had to make sure that if she compromised anything, she didn't compromise that. Then her heart would be safe. Never need anyone who doesn't need you and never sacrifice anything you can't afford to lose. Her father had taught her that lesson as a child, she had to make sure she didn't forget it.

She breathed out, her mind made up. 'I'll take the job.'

His eyes widened. She'd surprised him. Truth was she'd surprised herself more.

'Great.' He stroked her arm. 'That's fantastic. I'll get Monty to work up a contract and then we'll discuss your salary. But I guarantee you, it'll be enough to get you back to London next month in style with a nice chunk of change in your pocket.'

'Okay,' she said, the thought of going home so soon making her feel as if she were standing on the edge of a very deep precipice already.

'So we've got a deal?' he asked.

'Yes, I suppose we have.' All she had to do, really, was

make sure that, whatever happened between them, she kept a good, firm grip on reality at all times. That had always been her mother's mistake. It wasn't one she was about to repeat.

She thrust out her hand. He looked down at it, but shook his head. 'Not good enough,' he said quietly, pinning her with a gaze that scorched her skin. 'Not nearly good enough.' Threading his fingers through her hair, he tilted her face up to his, slanted his lips across hers.

The kiss was so sudden and so hot, it seared her down to her toes.

When he finally lifted his head, she felt as if she'd been branded.

'There,' he said, framing her face in large palms. 'Now we've got a deal.'

Twin tides of joy and dread swelled inside Kate as she stared at her new boss.

What had she gone and done now?

CHAPTER EIGHT

'WE'LL TAKE THE SHORTER one with the straps,' Zack announced to the overjoyed boutique manageress. 'Now let's see some of your evening wear.'

'Yes, sir, Mr Boudreaux,' the woman replied, snapping her fingers at the staff hovering around her. 'I'll get the models ready right away.'

Kate watched the woman and her minions rush off. The manageress's eyes had glazed over ten minutes ago, clocking up the dollar signs like a human cash register.

As soon as she and Zack were alone she turned on her boss, determined to make him see sense. She'd accepted his job proposal less than an hour ago and already she was starting to panic.

After taking a quick shower in his penthouse, she'd been whisked off in a limousine to one of Vegas's priciest and most exclusive designer boutiques. The merchandise here made the clothes she'd seen on Michelle's rail look like bargain-basement knock-offs.

'This is preposterous,' she whispered furiously. 'I don't need all these things. You must have spent thousands of dollars already. And there's no way that as my boss you should be responsible for buying my clothes.'

'Relax.'

He looked relaxed enough for both of them, she thought. His arm was slung casually across the back of her chair, one leg crossed with his ankle resting on his knee. How could he be so calm when he was spending a fortune?

'It's my money and I *am* the boss,' he continued. 'You need to look the part when we get to California.' His gaze drifted down her figure, taking in the T-shirt and jeans she'd bought from Michelle. 'The tomboy outfit's cute, but it's not going to cut it at The Grange.'

'But I could get the same effect for you for a lot less money. Remember how much you liked that dress I wore to dinner?'

'Yeah.' His voice deepened, making the single word sound like a caress. 'I don't think I'm ever going to forget it.'

'I got it at a thrift store for twenty dollars,' she said triumphantly, sealing her argument. Or so she thought.

He chuckled. 'They say the Lord works in mysterious ways. I guess I know what they mean now.'

'Don't be ridiculous, you don't have to—' she started, only to be silenced when he placed his forefinger on her lips.

'Quit arguing.' His lips quirked. 'This is all part of the deal, so you're going to have to stick with it, sweetheart.'

'Oh, for Pete's sake.' She slumped back in her chair, pouting. The man was completely intractable. 'I was only trying to save you some money.'

'Well, don't,' he said. 'That's not your job. Anyhow, the way I see it, it's money well spent. I'm getting a real kick out of imagining you in some of this stuff.'

'Oh, you are, are you?' Her own lips twitched. She was unable to resist his teasing any longer. He was behaving like a child in a sweet shop—and making her feel like a flipping walnut whip. Light and fluffy and completely nuts.

He grinned. 'Honey, my knicker fetish and I are gonna have a ball when they bring out the underwear.'

* * *

After making her protest, and having it comprehensively shot down, Kate gave in. Who knew she'd have so much fun doing it, though? She'd always had a passion for beautiful clothes, had spent years poring over glossy women's magazines unable to afford so much as a handkerchief. Once she'd started picking out garments, she hadn't been able to stop.

If Zack was bound and determined to buy her a whole new wardrobe, she might as well have some input, she reasoned. After all, she was the one who was going to be wearing the clothes. And she hadn't failed to notice Zack's taste leaned towards the more revealing end of the spectrum. If she left all the choices up to him she'd end up looking more like his mistress than his PA, and freezing to death to boot. It might be sweltering in Vegas in May, but she doubted it would be that hot on the Californian coast. He welcomed her suggestions, encouraging her to pick out whatever she wanted and—true to his word—didn't seem remotely bothered by how much they were spending. Consequently, Kate decided to lay the blame at his door when they got back into the limousine an hour later and she watched the boutique's doorman load box after box of their purchases into the boot.

Why had she let him buy all those clothes for her? It felt rash and indulgent. And what did it say about her precious self-sufficiency?

'What's the problem?' Zack watched Kate's teeth tug on her bottom lip as she gazed out of the limo's back window. She looked dazed.

He'd had a whale of a time buying the clothes—and not just because he wanted to see her in them. Watching the way she enthused over fabrics and designs, checked the texture of every item, marvelled over the stitching and the craftsmanship, had reminded him of the passionate way she made love—with nothing held back. It was a shame she couldn't be like that all the time.

Seeing her let go of the hang-up she had about money, if only for a little while, had made him wonder about it. Someone must have hurt her deeply once, for her to be so cautious, so careful about her independence—and he was certain it went a lot deeper than that loser Rocastle.

She collapsed back into the seat, gave him a concerned smile. 'I'm wondering how I can justify spending so much when I'm only going to be working for you for two weeks.'

'Simple,' he said, enjoying her confusion. He'd bet she'd never treated herself before in her life. 'You don't justify it. I spent the money, not you.'

She frowned. 'Actually, that makes me feel even worse.'

'You're going to look a million dollars in your new clothes. The money's not a big deal. Get over it.' He lifted her hand to his lips, buzzed a quick kiss across her knuckles. 'Now, how about we head back to the penthouse and have a nice long lunch?'

She sat upright, eased her hand out of his grasp. 'But I thought we were going to be working this afternoon. I need to start familiarising myself with everything. Aren't we leaving for California the day after tomorrow?'

'That can wait,' he said, knowing his indifference was going to bother her more. Somehow, teasing her was becoming addictive. He loved watching her blue eyes darken to a vivid turquoise and those plump, kissable lips get even more pouty. And anyway, work was the very last thing on his mind at the moment. 'There's a few other things I'd like to familiarise myself with first.' He pressed the driver's intercom button, resisting the chuckle as her forehead puckered up. 'Take us back to The Phoenix, Henry,' he said.

Zack clicked off the button, settled back in the seat. 'As I recall, we've got some unfinished business, you and I.' He toyed with one of the curls that had escaped Kate's pony-tail, loving the soft, silky texture of it. He was already anticipating the feel of it draped over his chest.

Panic closed Kate's throat. She could see from the possessive look in his eye exactly what he had in store for this afternoon and lunch didn't have anything to do with it.

She swallowed heavily. As much as she craved the thrill of what they could get up to in the privacy of his penthouse, she had to start setting some boundaries. For herself as well as for him. The limo, the designer clothes, the casual, proprietary way he looked at her, touched her, had already thrown her off balance.

If they leapt straight back into bed, it would only make that harder. She had to establish herself professionally, start showing him what she was capable of as his PA before she became anything else. Maybe it was pride, but she wanted him to see that he hadn't made a mistake hiring her, even if he had done it for all the wrong reasons.

He tucked the tendril of hair he'd twirled round his finger behind her ear. 'If something's bothering you, why don't you spit it out?' he said indulgently, putting his hand on her knee.

Her back went up even more. That confidence of his really did need to be taken down a notch. Another good reason not to go straight back to the penthouse and do just what he wanted, however hard it was going to be to say no.

She bit into her bottom lip, trying to find the right way to tell him. 'In the words of the great Mick Jagger,' Kate began, grasping for something approaching gravity, '"you can't always get what you want".' She lifted his hand off her leg, shifted away from him. 'And in some cases it's better if you don't.'

He laughed. 'Mick sure as hell never said that last part.'

'That's not the point,' Kate continued, determined not to be sidetracked. 'You hired me to do a job. I want to get a chance to do it before we... I mean, if we decide to...' She sputtered to a stop. Great—she sounded like a complete ninny now.

He was grinning at her, as if he found her incredibly amusing. 'If we decide to what?' he asked, raising an eyebrow. He placed his hand on her waist, stroked warm fingers under the hem of her T-shirt. 'If we decide to do this, you mean.'

Kate shuddered at the contact. She grabbed his hand, pulled it out. 'I'm trying to have a sensible discussion here,' she snapped.

'Your idea of a sensible discussion is misquoting Stones lyrics?' he asked.

Right, that wasn't a smile on his face any more. It was a smirk. She wasn't putting up with it any longer. 'I'm being serious.'

'Are you playing hard to get?' He leaned closer. 'Because I've got to tell you, it's turning me on.'

She put her hands against his shirtfront, pushed him back. 'I'm saying I don't want to make love with you this afternoon.' The words were shaky but distinct. She could see he had got the message when he frowned.

He sat back; his glance flicked down to her nipples. 'That's not what your body's saying,' he remarked calmly. Reaching up, he touched one rigid peak through the cotton of her T-shirt. She gasped as the spear of need shot straight down to her toes.

He dropped his hand, having made his point. Blast. He was still smirking.

'Why don't we cut to the chase?' he said. 'We both know you want me as much as I want you. We're two healthy, consenting adults who happen to be great in bed together. There's no reason why we shouldn't mix business and pleasure over the next few weeks.'

She took a deep breath, tried to steel herself to be as honest as she could. 'It's just…' She hesitated. 'I don't think jumping back into bed with you is a good idea.'

'I disagree.' He tugged on one of her curls again. 'I think it's a great idea.' He watched the tendril as it sprang back before looking at her face. 'Why don't you?' he asked so bluntly, she flushed.

She forced herself to ignore the fluttering in her stomach at the determination in his gaze. 'You said yourself you have a strict rule against sleeping with women who work for you.'

'Rules are made to be broken,' he countered.

'You'll be my boss—sleeping with you will complicate our working relationship.'

'No, it won't,' he said without a moment's pause.

Could he really not see the problem at all?

She was at a complete loss about what to say next when the chauffeur swung open the door to the limo and tipped his hat at Kate. 'We're here, ma'am.'

She stepped onto the pavement, heard the door slam behind her as Zack got out on the other side. He walked round the car to join her. 'I say we go up to the penthouse and discuss this further,' he said as he put a possessive hand on her back and led her towards the hotel's entrance. She obviously hadn't got through to him at all, she realised.

She stopped and turned, dislodging his hand. 'I'm not going to the penthouse with you.' There, she'd said it. Now all she had to do was stick to it.

His eyebrow lifted. 'You sure?'

From the self-assured look on his face, it occurred to her she absolutely had to win this round if she was going to maintain any kind of control on this relationship at all. She might be deluding herself about being able to resist him for two whole weeks. But she needed to prove to him she wasn't a pushover. He liked to dominate. She had to show him that he couldn't dominate her. 'Yes, I'm positive,' she said as firmly as she could manage.

He pushed a fist into the pocket of his trouser. 'All right. We'll leave this discussion for another time.'

'And until we go to California,' she announced hastily, 'I'd like a separate room, please.' That got another raised eyebrow, but nothing more. If he was annoyed, he was hiding it well.

'I guess that can be arranged,' he said, calmly.

'Thank you,' Kate murmured, feeling oddly dispirited. But as she went to walk into The Phoenix ahead of Zack she snagged her wrist and pulled her back. He leant over her, the whisper of his breath against her ear making the sensitive skin of her neck tingle.

'You can have it your way for now.' He pushed her hand behind her back, trapping her against him. 'I can wait,' he murmured, his lips inches from hers. 'I'm very good at waiting, until the cards fall the way I want them.' There was no mistaking the sensual threat before he pressed hot, firm lips to hers.

Her lips parted and his tongue thrust into her mouth, devouring her as her body moulded to his. Just as she felt herself losing control, the heat scorching her insides, he stepped back. He held her steady as her breath gushed out. Taking her hand in his, he pressed his lips to her hair, whispered against her ear. 'But I won't wait for ever.'

The kiss had been quick, fleeting even, but also devastating. Kate trembled as she walked across the lobby to the reception desk, unbearably aware of the man beside her.

Good Lord, she'd just been branded. Again!

CHAPTER NINE

'HE WANTS TO PAY ME four thousand dollars for two weeks' work! But that's completely ridiculous.' Kate gaped at the contract Monty had given her to sign.

Zack's business manager chuckled. 'I told you, he's a generous employer. Don't worry—knowing Zack you'll be working your socks off for it.'

Which was exactly the problem, Kate thought, slapping the pen down and thrusting the contract back across the desk. 'I can't sign it. That's far too much money.'

Monty looked at her for a moment, then grinned. 'You know, it's funny, but he said you'd say that.'

'He did?'

Was that why she hadn't seen him since their little disagreement yesterday morning? She dismissed the notion. Don't be daft. One thing Zack had never been was afraid of a confrontation with her.

The cold weight settled more firmly in Kate's stomach. There could only be one explanation for his vanishing act over the last day and a half. He'd lost interest in having anything other than a business relationship with her. Which was great, she tried to assure herself, even though she knew her pitiful behaviour that morning told a different story.

She'd been sent a curt note by one of Zack's secretaries

telling her to report to his offices. Assuming he'd be there, she'd spent a good half an hour picking out an outfit from her new wardrobe and preening in front of the mirror.

When she'd arrived in a silk wraparound skirt and blouse ensemble by Nicole Farhi only to find Zack gone for the day, she'd been miserably disappointed. It had taken a titanic effort to write notes on The Grange deal instead of second-guessing herself over the decision to make him wait. She shouldn't give a hoot that she'd blown it with him.

Then she'd been ushered into Monty's office and presented with Zack's ludicrously generous contract. And now she was all over the place again. What exactly did Zack think he was paying for? And why didn't she feel as indignant about it as she should?

Monty pulled open his desk drawer and lifted out a piece of folder notepaper. 'He told me to give you this if you put up a fight.'

Kate unfolded the heavy paper. Written in Zack's distinctive black scrawl were just three sentences. Kate read them, felt a surge of excitement and blushed scarlet.

Stop getting your proper knickers in a twist.

I don't pay for sex.

Z

PS: Especially if I'm not getting any!

A bubble of laughter burst out without warning. She slapped her hand over her mouth to hold it back and it came out as a snort.

'You okay, love?'

She eased her hand down, her face hot enough to fry an egg on as she took in Monty's concerned frown. Good grief, had Monty read the note? He probably thought she was a complete tart. She gave what she hoped was a ladylike cough. 'Yes, I'm fine, thank you for asking.'

'Ready to sign the contract yet?' he asked amiably.

'Of course,' she said, holding on to her composure. She took the contract, signed it with a flourish and pushed it back across the desk—the picture of cool, calm professionalism.

'Great,' Monty said, checking her signature and then standing up to offer Kate his hand. 'Good to have another Londoner on board.'

She grasped his fingers, mollified somewhat by the genuine warmth in his eyes. Maybe he didn't think she was a total slut.

As Monty led her out of the office and started introducing her to 'the team' Kate made herself a solemn promise. She would be the best PA Zack Boudreaux had ever had. She would work so hard over the next two weeks, Zack and everyone else at The Phoenix would be blown away by her efficiency, her industriousness and her unimpeachable work ethic. She was going to earn every single solitary cent of those four thousand dollars—so that no one could imply she'd got this job by sleeping with the boss.

'You know, you look really familiar. Are you sure we haven't met?' Kelly Green asked, sending Kate an inquisitive half-smile as she handed her yet another file on The Grange deal.

'I've been staying in the hotel—maybe you've seen me about,' Kate said, concentrating on the file to hide her guilty blush.

She'd recognised Kelly instantly. The plump, pretty secretary had been sitting outside Zack's office gaping when Kate had been marched up there in her underwear and a bathrobe. Luckily Kelly hadn't been able to place her. Yet. 'I must have one of those faces,' she continued, the insincere smile making her cheeks ache.

'Oh, well.' Kelly shrugged. 'I can already tell you're a lot nicer than Jill.'

'Who's Jill?'

'Mr Boudreaux's last PA. The one in the hot seat before you,' Kelly replied in a sing-song voice, obviously keen to chat.

'Do you know why she left?' Kate asked, more curious than she wanted to admit.

'Sure, she quit a couple of days ago after Mr Boudreaux blew up at her. But I think he would have kicked her out pretty soon anyway. Jill was a whiner—and he doesn't put up with those for long, let me tell you.'

That didn't sound too encouraging. Was Zack the sex god also Zack the slave-driver? In Kate's position, that might not be a good combination. 'He doesn't sound very sympathetic.'

'He can be hard on you if you don't get the job done right,' Kelly said, carefully. 'And he's famous for being ruthless in business. There's even rumours he used to be a professional poker player before he built The Phoenix,' she added, as if she were divulging a state secret. 'But he's never shouted at me before,' she finished, sounding almost disappointed.

'So Jill wasn't any good?' Kate asked hopefully. Her mission to dazzle would be easier if she wasn't replacing someone with a pristine reputation.

'That—and she was always coming on to Mr Boudreaux in the office.'

Kate blinked. Fabulous. So the man already had a history of sleeping with his PAs. Why was she not surprised? 'They had a relationship?' she asked dully.

Kelly looked round, making a quick check on the two other secretaries who were handling some filing on the other side of the office. She perched herself next to Kate's chair and said in a conspiratorial whisper, 'Jill always made out like they did to me. She went on and on about the trip to California, even booked them into the same cottage at the resort. Course, she knew we were all pea-green with envy.' Kelly sighed. 'He's such a hottie, who wouldn't want to spend two weeks alone with him in a hotel?'

Who indeed? Kate thought huffily. So much for Zack's strict rule about sleeping with his employees. It was lowering to realise she wasn't the first of his underlings to be charmed out of her knickers.

'But you know what?' Kelly continued, standing up. 'I think Jill was full of you-know-what. I never once saw him respond to any of her flirting. If anything it seemed to annoy him. I think she quit because she'd finally figured out he was never gonna be interested in her.'

Or she'd discovered Zack was replacing her with a newer model. The man was obviously a serial seducer of his staff.

'I see,' Kate said, giving Kelly a sympathetic nod and trying not to feel hurt. What had she expected? He'd talked her into bed in less than a day. And she could hardly pretend she hadn't enjoyed every minute of it. 'Thanks for telling me all this. It's always good to know the lay of the land on a new job.'

'No problem,' said Kelly. 'My advice would be, do your job the best you can and don't flirt with Mr Boudreaux. But then I can tell you're a lot classier than Jill. That must be why he hired you.'

Not quite, thought Kate, feeling more compromised than ever as she watched Kelly walk back to her own desk. She opened the file Kelly had handed her, but the words and figures blurred as she considered her position and exactly how impulsive she'd been up to now.

She hadn't exactly been very classy either, but she was going to do her best to be classy from here on in. Which meant no more recreational sex with the boss whenever he clicked his fingers. She was not about to become another notch on his bedpost.

Kelly was right about one thing. Until Kate knew how to handle Zack, and her overpowering attraction to him, there could be no more flirting.

CHAPTER TEN

'MONTY SAYS YOU SPENT yesterday getting up to speed on The Grange deal,' Zack said, unfastening his seat belt.

'That's right,' Kate replied. She smoothed her skirt down, noticed the way his eyes followed the movement. She cleared her throat, ignoring the dancing butterflies in her stomach. Surely the weightless feeling was only because Zack's private jet had just reached its cruising altitude.

Luckily, Zack had been all business since meeting her at the airport, which was handy, because her resolve not to flirt with him had already taken a few hard knocks. He looked tall, dark and delicious freshly showered and shaved and wearing a navy-blue perfectly tailored Hugo Boss suit and white shirt. Her heart had been beating double time ever since they'd entered the jet, the subtle scent of his aftershave making the luxury tan leather interior unbearably intimate. She hadn't bargained on being alone with him so soon, but he'd dismissed the cabin attendant right after take off.

What she needed to do now was keep the conversation as businesslike as possible or she'd be totally sunk. Heated looks like the one he'd just flicked down her legs would be ignored at all costs.

She pulled the report she'd been working on the previous evening out of her carry-on bag. 'I've typed up my notes on the history of the negotiations,' she said in her most forthright, no-nonsense voice. 'Monty said it would be useful for you to have it all in writing. All the aspects you've already agreed with Westchester and anything that's still to be decided before the signing.'

His eyebrow lifted but he took the file. She jerked when his fingers touched hers on the document and prayed he hadn't noticed her reaction.

'You've been busy,' he said at last, leafing through the pages. 'This looks very thorough.'

'That's what you're paying me for, remember,' she said tartly, and instantly regretted it.

His lips curved. 'So you got my note?'

'Yes, I got your note,' she replied, flustered. This was the last thing she should be talking about. 'I thought it was completely inappropriate,' she said, aiming for outrage and getting breathless instead.

He dumped her report on the coffee-table and, crossing one leg over the other, tapped his open palm on his ankle. 'As I recall,' he said, 'appropriate behaviour isn't your strong suit.'

'It is now,' she said, trying to convince herself.

'There's no need to change your ways on my account,' he said, a devilish glint in his eyes. 'I'm a big fan of your inappropriate behaviour.'

'I don't have time for that any more,' she said recklessly, layering as much simpering subservience into her voice as she could muster. 'I'll be too busy working.'

He flashed her a laser-sharp grin. 'Well, hell, Kate. I thought a good PA knew how to multitask.'

'I'm superb at multitasking,' she said, determined to ignore the innuendo. 'My shorthand and typing are exemplary, as are my communication skills.' Businesslike and abrupt ought to shut him up.

He gave her a deliberate once-over. 'As you know, I'm more interested in your other skills.' A shiver of awareness shot up Kate's spine.

The man had no shame. Why wasn't she outraged?

'Yes, but you're not paying me for those, remember?'

'I know I'm not.' He reached across the table and brushed a knuckle across her cheekbone. 'I was thinking more in the region of a free trade.'

The soft touch and suggestive comment had images of their one night together blasting into Kate's mind.

'I don't think so,' she said. Could he sense the fireball of need searing her insides? She saw the challenging grin and decided retreat was her only option.

Fumbling with her seat belt, she leapt up and walked to the aeroplane's window with as much poise as she could manage. Staring at the candyfloss clouds, she tried to even out her breathing. Well, her attempt at classy and businesslike hadn't exactly been a roaring success.

'Look at me, Kate.'

She turned to find him standing close. Too close.

'Why are you sulking?' he asked, amused and indulgent.

And so much for her grand plan to put him in his place. 'I'm not.'

'Sure you are.' He slid his finger under her chin, lifting her face, then stroked his thumb across her lower lip. 'The pout's sexy as hell, you know.'

'I'm not pouting, either,' she said, pulling away. 'This is me looking annoyed.'

'Yeah?' He curled his fingers round her nape. Her sex throbbed hot as he got closer still. 'Then I guess I better annoy you some more,' he murmured against her lips.

The smart thing to do would have been to push him away. Her mind registered the thought, but then his mouth covered hers, his tongue pressing against her lips, demanding entry—

and smart crashed and burned. She let him in on a sigh, her fingers clutching at his shirt.

Why did he have to be such a fantastic kisser?

He dragged her against him. The blatant evidence of his arousal, hard against her belly, had her sanity returning. She wanted his respect, and she wasn't going to get it if she melted the instant he crooked his finger. The realisation brought the thought of Jill Hawthorne and all his other conquests to mind. She let go, pushed him back.

He dropped his arms. 'Still sulking?' he asked mildly, his breathing only slightly uneven. Did the man never lose his cool?

'I have no intention of becoming one of the herd.'

His brow furrowed. 'What herd?'

'How about we start with Jill Hawthorne?'

'What about Jill Hawthorne?' He looked genuinely stumped.

'You know, your previous partner in multitasking,' she announced, getting a good firm grip on her indignation at last.

'My…?' His eyebrows shot up and then, to her astonishment, he laughed.

'It's good to know you find it funny,' she snapped. At least he could have the decency to be ashamed of his track record. 'I bet Jill didn't.'

'That's so cute.' He took her arms, still chuckling as he rubbed his palms up the thin silk. 'You're jealous.'

'I most certainly am not jealous,' she said, trying to shove the green-eyed monster back down his hole.

'Yeah, you are,' he said. 'And I think I like it.' He paused for one last chuckle. 'But I've got to tell you it's misplaced. Jill and I never multitasked.'

'You didn't?' She would not be glad.

'I told you already. I don't sleep with my staff.'

'But what about me?'

'You're the exception to my rule. The one and only exception so far.'

'Really?' She would not feel special either.

'Yeah, really.' He took her hand and led her back to her seat. 'But you're right about one thing.'

'I am?'

He waited for her to sit down and then sat in his own seat. 'We should have talked about this before, but I got distracted.' He gave her a sheepish grin. 'I always do with you.'

And she absolutely, definitely would not be charmed.

'Talk about what?' Kate asked, trying and failing to stifle the warmth spreading up her torso from the gruff intimacy in his voice.

'Our sexual histories. This is the twenty-first century and it's the smart thing to do.'

'Oh,' Kate exclaimed, not sure what to say. This conversation threatened to be even more dangerous than the last one. And look where that had got her.

'To put your mind at rest,' he carried on, in the same supremely confident tone, 'I always use condoms and I'm not quite as prolific as you think. The last woman I dated was over three months ago and we only lasted one night.' He gave her a crooked smile. 'She was nowhere near as distracting as you.'

'Oh, well, that's good,' Kate said, a blush spreading up her neck again. For goodness' sake, she was not a blusher, but she'd done more blushing in the last few days than the whole rest of her life put together.

He rested his forearm on his knee. 'So, what about you and Rocastle? Were you sleeping together?' The question sounded casual. A bit too casual.

'No, we certainly were not.'

'Good.' He sat back, looking pleased. 'Any guy who treats a woman like he did—whether she's his employee or not—is a jerk.'

'I know,' she said, grateful for his support, even though it seemed a bit misplaced. 'But to be fair to Andrew, he didn't put nearly as much effort into seducing me as you are.'

'His loss,' he said, apparently not taking the hint. 'So how long had it been for you?'

Kate's blush intensified. She was not about to tell him her last sexual relationship before him had been well over two years ago. He'd gloat. And it would put her at even more of a disadvantage. 'I don't want to answer that question,' she said, delicately.

'That long, huh?' he said, gloating.

Drat, was he a mind reader now, too? 'Could we please stop talking about this?'

'Sure,' he said, sounding even more self-satisfied. He picked up her report from the coffee-table. 'Why don't you call the flight attendant and organise our lunch while I read this?'

And just like that, they were boss and PA again. Kate should have been overjoyed, but she wasn't. The abrupt turn-around provided more proof, if proof were needed, that he was the one in charge. He set the agenda for their relationship and she didn't seem to be able to do a thing about it.

She opened her mouth to speak, to protest his high-handed attitude, when he reached into his jacket pocket, pulled out a pair of horn-rimmed spectacles and put them on.

He glanced up at her sharp intake of breath. 'What is it?'

'You... You wear glasses?'

She'd never been particularly attracted to guys in specta-cles before. But, good grief, those piercing green eyes were even more devastating in the slightly nerdy frames. They made him look vulnerable. Which was an illusion, of course, but a very sexy illusion nonetheless.

'I'm near-sighted,' he said matter-of-factly. 'I don't wear my contacts on the plane because of the dry air.'

'I see.' She recrossed her legs, tugged her skirt down over her knees.

Get a grip, woman. Stop picturing yourself ripping his clothes off and ravishing him in nothing but his glasses right this instant.

She stabbed the intercom button and arranged their refreshments with the flight attendant while Zack bent his head to study her report.

What had happened to her carefully laid plans for getting this situation back under control? It was more out of control now than ever. Thank goodness he hadn't spotted her ludicrous reaction to his specs. It would be like a red rag to an already very confident bull.

As Zack studied Kate's impressively comprehensive report he couldn't resist a wry smile. So the glasses got her hot. Good to know. Just as it was good to know she hadn't slept with Rocastle—or anyone else for quite a while. He wasn't usually a possessive guy, but with Kate it was different.

He'd done the right thing offering her the PA's job. And, as tough as it had been yesterday to stay away from her, it had been a smart move to give her some space too. He didn't want to scare her off. He wasn't usually a pushy guy, but Kate's artless sensuality had got to him. Hell, he'd needed a little space himself.

He flicked a page over, smiled some more. After that kiss, it was clear she wasn't nearly as afraid of him as she was of herself and her reaction to him. All he needed to do was stoke that fire every chance he got and she'd come to him.

Having to wait didn't bother him one bit. Hell, anticipation was nine-tenths of the fun—and Kate's quick wit and sassy mouth would make the victory all the sweeter.

For the first time ever he could appreciate the old saying that it wasn't the winning that counted, it was playing the game. Then again, he could afford to appreciate it, because no way was he going to lose.

CHAPTER ELEVEN

THE WIND WHIPPED at Kate's cheeks as the rocky splendour of Big Sur rushed past. Unfortunately, the elemental beauty of the California coastline wasn't the only thing taking her breath away.

The roar of the convertible's engine dulled and Kate watched Zack downshift to take another hairpin bend. As the glory and spectacle of America's legendary Highway One flashed past, the spring sunshine glinted off the Ferrari's glossy red paintwork and seemed to spotlight the man beside her. Even though he'd finally taken off those sexy specs, all her senses seemed to be heightened, her awareness of him humming through her veins like a potent narcotic.

She studied his profile, the slight cleft in his chin, the hint of a five o'clock shadow on high slashing cheekbones, the Armani sunglasses that didn't quite hide the tiny laughter lines around his eyes. She battled back the heady sexual thrill that had paralysed her on the plane and took a deep fortifying breath of the fresh sea breeze.

As the car rounded another treacherous bend the dense chaparral bushes on their right gave way to a meadow of lupines, poppies and wild lilacs, blanketing the forbidding cliffs in cheerful blue and purple blossoms. Her heart slowed. What a glorious sight.

Kate closed her eyes, turned her face into the wind and tried to force herself to think sensibly. Okay, this was easily the most romantic place she'd ever been and with the sexiest man she'd ever met. She shoved her hair back, held it behind her head and took another long, calming breath of the salty air. She had to stop herself from being completely and utterly swept off her feet.

She'd known from the start how skilled Zack was in the art of seduction. What she hadn't realised was how single-minded he could be and how used he was to getting his own way. It seemed nothing could put a dent in that self-confidence. And if his towering ego wasn't already a big enough mountain to climb, the fact that she was so over-whelmingly attracted to him meant she was trying to scale Mount Everest with one hand tied behind her back.

As the coast road wound around the cliffs like an asphalt ribbon Kate peeked over the edge. It was a long drop to the secluded coves softening the ancient rocks below. But the truth was the whisper of nerves thrilled her as much as they terrified her.

Make that two hands tied behind her back.

The pressure of Zack's hand on her thigh made her pulse scramble. He squeezed her leg, shot her a quick grin. 'Awesome isn't it?' he shouted above the powerful hum of the Ferrari's engine and the rushing wind.

'Absolutely.' And the view wasn't the only awesome thing on offer. 'How far is it to The Grange?'

'About ten miles.' He rubbed her thigh. 'Wait till you see it. The location's to die for.' He put his hand back on the gear stick. 'Sit back and relax, not long now.'

Kate settled into the car's bucket seat and let the sun warm her cheeks—but she knew she'd need knockout drops before she'd be able to relax.

* * *

'Welcome to The Grange.' Harold Westchester's sherry-brown eyes glinted with appreciation as he gave Kate's hand a dignified peck.

The elderly owner of The Grange straightened and shook Zack's hand. 'It's good to meet you in the flesh at last, Boudreaux. I was starting to think you were going to let Robertson close the deal without ever seeing the place.'

Kate caught the mild note of censure in Westchester's tone. The old guy was clearly miffed Zack had never visited before. The news surprised Kate. The files on The Grange deal showed Zack had been angling to buy the place for over two years. Given his reputation for thoroughness, it seemed odd he had never come to inspect the investment in person.

Maybe that was why he seemed a little agitated. As soon as they'd taken the turn-off leading to the resort, he'd been silent and tense. He'd even stalled the car when they'd parked at the entrance to the hotel lobby.

Westchester had been waiting for them, directing an army of bellboys to handle their luggage. Kate had instantly warmed to the older man. He reminded her of her Grandad Pete, her mother's father. A wily old fella who would tell it to you straight and always had a ready hug. The fact Westchester didn't seem the least bit overawed by Zack's status endeared him to her even more. Nice to know one other person who wasn't prepared to drop to their knees and start genuflecting as soon as Zack appeared. She might have found an ally.

'I thought you were coming with Robertson during his visit last week?' Westchester continued, still sounding starchy.

Zack stiffened almost imperceptibly. 'I was tied up.' The denial sounded defensive to Kate, which wasn't like Zack at all.

'Well, at least you're here now, young fella.'

Kate had to control the giggle at the old guy's irascible tone. No, he definitely was not in awe of Zack.

'I guess we better get you and your pretty assistant checked in,' Westchester said, winking at Kate.

After signalling his bellboys, he led Kate and Zack into the hotel's wood panelled lobby. A huge central fireplace accented the high vaulted ceilings, making the place look both spacious and homely at the same time. It was neat and clean and the profusion of wild spring blooms spilling out of the wall-hangings gave it a fresh, cozy ambience. It was beautiful in a sweet, uncomplicated way, but so unlike the sleek exclusivity of Zack's Vegas hotel Kate wondered what had made him so determined to buy the place and relocate here.

Westchester introduced them to the reception staff using their first names. Kate wondered if the informality was another little dig intended to cut Zack down to size. If it was, Zack didn't seem to notice.

'Now, then,' Westchester began. 'The Ms Hawthorne who made the reservations said you'd need a two-bed cottage because you'd probably be working late together. So I stuck you in Terra Del Mar. It's got a shared bath, but it is real pretty. Hope that's okay?'

The blood surged back into Kate's cheeks. Mount Everest just got bigger. How on earth was she going to resist Zack's advances if they were sharing a cottage—and a bathroom?

'That's great,' Zack said, stroking a hand across Kate's back. In a lower voice, he added, 'I expect we'll be having a lot of late nights.'

If Westchester heard the innuendo he didn't let on. 'That's settled, then. How about we get some tall drinks in my quarters while your luggage is taken to your cottage?'

Kate was about to accept when Zack interrupted her. 'Kate's tired from the trip. We'll take a rain check on the drinks.'

'All right,' said Westchester evenly.

'Don't be silly.' Ignoring Zack, Kate put a hand on

Westchester's arm. 'I'd love to have drinks. I'm not the least bit tired.' And she had no intention of being alone with Zack again so soon. She needed more time to marshal her defences.

'I'm glad to hear it, young lady.' Westchester tucked her arm under his, patted her hand. 'I make a mean martini if I do say so myself.' But as the older man turned to make the last of the arrangements with his receptionist Zack mouthed the word 'chicken' at her.

She blinked at him. Who, me? she mimed back.

He shot her a provocative smile and raised his eyebrows. Her blood pressure soared. Oh, dear.

'I do hope you like martinis,' Westchester said as he escorted Kate down the corridor to his private quarters.

'I adore them,' Kate replied, having never tasted a martini in her life.

Despite all her efforts to keep the drinks with Westchester going as long as possible, Kate found herself alone with Zack in the Terra Del Mar suite less than an hour later.

Just as Kate had suspected, the place was a romantic dream. Zack couldn't have picked a better love-nest if he'd arranged it deliberately.

While Zack tipped the bellboys, she inspected the deluxe two-bedroom bungalow. Westchester had called it a 'cottage', but she thought the term a little quaint. A large sitting room with an open fireplace led onto a cliff-top terrace. Glancing into the master bedroom, she spotted a huge four-poster bed Sleeping Beauty would have been proud of. The image of her and Zack entwined on the coverlet came to mind and had her slamming the door shut.

'You want the double or the single?'

She whipped round at the sound of Zack's voice. He looked relaxed and amused with his butt propped against the back of an armchair. He'd taken off his jacket and slung it over the chair—and was studying her with an intensity that made her wonder if he'd just read her mind, again.

'I…' She stopped, cleared her throat. 'I'll take the single, thank you.'

He began rolling up the sleeves of his shirt, displaying tanned, muscled forearms sprinkled with dark hair. Kate's mouth dried up.

'You sure?' he asked, crossing his arms. 'Maybe we should conserve energy and share the double?'

'That's more likely to generate energy than conserve it,' she shot back.

He laughed. 'You've got that right.'

Her face wasn't the only thing starting to heat up and she suspected he knew it from the way he was watching her. Tearing her eyes away, she walked past him onto the terrace.

'Wow, this view is incredible,' she exclaimed, maybe a bit too loudly as she walked across the redwood deck.

Although she was far too aware of the man behind her, she wasn't wrong about the stunning natural beauty before her. Leaning on the rail, she gazed out over the rocky promontory. The ocean swirled below them, the waves crashing onto a sandy cove accessed by a steep wooden staircase anchored into the cliff. Secluded and spectacular, the cottage seemed to cast almost as potent a spell as the man. Spotting the bubbling hot tub at the end of the terrace, Kate deliberately turned away from it and let the brisk breeze cool her cheeks. Okay, probably best not to go there yet either.

The soft thud of his footsteps on the wooden boards seemed louder than the crash of the ocean below her. Warm hands smoothed over her belly and pulled her back against a solid chest. Zack's breath whispered against her ear as his arms hugged her midriff. 'You can't run away for ever, you know.'

She shuddered as his thumbs traced her hip bones. Her breath hitched. She fought back the swell of pleasure, turned in his arms. Seeing him so close, the deep green of his eyes, the harsh demand on his face, smelling that tantalising scent of soap and man and sexual intimacy, she realised he was right. But letting him know it was another thing entirely. After allowing him to get the upper hand on the plane so easily, she had a lot of catching up to do.

'I'm not running away. I'm standing my ground,' she said tartly. 'It just so happens I don't like to be pushed. And up till now you've been a bit pushy, Boudreaux.'

Passion flared hot and intense in his eyes as he pulled her hard against him. 'See that's where you're wrong. I'm not being pushy. I'm being honest.' He sank his fingers into her hair, scraped it back from her face. 'Unlike you.'

Fisting his fingers in the wayward curls, he captured her lips in a raw hungry kiss. Her mouth opened involuntarily and his tongue swept inside her mouth as every single nerve-ending in her body stood to attention.

Her breath panted out, the flames burning so strong, so fierce, she knew she would soon be overwhelmed. Her hands gripped his shoulders, felt the hard, unyielding muscle, the tensile strength beneath the smooth linen of his shirt, and held him back as she tore her lips away.

So much for fighting fire with fire—all she'd done was set off an inferno.

'I want you,' he murmured, his hand stroking her backside. 'Let's stop playing games.'

'I'm not the one playing games. You are.'

He stared at her. 'How do you figure that?' His breathing was a little harsh, his voice huskier than before. The knowledge gave her a much needed burst of power.

Maybe she couldn't throw his confidence, his arrogance, his conviction that he would soon have her again back in his face. After all, her erect nipples were practically boring a hole in his chest, her sex was so swollen and ready for him she had to clamp her thighs tight to stop her knees from giving way. And the heady masculine scent of him was making her head spin. But she could at least get things back on an even footing.

'I'm not prepared to jump every time you click your fingers, Zack. I want some ground rules.'

'What rules?' he asked, incredulous, his eyes skimming down her figure. He didn't sound quite so calm and in control any more. It was music to Kate's ears.

'Rule Number One,' she announced, easing his arms down. 'Just because Zack is the boss in the boardroom, does not mean he's the boss in the bedroom.'

He let her go. 'You ought to know by now, I don't play by anyone's rules but my own.' He cursed softly and raked his fingers through his hair. 'But I guess I can give you some more time to figure that out.'

She wanted to argue with him, to take offence at his dictatorial manner, his cast-iron confidence, but not a single word would come out of her mouth. Because she knew, if he'd pressed the point, they'd already be breaking all the rules. And her body wouldn't be putting up an argument.

He left her standing at the rail and marched back into the cottage. He turned in the doorway and her eyes took in the impressive bulge in his trousers. 'You've got a little while, Kate, to get used to the idea. But after that I intend to have you again. And by then, you won't want to stop me.'

She stood dumbstruck as he walked off to the smaller bedroom, snagging his suitcase on the way. Now why did the audacious statement sound more like a promise than a threat?

CHAPTER TWELVE

'TAKE OUT THE second clause here,' Zack said, pointing at the document over Kate's shoulder. 'And rephrase the third paragraph according to the attorney's instructions.' The cotton of his shirt sleeve brushed against her cheek. 'When that's done, I'll take another look.'

'Yes, boss,' Kate murmured without thinking, all too aware of the sudden drop in temperature as he straightened away from her.

'And no cheeky remarks,' he said, walking around the terrace table to sit in the chair opposite Kate's.

'No, boss,' she said, a flirtatious smile lifting her lips.

He pulled his glasses down, eyed her over the top of the horn-rimmed frames. 'Watch it,' he said, his voice lowered in warning. 'I might think you want to play.'

She bit back the provocative reply that wanted to burst out and ducked her head to start typing in earnest.

She had to stop goading him. But how could she when he was driving her insane?

Maybe it was the sleepless night she'd had, unable to get comfortable on the huge, empty four-poster bed, or the fact that he'd been ordering her about for the last twenty-four hours.

Problem was, every time he gave her another order, the promise he'd made yesterday afternoon kept running through her head. That he didn't have the slightest qualm about touching her, leaning over her, and generally getting into her personal space every chance he got, wasn't helping much either.

Much more frustrating, though, was the fact that he seemed a lot better at playing this waiting game than she was. He hadn't talked once about their personal relationship since yesterday's ultimatum. Last night he'd wished her a pleasant evening and walked off to his bedroom alone without a backward glance.

When they'd gone to dinner earlier in the evening at the hotel's restaurant, he'd watched intently as she'd licked lobster butter off her fingers, but had kept the conversation on his plans for moving his business to California. By the end of the evening, Kate had been hyperventilating. Finding six packets of condoms neatly stacked in the bathroom cabinet this morning had made things even worse. She hadn't been able to stop thinking about them and him—and what he intended to do with them—all day long. And to top it all off, he kept wearing those damn glasses. All he had to do now was take them out of their case and twirl them in his fingers and she got aroused. It was mortifying.

The only thing keeping her from giving in to the sexual tension crackling in the air was pride. She didn't want to lose this game of cat and mouse—with Zack in the role of tomcat and her in the role of obedient mouse.

He was toying with her, waiting for her to show a weakness and then he would pounce—and she didn't want to be pounced on. Well, not quite yet anyway—not until he showed a weakness too. But she was beginning to think he didn't have any. And the strain of holding back was making her crazy. Why else would she have this reckless urge to flirt with him again?

She clicked the laptop's keys, forced herself to concentrate on the job at hand and ignore the liquid pull in her belly. At least she'd managed to keep abreast of all the work he'd set her as his PA. She'd typed so hard her fingers ached, made so many phone calls she was worried she might be going deaf in one ear, and had started reciting Zack's business diary in her sleep. The job was challenging and exciting and she knew she'd impressed him with her efficiency. And he couldn't possibly know how much sexual energy she was channelling into her job to keep from leaping into his lap.

Zack watched Kate's fingers fly across her keyboard and admired the titanic effort she was making to get back on task. Good to know he wasn't the only one performing at the top of their game thanks to a raging case of sexual frustration. His groin had ached like a sore tooth the night before when they'd got back from their meal. He'd spent most of the evening staring at her lips all shiny with melted butter. He'd taken his second cold shower of the day as soon as he'd wished her goodnight, only to step out of the cubicle and be assaulted by the smell of Kate's rose-petal perfume. Had she sprayed it round the bathroom to drive him nuts? But still he'd stuck to his guns and resisted the urge to march straight into her bedroom.

She was damn well going to come to him this time.

He'd made his feelings clear. He knew she wanted him as much as he wanted her. As soon as she admitted it, they could stop kidding around. He hadn't liked her accusation that he was being too pushy with her. He was never pushy with women. They could either take what he had to offer, or leave it. It was always their choice. With her the lines had gotten a little blurred. All right, maybe more than a little blurred. As soon as she came on to him the way he knew she wanted to, they'd be crystal-clear again. He tore his eyes away from her rattling away on the keyboard and looked out over the terrace rail.

The glorious spring weather and the comforting smell of

pine resin and sea salt he remembered from his childhood lifted his spirits some more. It was good to be back. And despite the havoc Kate was causing to his libido, she'd also been lively company, a worthy adversary and a dynamo at work. He'd never had a better PA. All of which amounted to a great distraction when he needed it.

He'd expected the jolt when he saw Harold Westchester again, but he hadn't quite bargained on having all those emotions he'd spent years burying deep being wrenched back to the surface. The games he'd been playing with Kate had done a great job of taking his mind off the ghosts of his past.

He started to scroll through the emails on his laptop while letting the feeling of anticipation wash over him. The last few days of torture were going to be worth it in the long run. In fact, now might be a good time to turn up the heat on Kate. After that flirtatious little smile a moment ago, he figured she was real close to throwing in her hand.

'It's finished,' Kate said. 'Do you want to take a look at it before I print it out?'

'Sure,' he said, levering himself out of his chair. He braced his hands on the desk on either side of her, his cheek almost touching her hair. God, she smelled good.

'This looks great,' he said, scanning the copy and savouring the spurt of satisfaction when she tensed. Nope, it wouldn't be long now before she folded. 'I can't see Hal putting up any more resistance,' he said, inhaling the scent of her hair and thinking the deal with Westchester wasn't the only thing about to get settled.

'Who's Hal?' she asked, turning to face him.

'Hal Westchester, the old guy whose hotel we're buying,' he said absently. She was close enough for him to see the beguiling rim of purple round her irises.

'I thought his name was Harold.'

'Hal's his nickname. That's what I called him when—' He stopped, clamped his mouth shut. What the hell was wrong with him? He'd nearly blurted out something he hadn't spoken about in more than twenty years.

What had he been about to say? Kate had never seen him flustered before, but he'd paled beneath his tan. He pushed away from her, straightened. 'Why don't you email the—?'

'I didn't know you and Harold Westchester knew each other,' she interrupted, intrigued. What had put that haunted look in his eyes?

'It was a long time ago.' His face went hard and expressionless.

She swivelled in her chair. 'Why did you both pretend you'd never met?'

His shoulders tensed. 'Hal wasn't pretending.' His eyes flicked away. 'He doesn't remember me.'

Apprehension churned in Kate's gut. What was really going on here? Why couldn't he look at her? Was that guilt she'd heard in his voice? Did he have some ulterior motive for buying Westchester's resort? Kelly had said he was ruthless in business. But how ruthless?

'Why didn't you tell him you've met before?' she asked.

It occurred to her in that moment that, although she'd spent one unforgettable night of passion with this man—developing a major sexual obsession for him in the process—and had travelled all the way to California with him, she knew next to nothing about him. Because she hadn't asked. It was about time she stopped letting her hormones make all her decisions for her.

He turned back, studied her face. 'Stop looking at me as if I just drowned a kitten,' he said impatiently.

'Well, stop avoiding the question, then,' she replied.

His eyes narrowed and he sank his hands into his pockets. 'I don't have to explain myself to you.'

The curt statement hurt in a way Kate would never have expected. 'I know that, but we have been lovers and…' she hesitated, took a deep breath, knowing what she was about to say would end the game for good '…and we're going to be lovers again.'

The flare of arousal turned his eyes a dark jade-green. Taking his hand from his pocket, he brushed a finger down her cheek. 'Good to know you've finally accepted the inevitable.'

She pulled away from his touch. 'What's your history with Harold Westchester?'

He shoved his hand back into his pocket. 'The connection between Hal and me is old news. It hasn't got a damn thing to do with us.'

Kate acknowledged the hit. 'Of course it does. I'm not about to jump into bed with a guy who might be doing something unethical.'

'Unethical!' he shouted, genuinely outraged. 'What the hell are you talking about? There's nothing unethical about this deal. Westchester's getting a good price for the resort, more than a good price. I would never cheat him, he means—'

He stopped abruptly, turned away. He gripped the terrace rail, his knuckles whitening. She wasn't sure what she'd unearthed, but this was the first time she'd ever seen him lose that implacable cool. She wasn't about to let it drop now.

He'd collected himself when he turned back. Crossing his legs at the ankle, he leant against the rail. She could see he was trying for casual indifference. 'Look, Kate,' he said. 'It's no big deal.'

'If it's no big deal, why are you scared to talk about it?'

He shot upright, casual biting the dust in a big way. 'I'm not scared, damn it.'

'Then tell me.'

'All right. Fine.' He threw up his hands, frustration pumping off him. 'When I was eight years old, my old man checked us in here, then split. He didn't show up again for six months. That's it.'

Kate didn't know what she had been expecting, but whatever she'd been expecting it wasn't the anger that blindsided her. 'Are you saying your father abandoned you here?'

'No, not exactly.' He gave a harsh laugh. 'Jean-Pierre wasn't a bad guy. He just wasn't cut out to be anyone's father. He was a gambler. When he was on a roll, he forgot about everything else. It's no big secret. Now can we drop it?'

Not on your life, thought Kate. She'd caught a glimpse of the man behind that super-confident mask. It both stunned and fascinated her. 'Where was your mother?' she asked quietly.

He sat down opposite her, sighed. 'Do we have to talk about this?'

'Yes, we do.' More than he could possibly know.

He shrugged and looked out at the dusky light. The evening was closing in, scarlet clouds bleeding into the blue of the ocean on the horizon. The shadows on his face weren't just from the dying day, Kate realised.

'My mother died when I was a baby. I don't remember her.' He looked back at her. 'It was me and my old man and it worked fine, most of the time.'

'*Most* of the time?' she said, hating the feckless reprobate. 'Did he forget about you more than once, then?'

'Never for more than a couple of days.' He shrugged. 'Until we landed here.'

'But that's appalling.' How vulnerable and alone he must have been. A little boy abandoned by the one person who should have been looking after him. Was that why he fought so hard for control now, because he'd once had so little of it as a child?

'JP signed us in under false names, then did his vanishing act. After he'd been gone five days, I panicked.'

'What did you do?'

He gave her a crooked half-smile. 'I tried to steal some money from the motel register. Hal caught me and figured out the truth.' He sighed. 'I freaked out, swore at him, kicked him in the shins, tried to run away. I was a real brat.'

'You were frightened,' Kate said gently.

'Maybe,' he said casually, as if his feelings hadn't been important. 'I thought they'd turn me over to the cops. But they didn't. They took me in.' Astonishment tinged his voice. 'Hal's sitting room still looks exactly the same as it did back then.'

No wonder he'd been so tense when they'd walked into Harold Westchester's parlour.

'What happened when your father returned?'

He leaned his forehead on his open palm, ran his hand down his face. It seemed this memory was the hardest. 'It wasn't pretty,' was all he said.

'You should tell Hal who you are.'

He stiffened. 'No.'

'Why not?'

'Because I don't want to,' he said with a vehemence that shocked her. 'I'm not that miserable brat any more. I left him behind years ago.'

She wanted to ask him why he hated that desperate child so much. From the closed look on his face, though, she knew he wouldn't answer the question. She decided to approach the problem from a different angle. 'Why did you want to buy The Grange so much, then?'

'Honestly? I don't have a clue. I decided a while back to sell up in Vegas. But I don't know why I chose this place.' He pushed his chair back, got up. 'It was just some dumb impulse I couldn't stop.' He paced over to the rail, leaned against it, his body stiff with tension. 'When Monty started the negotiations, I got him to check out what Hal knew. I didn't want Hal connecting me with that kid.'

'I can't believe Hal would forget you so easily.'

'Hal and Mary never knew my real name.'

'You mean you never told them, all the time you were living with them?'

'No, I never did.' He paused, as if debating whether to tell her more. Was this where the guilt had come from? 'They thought my name was Billy Jensen. At first I didn't tell them my real name because I thought it'd be safer, but then...' He sighed. 'I don't know. It was like I'd become a different person.'

'You were a scared little boy,' Kate said gently. 'Believe me, Hal's not going to hold it against you if he's the man you described to me.'

'How can you know that?' His voice broke on the words, and she realised that inside the tough, commanding man there was still a tiny part of that abandoned child—who didn't think he was worth the trouble to love.

She crossed to him, laid her hands against his chest, felt the hard pulse of his heart. Her own heart squeezed in response. 'You have to tell him who you are,' she whispered. 'You have to tell him the real reason you're buying The Grange.'

'What do you mean, the real reason?'

'You want a home,' she said simply. 'And this is the only one you've ever had.'

Zack was dumbfounded. It was as if she'd reached into his soul and pulled something out he didn't even know was there. A secret yearning he'd never once admitted to anyone, not even himself. He turned away from her, stared out to sea, the conflicting feelings of guilt and remorse and longing making his stomach pitch like the surf below.

Her hand rested on his back, smoothed over his spine. 'Hal's the real reason you came back.'

He bent his head, his fingers clenching on the warm solid wooden railing. The earth had just shifted beneath his feet. It made him feel exposed and needy, the way he'd felt as a kid. The way he'd sworn he'd never feel again.

He swung round and her hand fell away. 'You're wrong. I don't need a home and I don't need Hal Westchester.'

And I don't need you either, he thought desperately. He couldn't. She'd made him feel things, think about things he didn't want to think about. It was way past time he stopped messing about and took what he did want. Her body.

He pushed back the panic, reached for her. 'How about I order us some supper?' He slid his hand down her arm. 'This sunset's too pretty to waste on work.'

The deliberately seductive rumble of Zack's voice rippled across Kate's senses. The brush of his fingertips made her skin tingle.

What she'd said had shaken him, and he was trying to hide it by changing the subject. She didn't understand why, but that glimpse of vulnerability made her want him now more than ever. The depth of her attraction still frightened her, but she was finally willing to admit that it excited her more.

'Dinner would be lovely,' she said, hurling caution to the wind. What had it done for her anyway except leave her on a knife-edge of unfulfilled passion? 'I'm famished.'

She welcomed the swift kick of lust as she watched him walk into the cottage to order room service. Her imagination ran hot as she tidied away the laptops, stacked their work papers on top.

Zack had won another hand, but they'd both be reaping the reward.

CHAPTER THIRTEEN

'I'M STUFFED,' Kate said, dropping her fork onto her plate.

'You finished already?' Zack said, glancing at her mound of uneaten pasta. His eyes fixed on her lips. 'I thought you were starving?'

Kate didn't miss the deliberate innuendo.

It was a miracle she'd been able to eat anything at all with Zack watching her like a hawk all through supper. Knowing what was in store for tonight was playing havoc with her appetite—for food, anyway.

She picked up her glass of Pinot Noir, took a hasty gulp and searched for an innocuous topic to calm her nerves. Now they were so close, she was getting jumpy.

'Is it true you were a professional poker player before you built The Phoenix?'

'You sound surprised,' he said, taking a leisurely sip of his own wine.

'I am a bit,' she admitted. 'You don't seem the type to risk everything to luck.'

'If you stay focussed and play the cards right, luck can be tamed.'

He said it with such confidence, she was honour-bound to contradict him. 'I don't believe that. If you're not dealt the cards it wouldn't matter how you played them. You'd still lose.'

'How about we have a game of five-card draw and I'll prove you wrong?'

'I don't think so.' Did she look stupid? 'I haven't got any money—and I'm not even sure I know the rules, so I'd be at a huge disadvantage.'

'We don't have to play for money.' He ran his fingertip down the stem of his wineglass. 'And I can tell you the rules.' When she didn't reply he arched one tantalising eyebrow. 'Unless you're chicken?'

'Of course I'm not,' she said, loudly. She wished he would stop caressing his glass like that. 'But what else can we play for?'

A sinfully sexy smile spread across his face. 'Items of clothing.'

She blinked. 'You're not seriously suggesting we play strip poker?'

'I've waited close to a week to get you naked again,' he said. 'I'm getting desperate.'

But he didn't look desperate, he looked like a tom-cat with a bucket full of cream in his sights.

Kate's cheeks pinked and her pulse began to race. But she couldn't get the picture of Zack naked and at her mercy with that cocksure grin wiped off his face out of her head. Surely, this was too good an opportunity to miss.

But did she dare?

She leaned round the table and assessed the situation. He had on chinos, a shirt, a belt and some Magli loafers, no socks. Assuming he also had a pair of boxers that was still only six pieces of clothing. She did a quick mental calculation of her own wardrobe. Including her earrings—counted individually, of course—and five bracelets, it made a grand total of twelve items. 'And we count everything—including jewellery?' she asked.

He laughed, his gaze flicking to her wrists. 'Sure, we can even count buttons if you want.'

Kate glanced at her cotton print dress which had about twenty-five tiny pearl buttons from the neckline to the hem and the cardigan she'd put on to chase away the night chill. Another six buttons there. His shirt couldn't have more than ten and the top two were already undone. He really was full of himself.

'That sounds fair,' she said, already savouring the thought that his confidence was going to be his undoing—literally.

'All right, then.' He stood, dumped his napkin on the table and picked up the bottle of Pinot and their wineglasses. 'So we've got a game?'

'Absolutely,' Kate said as he held her chair for her.

He steered her into the cottage's living room. After lighting the small fire in the fireplace, he went to get a deck of cards. Kate perched on the couch and studied the fire. He hadn't turned on the main light switch, leaving the licks of flame to light the room with an amber glow. Added to the luxurious silk-weave rug on the floor, the half-full bottle of rich red wine on the coffee-table, and the night perfume of jasmine and lavender drifting in from the terrace, Kate didn't think he could have set the scene for seduction more perfectly.

The flicker of arousal that had been taunting her for days flared up as he walked back into the room. He toed off his shoes and sat cross-legged on the rug, the fire highlighting the harsh line of his jaw. She stared at the bare foot peeking out from beneath his folded knee. Did he realise he'd just given her another two item advantage?

He fanned out the cards, flipped out the jokers, then shuffled with a dexterity that suggested years and years of practice. As she watched his long dark fingers handle the cards with consummate skill, Kate felt the bottom drop out of her stomach.

Why did she get the feeling she'd just been hustled by a pro?

He looked up, his gaze penetrating, and beckoned her with his finger. 'Sit on the rug, it'll be easier to deal.'

She sat facing him, tucking her legs under her butt and trying to ignore the tickle of silk under her calves and the heavy thud of her heartbeat.

Why did she feel as if she were stark naked already?

He dealt them five cards each, face down, then poured them both another glass of wine while he explained the rules. As Kate picked her cards up she didn't feel like a mouse about to be pounced by a tom-cat any more, she felt like a mouse at the mercy of a big, bad, poker-playing wolf.

'But I've got two aces!' Kate cried. He could not have beaten her again. So far she'd lost both her shoes, all her jewellery and her cardigan—and her dress was being held together with one hand while she played with the other. He'd only had to undo four measly shirt buttons.

'And real pretty they are too,' he said as his eyes swept over the gaping neckline of her dress. She scrambled to cover the pink lace of her bra. His gaze moved back to her face. 'But two aces don't beat two pair.'

'But they're only twos and threes. That's ridiculous,' she argued. She couldn't lose her dress. She'd be down to her bra and knickers.

He chuckled, scooping up their discarded cards. 'By my count you've got three items left,' he said smoothly. He looked at her, his gaze piercing enough to make the thin cotton of the dress even more redundant than it was already. 'You want me to help you out of the dress?'

'No, thanks,' she remarked tartly, covering the hitch in her breath with bravado.

The way things were going, she might as well have offered to do a striptease for him. The fact that she felt unbearably turned on only made the situation worse. Her plan these last few days had been to make him realise he couldn't always be the boss. But he was more in charge now than ever, and she'd handed over control like a lamb leading its own way to the slaughterhouse.

What made it all the more mortifying, though, was the fact that he had stayed focussed just as he'd said he would, while she'd been distracted by every single hot look he'd sent in her direction.

The brush of his fingers on her leg made her jump.

And he still had that cocky grin in place.

He stroked his open palm over her knee. 'You're not a welcher, are you?'

She shivered. 'Of course not,' she said, pride warring with nerves as she got up on shaky legs. His gaze took its own sweet time working its way up her figure. Everywhere his eyes touched burned as she edged the dress off her shoulders, held it close and then let it go. It dropped to the rug, billowing around her feet. His jaw hardened and his eyes flashed with green fire before he looked down to shuffle the cards.

She stared at the waves of dark hair on his head, his shoulders broad beneath the white linen. From this angle she could see the ridged muscles of his abdomen through the opening in his shirt.

Hang on a minute. Why wasn't he looking at her? And why hadn't he said anything?

Her nipples peaked against her bra and goose-bumps pebbled across her flesh despite the warmth of the fire. Could he really be so unaffected when she was about to explode?

But then she noticed a muscle clench in his cheek and the small adjustment he made to his trousers as he shifted his sitting position.

Maybe he wasn't quite as comfortable—or as focussed— as he wanted her to believe.

She silently cursed her own stupidity. What was wrong with her? She'd been an easy mark. She should be using all this bare flesh to her advantage instead of behaving like a shrinking violet. She sucked in a breath. It was about time she gave him a run for his money.

Kicking the dress to one side, she knelt on the rug. Placing one hand flat, she braced her arm against her chest, pumping her breasts up until they were practically bursting out of the pink lace. She cleared her throat. Zack glanced up and his eyes widened. The muscles of his jaw tightened even more. Well, he was certainly looking at her now.

'Why don't I deal?' she said, doing her best imitation of Marilyn Monroe.

He raised an eyebrow but then his gaze strayed back down to her cleavage. He coughed. 'No problem,' he said, his voice strained as he handed her the deck.

She ran her nails across the back of his hand as she took them, felt the ripple of reaction. That was more like it. Poking out the tip of her tongue, she slid it across her upper lip while she dealt the cards. She could have sworn she heard a muffled groan.

As he reached forward to collect his cards she shot a quick look below his belt.

The rush of feminine power made her feel more confident than she had in days. Just as she had suspected, her opponent wasn't nearly as focussed as he was pretending to be and she had some very impressive evidence to prove it.

Her luck was about to change.

She fanned her cards and spotted two queens.

Skill and focus be damned. He was going to lose his shirt— and a lot more besides.

Kate watched Zack frown at his cards and couldn't resist a grin. Another bum hand for Mr Poker Man. After she had tried every seductive trick she could think of in the last twenty minutes his game had gone to pieces.

Pretending to study her own more than adequate pair of

tens, she slipped her fingertip under the lacy edge of her bra and ran it down the plump swell of her breast with a lazy sigh.

He swore under his breath.

'Pair of twos says you take the bra off, now,' he snapped, throwing the pitiful hand face up onto the rug.

'Well, what do you know?' Kate waved her cards in his face, savouring her moment of triumph. 'It appears my pair of tens wins.' All he had left on were his Calvin Klein boxer shorts. She pointed at the obscenely stretched cotton, her own sex throbbing with anticipation. 'Hand over the Calvins, buster.'

'Not till I get the bra.'

'Sorry, no can do.' She flapped her tens at him again. 'I won.'

To her utter shock, he clamped strong fingers round her wrist, whipped the cards out of her hand and flung them into the fire. 'Game's over, sweetheart.'

'You can't do that!' she shouted, staring at her winning cards as their edges curled up in the flames.

'Wanna bet?' he said, standing up and hauling her with him.

In one smooth move, he trapped her arms behind her back, manacled them in one hand, and covered her gaping mouth with his.

She struggled, panting, consumed by fire as his tongue thrust into her mouth and she was crushed against the broad, unyielding chest she'd been ogling a minute ago. He tasted of wine and frustration. Hunger seized her and she pressed into him, her mouth accepting the dominance of his tongue, her belly melting against the hard ridge in his boxer shorts.

The sharp snap hurled her back to reality. She tugged her arms free, mortified to see her breasts spilling out of the bra cups. He pushed the lace straps off her shoulders as she grabbed for the bra. The struggle lasted less than a second before he whipped it away and flung it over his shoulder.

'Give that back,' she cried, clasping her arms over heaving breasts.

'You cheated,' he announced. 'You pay the price.'

'I did not cheat,' she said, outraged as she scrambled back.

'Deliberate distraction and provocation counts as cheating.' He stalked towards her.

'It does not. You made that up.' She slapped her palm against his chest to ward him off. But then the backs of her knees hit the sofa and she collapsed onto it.

He pounced, pinning her arms down and pushing her into the cushions with the weight of his body. 'Now for your punishment,' he murmured, dipping his head. His rough tongue lathed across one swollen nipple.

She shuddered, moaned as he captured the peak and suckled hard. All her righteous indignation was incinerated in a firestorm of lust. He transferred to the other breast, stroking the underside before tugging the turgid flesh with his teeth. She choked out a sob, need soaking her knickers.

His weight disappeared suddenly and she opened her eyes. Yanking her upright, he lifted her effortlessly over his shoulder.

'What are you doing?' she demanded in a daze, her hands braced against the firm muscles of his back as he carried her into the bathroom.

She could hear him opening the bathroom cabinet. The packets of condoms she'd spotted earlier that day flashed into her mind. 'Getting supplies,' he said. 'It's going to be a long night.'

She barely had a chance to register that shocking announcement before he'd marched her through into the bedroom and dropped her onto the four-poster bed. Two boxes bounced next to her. Six condoms!

He knelt on the bed, making the mattress dip. His fingers clasped her ankle and he dragged her towards him. 'We've got a lot of catching up to do,' he said. The hooded look he gave her carried both promise and threat now.

Her time was up.

Kate debated her options—fight, flight or surrender—for about two seconds. Then accepted the inevitable as strong, insistent fingers stroked up her legs.

'Anything you say, oh, lord and master,' she said, batting her eyelids.

She laughed at his surprised expression, then gasped as he hooked a finger in her knickers and ripped them down. He cupped her and her hips lifted instinctively.

'Good to know you finally figured out who the lord and master is around here,' he said, chuckling.

Drawing his fingers through the moist folds of her sex, he circled her clitoris. A lightning bolt shimmered through her body. She bit her lip, fighting to hold back her climax. Writhing away from his probing fingers, she got onto her knees, reached blindly for the waistband of his boxers. She might have given up the fight, but she intended to go down swinging.

But as she leant forward he cradled her breasts in warm palms, his thumbs stroking the engorged nipples. She moaned—and completely lost track of what she was doing.

He bent his head, nuzzled her neck. 'Keep going, honey, you've only just started.'

A pithy response to his teasing came to her lips, but she couldn't catch her breath as his teeth bit into her earlobe and his fingers plucked at her nipples.

She pushed frantically at the waistband of his boxers, struggled to free his powerful erection as the flames blazed down from her breasts to her core.

She stared at the magnificent column, then wrapped her fingers round the thick, solid length. She drew her hand up and touched the drop of moisture at the tip. His penis leapt in her hand and he groaned.

'You still owe me those Calvins,' she whispered.

He looked at her, his sensual smile tempered by the intensity in his eyes. Getting off the bed, he took them off and handed them to her. 'About time, too,' she said, then flicked them over her shoulder and reached for his penis again. He grabbed her wrist, held her hand away, his smile strained. 'No, you don't.'

He pulled her arm above her head, forcing her to lie back on the bed, and then settled beside her. She reached for him with her other arm, but he simply caught that wrist too, held both hands above her head.

'Remember who's boss,' he said, his free hand caressing the curve of her hip as if to emphasise his mastery over her.

She bucked beneath him, but he only chuckled.

'Let me go—this is silly,' she cried. 'I want to touch you, too.'

His teeth nipped her bottom lip. 'Not yet.' She could feel him, hard and ready, prodding her thigh.

'Why not yet?' Desperation edged her voice.

'Because I want to savour you.'

What about what I want? she almost shouted, but then his fingers delved into her sex, found the pulsing nub of her clitoris, circled it and then stroked. She shattered, the vicious climax exploding inside her. Her cries of fulfilment echoed in her ears as she convulsed against him, letting the long-denied orgasm rip through her with the force and fury of a hurricane.

Zack released her wrists and took in the beauty of Kate's face, soft and serene with afterglow. Her lithe, lush body was still shuddering in the aftermath of her climax. The pounding need to have her made him ache, but right alongside it was the fierce surge of possessiveness and pride and the underlying thread of fear. He'd never seen anything more incredible in his entire life.

He'd intended to prove he could take it slow, wanted to show that he could handle her as he'd handled every other woman before her. As a child he'd been a victim of his emotions. He'd never wanted to feel that way again. He had never considered that returning to The Grange might bring those feelings back. But it had. Kate's lusty, quickfire response to him only made him feel more exposed, more needy. And so he'd forced himself to step back, to prove he was the one calling the shots in this relationship. But his driving need to control her, control himself, had backfired spectacularly.

He wanted her now more than ever.

What if he could never get enough of her?

Shoving the disturbing thought aside, he gripped her hips, rolled onto his back and pulled her on top of him. Her fragrant curls curtained across his face as she braced her hands on either side of his head and smiled down at him, that overblown mouth of hers making him crazy. She sat up, straddling him. The moist heat cradling his engorged penis threatened to send him shooting over the edge before he'd even got inside her.

He adjusted her weight, trying to ease the torturous pressure while he grappled with the packet of condoms. But as he ripped at the foil packet, she lifted up and shimmied down his legs.

'No need to rush, Zack,' she murmured, her breath cool on his heated flesh as she nibbled kisses across his collarbone, 'because as it happens…' her tongue found his nipple and his blood throbbed harder in his groin '…I really want to savour you now.'

He cursed as her lips shimmered across his abdomen. Tantalising him, torturing him. His breath came in harsh pants as he fumbled with the condom. He couldn't think, couldn't feel anything except the soft sultry licks, the delicious torment. Then her tongue touched the head of his penis. The moist pressure speared through him like lightning and he shot upright.

'Stop it.' He grasped her head in his hands, his whole body shaking with the battle to control himself. 'Not like that. Not this time,' he said, hearing the alarm in his own voice.

She started to protest, but he took hold of her shoulders,

pulled her up and rolled over again. Trapping her under him, he covered her mouth with his, swallowing her words as he sheathed himself with the condom.

He settled between her thighs and, gripping her buttocks, thrust into her, making her take all of him. She was so tight, so hot, he could feel the rapid beats of her heart as her muscles clenched around him. He gritted his teeth, struggled to hold on to that last thin thread of control. He pumped violently, hearing her gasping sobs as he forced her to orgasm. Then his control shattered, and the surge of his own climax gripped him in a mighty fist and pounded him into bloody pulp.

Kate felt as if she'd been in a war. Her breath shuddered out in ragged gasps while her heart kicked in her chest. The aftermath of an earth-shattering climax swept through her blood like brush fire.

Zack flopped back onto the bed and draped his forearm over his eyes.

She studied him, feeling stunned and wary. What had just happened?

As her breathing finally evened out she propped herself up on an elbow and stared down at him. Short locks of dark hair damp with sweat clung to his forehead. She brushed them aside, drew her finger down his cheek and laid her palm on his chest. She could feel the staggered rise and fall of his breathing. He'd lost control, she'd made him lose control and the realisation had excited her beyond belief. But it frightened her too.

During their first night together the sex had been fun, carefree. This time there had been an urgency, an intimacy that hadn't been there before. It terrified her.

'That's what I call a game of strip poker,' she murmured, trying to keep her voice light.

Zack drew his arm down and looked at her. His lips curved in a lazy smile, but Kate wasn't fooled; his heart still raced beneath her palm. 'You okay?' he asked as his hand curled round her bottom, gave it a possessive squeeze. 'I was kind of rough at the end.'

'Don't be silly, I'm great,' she said, trying to persuade herself it was true. The tenderness, the longing she felt was just an extreme case of afterglow.

She pulled the sheet up, determined to ignore the emotion tightening her chest. She shouldn't feel this content, this complete. All they'd shared was good sex. Okay, stupendous sex. She turned on to her side away from Zack, feeling disorientated.

He lifted the satin cover over them, then his hands smoothed across her abdomen and he pulled her against him. 'Come here,' he whispered against her hair as his big body enveloped hers. His chest pressed against her back, the hair of his legs bristled against her thighs and she could feel the distinct outline of his penis still semi-hard and snug against her bottom.

Kate tried to shift away but his arms only tightened. Normally, she didn't cuddle after sex. She didn't like it. It felt too intimate. She ought to tell him so, but while she was debating what to say the sound of his breathing slowed, deepened and the possessive hand cupping her breast relaxed in sleep.

She yawned and her own eyelids drifted closed. She snuggled deeper into his embrace, her limbs suddenly unbearably heavy. Maybe she'd have a quick nap. She'd move away from him in a little bit, she reasoned dully.

Zack woke her twice during the night, driving her to new heights of sexual pleasure. But when Kate awakened in the morning she was still cradled in his arms.

CHAPTER FOURTEEN

'I SHOULD HAVE a word with your boss, young lady. Boudreaux works you too damn hard.'

Kate covered another jaw-breaking yawn with the back of her hand as Harold Westchester scowled at her. She'd been shadowing him for the last few days to write a report on The Grange's current operating practices. They'd hit it off instantly, but this wasn't the first time Hal had noticed how tired she was.

'Really, I'm fine,' she said, stifling another yawn.

'You two working late again last night?' the elderly hotelier asked.

The blush blossomed in Kate's cheeks. Well, that was one way of putting it.

Since their strip-poker night, Zack had proved to be a demanding boss and an even more demanding lover. And Kate had met every demand with lusty enthusiasm. But while Zack seemed to be able to operate on next to no sleep, she was starting to flag. Tonight, she had to tell him she needed a rest. Her work was starting to suffer. She might be sleeping with the boss, but she had no intention of slacking off on her job. But satisfying Zack's sexual appetite, as well as fulfilling all her duties as his PA, was exhausting her.

'We weren't up all that late,' she said.

Hal's eyes narrowed. He wasn't buying it. 'If you turn up here tomorrow yawning again, I'll have something to say to Boudreaux about it. You can tell him that from me.'

Kate nodded, feeling touched that Hal would be so protective of her. But it wasn't the first time he'd said something snarky about Zack. She put her notebook down on his desk. 'Why don't you like Zack?'

He didn't seem perturbed by the question. 'Don't like him or dislike him. I don't know him,' Hal said. 'And that bothers me. I'm not sure I trust him.'

Kate had suspected as much since her first meeting with Hal. That Zack was still avoiding the old man and had made no attempt to resolve the situation bothered her. Maybe she could put some of Hal's fears to rest.

'Why don't you trust him?' she asked carefully. 'He's a well-respected businessman.'

'That's as may be, but I judge them how I see them,' Hal said belligerently. 'When The Phoenix started looking to buy my place, I did some enquiries of my own. I found out things about your boss that didn't sit right with me.'

'Such as?'

'He used to be a gambler. I don't like them.' Hal gave Kate a penetrating look. 'I knew a gambler over twenty years ago. A real nasty piece of work, this guy. Selfish, violent and ruthless as hell.' Hal sat back in his chair, his cheeks mottled red, his eyes sharp. 'I wasn't about to sell my place to a guy like that.'

'What made you change your mind?' she asked, taken aback by Hal's outburst.

He picked up his pen, tapped it on the desk. 'I went to visit Boudreaux's place in Vegas. Incognito, of course. I was pleased with what I found. I got to thinking maybe Boudreaux wasn't like the gambler I used to know, but just a man willing to take risks.' A self-satisfied smile softened Hal's face. 'And the final offer I got out of him didn't hurt.'

Kate laughed, wondering if Zack realised he'd met his match in Hal Westchester. Then something else he'd said came to mind. 'How did you know this gambler?' Could Hal be talking about Zack's father?

The smile disappeared. Hal sighed and eased himself out of his chair. 'It's a long story, and not a happy-ever-after one, either.' He walked slowly to the open terrace doors, stared out of them. For the first time since Kate had met him he looked every one of his sixty-five years.

'If you don't want to talk about it, I understand,' she said quietly, guilty at having brought back what was clearly a painful memory.

'You know, I haven't talked about what happened back then since Mary died.' Hal turned back to her, his eyes shadowed by grief. 'But you're a straight shooter and I like you. Maybe I need to talk about it. I don't know why, but it's been bugging me recently.'

She rose, walked to him. 'I'd be happy to listen.'

They settled at the wrought iron table on Hal's terrace and as the sea breeze ruffled Kate's hair she sipped the tea Hal ordered and listened to what he had to say. Once he'd finished the first sentence, she knew exactly who he was talking about.

'The guy I was telling you about had a little boy. They checked in here one summer and right away Mary noticed something wasn't right. The kid had these hollow eyes, his clothes were dirty and he was stick thin.' Hal put his teacup down, a wistful smile tugged at his lips. 'Mary kept badgering me about the boy. Why hadn't we seen his father since they arrived? Why did the kid never come out of the room? The cleaning service hadn't been able to get in for four days because the do-not-disturb sign was always out. Still I didn't pay it much mind until I caught the little scamp trying to steal from my till. The kid went wild, so I locked him in my office.

I was all ready to call the cops, but Mary stopped me. Insisted we go check the room. What we found…' Hal shook his head, the look of remembered horror making Kate's heartbeat skitter painfully in her chest. 'The father's bed hadn't even been slept in. He'd skipped out that first night and left the poor kid to fend for himself.'

'What happened?' Kate felt like a fraud for asking the question. Torn between telling Hal what she knew and not breaking a confidence to Zack.

'We kept him,' Hal said simply. 'He had terrible nightmares at first, and when Mary finally got him to have a bath she found bruises all over. The boy was smart as a whip too, but he couldn't read. It took a while, but eventually Billy began to trust us.' Hal smiled. 'Billy, that was his name. And after a while longer, he just became ours. Mary said, it all made sense, why we'd never had kids of our own. That Billy needed a family and we were it. I knew it was a dumb idea. We should have told the authorities. But Mary was so happy, and so was I. Watching him fill out, watching him lose that hollow look, it seemed worth the risk.' Hal paused, poured them both a fresh cup of tea. 'After he'd been with us about three months, I was giving him some book learning and he read his first full sentence. I told him how proud I was of him. He just crawled into my lap and held on. It was the first time he'd let me hug him.'

Kate could see the sheen of tears in the old man's eyes.

'Well—' he huffed out a breath '—I'm not ashamed to say I was a grown man and it got to me. It still does. I felt like a father that day.'

'Probably because you were,' Kate said, gently.

'It didn't last. The gambler came back.' Hal's voice deepened with anger. 'He'd called once, early on, couple days after we'd first discovered Billy. I told him what I thought of him and his parenting skills. He laughed. Told us we could keep the little brat for all he cared and hung up on me. I didn't think we'd ever see him again. But six months later, he turned up on our doorstep. Said he wanted his son back.' Hal's soft brown eyes hardened with fury. 'You want to know why?'

'Why?' Kate asked, sure she didn't want to hear the answer.

'The guy's luck had gone bad while he'd been away. He figured the kid was his good-luck charm.'

'That's hideous.' Kate felt disgust and fury churn in her own stomach. The picture Zack had tried to paint of his father was of a happy-go-lucky charmer who couldn't quite live up to his responsibilities—the man Hal described was nothing short of a monster.

'I had no intention of letting him take Billy,' Hal continued, the words brittle with anger. 'I'd never have willingly let him go back to that. But his father was younger and meaner and he knew how to fight dirty. He beat the crap out of me. Hit Mary too, slugged her across the face when she tried to hold on to Billy. The boy was crying, hysterical. I remember seeing the father slap the kid so hard his head snapped back. I tried to rise, but Mary held me down, weeping. She knew there was nothing we could do, and the more we tried, the worse it would be for Billy.'

Kate bit into her hand, hardly able to breathe round the boulder of outrage and agony in her throat. How had Zack endured this man's brutality? How had any of them?

'We never saw the boy again. It devastated Mary and I. We missed Billy something fierce, feared what had happened to him. We called the cops, but they never found a trace of them. Eventually we had to get on with our lives. It's the guilt I can't get over, though, even now.'

'What guilt?' Kate brushed the tears from her cheek. 'What have you got to be guilty about?' she demanded.

Hal stared at her, misery shadowing his face. 'We should never have kept him. If we'd turned the boy over to the authorities like we should have, his father wouldn't have been able to take him back. Billy would have been safe. We were selfish and he suffered because of it.'

Reaching across the table, Kate grasped Hal's hand, squeezed hard. 'You're wrong, Hal. So wrong. You gave that child something he'd never had. You gave him a home.' She wanted so badly to tell him who Zack was. Knowing she couldn't made her feel partly responsible for the old man's pain. 'You weren't selfish.' She sniffed, desperate to make him see how wrong he was. 'You did the right thing.'

'But—'

She squeezed harder. 'No buts, Hal. You can't blame yourself for another man's crime. The only villain was Billy's father.'

'Do you really think so?'

'I know so.' She let go of his hand, gave him a watery smile. If only she could tell him how she knew.

Hal's face brightened, his shoulders losing some of their stoop. 'Gosh.' Hal gave a half-laugh, scrubbed his hands down his face. 'Thanks for that. It's made me feel...' he shrugged '...I don't know—better somehow.'

'I'm so glad.'

'You're a good listener.' He patted her hand. 'I guess that's one of the skills of a great PA.'

'I suppose,' she said, her heart lightening at the affection on Hal's face.

No wonder Zack had fallen in love with this good, strong, loving man. She couldn't think of a better role model, a better father for any young boy. It was a tragedy Zack and Hal had been given so little time together, but it occurred to her that those six months had been enough to change Zack's life. He could have become like his father, but instead he'd become like Hal.

If only Hal knew how much he'd really done for that little boy.

She had to get Zack to tell Hal the truth.

* * *

After giving Hal a goodbye hug, Kate walked back through the hotel gardens and ran possible scenarios through her head. How and when to approach Zack. How to get him to talk about Hal again. How to persuade him to tell the old man who he was.

She steadfastly ignored the niggling voice in the back of her mind that whispered: Why are you getting involved in Zack's personal life? You and Zack are just casual lovers. This isn't any of your business.

She wouldn't worry about that now, she was on a mission.

CHAPTER FIFTEEN

'I CAN'T BELIEVE this is the slum Steinbeck wrote about.' Kate peered over the balcony of the Fisherman's Wharf restaurant into Monterey Bay. The afternoon sunshine glittered on the water and caught the shiny brass fittings of a luxury yacht bobbing next to functional fishing boats draped with netting. Kate grinned as she spotted the whiskered snout of an inquisitive seal. The crying of seagulls on the lookout for lunch filled the air but couldn't compete with the seal's hungry bark.

'It's clean and pretty,' she said wistfully, 'but not quite as colourful as I expected.'

Zack smiled at her across the table. He took off his sunglasses. Those killer green eyes sparkled with humour and affection. 'You're the only woman I've ever met who'd prefer to eat in a flophouse than a five-star restaurant,' he said, picking her hand up.

'I didn't say I'd prefer it.' Her belly fluttered pleasantly as he threaded their fingers together. 'If we'd eaten here in Steinbeck's day we would have got food poisoning.'

'My point exactly.' He chuckled.

As she watched him playing with her fingers Kate realised how much she had come to enjoy Zack's company, to depend on it even, in the last week. She knew it wasn't wise. But after the fabulous morning they'd spent browsing the brightly coloured curio shops along Fisherman's Wharf and visiting Monterey's awe-inspiring aquarium—not to mention the two glasses of Californian Chardonnay she'd polished off over lunch—she couldn't summon the will to care. She'd worry about it a week from now, when she was on her flight back to England and this all became an impossible romantic dream.

'So, you ready to hit some more shops yet—' he grinned, turning her hand over '—or do you want to go home for a nap?' He bussed her palm with his lips.

Her heart swooped in her chest at the casually intimate gesture. She dismissed the jolt to her system as lust, pure and simple. They hadn't indulged in their usual morning escapades today because she'd been so exhausted and she'd missed it.

'Why do I get the feeling your idea of a nap is liable to tire me out more?' she teased, determined not to read too much into the smouldering look he was giving her.

This was about sex, nothing more.

'You could be right about that,' he said, keeping his eyes on her as he signalled the waitress. 'Let's hit Cannery Row, then.'

As he asked for the bill the memory of how sweet he'd been that morning came back to her. He'd let her lie in, brought her breakfast in bed and had then insisted they took a day away from work so she could 'recharge her batteries', as he'd put it. Her heart squeezed as it had that morning and she curled her fingers into a fist in her lap.

Stop reading so much into it. He was just being a nice guy—and she had been almost comatose after burning the candle at both ends for days. The way he'd taken care of her didn't mean a thing. But it still bothered her that she'd enjoyed being pampered so much.

The waitress slid the bill onto their table and told them to 'have a nice day'.

Zack pulled his wallet out of his back pocket and began to

count out some bills. As usual he'd decided to pay the tab without consulting her. She ought to call him on it, but they'd already had several disagreements about what constituted a legitimate business expense since they'd arrived in California and Kate knew she wouldn't win.

Reluctantly she let it go this time and indulged the urge to study him instead. He hadn't bothered to shave today and the stubble on his chin, coupled with the T-shirt and faded Levis he had on, gave him a rakish, dangerous look even sexier than his usual smooth, commanding, captain of industry image. No wonder she was having trouble distinguishing reality from fantasy.

She needed a distraction before she gave in to her raging hormones and jumped him in broad daylight. Surely there couldn't be a better time to talk about Hal.

She gathered her courage, knowing what she was about to say might spoil the sexy, easygoing companionship between them. 'I had an interesting conversation with Hal yesterday.'

He stiffened slightly as he stuffed his wallet back into his jeans. 'Yeah?'

'About an abused and abandoned little boy named Billy who he's never been able to forget.'

He swore. 'Kate, I told you not to interfere.'

She pushed the hurt to one side. 'I didn't bring it up—he did. His version of events was a bit different to yours, though.'

'I don't care,' he said, shutting her out.

'Well, you should. He's never stopped worrying about you, you know.' She reached across the table, laid her hand over his. 'You should put his mind at rest. Don't you think you owe him that much?' It was a low blow and she knew it, but she had to try and make him see reason.

He pulled his hand out from under hers, stood up. 'I'm not talking about this now.'

She stood, too, thrusting her chin out. 'When are you going to talk about it, then?'

He gave a harsh laugh, shook his head in disbelief. 'You know, that's rich coming from you. The woman who's better protected than Fort Knox.'

'What's that supposed to mean?'

'How about I show you what it means?'

He didn't look angry any more; he looked determined. In Kate's experience that could be dangerous. 'Show me what?' she asked, warily.

'Uh-uh.' He tapped her nose. 'If you want to talk about Hal you'll have to come with me first. Then we'll see.'

Okay, this definitely did not sound good. 'We'll see is too vague.'

'Fine.' He held her upper arm, propelled her out of the restaurant with him. 'I promise we'll talk about Hal—' he shoved open the restaurant's door, guided her through '—after you've done something for me. That's the deal, take it or leave it.'

Kate's skin began to itch. Something definitely didn't feel right. What exactly was all this about? But then she thought of Hal. Good, kind, honest Hal who had a right to know about the little boy who still haunted him. Whatever Zack intended, she couldn't let Hal go on suffering because of Zack's obstinacy. 'I'll take it,' she said.

The itch instantly got worse.

Zack held on to Kate as they walked through the tourist Mecca of the once-rundown Cannery Row. Silversmiths and designer boutiques vied for attention with souvenir shops and candy booths. The eclectic mix might be more picturesque than in Steinbeck's day but Kate was wrong about the atmosphere. The tourists and the locals alike exuded the same happy-go-lucky air that Doc and his pals had done in Steinbeck's imagination. All except Kate, who was stiffer than a street light by his side.

He knew how much she hated being manoeuvred into things—and how hard she found it to relinquish control. Tough. He hated it too, but that hadn't stopped her sticking her cute little nose into his personal business.

He didn't want to talk about Hal. Hell, he didn't even want to think about Hal. The shame and guilt over what had happened the day JP had come back had haunted him for years afterwards. He'd become a wild and angry teenager, hating himself and living on the edge of his temper, until he'd found an outlet in the poker parlours of Europe. It had taken him too many more years to channel it into something genuinely productive. He was within weeks of finally burying that miserable part of his life for good. He didn't want to open that can of worms all over again.

But in the last few days, his perspective had changed. He still didn't want to risk telling Hal the truth, but he might be persuaded to do it, if he could get one thing in return. And that one thing was Kate's trust. He'd enjoyed the light, teasing nature of their relationship in the last week. Hell, the sex alone had been phenomenal. But it wasn't enough any more.

He could feel the curve of her hip beneath the linen of her dress, stroked his palm over the fabric. Even above the bustle of the crowd, he heard her breath hitch and smiled. Her response to him was so instant and so dramatic. Every night they made love with a violent passion that still staggered him. He frowned, his hand tightening around her waist—and afterwards she always tried to wriggle out of his arms. He never let her, of course, but each time she tried it made him want to hold her even closer.

And then there was her damn hang-up about money. He'd always enjoyed giving lavish gifts to the women he dated. He liked to show a woman she was appreciated. With Kate he'd never even broached the subject because he knew what her reaction would be. She'd even got huffy the last few days about what meals and services he was paying for, which was ridiculous. No way was he letting her pick up the tab on a business trip.

He guessed that non-materialistic side of her, that stubborn, unflinching independence, was one of the things that had captivated him at first. But there was independence and there was pigheadedness. And her arguments every time he paid for anything were starting to bug him. He knew it was all part of that invisible barrier she'd put up to stop him getting too close. The higher she built it, though, the more determined he became to knock it down.

The exclusive jewellery store he'd been looking for came into view at the end of the street. Taking his arm from around her waist, he clasped her hand and led her through the crowd.

'Where are we going?' she asked, her step slowing.

'It's a surprise,' he replied, tugging her along behind him.

Kate's heartbeat kicked up as Zack pulled her towards the seafront. She was more wary than ever now. She still hadn't been able to figure out what this was all about.

'I don't like surprises,' she said cautiously.

He glanced over his shoulder. 'Stop looking so scared,' he said with a quick grin. 'You'll like this one.'

She decided to reserve judgement on that as he marched off again, still hauling her along.

The old-fashioned frontage of the silversmiths' shop looked sedate and chic sandwiched between a powder-pink arts store and a sportswear emporium. The sign out front stated it was a supplier for the local designers, but Kate had barely had a chance to glance at the window display before Zack had pulled her inside. With the lighting dimmed, an old *Mamas and Papas* tune playing softly in the background and a young saleswoman the only other person in the shop, it was an oasis of calm and good taste from the seething swell of afternoon shoppers and tourists outside.

Her misgivings momentarily quashed by curiosity, Kate wandered over to a long glass cabinet. Her breath caught as she examined the exquisitely detailed and expertly crafted pieces on display. Silver dolphins cavorted on a charm bracelet carved in a sea swell motif. Tiny rubies winked red fire at her in a necklace intricately crafted from white-gold filigree.

'What do you think?' Zack's hand settled on the small of her back.

Kate eased out the breath she'd been holding. 'They're exquisite. You should buy some cufflinks or something.' She'd already spotted some beautiful ones.

He folded her hand in his. 'I've got something to show you.' He led her to the end of the case and pointed at a necklace laid out on black satin.

Kate's heartbeat pounded in her ears. Clusters of tiny freshwater pearls cascaded down from a series of interlinked waves fashioned from sterling silver. She imagined the hours the designer must have spent creating such an incredible piece. The pearls looked like teardrops falling from a savage sea. It made her think of the surf the day before on their private beach.

'Why don't you try it on?' Zack said next to her ear.

She touched the glass, unbearably tempted. 'I'd love to.' She stole a glance at the shop assistant who had kept a discreet distance. 'It seems a bit cheeky to put her to the trouble, though.'

'Don't worry about that,' he said. 'She's paid to go to the trouble.'

Spoken like a man who's never had to wait on anyone, Kate thought wryly. But just this once she wanted to forget about who she really was and pretend to be a woman who could afford something as exquisite as the necklace shimmering seductively at her.

Zack signalled the young woman, who was only too eager to get the pearls out of the display case.

'It's called Sea of Dreams,' the assistant said in hushed

tones as she draped the necklace around Kate's neck and clipped the clasp closed. The young woman picked up a mirror from behind the counter, angled it so that Kate could see her reflection. 'It looks sensational on you.'

Kate's hand came up to touch the pearls, which glowed warm against the skin of her cleavage. She noticed for the first time the delicate, painstakingly fashioned silver chains attaching the pearls to the necklace. 'It would look sensational on anyone,' Kate whispered.

'Let me see.' Zack turned her towards him. His eyes lowered to her breasts. He reached up and ran the pad of his thumb under the pearls. Her skin sizzled with awareness, her nipples pebbling into hard points as his eyes met hers. 'It suits you,' he said, his voice low and husky, the green of his eyes smoky with desire. 'You're beautiful, Kate.'

Desire and something far more dangerous made Kate's skin flush with colour.

Zack glanced at the shop assistant. 'Box it up. We'll take it now.'

'What?' Kate said, shock tightening her voice.

'Certainly, sir,' the young woman replied eagerly and began to unclasp the necklace. 'Will that be cash or charge?'

'Wait.' Kate flattened her hand on the necklace, pushing the pearls into her skin. 'You're not buying this.' Had he gone completely mad? He hadn't even asked the price.

'Charge,' he said to the assistant, ignoring Kate.

The woman took the necklace delicately from Kate's numbed fingers. 'I'll put it in its case for you, miss,' she said.

Kate watched her walk off, stunned. 'Zack, don't be ridiculous. I can't accept it.'

His lips quirked. 'It was made for you,' he said, as if she hadn't spoken. He stepped closer, ran a knuckle down her cheek. 'When we make love tonight,' he whispered, his fingers curling round her nape, 'I want you in nothing but those pearls.'

The erotic vision sent heat spiralling down to her core. She forced herself to step back, to let his hand fall away. 'I don't want it.'

She'd expected to see temper, had been more than prepared to meet it. But instead his gaze softened. He shook his head. 'Yes, you do. But you won't admit it.' He cupped her cheek in his palm, the gesture so gentle it made her ache. 'Why?'

'I…' The tenderness in his eyes almost had her blurting out the truth. She stopped, swallowed the words. She couldn't let him see how needy she was. It would give him too much power. 'It's too expensive.'

He dropped his hands to her shoulders, slid them down her bare arms. 'That's not why and you know it,' he said. 'I thought we had a deal.'

So this was what he had meant. He wanted her to expose herself, to let him delve into the rawest corner of her heart. To take that last little bit of control away from her. 'I can't…' She stood rigid, restraining the urge to step into his embrace. 'I need some air.' She tore herself away and rushed out of the shop.

She could see the young assistant staring at her as if she'd lost her mind. Maybe she had.

She weaved her way through the crowds to the sea rail that edged the wharf. Gripping it until her knuckles ached, she stared into the bay. The sun shone warm on her face, but chills shivered up her spine—a reminder of old demons she'd thought she'd conquered a long time ago.

She stood frozen in place, only jerked back to reality when Zack's palm rested on her hip. 'You ready to talk about it yet?'

She huffed out a breath. She might have guessed he wouldn't give up so easily.

The slow rub of his hand radiated heat, warming her at last. She spotted the bag he carried. 'You bought it?'

He nodded.

She wanted to be angry with him but somehow she just felt drained. And scared. And hopeless. Because she wanted to take his gift, and she knew she shouldn't. Zack was a rich man. A thousand dollar necklace probably didn't mean much more to him than a spray of flowers, but it would mean so much more to her.

'Kate, it's just a gift,' he said.

But it wasn't, not to her. And if she accepted it, she'd be giving something in return she could never get back.

'I want you to have it,' he continued. 'Why don't you trust me enough to take it?'

It's not you I don't trust. It's myself, Kate's mind screamed, the plaintive cry of a tern echoing the yearning in her heart. 'I don't want you spending loads of money on me.'

'Who hurt you? At least tell me that much.'

Tears burned her throat, welled in her eyes. She blinked them back, hoped he hadn't noticed. No such luck. He pulled a handkerchief out of his pocket. 'Here you go.'

She sniffed, took the square of linen, inhaled his scent as she wiped her eyes. 'I'm sorry,' she said, her voice hitching. 'I guess I'm still a bit tired and over-emotional.'

'Don't lie to me.' He tucked a finger under her chin, lifted her face. 'You don't have to.'

The compassion, the understanding in his gaze was her undoing. Her lips quivered and the tears flooded over, streaming down her cheeks like a river breaking its banks.

He tugged her against him, wrapped strong arms around her and held her tight. So tight she could hear the strong, solid beat of his heart, smell the woodsy aftershave he used and the clean scent of his worn T-shirt.

She clung on, unable to deny herself his strength, his support, any longer.

Eventually, she choked back the last of her tears. His hands were rubbing her back, making her feel secure and at the same time unbearably needy. She pulled back, embarrassed by the wet spot on his chest.

'I feel like an idiot.' She dabbed at the moisture with the hankie. 'I'm sorry.'

He stilled her hand, looked down at her. 'Now will you tell me why getting a pearl necklace makes you bawl your eyes out?'

She sent him a weak smile, wiped her cheeks. 'You must think I'm completely bonkers.'

'Well, no woman's ever reacted that way to a gift before.'

She gave a half-laugh. 'I'll bet.'

His hand rubbed a circle of warmth on her hip. 'Talk to me, Kate.'

She sighed, looked out across the bay. Would it be so terrible to tell him this much at least? 'My father sent me gifts. Every birthday, every Christmas, at the boarding-school he sent me to. Because he preferred me to stay there than to come home.' She blew out an unsteady breath. 'He called them his tokens of affection.' She laughed, but it sounded as hollow as she felt. 'Which is quite funny, seeing as he didn't even like me.'

Zack felt tension knot up his spine at the misery on her face and her desperate attempts to disguise it.

She pushed her hair back. 'You see how pathetic I am. I'm twenty-seven and I'm still obsessing about the fact that my daddy didn't love me.'

'How did you know he didn't love you?'

She leaned back against the rail, balled his handkerchief in her fist. 'Honestly, Zack. You don't really want to hear all this do you?'

'Hey, you know all about my miserable childhood,' he said, struggling to keep his voice light and undemanding.

She heaved a heavy sigh. 'I knew he didn't love me, because he told me.'

'You're kidding.' He couldn't hide his astonishment.

She gave a weak laugh. 'No, I'm not. He never wanted me. When I had to go and live with him, he made it clear I wasn't welcome and sent me straight off to boarding-school.'

'Why did you have to live with him?' he prompted.

She jerked a shoulder. 'When I was thirteen, my mum died and…' she paused, quickly masking the flash of anguish, of grief '…there was no one else. I hardly knew my father. He'd visited us over the years, to see my mother, but he'd never shown the slightest bit of interest in me.'

How could any father be uninterested in such a beautiful, vibrant young woman? Zack wondered, but didn't say so. He'd already figured there was a lot about her parents' relationship she wasn't saying.

'How did you feel about him?' he asked carefully.

I wanted him to love me. I wanted him to need me, Kate thought, but stopped herself from saying it. It would make her seem even more pathetic. She couldn't bear to let Zack know how little protection she had once had. Not now, when her defences were so low again.

'We were strangers. I didn't really feel anything for him.' Or at least she'd tried hard not to. 'By the time I was seventeen I'd finally figured out that would never change.'

'What did you do?'

'I left school and never saw him again.' She held on tight to the sea rail. The surf rippled lazily in the bay, the seagulls wheeled above, ready to swoop on any unwary fish, but all she could see was her father's uninterested face telling her he didn't care what she did.

'So that's why you're such a pain in the butt about your independence,' Zack said beside her, making her smile.

'Yes, it's very important to me. And that's why I don't like accepting gifts. Because there are usually strings attached.'

She thought she'd made her point, and convinced herself to stick to her guns. But when she saw the determination in his eyes she wasn't so sure.

'There are no strings attached here, Kate. You'll have to trust me on that. Just tell me one thing. Do you like the necklace?'

She shuddered out a breath. 'Yes, I do.' He reached into the gift bag, but she grasped his wrist, stopped his hand. 'Let me tell you another story from my childhood, Zack.' At least this one wasn't so raw, so revealing. 'When I was ten, I found a baby kitten in the gutter outside our mews cottage in Chelsea. I begged and begged my mother to let me keep it, and eventually she gave in.'

'So that pout was lethal even then,' he murmured, bending his head to give her a fleeting kiss.

She eased him back. 'The cat was feral. It shredded my mum's antique furniture, bit me so badly I had to have a tetanus shot and then ran off after a week.'

Zack chuckled. 'I won't bite you, I swear. Not unless you want me to.'

Kate huffed, charmed despite herself. 'For goodness' sake. Can't you see what I'm trying to say? This thing we've got is going exactly nowhere. We both know that. I don't want to accept your gifts. I don't want to need them.' Or you, she thought silently. Please don't make me need you.

Zack stroked his open palm down her hair, brushing the wayward wisps behind her ear. The gesture carried a tenderness that made Kate's heart plummet in her chest. This was just what she was afraid of. With one look, one touch, one simple gesture, he could shatter her defences. Make her want things she could never have. She couldn't risk offering her heart to another man who didn't want it. Didn't need it. It could very well destroy her.

She opened her mouth to protest, but he placed a finger on her lips. 'Shh.'

The kiss was soft and gentle and only frightened her more. A fresh tear streaked down her cheek. He lifted it off with his thumb. 'You know what? If that kitten had stuck around it would have found out what it was missing.'

'But…' She tried to stop her heart from plummeting even further, but she was very much afraid it was already in free fall.

'But nothing,' he said. 'I'm not making any guarantees. This is as new to me as it is to you. But it feels right at the moment and it feels good. I say we see where it takes us and enjoy the ride for as long as it lasts.'

When they made love that night, Kate let Zack fasten the pearls round her neck. She could feel the weight of them, cool and heavy against her fevered flesh, symbolising much more than they should as Zack brought her to a staggering orgasm.

As she lay anchored in his arms, listening to his slow, steady breathing and inhaling the musky scent of recent passion, Kate realised she no longer had the will to even try to pull out of his embrace.

And she hadn't managed to get him to talk about Hal as he'd promised. But as she drifted off to sleep she knew she couldn't afford to worry about Hal's heart any more; she was going to be too busy trying to protect her own. Even though she was afraid it was already far too late.

CHAPTER SIXTEEN

'THE GRANGE IS YOURS, young man.' Harold Westchester put the pen down on his desk and stood up to shake Zack's hand. 'Feels damn strange, thirty years of my life, gone in a single signature.'

'You drove a hard bargain,' Zack said, letting go of the old man's hand. Kate noticed the way his eyes didn't quite meet Hal's. 'The Grange is in safe hands,' he continued. 'We'll honour its tradition of good service and honest hospitality.'

Hal nodded. 'I know you will. You know, despite your past I think you're a man I can trust.'

Zack's eyebrow lifted. 'My past?'

'As I told Kate—' Hal inclined his head towards her '—I've never been real keen on gamblers.' He sighed and sat down. 'And I always had this dream I'd be able to hand the resort over to my son some day.'

Zack shifted in his seat. His Adam's apple bobbed as he swallowed. 'I didn't know you had children,' he said carefully.

This was much harder for him than he'd anticipated, Kate realised. Her heart went out to him, even though she knew it shouldn't. Couldn't he see he had to tell Hal the truth?

'I don't, not really.' The absent smile that wrinkled Hal's lips seemed desperately sad to Kate. 'There was a boy once. He was like a son to Mary and I. He couldn't stay, but I always had this dumb notion he'd come back one day.'

Zack tensed. Kate reached across and covered the clenched fist in his lap with her hand. His eyes whipped to hers.

Tell him. She shouted the words in her mind, willing him to understand. To her surprise, he turned his hand over in hers and held on. Then he looked at Hal.

'He did come back,' he murmured.

A lump of emotion formed in Kate's throat.

Hal's eyes fixed on Zack's face. He inclined his head. 'What did you say?'

'He did come back,' Zack said, louder this time. He let go of Kate's hand. 'I'm the kid you're talking about.'

'Damn.' Hal's eyes glazed with shock. 'I knew there was something about you. It bothered me right from the first time we met.' He searched Zack's face. 'You are. You're my Billy,' he said, finishing on a note of astonished wonder.

Zack scraped the chair back and stood up. 'I've got to go.' He gave a stiff nod and headed for the door.

Hal's shout stopped him in his tracks. 'Don't you run out on me, Billy. Not again.'

Zack's hand fisted on the door handle, but he didn't turn it. He rested his forehead on the wood, the air whooshing out of his lungs. 'I'm not Billy,' he said on a broken whisper. 'I never really was.'

'Of course you are.' A huge smile bloomed on Hal's face as he walked over to Zack. Kate gulped down tears. 'You should have told me who you were two years ago, son.' Hal chuckled. 'I would have given you the damn resort for nothing.'

Hal rested a gnarled hand on Zack's back. A tear spilled over Kate's lid as she saw Zack stiffen. 'I don't want it for nothing,' he muttered, the sound muffled against the door. 'I don't deserve it.' Finally he turned and Kate could see the remorse in his eyes. 'I should have contacted you years ago. To say I'm sorry. But I was too much of a coward.' His shoulder hitched. 'I guess I'm not as different from my old man as I thought.'

'You were never like him,' Hal said, his voice thick with emotion. 'And what have you got to be sorry about anyway?'

Zack gave his head a bitter shake. 'I hurt you. And Mary. I didn't mean to.'

Hal rested his hands on Zack's shoulders. 'You were a child and we loved you. What happened was never your fault.' So saying, he pulled Zack into a manly hug.

Zack's shoulders softened as he accepted the older man's embrace and Kate felt a lone teardrop run down her cheek. She wiped it away and bit her lip hard to stop herself from bursting into tears. Goodness, she'd cried more in the last few days than she had in years. She pushed the thought away, unwilling to analyse why Zack's actions had touched her so deeply. She had no real stake in this relationship, this reunion. Why did it feel as if she did?

Zack heaved a shuddering breath. Hal didn't hate him. The relief was so huge it made his knees feel a little shaky.

The scent of peppermint and sea salt—so different from the smell of cigarettes and whiskey that had always clung to Jean-Pierre—propelled Zack back to those few brief months in his childhood when he'd felt truly happy, truly secure. As Hal continued to hold him, to pat his back, the knot of guilt, of anger, that had been lodged inside him for more than two decades finally began to unravel.

Hal stepped back, patted Zack's arms one more time, then let go. His gaze roamed over him. 'You sure are a heck of a lot taller than I remember.'

Zack laughed. 'I grew,' he said, realising that his palms, which had been clammy with sweat moments before, were dry.

'I should leave you two alone,' Kate said, gently.

Zack looked past Hal to see her standing by the desk, tears shimmering on her lids. She walked to them and he took her hand, linking his fingers with hers. 'You don't have to,' he said.

She was the one who'd made this possible. If she hadn't come to California with him, he never would have got up the guts to tell Hal the truth.

'You guys have a lot of catching up to do,' she said, a smile of reassurance brightening her face. 'I'll be at the cottage if you need me.'

She released his hand and spoke to Hal. 'I'm so sorry I couldn't tell you who Zack was, but I couldn't break a confidence. I hope you can forgive me.'

The old man beamed back at her. 'No forgiveness necessary,' he said, lifting her hand to his lips.

Zack watched her leave the room. She'd be at the cottage if he needed her. It scared him to realise how much that meant.

'That's one beautiful woman, inside and out,' Hal said as the door closed behind Kate. 'She reminds me of Mary. She'll make some lucky man a fine wife one day.'

The bubble of contentment burst inside him. He didn't want to think of Kate belonging to anyone else.

'Let's sit down, son,' Hal said, directing him to two armchairs on the far side of his office. 'These old bones aren't as spry as they used to be,' he remarked, settling slowly into one of the chairs.

Zack sat in the other.

Hal chuckled. 'Boy, but it's good to see you.' He thumped Zack's knee. 'You've really made something of yourself. I'm proud of you.' The words pleased Zack more than he wanted to admit. 'And Kate's a treasure.'

Zack's mood faltered. He didn't want to talk about Kate.

'I'm surprised a good-looking young fella like you hasn't snapped her up. And not as your PA,' Hal continued, giving Zack a wistful smile. 'Why, if I was thirty years younger, I'd—'

'She's not *just* my PA,' Zack blurted out.

Hal's smile faded. 'You're dating her?' He gave Zack a sober look.

'Yeah, I guess.' Although Zack figured 'dating' was too tame a term to describe what he and Kate had been doing.

'But she works for you.' Hal shook his head.

Where had that accusatory look come from? Zack wondered.

'You disappoint me,' Hal added. 'Sounds to me like you're taking advantage of her.'

Zack shifted, feeling as if he were seated on an iron bar instead of the well-stuffed cushion. 'No, I'm not,' he said. Then the image of Kate's expression yesterday—vulnerable and scared, when she'd tried to refuse the necklace—slithered across Zack's memory. Why were his palms sweating again? He rubbed them on his trousers. 'The attraction is mutual.'

'You're her boss, son,' Hal said firmly. 'You have sex with her, you're taking advantage. However mutual the attraction.'

Zack's blood pressure spiked. 'It's not like that. It's not just sex,' he said, not sure why he was justifying himself.

'You saying you're in love with her?'

The muscles in Zack's spine went rigid, his palms got even damper and his pulse zipped into overdrive. 'I…' He hesitated, had to force the denial out. 'I never said that.'

Hal frowned. 'It's either love or it's just sex, Billy, there is no in between.'

'My name's Zack,' he snapped, feeling cornered.

'You'll have to forgive an old man,' Hal replied, unfazed by Zack's show of temper. 'You'll always be Billy to me.' Hal's eyes softened. 'So what is it?'

'What's what?'

'Are you in love with the girl or not?'

There it was again, that dumb question. Zack shot out of his chair, paced over to the parlour's open terrace doors, suddenly feeling like a caged animal. Tension vibrated through him. He shut his eyes, the scent of lavender and brine flowing in on the breeze suffocating him.

He pictured Kate's face. Comforting and compassionate when she'd held his hand a few minutes ago. Bright and defiant whenever they argued. Sexy enough to make his heart stop when they made love.

He wanted her, sure. But was he falling in love with her?

Over the last week he'd been pretty much cross-eyed with lust, but right along with it had been a surge of longing and bone-deep contentment he still didn't understand. After all, she was easily the most difficult, the most impossible woman he'd ever dated. She used her independence like a shield and never let him get away with anything. That her obstinacy thrilled him as much as it infuriated him probably meant he was losing his mind.

'You figured out the answer yet?' Hal asked, touching his shoulder.

Zack glanced round to see an 'I told you so' smugness in the old man's face. 'We're not in love with each other,' he said, frustration sharpening his voice. 'We're friends. Nothing more.'

And that was the way it was going to stay. He wasn't going to let his heart get ripped out and torn to shreds. He knew what it felt like, had known since he was eight years old. No way was he ever going to leave himself open to that again. If he'd learned one thing from JP, it was that love was for suckers.

'If you say so,' Hal said gently, interrupting Zack's thoughts. 'But she's my friend now, too. So I'm going to ask you a favour.'

'What is it?' Zack asked, warily.

'When you two get the passion out of your system—when you decide to let her go—I'll be expecting you to make sure she doesn't get hurt.'

Zack nodded, but the hair at the nape of his neck bristled. One thing was for damn sure. Kate wasn't out of his system yet—and until she was, he wasn't about to let her go anywhere.

CHAPTER SEVENTEEN

As KATE WALKED along the crushed rock pathway back to the cottage she inhaled the fresh resin scent of the Monterey pines and finally faced the truth.

She'd fallen hopelessly in love with Zack Boudreaux. Super-cool, super-confident, super-sexy Zack. Her boss, her lover and a man who would never, ever need her the way she needed him.

She'd made some pretty spectacular mistakes in her life up to now—trying to win her father's love, trusting Andrew the rat—but this was easily the most catastrophic one so far.

She'd feared the worst yesterday when she'd accepted his necklace. But she hadn't realised the full extent of her idiocy until she'd watched him stiff and vulnerable in Hal's arms and the wave of love, of longing, that had welled up inside her had left her feeling punch-drunk.

A plump quail and its chicks waddled out of the long pampas-grass in single file, scratching for seeds. Kate watched them cross the path. The sight didn't make her smile as it had the day before.

How could she have been such a fool? Hadn't she always promised herself she would never make the mistake of falling for someone who didn't love her? She'd seen what it had done for her mother—tied her for life to a man who had ended up destroying her. Of course, Zack was nothing like her father. He might be arrogant, ruthless even, but he wasn't cruel and manipulative. He'd been generous and caring in his own way, he'd even held her when she'd needed it. But she knew he didn't love her back. He'd never given her any indication that this meant more to him than a casual—and temporary—fling.

She opened the cottage door and walked through the living room, slanting her gaze away from the fireplace as the memory of their strip poker game assaulted her. She paused by the French doors, pushed them open. The bougainvillea and trumpet vines gave off a sweet perfume, making her feel like a princess in a tower. The rocky cliffs gilded with spring flowers and the drama of the dark blue sea below completed the enchanting spell.

Kate let go of the rail and stepped back from the edge. There she went dreaming again like some naïve teenager. She wasn't Rapunzel waiting for her prince. This wasn't a dream. It was an illusion, that was about to suck her in and destroy her. She'd always prided herself on her independence, her self-sufficiency. She needed to cling on to the last remnants of it now if she was going to survive this.

She had to protect herself. She gave a quiet huff of breath, felt her heart crack. Which meant not begging Zack for a commitment he couldn't give. She had made that mistake once before, with her father, and it had cost her dearly. She already knew Zack's rejection would cost her a great deal more.

Drawing her shoulders back, she walked through the cottage to the bedroom she'd been sharing with Zack. She dragged her suitcase out of the wardrobe with leaden arms and began gathering up the clothes scattered around the room. She pulled her clean undies out of the dresser, threw them in the case.

The first step to a stronger, more resilient, more self-aware Kate was a Kate who didn't give in to her rioting hormones. Starting now, she had to stop sleeping with Zack. After all, the incendiary sexual chemistry between them had got her into this fix in the first place. She zipped the lid shut and wheeled the case through the bathroom and into the smaller of the two bedrooms.

The fantasy was over. She lifted her case onto the bed's down comforter, flopped down beside it. She had to start facing reality.

She'd taken a gamble sleeping with the boss, but now she'd fallen in love with him all bets were off.

Two hours later, Zack skidded the Ferrari to a stop in the cottage's driveway and yanked on the handbrake. Ignoring the crisp wind and the darkening sky on the horizon, he left the top down and jumped out of the car. He felt revved up, excited about what the future held and no damn rain cloud was going to dampen his mood.

After spending an hour chatting to Hal—and taking the first tentative steps to reforging the bond they'd once shared—he'd gone for a drive to clear his head. And to plan what the hell he was going to do about Kate. It had taken him a while to calm down enough to think it through rationally—surely just a result of the emotional jolt from his reunion with Hal—but once he had, everything had fallen neatly into place.

He didn't love her, any more than she loved him, but what they had together was way too good to throw away. He adored her company, her companionship, even her smart mouth, and they made a fantastic team—both in business and in bed. The simple solution to the problem had hit him like a brick as he'd handled the powerful car through the heart-stopping scenery of Big Sur.

He'd make her his permanent PA.

She could work for him during the day and they could play together at night. It would be the perfect partnership with no messy emotional entanglements. Kate was the most practical, pragmatic woman he knew—right down to those proper knickers. She'd see the benefits and wouldn't be sidetracked by loads of dumb nonsense about true love. She valued her independence. She wouldn't need more from him than he was willing to give.

He whipped his key card through the cottage lock and flung the door open. 'Hey, Kate, where are you?'

Damn, he'd never been so excited about offering someone a job before. His blood pumped through his veins as he strode through the living room, making him feel more alive than ever.

His enthusiasm had dimmed, though, by the time he'd checked out the terrace, the bathroom and their bedroom and hadn't been able to find Kate. Where had she got to? She was supposed to be here, waiting for him, so he could tell her about the great new opportunity he was about to give her.

As he turned away from the bed, though, he noticed something that sent a chill skidding up his spine. Where was the silk camisole he'd stripped off her this morning while taking her back into bed? He turned in a slow circle. And where were the rest of her clothes? Walking over to the armoire, he pulled open the doors, saw the empty space where her suitcase should have been. Every last molecule of blood seemed to drain out of his head. He blinked, tried to focus past the roar in his ears, the panic ripping at his gut. He swore viciously, the obscenity slicing through the ominous stillness like a jagged blade. The room seemed to fold in around him, and suddenly he was eight years old again, waking up to find the bed beside him empty and his father gone. He tried to force the memory down, but the panic crawled up his chest and sank its teeth into his throat.

Calm down, damn it. She hasn't left you, she can't have.

Slamming the armoire door shut, he stormed through the living room and out onto the terrace, his hands fisting at his side. He whipped round as the flash of blonde caught his eye in the cove below.

He took a deep breath, eased it out. Finally the choking panic began to fade, but the bitter bile of temper rushed up to replace it.

He took the steps down to the beach, two at a time. If she ever scared him like that again she was going to regret it. And, anyhow, what the hell had she done with her stuff?

CHAPTER EIGHTEEN

KATE PERCHED ON the slab of grey granite and stared out at the Pacific Ocean. The timeless rhythm of white surf foamed around the rocks topping the dark, angry blue peaks. A chilly mist hung low as storm clouds frowned over the coastline.

Kate knew just how they felt.

She wrapped her arms round her knees and swallowed down the tears that had been tightening her throat ever since she'd decided her fling with Zack had to end. She had to shake this ridiculous melancholia before she saw him again. Carefree and flippant was how she'd decided to play it. He'd be irritated she didn't want to sleep with him any more, but he'd get over it. They had less than a week left in California. Surely she could hold out against him that long, now she knew how much was at stake.

The knowledge that the days to follow would be agony only made her more determined to keep things dignified. She must not break down in front of him. She mustn't let him know how she felt. Pride, after all, was the only thing she had left. She shut her eyes, pulled her skirt over her knees and hugged her shins as the first drop of rain splashed onto her cheek.

'What are you doing out here? It's about to pour.'

She looked round to see Zack jogging towards her across

the sand, devastatingly sexy in an open-necked shirt and black trousers. Why did he have to look so flipping irresistible? It wasn't fair.

She forced a smile onto her face, climbed off the rock. 'I fancied a walk.'

One black brow arched as he got closer and studied her face. A raindrop splattered down and clung to his lashes like a tear. 'What's wrong?' He wiped the moisture away. 'You look like you're about to cry.'

So much for carefree and flippant. She looked past him, her throat closing on the words she needed to say. 'We better go inside before we get soaked.' She tried to walk by him but he took her arm, pulled her round to face him.

'Where's your stuff?'

She shivered, his confrontational stance as much to blame as the spots of rain dampening the light sweater and skirt she wore. 'I've decided to move into the other bedroom.'

The emerald-green of his eyes darkened to match the ominous clouds overhead. 'What the hell for?'

She dipped her head—and felt the instinctive response at the sight of his chest outlined by the damp splotches on his shirt. This was exactly why she had to stand her ground. She was addicted to him. Her head came back up. 'I think we should stop sleeping together.'

'Yeah?' The single word sliced out. This wasn't irritation, Kate realised, but something much more volatile. 'Well, what if I don't?' he finished.

'Please, let's go inside?' she said, struggling for calm. Matching his temper with her own would only make the fire between them flare hotter. 'We're getting wet.'

He looked ready to argue, but then the rumble of thunder signalled a deluge that drenched them in seconds. But as they raced up the cliff steps he kept hold of her arm, only letting go once they were inside the cottage.

'Stay put. I'll get the towels,' he said, his voice now rigid with control.

She stood frozen in place as he stalked into the bedroom. The soft pat, pat, pat of rainwater dripping from her hair onto the floor galvanised her into action. She peeled off her soaked cotton sweater, clasping her arms over her chest as Zack walked back into the room, only too aware of her bra made transparent by the rain.

He'd taken off his shirt and was rubbing a towel across his chest. She swallowed, feeling the familiar flames burn hotter. Terrific. Now she would have to argue her case while they were both practically naked. Why couldn't anything in her life be easy?

'Here.' He threw her the extra towel he'd slung round his neck. His gaze slid down to her breasts, making the heat throb harder. She pulled the towel around her shoulders.

'I thought we could grab a shower together,' he said, his voice cool, but his gaze more penetrating than a laser beam. He leaned against the sofa and folded his arms, giving her a stiff smile. 'Then we'll talk about our sleeping arrangements.'

Kate felt indignation flare alongside the desire. He was trying to ride roughshod over her. Typical. Well, this time, finally, she was going to get her own way. Pheromones or no pheromones. She had to.

'I'll shower alone, thank you. And then I'd like to make a few calls. I'll be back in Britain at the end of the week and I need to line up a new job.'

He straightened, the smile wiped off his face. 'You're not going back to Britain. I'm giving you a permanent contract as my PA.'

'But…' The implication of what he'd said sank in. She bit into her bottom lip, forcing down the spurt of hope. She couldn't stay with him, however much she might want to. It would only make things harder in the end. 'Why are you offering me this now?'

'Isn't it obvious?' Zack dropped his arms and gripped the armrest, tilting his upper body towards her. 'You're doing a fantastic job.' His gaze intensified. 'And we make a great team.'

'I…I can't accept it,' she said on a shuddering breath, feeling her resolve dripping away like the raindrops from her hair.

'Don't be stupid.' He pushed away from the sofa, stepped close. His body heat felt almost as overwhelming as the force of his will. He stroked open palms up her arms. 'I'm offering a good salary.'

Her heart plunged as he pushed her wet hair back and framed her face.

'You'll have your independence.' He pressed his thumb against her bottom lip. 'If that's what's bothering you.'

She heaved out an unsteady breath.

'I want you with me,' he said, pushing the towel off her shoulders, throwing it away.

She shivered violently.

'You're cold,' he murmured, holding her steady. But she knew she wasn't. What she was was weak. He took her hand, led her across the living room. 'Let's get you warmed up.'

But as they walked towards the bathroom her dazed mind registered one thought. He was wrong. She wouldn't have her independence. Despite the salary he was offering, despite the trappings of independence, she would be little better than her mother. A woman who'd sacrificed her identity, her individuality, for a love that had never been real.

Clinging onto the thought, Kate tugged her hand out of Zack's. 'I'm not doing this. I'm not taking the job.'

'Why?' Temper still simmered in his eyes, but with it was confusion.

She drew in a deep breath, gathered her courage like a shield around her heart. 'Because you don't just want a PA, you want someone to share your bed. And I don't want to be your convenient bed partner any more.'

He gave a harsh laugh. 'You're not what I'd call conve-nient.' He stepped forward and she bumped back against the wall. 'And, anyhow, you're lying.' His hands grasped her hips, held her still. 'I know you want me.'

'Stop it, Zack.' She wriggled.

He dragged her against him. 'You want to know how I know?'

She flattened her hands against his chest. 'No, I don't.'

His big body held her back against the wall. 'Your eyes get this ring of violet around the iris when you're aroused.' He captured her chin in his hand when she tried to turn away. 'And your lips get plumper.' He bit her lower lip softly as his thumb and forefinger skimmed down her neck. 'Your breath-ing gets rapid.'

Her breath panted out in ragged gasps.

'And your nipples get so hard.' He cupped her breast, lifted it. 'It's like they're begging for my touch.' He bent his head, took the swollen peak into his mouth, the hot suction scalding her through the cold, wet lace.

She moaned, the sexual thrill spreading through her like wildfire. 'I can't. I can't do this.' She choked on the words, unable to hide the quiver of longing.

He lifted his head. 'Yes, you can.' His arm closed around her waist as one powerful thigh pushed between her legs, forcing them apart, and rubbed against her sex. 'Put your arms around my neck.'

The harsh demand sliced through the fog of arousal and her arms lifted of their own accord. She clung to him, feeling the press of his erection through his trousers. Her legs quiv-ered as her insides melted, surrendering against her will.

His lips crushed hers as his hands pushed under her skirt and kneaded her buttocks. The swift, heady rush of heat had her fingers fisting in his hair. Her mind screamed at her to stop him, but her body wouldn't listen. Like a kamikaze moth dive-bombing into the flame she held his cheeks, dragged him closer. Her breath shuddered out and her eyes closed as their tongues tangled in a kiss full of hunger, heat and mutual demand.

His fingers ripped at her knickers and then plunged into her. She bucked, cried out, already on the verge of coming apart. Humiliated by her inability to resist him, she let go of him, pushed against the hard planes of his chest.

'Please.' She gasped. 'Don't. I can't.'

He reared back, his face fierce. 'Yes, you can. You're soaking wet.'

He cradled her head and took her mouth again. Stamping his claim on her. The tidal wave of desire was so strong she couldn't hold it back any longer. She trembled, sobbed with need as his thumb pressed against her swollen clitoris and stroked hard until she cried out her release.

Dazed by the strength of her orgasm, she watched as he pushed her bra up, suckled the engorged nipples. She writhed against him, the fire streaming down to her already aching sex. She heard the hiss of his zipper as he freed himself from his trousers.

'Open your eyes,' he ordered.

Her lids fluttered open to see him watching her, his eyes feverish with desire, his face harsh with demand. 'You're mine,' he said, his fingers digging into her hips as he lifted her. 'You hear me, Kate.' She was trapped against him, her legs wrapped around his waist. The blunt head of his penis pressed against the folds of her sex. 'Tell me you want me,' he said.

'I want you,' she whispered, her sanity overwhelmed by the need clawing inside her and clamouring for release.

He thrust inside her. The slickness of her recent climax eased his entry but still it was difficult, painful in its fullness. She sobbed, tried to buck him off, as she felt herself losing that last gossamer thread of control. That last tiny portion of self.

She shook her head from side to side. Struggled to deny

the sexual frenzy, but then he plunged deeper. The brutal pleasure intensified and she gave a moan of defeat.

'Shh,' he crooned. 'It'll be okay in a minute.' And then he was fully inside her, stretching her unbearably.

He began to move, the tormenting rhythm bumping the place inside her he knew would trigger her orgasm. It roared through her, forcing her over the edge and dragging her back up. She cried out, breaking into a billion quivering pieces. Ecstasy and agony made one in her quaking body. He shouted out his own release as he emptied inside her.

'Are you okay?' he asked softly, his breathing harsh, his penis still thick, still firm inside her.

She pushed against his shoulders. 'Let me go.' The tears misting her eyes, closing her throat, only humiliated her more. She'd let him do it again.

He pulled out of her in silence. She flinched, her sex tender as it released him. She pushed her bra down, her fingers trembling as she fumbled with her skirt. She willed herself to stop shaking, heard him refastening his trousers.

He touched her cheek, a tender smile on his lips, but she could see the triumph in his eyes. 'I'll get Monty to sort out a new contract when we get back to Vegas.'

The words hit her like an icy slap. The horrible truth of what she'd done, of what she'd let him do, dawned on her with shocking clarity. Her own body had betrayed her.

She lurched away from his touch. 'I won't sign it. And I'm not going to Vegas with you.' She scrambled away from him. 'I'm leaving. I'm leaving now,' she said frantically as she rushed towards the smaller bedroom.

'Come back here.' She heard the pained shout but kept on going.

She slammed the bedroom door shut, shame and heartbreak turning to smothering rage. Suddenly, she was as mad at him as she was with herself. She ignored the loud crash as the door flew open behind her and slapped back against the wall.

'What the hell has gotten into you?'

She unzipped her case, pulled out a new top, refusing to look at him. 'Apart from your insatiable penis, you mean?' The words were crude, ugly, but it was how she felt. He'd used her desire, her love, against her and part of her hated him for it.

'Stop it.' He ripped the blouse out of her grasp. 'You came apart in my arms in there and now you're acting like some outraged virgin.' His fingers fisted on her arm. 'What the hell is going on?'

'I've fallen in love with you.' She hurled the words at him. 'Now do you get it?' Humiliation turned the shout to a whisper.

'What?' His fingers released her, the look of shock and confusion on his face made the last of the anger drain away until all that was left was a grinding, lancing pain where her heart should have been.

'I love you. And that means I can't stay with you. As your PA, as your handy bed companion or as anything else.' She picked up her blouse, tugged it on, tried to button it with trembling fingers. 'I saw what it did to my mother. I won't let it happen to me.'

'For heaven's sake, Kate.' His fingers stroked her arm. 'You're not making any sense.'

She looked at him then, saw compassion and it almost undid her. 'You don't understand because you don't know what it's like. To love someone and have them not love you back.' She sniffed, wiped her eyes hastily with her fist. For goodness' sake don't cry now, not when you've finally got up the courage to tell him the truth.

'So your father didn't love your mother. What has that got to do with us?' he asked, sounding exasperated.

'She was his mistress, Zack. His kept woman. He paid for her clothes, her food, the house we lived in. She would beg him to marry her, to acknowledge me, but he wasn't interested, because the only thing he wanted from her was sex. He never wanted her love—and he didn't want mine either.'

'Damn, Kate. I'm sorry,' he said. He pushed the curls from her forehead. 'But I still don't see what all that's got to do with—'

She pressed her fingers to his lips, the hopelessness of the situation tearing her apart. 'I love you but you don't love me. Can't you see? In the end it's the same thing.'

'But I'm not like him. I'm offering you a good job. I'm not trying to turn you into my mistress.'

'Just answer me one question. Do you need me, Zack? Really need me?'

His brow furrowed as he dragged his fingers through his hair. She felt her heart splintering. 'I care about you,' he said cautiously. 'I want you—you know that.'

'It's not enough,' she said miserably.

He reached for her but she pulled away.

'You want me but you don't need me,' she said. 'You don't love me.' She hugged herself to try and stop the shaking. 'Every time you touch me, every time you hold me, every time we make love, knowing you don't will chip away another little piece of my self-confidence, another little piece of my self-respect, until I'll be just like her. Begging for scraps when I deserve a banquet.'

'Damn it, this is stupid. You're not seriously going to throw away everything we've got for the sake of a few dumb words.'

She felt her heart shatter. 'Please leave, Zack. I want to have a shower and get changed—and then I need to arrange things so I can leave.'

No way was she going anywhere tonight, or any night. But Zack could read the misery on her face and see the goose-bumps on her arms. She was emotionally distraught and she was shivering. He doubted he'd be able to talk any sense into her at the moment—and he didn't want her catching pneumonia.

'I need to get some dry clothes on myself.' He nodded towards the bathroom. 'Have your shower. Then we'll talk.'

'There's nothing left to talk about,' she said wearily.

They'd see about that, he thought as he walked out of the room. Frustration and panic burning like lava in his gut.

CHAPTER NINETEEN

'I'LL SEE YOU in twenty minutes. Yes, that's right, San Francisco airport.' Kate put the phone down, heard the annoyed huff from behind her.

Zack stood in the doorway to their bedroom, his hair still damp from his shower and furrowed into rows. His feet were bare and he wore the T-shirt and faded jeans she remembered from their date in Monterey. The day he'd bought her the necklace. The painful stab of memory was just one of many she would have to endure over the coming weeks.

He propped his shoulder against the door jamb. 'You're not going through with this,' he said with so little inflection in his voice she wanted to scream at him. It wasn't a question. It was an order. She bit back the angry words that hovered on her tongue, forced herself to remain calm. Hysterics would only make it worse.

'Yes, I am. I phoned Monty and he said he'd already wired my salary into my credit card account.'

He looked at her, his eyes giving nothing away.

'I know I haven't worked the full two weeks,' she continued, as conversationally as she could manage. 'So I'll repay you what I owe you as soon as I get home.'

He swore viciously. 'This isn't about the money or the

damn job.' He didn't look indifferent any more. 'You're not going anywhere.'

'Yes, I am.'

He walked towards her. She stood her ground.

'We just had sex without a condom. What if you get pregnant?'

Heat pumped into her cheeks. She hadn't even considered the possibility. 'I won't.'

'You're forgetting, we've been living together for the last week. I know you haven't had a period and I also know you're not on the pill. So that won't wash.'

'So what if I do get pregnant?' She thrust out her chin, forced her eyes to meet his. 'It wouldn't make any difference.'

He gave a hollow laugh. 'Think again. I'm not letting you out of my sight while you might be carrying my baby.'

'You haven't listened to a word I've said, have you, Zack?' She suddenly felt unbearably weary. Could he really understand so little about what she wanted, what she needed? 'I would never bring a child into the sort of relationship my parents had. I know what that's like.'

His eyes narrowed. 'You better not be talking about abortion.'

She hadn't been, but it hardly mattered now. 'This is all hypothetical, anyway. It doesn't change a thing.'

She glanced at her watch, struggled to keep her voice even. 'The cab's going to be here in fifteen minutes and I wanted to say goodbye to Hal before I go. If you'll excuse me.'

She tried to walk past him. He stepped into her path.

'You can't leave me.' The anger in his voice surprised her, but more shocking was the anguish swirling in his eyes.

'Please, Zack. Don't make this any harder than it already is.'

'I don't want to lose what we have.'

He cupped her cheek. She jerked away. 'All we ever really had was great sex. Believe me you can find another playmate.'

The tears she refused to shed clogged her throat. 'They'll be lining up round the block once I'm gone.'

He shook his head slowly. 'But they won't be you,' he said. Was that pain she'd seen in his eyes? Before she could be sure, he turned away, walked towards the terrace. He stopped at the French doors, his back to her, braced his hand against the frame and bowed his head.

'This is so damn hard,' he muttered.

He looked tense and defensive, reminding her of how he'd been during their meeting with Hal.

She stood behind him, her voice shaking. 'What are you trying to say, Zack?'

'I promised myself when I was eight years old that I'd never let this happen again.' He was still muttering, his back rigid as he looked out into the storm-shrouded sky. 'And now it has and there's not a damn thing I can do about it.'

He sounded so frustrated and so annoyed, but if there was even a slim chance, a slight hope—she let the feeling of anticipation rise like a star in her chest.

'I don't understand.'

He shot round, pinned her with his gaze. 'I'm saying I'm in love with you and it's all your fault.'

His fingers fisted on her arms and he held her upright as her knees gave way. He shook her, the emotional battle etched on his face. Her heart thumped so hard she was sure it was about to burst out of her chest. Could he be telling her the truth?

'I was rich beyond my wildest dreams,' he said, accusation weighing down every word. 'I didn't have to live on the turn of the cards any more. I was doing just fine. And then you come along in your bra and thong and ruin everything.' He sounded so angry. 'I need you so damn much, it scares me to death,' he said, his voice even harsher, but the truth shone in his eyes, lighting her from within.

'Welcome to the club,' she said softly, sniffing back tears

of joy. 'You happen to be the most arrogant, overbearing man I've ever met.' Her breath hitched as a smile curved her lips. 'And if I could have chosen someone to fall head over heels in love with there's no way on earth I would have picked you.'

He yanked her against him, wrapping his arms around her so tightly her breath gushed out. She could feel his heart, pounding sure and steady. She clutched at his back, wanting to mould herself to him.

Finally he touched his forehead to hers. 'What the hell are we going to do?' He sounded more confused than ever.

'We're going to love each other.' Wasn't it obvious?

He hugged her close, cursed softly. 'I'm so sorry, Kate.' The words shuddered out against her hair.

'What for?'

'For being such a damn coward. I didn't want to love you, didn't want to admit it, even to myself, because it hurt so much before.'

She pulled back, took his face in her hands. 'What do you mean, before?'

He put his hands over hers, drew them down. 'They were such good people and he hurt them. I hurt them.'

'It wasn't your fault. It was never your fault.'

He shook his head. 'You don't understand. Hal's eye was all swollen up, he had blood on his lip. And Mary was crying. I carried that picture in my head for years. I hated JP after that. And I hated myself, too. I went off the rails when he died. Gambling, living in the darkness, taking dumb risks to make an easy buck. Just like he did.' He sighed. 'I turned my life around, eventually. Thought I was finally free of him. But I wasn't.'

The self-loathing in his voice made her heart bleed for him. 'Why do you say that?'

'Because I was still living by his philosophy of life. Never be dumb enough to love anyone.'

'You're not living by that philosophy any more, though, are you?' she said smugly.

A wry smile curved his lips. 'No, I'm not.' He held her chin in his fingers, stroked his thumb down her cheek. 'I guess I've got a certain lady in her bra and thong to thank for that.'

'Don't sell yourself short, Zack.' She hugged him close, her love and commitment even stronger than before, if that were possible. 'You've got you to thank for that.'

His hands caressed her bottom and she felt the wonderfully predictable swell of his arousal against her belly. 'And anyway—' she smiled against his chest, lifted her face to his '—those were proper knickers.'

'So you keep saying.' He pulled her skirt aside, slipped warm fingers under the waistband of her panties.

She jumped at the intimate contact. 'What are you doing?'

'Just checking,' he said, chuckling as she melted in his hands.

EPILOGUE

'HOW'S THE BUMP?' Zack murmured against the back of Kate's head.

'The bump's fine.' She grinned as broad fingers caressed the slight swell of her belly through the satin of her bridal gown. 'Now keep your voice down. I don't want everyone thinking this is a shotgun wedding.'

Zack gave a wry chuckle as the heat tinted her cheeks. 'You know, until this morning I never knew you were such a scaredy-pants, Miss Proper Knickers.'

'That's Mrs Proper Knickers to you,' she said, loving the feel of him pressed against her back, and feeling too mellow to rise to the bait he'd been dangling since their little disagreement that morning.

After all, this was her wedding day and it had been picture perfect. She took in the gardens of The Grange, breathtaking in their summer glory, and the specially erected gazebo bedecked with flowers where she and Zack had said their vows only half an hour ago. She smiled at the sight of Monty and Stella, their live-wire son Joey, Hal and a few other carefully selected guests enjoying champagne and canapés in the bright sunshine while beyond the cliffs the waves crashed onto shore in their timeless, never-ceasing rhythm.

Not unlike the rhythm of Zack's heartbeat, which she could

sense matching her own in the summer stillness. This place and time had a raw, elemental beauty that she would hold in her heart for ever, much like the man behind her.

She'd decided to ignore the fact that he wouldn't stop goading her about her request not to announce the pregnancy yet. Even the thought of it made her blush.

For goodness' sake, they'd only been together for three months. She still wasn't quite over the shock of discovering she was pregnant in the first place. Telling everyone else was too much for her. What if people thought they were only getting married because of the baby? Of course, she'd mentioned all this to Zack this morning. He'd finally agreed to keep the news to himself, for today. But she'd known from the pained look on his face, he was just humouring a pregnant lady—and he was unlikely to let it drop for long.

His fingers spread out across her abdomen, rubbed the silky fabric. 'You're not going to be able to hide it much longer. And I still don't see what the big deal is anyway.'

She turned in his embrace, cradled his cheek. Good Lord, he looked gorgeous in the Armani suit he'd worn for the ceremony, especially now he'd taken off his tie and she could see his chest hair where he'd undone the first three buttons of his dress shirt. 'I know you don't,' she said. 'But for today I want it to be our secret.'

He frowned. 'You're not scared about the baby, are you?'

'Right down to my toes, but I'm excited too,' she added quickly as she saw his frown deepen. 'It's just, the last few months, there's been so much to take in.' She'd been floating on a cloud of heart-bursting love, mind-blowing passion and soul-deep contentment and her feet still hadn't touched the ground. She was beginning to realise they probably never would.

There'd been the job Zack had offered her, not just as his PA but as part of his management team. There'd been the stunning glass-and-wood house he'd bought just down the coast road from The Grange, plus the marriage proposal and the frantic arrangements for the wedding when he'd decided he couldn't wait. And then, last but by no means least, the confirmation a week ago that they were starting a family—rather sooner than they would have planned. All thrilling, all wonderful and all scary as hell.

'Don't be scared, Kate.' He brought her fingers to his lips. 'I found out a long time ago, you make the most of the cards you're dealt in life. I figure we've been dealt four aces. All we have to do now is sit back and play them slow.'

'Umm-hmm.' She nodded. Oh, God, she thought, I love this man so much, I'm even turned on by his poker analogies. She fluttered her eyelashes at him. 'Well, if you've dealt me more than one ace, honey, you're going to be in big trouble.'

He chuckled. Letting go of her hand, he rested his palm on her shoulder, skimmed his thumb down her throat. 'Are you saying you don't want a pair of babies, or trips?' he said. 'Just think how big you'd get.' His eyes dipped, following the path of his thumb as it outlined the curve of her breast, already swollen in pregnancy. Her nipples peaked against the snug satin of her bodice.

She huffed. 'What is it with guys and enormous boobs?' she said, trying to put some indignation into her voice although she was getting breathless.

'You look great pregnant,' he said, his voice so husky the heat built at her core. 'And it's not the size of your boobs, so much as the sensitivity.'

The flush spread up her chest and her nipples tightened even more as she recalled what had happened the night before when Zack had decided to test how sensitive her breasts had become.

He pressed his thumb against her nipple and the heat lanced downwards. She gasped and grabbed his wrist. 'Behave yourself, we happen to be in public—and it's the middle of the day.'

'Sweetheart.' He folded her into his arms, laughing. 'We're married now. Public displays of affection aren't just allowed, they're encouraged.'

'Is that so?' She grinned up at him.

'Yeah. Anyhow, I'm the boss and I say married guys are allowed to come on to their wives any time they want.'

'Who made you the boss?' she demanded, raising a coquettish eyebrow.

'I did,' he shot straight back at her.

'I may have to dispute that.'

He lowered his head, his breath feathering her lips. 'I was hoping you'd say that,' he murmured, before capturing her mouth.

She wrapped her arms around his neck, welcoming the invasion of his tongue and revelling in the heat of the kiss. She matched his need, his desire, with her own while every single thought flew right out of her head. Bar one.

When it feels this good, I don't care if he is the boss.

But she had no intention of telling him that.

Caught on Camera with the CEO

NATALIE ANDERSON

Possibly the only librarian who got told off herself for talking too much, **Natalie Anderson** decided writing books might be more fun than shelving them—and, boy, is it that! Especially writing romance—it's the realisation of a lifetime dream, kick-started by many an afternoon spent devouring Grandma's Mills & Boon® novels...

She lives in New Zealand, with her husband and four gorgeous-but-exhausting children. Swing by her website any time—she'd love to hear from you: www.natalie-anderson.com.

For the best apple pie and chocolate chip biscuit baker in the world: Aunty Margaret.
No one makes 'em like you do.
And no one laughs as infectiously as you either.
Thank you for all your support.

CHAPTER ONE

'YOU'LL have that for me by three? Fantastic.'

Dani forced her body to freeze at the sound of that voice. 'No problem.'

Dani knew the breathless assistant would have it for him by two at the latest—just as she would if he'd asked her.

Alex Carlisle, CEO of Carlisle Finance Corporation, on his rounds again—gliding through the open-plan area and bewitching his staff so they performed above and beyond. She wondered if he even knew the effect he had on his legions of adoring employees.

And Dani was the latest. Not looking was impossible. Her lashes lifted.

Truthfully she was probably the only one whose work was *suffering* because of him. She found him so distracting she wasn't getting half as much done as she should. Half of her wished he'd go away so her insides wouldn't be so pummelled, but all of her wanted him to stay.

He was so good to look at, she'd been watching him all week. She'd seen how he abandoned his lavish office suite at the top of the building and came to talk with his worker ants— all of whom then frantically tapped faster at keyboards to get the work done for him. Charismatic, confident, Alex Carlisle got everything he wanted, every time. And if the water-cooler gossip she'd got from one of the secretaries was anything to go by, women were a big part of what he wanted—beautiful, high-flying, high-society women. He played a lot, apparently. And all his female employees wished like crazy he'd play with them.

Dani totally understood why they did, but she wasn't going to admit she was floored by him too. So predictable. Anyway she couldn't afford to fixate like this. She checked the time. Only a few minutes and she could go to lunch. She'd never clock-watched before, usually enjoyed her work so the hours flew, but she had a mission to fulfil. Besides, something about this place made her antsy. OK, it was him. She was waiting, always waiting for him to appear. Now he had, she couldn't wait to bust a move, so restless it was as if she had creepy-crawlies infesting every inch of her clothing.

Unable to resist the compelling force of him, she lifted her head and looked again. She was such an idiot. It was as if she'd been tossed into a stormy kind of teen crush—she'd never experienced one in her youth, but it seemed there was a time for everything. She only had to hear his voice for her heart to thunder and the adrenalin to flood her system, so sitting still was no longer possible.

Concentrate, you fool.

The excitement was a waste of energy anyway. The water-cooler woman had also informed her that, while the man might play fast and loose in his own social set, he never ever fooled around at work. Big shame. She watched as he stood talking with her supervisor. He was tall; his tailored trousers seemed to go on forever.

Yeah, Dani, all the way to the floor.

But her self-mockery didn't stop her looking. He'd shed his jacket so he wore just the pale blue shirt, sleeves rolled partially up his arms—the ultimate ad for corporate wear. He turned. Caught her look on the full. And then held it prisoner.

Oh. Wow.

All but his face blurred. The low noise of the office became a distant hum. The sudden silence was nice and her antsy body stopped still, bathed in his gaze. Dani's favourite colour was green. And Alex Carlisle's eyes were very, very green.

He moved, one small step. Was he coming over? To talk to her?

Someone called his name. He turned away, his smile flashing back on. And it was gone—the stillness, the warmth, the quiet. All disappeared the instant she blinked.

Good grief, what was she doing sitting there like a *Muppet*? Unable to move or speak or even breathe? She shook her head and released the air held too long in her straining lungs.

Ridiculous.

But how glad was she that he hadn't come over? Because when he'd looked at her she'd been unable to think of anything. Not a thing. All power had gone from her brain to somewhere else entirely—and was warming her up. She couldn't see how any of them got any work done when he was on the floor.

OK, so it was two minutes 'til lunch. But she'd arrived early, as she always did, and had already promised to work late tonight, so she needn't feel guilty about stepping out now. Because she desperately needed to get outside and gasp in some fresh air.

She walked down the length of the floor to the lift, keeping well to the side of the room. She was short enough not to be noticed and she was only the temp, after all. She moved fast. Usually she took the stairs but he was near the stairs and, as much as she was drawn to him, her instinct told her equally loudly to stay well away. And this instinct was just strong enough to beat the one that made her avoid small, confined spaces. She could do it. Sure she could.

But when she got to the lift and pressed the button, her nerves sharpened. She counted to ten as she waited, trying to slow her breathing to match it with her mental chanting. It was only a lift. People went up and down them millions of times a day without accident. People didn't get trapped in them.

Trapped. Her scalp prickled as if she were under one of those huge cover-your-whole-head driers at the hairdresser— and it was on too hot and she couldn't get it off. She didn't want to be trapped.

She redirected her thoughts. Forced the fear to the back and focused on a plan. If she ate on the run, she'd have time to go to the public library and be able to check the message boards on the Internet. The search was all that mattered.

The lift chimed and she made herself move into it, closing her eyes as the doors slid together. It would be over in a whirl. Such fears were childish.

But there was a noise. She opened her eyes again in time to see the doors sliding back again. An arm was stretching out between them—making them automatically reopen. And stay open.

'I'll be back shortly.' The arm held firm. 'Email the guest list through to Lorenzo, as well, will you? And make sure the catering staff have the right number of vegetarians this time. We don't want to upset anyone again. Oh, and can you make sure Cara gets the message about Saturday?'

Jeez, the lift could have been down and back up again in that time—well, almost. At last, the rest of him stepped in.

He smiled at her. 'Sorry about that.'

Was he really? Or was that just his polite upbringing

talking, hiding the real ramifications of his childhood—that he had the right to make others wait, that his time was more important than hers? Dani only had an hour—unpaid and all—and she had to make the most of it. But that thought and every other disappeared as the doors finally slid shut.

Dani stepped right back, standing stiffly against the far wall of the lift. Would the fear never leave her?

He leant his back against the side wall so he was at right angles to her. Not even covertly looking at her. No, his gaze was open, intense and relentless.

She kept her eyes fixed on the doors, trying to stop the sensation that they were closing in on her. At least the lifts in this building were science-fiction fast—once they were allowed to get started. But the sense of airlessness closed in too.

He pressed the button again and finally it began its swift descent.

Dani gritted her teeth, sweat sliding down her back.

'Are you OK?'

Dani couldn't answer. Too busy holding her breath. Five, four, three...

There was a groaning sound—a metallic moan that, although slow, was definitely getting louder. Dani's muscles flexed. The lift stopped, dropped another foot and then stopped again. Dani's stomach just kept on falling.

She looked at the lights—no floor indicated. The doors half opened and she had a glimpse of metal and concrete. Between floors. She was damn glad when the doors closed again.

There was a second of complete silence.

'I'm sure it won't be long.'

'I'm not worried,' she lied, flicking a glance his way and looking straight back at the doors again when she registered he had a smile on. His smiles weren't good for her blood pressure. Nor was being stuck in a very small space. Adrenalin rippled through her muscles but the nausea rose faster. She inhaled through her nose, aware of every inch of her body. Surely those few years of physical training would stand her in good stead. She could overcome fear. She could breathe.

He'd lifted away from the wall. 'No, really, it won't be long.'

Sure. No matter how stiff she tried to stay, her limbs insisted on shaking. Her heart was shaking too, the beats falling over themselves, and she couldn't breathe fast enough. She couldn't get any oxygen in.

'We never have trouble with these lifts.'

Oh, yeah? Well, they were now. 'You probably confused it by making it wait so long with its doors open,' she said. The spark of anger pushed the bile back down.

'It's a machine. Machines don't get confused. Only people do that.'

She was confused now—her body wanting to run, her brain wanting to shut down altogether, her stomach wanting to hurl its contents.

'You're new here,' he said. 'I've seen you in the office.'

Distraction. Excellent. 'Yes,' she said, barely controlling the wobble in her voice. And after another stumbling beat she looked from the doors to him.

His eyes were very wide and very green and filled with a painfully gentle concern. He took a step towards her. 'My name is—'

'I know who you are,' she cut him off. She couldn't think enough for conversation.

'You do?' His eyes narrowed and his smile twisted, bitterness thinning his sensual lips. 'Then you're one up on me.' He took the last step closing the gap between them. 'I have no idea who I am.'

The bitterness surprised her, blasted the smothering fog from her head. She looked closer at him. 'You're Alex. And you're stuck in a l-lift.'

She glanced at the walls; they were nearing her again. The fear crept back up. She gulped in air. Were they running out of oxygen already? And had she just whimpered?

'There's no need to be afraid.'

Wasn't there? Didn't she know exactly how frightening it was to be stuck in a small place for too long?

'Hey.' He put his hands on her shoulders. 'It's going to be fine.'

At his touch she looked back into his face. Green eyes gazed at her, deepened by the dark lashes that framed them. Everything else in the world receded again. Yes, she'd look at him, focus on him, forget everything…but green eyes. The colour swirled, the black centre spread. His gaze flickered, dropped to her mouth. Made her realise it was dry. She touched her tongue to the corner of it and then she found she was looking at his. It was extraordinarily fine, with lips that were currently curved up in a smile.

'You OK?'

She couldn't take her eyes off him. She couldn't answer.

'Sweetheart?'

Funny how just one word, said in just the right way, could change everything.

She gazed at him, feeling that restlessness inside roar, and her chin lifted.

His hands moved, dropping to circle round her waist.

'It's going to be just fine,' he said. And then slowly, so slowly, giving her all the time to turn away, he lowered his head.

But she didn't turn.

His lips were warm, firm but not forceful, not invasive, just gentle. He lifted his head a millimetre and his green eyes searched hers. 'See?'

Still she said nothing, but the smallest of sighs escaped as she lifted her chin back up to him.

Those strong hands at her waist then lifted her right off her feet. Automatically she put out her own hands—not to punch, but to steady. Her fingers connected with cotton and curled around the hard muscles. The heat of him burned through the shirt. She spread her fingers wider—wow, he was broad. All she could hear was her breathing—too short, too fast.

Their gazes remained locked all the while he lifted her, sliding her up against the back wall of the lift until her eyes were almost level with his. Her heart thundered while her toes stretched down, vainly searching for something solid— like the floor.

This time when he kissed her he stayed, his lips moving over hers slowly teasing. Oh. Her eyes closed as again and again his mouth caressed hers, making her brain go so mushy. And then Dani had to move: softening, opening, relaxing yet seeking at the same time—*more*. And he gave it, his tongue sweeping into her mouth and curling with hers. It was like feeling all her favourite things at once—the heat of a summer's day, the freshness of sea breeze and the sensation of diving into the deepest warm water. Only it was better. It was all-in-one. And it was real.

Her hands slid over his arms, her fingertips exploring his strength and heat, the breadth of his back. She lifted a hand, ran it through his hair. Short, dark, gorgeously thick. She moved, resting her palm on the back of his neck—so warm. Both hands lifted to hold his face close and the kisses changed again— deeper, more hungry, *fevered*. Now every inch of her wanted every inch of him hard up against her. She wanted to feel his body above her, beneath her—all around. But she couldn't tear her mouth from his. She didn't care about the tightness of his hands bruising her waist. She just didn't want the soaring feeling to end. It was as if a veil had been lifted to reveal a bottomless need she hadn't known she had. To be close.

And his need, too, seemed as strong. His kisses on her face and neck were fast, passionate, until their lips connected again and they could plumb the depths of each other in a long, long carnal kiss.

He pulled her away from the wall, close against his body. One hand quickly moving beneath her bottom to take her weight so she didn't fall from his hold. She responded automatically, hooking her legs around his waist. Gasping at how good it felt to have his body between hers. He was big, strong and fantastically hard. Basic instinct screamed at her now. Bursting with need for bare skin, she pressed her mouth harder against his, her fingers fighting with his shirt.

But then she felt him stagger. He pushed her, lifting her away and down until her feet hit the ground. But then the ground itself bumped up and down.

Oh, no, that was right. They were in a lift. Dani tore her gaze away from him. Looked beyond to the lights, to the door. The lift had finally moved again, descended. And now those doors were opening.

'I—'

He didn't get a chance to say whatever it was he was going to say. There were people—bankers, a couple of technicians. All chorusing his name.

'Alex!'

Dani knew when to make the most of an opportunity. Her legs might be short but she could move them quickly. And, breathless though she was, she had a huge hit of adrenalin to see her through. Energy was an inferno inside her roaring for release. Her high heels clipped on the polished floor. As she exited through the big glass door she glanced back. He was still caught talking to the group. Frowning this time, no smile. And he glanced up frequently, tracking her, she knew. Sparkling light tumbled from his eyes towards her. She walked faster. Pulled her mobile from the bag that miraculously was still slung over her shoulder. She'd phone the agency. Find another job. Snogging the boss was so not allowed. But it wasn't her flouting of that convention that made her move so fast. It was the fear of that bottomless need he'd uncovered. And the truth that she was desperately trying to ignore: it hadn't been a *snog*, it had been heaven.

Alex lifted the cup and sipped—yick. He might be sprawled in a big chair in the first-class club but the coffee was still thin, airport dross. He glanced at his laptop on the table beside him. The screen saver had been dancing for a good twenty minutes now—hiding the report he should have finished already. But focus had been impossible when distraction had such curves. He should be working. And if he wasn't working he should be worrying about Patrick's bombshell last week and the horrendous ramifications of those test results. He should be dealing with it.

Instead he was indulging in a wicked fantasy and debating how he was going to turn it into reality. There simply had to be more—wrong though it was. But those minutes in the elevator with that petite temp had been magic, and not anywhere near enough. Since when did he start kissing random women in elevators? Especially an employee? Just because she'd been nervous?

Well, it had seemed like a good way of distracting her at

the time. And himself. But that irresistible distraction had turned searingly, mind-blowingly incredible—how was he going to ensure he got more?

His mobile chimed. Lorenzo. Alex answered promptly. 'Hey.'

'Where are you?'

'Sydney Airport.'

'Man, you're hardly ever home these days.'

Alex sighed. 'I know. Just waiting for the flight back.'

He'd arranged this business trip after Patrick had called out of the blue. After years of only occasional correspondence, he'd rung to tell him the 'truth'—thirty years too late. At first Alex hadn't believed him, had insisted on the tests. It had only taken twenty-four hours. After seeing it in black-and-white he'd had to get away. He could have done the deal with conference calls, but he'd used it to avoid everyone for a few days. But now the job was done and he was aching to get back to Auckland. He had unfinished business to tend to and it wasn't the paternity nightmare.

'There's something you've got to see.'

Alex sat up, registering the thread of tension in Lorenzo's usually dry-humoured tones. Instinctively he pressed the phone closer to his ear to catch the nuances better. 'What is it?'

'You need to see it. I've sent you the link. You should have it now.'

He reached out and tapped a couple of buttons on the laptop, Lorenzo's email opened up and he grimaced—a YouTube video. 'Its not some stupid joke, is it?'

'I don't think so.' For once Lorenzo actually sounded unsure.

'Not porn?' He might be the boss, but the 'inappropriate use of office computers' clause applied to him too.

'Uh, well, I don't think so.' There was a laugh now. 'Just watch it, Alex.'

He read the title 'Get Stuck, Get Snogged—is this the hottest kiss ever?' and groaned. 'Lorenzo, it is porn.'

'Just watch it.'

He clicked on the play button and waited a moment for it to load. Turned the speaker up a touch on his computer and frowned at the poor quality of the picture on screen. It was black-and-white. And then he recognised what that small space was—an elevator. And then someone walked into it. And as if he was were trapped in it again, freefalling, his stomach dropped.

Hell.

That awful music hadn't been playing. Muzak didn't play in the lifts at all; no point when they whisked you up and down the many stories so fast—or at least they did if they weren't faulty and hadn't stopped between floors.

When that had happened, five days ago, it had been silent, save her breathing, which—despite her efforts to control it—had spiked. So whoever had lifted this footage had added a cheesy soundtrack—rich, melted chocolate, 'in the mood' kind of music. It didn't fit.

He leant closer to the screen as she waited in the lift. Her face was clear in the frame, and now so was his as he stood side on, until he turned and faced her. She didn't look nervous in this, but up close she'd been shaking like a leaf. Their mouths were moving, but the security camera recorded images, not sound. Even so, he knew exactly what was being said. He'd replayed that too-brief exchange a million times every sleepless night since.

And he knew her face too well. He'd been prowling the floor more than usual just to get a glimpse after spotting her in the open-plan office on Monday. Her glossy black bob with the too-long fringe had caught his eye, and then her oh-so-professional man-style shirts hinted at the most luscious curves.

The last thing he should be doing was chasing skirt—walking through the office a zillion times a day on the lamest of excuses. But while waiting on those blood results he'd been only too happy to be distracted. For five minutes he hadn't wanted to think at all. So he hadn't. And the moment he'd touched her, all remaining rational thought had fled. Her shape was more wicked than he'd suspected—slim, soft, devastatingly curvaceous. It hadn't taken much effort at all to lift her against the back wall of the elevator, raising her high enough so her eyes were almost level with his. Beautiful big brown eyes burnished with a caramel gold—and filled with a challenge he'd been utterly unable to resist. He'd been thinking about what she'd feel like in his arms—dreaming of her curves spilling into his hands. Damn it, he was still dreaming of that.

Alex blinked, came out of the haze and watched, seeing now what he'd felt so gloriously at the time. His back was to the camera but you could see her face as he kissed her lips, her jaw, her neck. Her eyes were closed, her hands caressed his shoulders, his hair. Passionate. Beautiful. And then came the moment, her legs parted, wrapped around his waist and his body reacted now as it had then. Instantly hardening, instantly burning, insisting on getting closer.

And then the bloody lift moved. It had been over far too quickly.

'You're watching it again, aren't you?'

Alex flinched. Hell, he'd forgotten Lorenzo was still on the phone. He'd forgotten he was sitting in an airport lounge. Fortunately it was a midweek red-eye flight and the other patrons were too busy slurping the rotten coffee to pay any attention to him.

'It looks pretty good,' Lorenzo added blandly. 'You're getting some star ratings.'

Alex scrolled down, read the first few comments and felt his face fire up like some mortified teen caught making out with his first girlfriend—by his grandma.

'Who is she?' Lorenzo might sound indifferent, but Alex knew his friend was as agog as he got.

'I don't know.'

'What do you mean you don't know?'

'She's a temp. Started last week. I don't know her name.'

Lorenzo's chuckle didn't help. 'Well, you better find out—this thing is doing the rounds of every inbox in the office.'

'You're kidding.'

'Wish I was, but I've been sent it three times already this morning—and once from a colleague in Hong Kong.'

Anger surged into Alex's veins. He didn't need this and she didn't deserve it. It had been a whim—a crazy, lusty whim and one right on the edge of his code. Alex Carlisle never seduced temps or coworkers—too messy. Especially given he was the boss. But the irresistible force of her had felled him. And was still affecting him—wasn't that why he was sitting here now doing nothing? Despite having been up for hours he hadn't achieved a thing because he was too busy plotting how he could get close to her again as soon as he got back to Auckland. How did he do it without breaking his own rules?

'What would your old man say?' Lorenzo laughed again. 'Screwing around in the office, Alex, bad you.'

Alex iced over and pressed pause on the playback. He hadn't told Lorenzo what he'd found out. It was proved—the chance of the DNA results being wrong were so tiny no lawyer in the land would dare argue it. Samuel Carlisle wasn't Alex's father. Instead it was his best friend who'd supplied the necessary chromosomes. The friend who'd been on the periphery of Alex's childhood—the honorary uncle, the godfather figure—

hell, he'd even been the one to offer advice when Alex had doubted whether he'd wanted to go into the family business.

'You're a Carlisle—it's in your blood.'

Patrick had lied so easily.

Alex had found out only a few years after that that Samuel couldn't be his biological father. When illness had struck, Alex had offered his body, his blood. But it didn't match Samuel's—*at all*. His mother had begged him not to tell, but she'd refused to say who his real father was. She'd taken that secret to the grave with her.

Alex couldn't then ask Samuel—couldn't destroy his last years. But Alex had been burnt through from the inside out by the betrayal. Anger, resentment had festered, his trust severed. And in the quiet dark hours the unanswered question had tormented him.

But now he knew. Patrick had been her lover. Patrick had fathered her child. The pair of them had lied for years to the man she was married to. They'd lied to him, their son.

And Alex would never forgive either of them for it.

He needed time before he could speak of it—even to his best friend. But before he got to that, there was now this situation to be sorted.

He forced out a half-laugh as he looked at the image on screen. Caught out the one time he went base at work. Just the icing on the way the last week had gone.

'I'm flying back shortly. Meet me at my place this afternoon.' He hung up before Lorenzo could say more. Stared at the way her hands threaded through his hair and her legs clamped round his waist.

The anger simmering beneath his skin spiked through. He wished he could storm into Security, find the culprits and fire them on the spot. Every single one of them. But going on the hunt would only inflame the situation. He'd have to make do with a memo reminding them of the 'Use of Internet' policy. He couldn't get rid of them—at least, not yet.

Damn.

The other person he couldn't sack was her—straight to litigation that would be. But it was going to be pretty messy with everyone in the office watching this little number. How was he going to protect her?

He didn't even know her name.

CHAPTER TWO

DANI wondered what it was she'd done wrong. She'd been temping here for over a week and until today they'd all been polite and friendly. All except Mr Alex Carlisle, that was. But she wasn't thinking about him. Definitely not fixated on what had to have been the craziest few minutes of her life. She'd forget it. He obviously had, because she hadn't seen him since—he'd disappeared from the floor, hadn't been down loitering by the managers' desks at all since The Lift. She refused to acknowledge the sting she felt over that. And she hadn't been able to swap to a placement with another company; there were no other placements—none that lasted as long and paid the same kind of money. So, embarrassed or not, she was here to stay.

But the looks she was getting from everyone else today. The number of people that had filed past her desk...and they'd all been rubbernecking. There was no way they could know what had happened. He wouldn't have told anyone, would he?

Maybe she had half her breakfast on her face. She ducked behind her computer screen and used a tissue. Surely they didn't know. How could they? They'd been alone. It hadn't been long—not nearly long enough for her starved hormones—only a few minutes. They'd been a metre apart when those lift doors opened because he'd been aware enough to move. She hadn't. So, given that he'd moved, he hadn't wanted them to be caught. Therefore, Dani reasoned, they couldn't know and she was just feeling paranoid. Besides, it was days ago now. And she. Had. Forgotten. It.

But there was an unnatural awareness about the place. She could feel them all watching her. And she couldn't help but think of him again. She'd been told he had a way with women, but she hadn't realised he had more pulling power than the sun.

She couldn't put all the responsibility on him, though, could she—hadn't she deliberately lifted her chin at him? Hadn't she deliberately looked him over as he had her? Hadn't she widened her stance—preparing for battle but also preparing for contact?

She had. And she hadn't exactly given him a cool, back-off response. She'd enjoyed every second of it, far more than she'd thought it was possible to enjoy a kiss. And that was ter-rifying. To want like that made you weak.

The office stirred, as if an invisible wave were working its way through. She glanced over her screen. Not invisible. This was a tidal wave and she was in its path—for that was the HR dragon, wasn't it, heading straight for her?

'Danielle? Could you come with me, please?'

For some reason a power-that-be like her could make Dani feel guilty just by the way she said her name. But Dani hadn't done anything wrong. OK, she hadn't been quite at her usual output level, but she hadn't been bad. Something was defi-nitely up. She was aware of the sudden stillness in the office—no one was talking, no one was moving. They were all, she realised, watching her. She lifted her head that little bit higher—*don't show weakness*.

'Shall we take the lift?' The dragon seemed to have a gleam in her eyes.

No way could she know about the lift. Could she? 'I'd prefer the stairs,' Dani answered quietly.

That was definitely a smirk. Quickly covered, but it had flashed in her eyes and on the edges of her mouth. Then there was nothing—just chilly silence all the way up the stairs to the executive level, even heavier silence in the corridor, only when the door closed behind her as she entered the woman's office was there the slightest noise. She wasn't invited to sit down. The woman just turned and spoke.

'I'm sorry but your recruitment agency has been in touch. Apparently there is a problem with your file.'

'A problem?' What kind of problem? Dani's blood ran cold. Surely it wasn't about her father. She'd passed bank security clearances in Australia despite his record. They'd investigated and known it was nothing to do with her—that she'd been a victim as much as the others he'd ripped off. But maybe in New Zealand they had different rules?

'I'm not entirely sure—you'll need to talk to your agent about that. However—' the woman was robot-like '—it means we're unable to have you working here any longer.'

'*What?*' She couldn't lose this job. She just couldn't. She was down to her last dollars. Literally—her last fifty or so. She'd come over too soon, hadn't saved enough, but she'd been so lonely and so desperate to find him. She'd waited long enough—so had he.

'The agency has the money for the days you've already worked this week. If you go and see them, you'll be able to collect it.' Her tone was utterly dismissive. Final.

'I'm to go now?' Dani gaped.

'Yes. Gather your belongings and leave immediately.'

Dani clocked the woman's impassivity. Wow—how could she ruin someone's life and look so uncaring?

She turned and left the room, tightening every muscle hard to stop the trembling from being visible. She walked back down the empty corridor to the stairs. This just couldn't be happening. It just couldn't. Her paperwork was totally fine; she was sure of it. When she'd registered with the agency they'd been pleased with her qualifications and experience. So, there was no problem—unless someone had taken a dislike to her?

Someone *important*?

She stopped. Swallowed. Turned and walked back—all the way to the corner office and to the fiftysomething woman sitting guard-like outside the sanctum.

'Is Mr Carlisle in?' Despite her determination it was only a whisper that sounded.

'He's overseas,' his PA answered crisply.

How convenient. Dani's suspicions grew, edging out the anxiety. 'When is he back?'

The PA lifted her head and looked at her. Behind the old-school librarian glasses she seemed to be reading her for a long moment before her lashes dropped. 'I believe he's due back here early this afternoon.'

And she'd be gone by then. Doubly convenient.

No way was this a coincidence. He didn't want to be embarrassed at work—was that it? Had she been so all over him he was trying to get rid an awkward situation before it got even more complicated? What was he afraid of—that she'd go psycho stalker on him?

She turned on the spot and marched back down the stairs to her floor. She'd go straight to the agency and clear it up. She needed the money more than he needed a clear-conscience office.

'Hi, Danielle.' One of the young bankers gave her a leery grin when she walked past him. He hadn't spoken to her before. She caught the grins then swapping between him and some of the others. It had probably been a bet. She knew about boys and their bets—ones made at her expense.

She didn't have the time or capacity to deal him even a cool look. Too busy trying to stomach the sick feeling. She'd been in the country less than a fortnight, was on the bones of her butt in terms of funds and now she'd just lost her job. And she needed to know *why*.

It only took two minutes to get her jacket from the back of her seat and the bag she'd tucked under the table. She logged off her computer.

She turned. The office was so quiet she would have heard her now ex-colleagues blinking—if they weren't all staring totally bug eyed at her. Wow, the ones down the far end had actually risen out of their chairs to get a better look. What on earth was going on?

She tossed her head, determined to hide the freak-out thudding of her heart. So what if her cheeks were purple with embarrassment—she could still walk, right? OK, it was a run/walk to the door and after that she basically threw herself down the stairs, letting the adrenalin fly to her feet.

The recruitment agency was only a ten-minute walk away. Dani did it in seven. Red cheeked, breathless, trying to suck up the desperation pouring out of her.

Then she had to wait ten extra-long, make-you-sweat minutes.

'What's the problem with my file?' Dani asked as soon as she was shown in.

'There are a couple of issues.' The agent wouldn't look her in the eye. 'One is misconduct.'

Misconduct? Dani frowned, that she hadn't expected. 'What kind of misconduct?'

The woman smiled then—it wasn't a kind smile. 'Have you seen this?' She angled her computer screen so Dani could see it.

Dani gripped her bag, pushing it hard on her lap as she waited for the clip to start playing. Why was she being shown a vid on YouTube? What was this all about?

She squinted at the black-and-white grainy images. Oh, no. It couldn't be.

Not *her*.

Not *him*.

OMG—it was! Alex Carlisle and her, Dani Russo, locking lips in that damn lift. Oh, *more* than locking lips. There was neck kissing, and touching and *moving*.

Heat prickled all over her body. From every pore popped a painful drop of blood. How had this happened? This just had to be a joke. Was she in a reality TV show and she didn't know it?

'Where did you get that?' she whispered, knowing she was damned.

'It was emailed to us. I believe it's been circulated around the company already.'

So that explained the staring, then. The embarrassment engulfed her, swamping the spark of anger she'd felt before.

The agent didn't stop the clip playing, just sat blandly waiting. Three and a half minutes of absolute agony. Dani couldn't look away from the screen. Had they been so passionate? Had she really jumped on him like that? Had she been so hungry? And what was that awful music?

Not going to cry. Not going to cry.

She hadn't in years. And she wouldn't, not 'til she was alone.

Finally it ended. Dani couldn't look at the woman.

'But this isn't why we're unable to place you in another position.'

Dani didn't understand. 'Pardon?' Still shocked.

'This was obviously a mistake and an embarrassing one, but we can deal with it with a simple warning.' The agent couldn't be crisper. 'Not on work time, not on work premises. Understand?'

Dani just nodded. Still unable to process what she'd just seen—they'd been filmed? How was that possible?

'The reason we've had to pull you from the job is because we haven't been able to get your school records verified.'

Dani jerked. Her *school* records? How were they relevant? She had banking qualifications that totally surpassed her achievements at school. Plus she had her security clearance from the Australian bank she'd worked at for the last three years—surely that was far more important than verifying her school-leaver's certificate?

'I can call the school,' she said. 'I can get them to fax whatever you need.'

'No, that's fine. We'll keep trying.' The woman smiled sharply. 'But until we do get it, we can't put you into another placement.'

It was then that Dani knew and understood. They weren't trying to contact the school; even if they did there would be some other obstacle that would arise. This was about that video—her fooling with the boss and getting caught. The school-records thing was an excuse. The walls were up. Her anger surged then, pushing back the embarrassment. 'I can go to other agencies?'

'Of course.' The woman smiled. 'But you might encounter the same problem.'

Dani looked at the computer screen again. Yeah, that was the real problem. She could see how many hits the clip had had. Too many just to be the bank staff and this agency—even if they had watched it over and over as she was quite sure some of those sleazy bankers had. No, this one had been doing the rounds; it would be a source of great amusement for anyone in the industries—both finance and recruitment. Alex Carlisle proving his legendary swordsman status with a temp at work.

There was nothing for it but to make a dignified exit. No way could she win this battle here and now. She needed to withdraw and come up with some kind of strategy.

She stood, stuck a small smile on her numb face. 'Thank you for letting me know. Please get in touch when you get my record confirmed. I'd like to get working as soon as I can.'

'Of course.' The agent stood and saw her to the door.

It was a complete fiction. They both knew they were never going to talk to each other again.

'You can collect your wages for the last couple of days from Reception.'

Dani made for the nearest café and ordered the biggest blackest coffee they made. She closed her eyes. The money she had would last less than a week. Her whole aim had been to work while she hunted because she hadn't wanted to wait any longer before trying to find him. But she had to be able to eat—to pay for her accommodation, and to pay for the search. How on earth was she going to find Eli now? How was she going to keep the promise she'd made to her mum?

It had been her final request—she'd given up that precious secret only in her last few days and it was the one last thing Dani *could* do for her. Dani wanted to honour that promise more than she wanted to do anything. And if she found him, it would be like having a part of her mother back.

She called a different agency. Then another. But once she'd told them the kind of work she wanted, then told them her name, the 'our books are full' line got handed to her. Was she going to have to move cities to get another job? She didn't even have the bus fare, and the best finance jobs for her were here. Or they had been. Now she was screwed.

Her anger fired even higher. What about Alex Carlisle? What about his misconduct? Had he been given a 'warning'— she bet there was no way he'd have got the sack. Oh, no— he'd just ensured he had a peaceful work environment again. She wasn't around to embarrass him anymore.

There was one person responsible for this. One person who owed her. One person who was going to pay.

Alex Carlisle was getting the bill.

'Kelly, I need you.' Alex called his PA into his office. 'The temp who was working on the Huntsman project last week—' He broke off. His super-efficient PA had a touch more colour to her cheeks than usual. But her brows lifted as if she were vaguely mystified.

As if.

'Temp?'

'Yes. Short, brunette bob.' Alex winced, hating to have to reveal that he didn't know her name. He watched Kelly's lips purse and sighed, frustrated. 'You've seen the clip, haven't you?' Now he felt his cheeks heating.

Kelly dropped the 'no idea' look and nodded. 'Yes. She no longer works here.'

'How come she's no longer working here? That project is months off completion.' Alex found he couldn't meet Kelly's eyes. Hell, what a mess. He'd never compromised himself at work like this. Socially for sure—he liked to play. But not at work. Kelly had worked for this company for more years than he'd been alive. She'd worked with Samuel, and his father before him. A Carlisle loyalist. There was nothing in the business that she didn't know. Alex remembered her giving him paper as a kid to entertain him while he waited for Samuel and him making darts to shoot at people walking past. The severe look she was giving him now wasn't so different from the one she'd given him then.

'I know,' Kelly said quietly. 'But there's a new temp now.'

Alex looked at her then, hearing the soberness in her voice. He didn't like the censure in her eyes, either. 'I think you'd better send Jo to see me.'

Kelly disappeared and Jo, the head of HR, was knocking at his door in less than a minute. Alex walked over to meet her. 'The temp that we had working on the Huntsman project last week—where is she?'

Jo looked distinctly uncomfortable. 'The temp?'

'Yes,' he growled. 'You know the one I mean.'

'Yes.' Of course she did. 'Her services were no longer required.'

'But there's a new temp out there now.' He'd walked through the floor as soon as he'd got in, run the gauntlet of knowing looks and smiles only to be completely disappointed when it had been some blonde at the desk and not the little brunette who'd been haunting him for days. 'So why did you get rid of the other one? On whose authority? For what reason?' He rapped out the questions, the nasty feeling in his gut growing.

Jo looked even more uncomfortable. 'It was the recruitment agency. They phoned and said they'd made a mistake with her file. They hadn't been able to verify her school qualifications so they pulled her.'

Alex stared at her, anger churning. 'So she's no longer working for the agency?'

'No. I don't believe she is.'

It was his turn to take a deep breath—he had to force his jaw apart to do it. 'They couldn't verify her school qualifications?' Alex shook his head. 'But we had security clearance for her? And proof of her banking exams?'

'Yes.'

So the records meant diddly, then. If she had her banking qualifications, then they didn't need to verify any other records—she couldn't have got the bank ones if she hadn't had the school ones. It was a trumped up excuse to get rid of her.

'So it wouldn't have had anything to do with this?' He strode to his desk and spun his computer screen round so the image he'd paused it on was viewable from her side of the room.

His head of HR went beet red.

Alex leaned back on his desk and folded his arms, hiding the fists. 'Don't tell me you haven't seen it. Everyone in the office has seen it. Haven't they?'

Jo nodded.

'And now you're telling me she's been removed for the most flimsy of reasons.'

'We're covered, Alex. It was the agency who removed her. Her dismissal had nothing to do with this…incident.'

Alex stared at her, unable to believe his ears. Like hell it didn't. She'd done nothing wrong. She shouldn't have lost her job. His fists bunched tighter.

'Does she have another job?' He could only hope she had a better one.

'I don't know.'

'Then you better phone the agency and find out,' he growled—he was not going to be able to rest until he knew. The job market was horrendous at the moment. That meant the temp market was even more vicious.

'Excuse me, Alex.' Kelly came back in, shutting the door

fast behind her and stepping forward. 'I have someone outside insisting on seeing you.'

'Who is it?' Alex asked crossly. 'I don't want interruptions now, Kelly.'

'I know you don't. But this one is different. It's her.'

'Who?'

'That temp.'

Alex froze. 'She's here?'

Kelly nodded.

'Now?' The ripple that ran through his body was pure testosterone. 'You. Out,' he barked at Jo.

She was out of there faster than a condemned prisoner getting a last-minute reprieve. But Alex was the one feeling the edge of desperation. He turned to the woman who knew more about what went on in the building than anyone. 'Kelly, please, what's her name?'

Kelly looked up at him through her half-glasses, her face as impassive and composed as always. When she finally answered, it was with marked deliberation. 'You really ought to know that already.' Then she left.

Alex stared at the door and wondered how on earth he was going to get away with it.

Dani perched on the edge of the chair—the one nearest to the exit. She shouldn't have come. What was she doing back here? Sweating for one thing and she was all shaky inside, as if it wouldn't take much for tears to sting. She couldn't let that happen—getting all emo was one sure way to come off the loser. She blinked and went rigid as the hideous HR dragon appeared from his office. She glanced at Dani but made no acknowledgement as she swept past. That was it—Dani was leaving. What had possessed her to attempt this? Oh, yeah, desperation.

Now the PA was standing in front of her. 'Mr Carlisle will see you now.'

Mr Carlisle. She swallowed, tried to quell the fluttering inside, told herself she had no need for nerves. But the moment before the door opened she had a second, a sliver of a second, when she thought she'd really rather die.

She pushed through, went in and it happened as it had all the last week. The large hand gripped her heart and squeezed, stopping the beat for two seconds too long, while lower in her belly someone switched on the heater.

He was in a suit. It was immaculate. He wasn't smiling.

But he was still brain-zappingly gorgeous and she was as bad as the thousand other women who fell at his feet—breathless, bedazzled. She tried to clear her mind of the clutter, to quell the hormones shrieking at her. Think Zen. Think power.

'Thanks, Kelly.'

Dani heard the door click. So it was shut. So they were alone.

He wasn't behind his desk; instead he stood on her side of it, in the middle of the room. 'My name is—'

'I know who you are.'

Their eyes met. His face was expressionless. But she knew he was remembering the moment after the last time she'd said that, just as she was. That time the spark in his eye had surprised her. The oh-so-relaxed boss, the charming playboy, had looked bitter for a half-second. She'd spent all that night wondering why—in between reliving the heat.

'Please sit down.' Quiet, firm and with that underlying note of authority.

Her legs moved towards the chairs without her instruction—just following his order. She seemed to have swallowed her tongue. Every sentence, the whole spiel she'd rehearsed as she'd steamed her way over here, had fled from her head. Mute, mindless, she was like some star-struck fan meeting her pin-up hottie in the flesh for the first time.

And then she saw it.

Every word, every angry thought, all of it came ripping back. She inhaled, trying to hold back enough to be able to tackle him with controlled fury rather than blind rage. Even so, she spat the words. 'Enjoying it?'

'What?'

'Your little home movie.' She pointed.

They were plastered across the screen. Her legs around his waist. Their tongues so entwined it was a wonder they'd ever managed to pull themselves free.

And he was watching it? Had spun the screen round so it was visible from right across the room?

As if the HR woman had just come to give him his warning—she'd come for a laugh, more like. Dani nearly choked on the rage that reddened her vision. Her face was so hot she was probably casting a glow into outer space. But that was nothing on the churning mass of fire in her belly. 'Why are you watching it?'

He hadn't known she was coming to see him. She'd only finally made her mind up as she'd walked past the building— had been regretting it all the five minutes since. She couldn't believe the whole nightmare. 'How did it happen?'

'What?' He took the seat next to hers. 'The kiss or the recording?' His mouth lifted at one end in a small smile.

She wasn't in the mood for seeing any kind of funny side— he wasn't going to defuse her with his attempt at good humour. 'The recording.'

'There are security cameras in all the lifts. Someone saw us, clipped the footage and put it up. As I think you know, it's been doing the rounds.'

'Yes, the viral video *du jour*,' she said bitterly. 'Was it a joke? Did you set it up for fun?'

'Of course not.' He went rigid. 'I'm the CEO of a large finance company. I think I have better things to do with my time than indulge in stupid pranks like this.'

He held her gaze a minute longer. Assessing. She withstood the scrutiny, tilting her chin that little higher. Refusing to be intimidated.

'Where have you been these last few days?' Assertive, that was how she'd be.

'Overseas.'

'How convenient for you—out of the country while the temp gets the boot and then can't find another job in the whole city.'

'What do you want me to do?'

'Give me my job back.'

He shook his head. 'Impossible.'

'How so?'

'You think you could sit there knowing they've all watched me kiss you like that?'

Kiss you. The words seemed to whisper over her skin, teasing her into greater awareness. She shifted in her seat, resettling her limbs in an attempt to stay in charge of them—and the whole nightmare. 'It was only a kiss, Mr Carlisle. It was nothing.' She shrugged.

His brows lifted for a second. 'You're not going back out there.'

Damn it, she *needed* this job. 'It was a moment. That's all it was. So some geek with nothing better to do made a mini movie with it. Not my fault.'

'You are not working on that floor again.'

'You're not understanding me. I need this job.'

'And I'm saying it's not going to happen.'

'Do you know what this is? Unfair dismissal. Sexual harassment.'

'That was not sexual harassment.' He pointed at the screen. 'You kissed me back. You wrapped your legs around me all by yourself.'

'But because of that video, I lost my job and I need my job. Because of that video, I can't get another. The world of recruitment agencies is really small here in Auckland, do you know that? The agents all know each other, all swap from company to company. And they send each other *emails*. Would you believe that?' Dani inhaled. 'That stupid kiss has cost me everything and I can't let it. How come you get to sit here in your fancy office and suffer none of the consequences while my life gets totalled?' She stood. 'It's not happening. This is unfair and I'll prove it's unfair. I'm going to a lawyer— see if you can say *"impossible"* to a court!'

She whirled and marched. She had no idea where to find a lawyer, whether she really did have a case, and she certainly didn't have the money to pay for it but she was bloody well going to find it somehow.

She opened the door but it was slammed shut again—his big hand spread wide on the wood above her head and firmly holding it in place.

'You don't shout at me and walk out without giving me a chance to respond.'

'Watch me.' She pulled on the door handle with all her strength. It didn't move.

'This is what happens. We talk. We negotiate. You're not leaving until you've let me think of an alternative.'

She turned to glare at him and discovered he was way too close. Right beside her, so all she could see was his body—

the jacket of his suit pulled wide by the way his arm was stretched out, revealing the breadth of his chest in the crisp white cotton beneath. His physicality was so potent, all she could feel was the warmth of him reaching out to her. The temptation to step closer was almost crippling—and totally wrong, wrong, wrong.

'What kind of alternative?' The woolly feeling was seeping into her head. She lifted her chin to be able to look into his face and the brain lethargy only worsened. His eyes were looking very green.

'Sit back down and I'll explain. If you want we can get my HR manager to sit in on the meeting.'

Reality returned with acute vividness. That cow? 'That won't be necessary.'

His lips twitched. 'My PA, then.'

Nope, not the boarding-school matron, either. 'Look, you and I both know that if you lay a hand on me, I'll be screaming the place down.'

His face suddenly lit up like a Christmas tree and his smile went so wicked she wouldn't have been surprised if he had a doorway to a den of sin hidden behind his desk. Or maybe that was wishful thinking—because when he looked like that all she could think about was bad, bad behaviour. Then she mentally replayed what she'd said and suddenly felt a need to clarify. 'Screaming in *horror*.'

'Ri-i-ight.' He nodded as if she were a delusional diva he had to humour. 'All outrage rather than ecstasy.'

She opened her mouth but before she'd thought of a comeback he'd lifted his hand from the door, and was holding it and the other up in the 'don't shoot' position, his mouth in a smile too cheeky to resist.

He'd be dead if her eyes had ammo. Sadly her eyes were

too busy gobbling up the gorgeousness before her to execute the death look. Her failing brain managed one last attempt to control the weakening of her body and she tried the door again. It still didn't move. She glanced down. His foot was jammed against it.

'I really have been overseas. I left the afternoon we were in the lift. The trip was unavoidable. I expected to see you when I got back. To talk to you.' His hands had dropped to his hips. She couldn't stop looking at his long fingers.

'What were you going to say?'

'It doesn't matter.' His fingers curled into fists. 'What matters is that I found out about the clip this morning and I found out about you being dismissed two minutes ago.'

She took a step back from the door so she could look into his face from a safer distance. 'You didn't know?' He hadn't ordered it?

'No. The clip was taken from the security camera in the lift. I don't know who did it yet, but when I find out you can be certain that *that* person will be in danger of dismissal.'

That sharp edge sliced back into his eyes for a second. She wanted it to stay—wanted him to truly understand the impact. 'It's had hundreds of hits. It got sent to the agency. I got a warning for it but by some great coincidence they can't complete the necessary verification on my paperwork.' Shaking her head, she walked into the middle of the room—the greater the distance between them, the better she could think.

'I know.'

'So what are you going to do?' It wasn't the unfairness of the ramifications that had brought her here, it was that she needed help and had nowhere else to turn. And she hated it.

'I'm not sure yet.'

That wasn't good enough. She spun and saw the wicked

smile was back on his face. He thought this was funny? He still didn't get how serious it was for her? She walked back to stand right in front of him, whipping the words out.

'Thanks to you I have no job and no hope of getting another one. Thanks to you I am flat broke. I'm in a strange country, I don't know anyone and suddenly I'm starring in some local sex clip and all you want to do is laugh it off.' Breathing hard, she glared at him—her eyes filled with the ammo they'd lacked before.

His grin was wiped. 'I don't think it's funny.'

'Oh, really? So that's why you're smiling like some satyr and watching replays like it's the joke of the century.'

'It wasn't a joke.' His eyes bored into hers so intently she couldn't move. His face hardened in the long seconds of silence. She sensed the rest of him becoming tense too—his body sending such strong vibes of tightly leashed energy that she could feel them pressing on her.

For a second her instinct screamed at her to run, but just as fast the urge was squashed. Other urges began to surge instead—and she needed a strong leash of her own to control them. Her whole body was aware of him, her whole focus was on him. His gaze dropped to her mouth and she felt it like a physical touch. He was remembering—as was she, and the fire arcing between them threatened to burn through her control. But she wasn't going to let this raging attraction muck up more of her life. She wasn't going to lose the little credibility she had left by letting it happen again.

She made her body move—away—a few steps back towards the door.

'You really can't get another job?' His voice sounded rusty.

'You really think I'd be here if I could?'

His brows drew closer as he regarded her. The angles of

his face became more pronounced. Suddenly, sharply, he moved. Walking to the window, he glared through it—she figured the glass would melt in moments if he still had that heat in his eyes.

'I might have another job for you. But not here. I don't think that's something you or I or anyone would be comfortable with.' He turned. It seemed he'd taken the time to ice over, for his face was schooled into blandness. 'Look, let's get out of here and go talk somewhere more relaxed.'

He opened the door and waited for her to pass through. Dani hesitated—relaxed might be a really bad idea. But if he could do cucumber cool, surely she could do better than melting jelly.

CHAPTER THREE

DANI kept three feet behind Alex as he strode past the PA.

'Please cancel that last appointment and take messages, Kelly. I'm out for the rest of the afternoon,' he said without slowing his pace.

'Certainly.' No surprise, no questions. The PA gave Dani a coolly professional smile but Dani was still too rattled to be able to match it.

Alex glanced at the lift. 'Shall we take the stairs?'

Dani was already at the door to them—hoped the PA hadn't heard his question. He'd laced it with the faintest hint of irony and if Dani were to look at him now and see him smiling she couldn't be held responsible for her actions—aggressive energy seemed to be bouncing round her body.

'Where are you staying?' He thudded downstairs swiping a security card to get them into the basement.

She gave him the name of the hostel and saw his frown appear.

'You don't know Auckland, do you?' He sent her a sideways glance. 'Because if you did, you'd know that's in a really dodgy part of town.'

It was a cheap part of town.

He unlocked the car—sleek, attractive, outrageously powerful, just like its owner. Dani got into the passenger seat. In seconds they were out of the garage and driving down the congested inner-city streets in awkward silence—he'd quickly cut the music that had roared louder than the engine. Dani wished he'd kept it on—better to listen to that than the silence between them or the voice in her head telling her how much of a mess she was in. The weather had turned, the rain drizzling and dampening her spirits further.

'Um…' he was drumming his fingers on the steering wheel '…I…'

Dani waited, surprised by his sudden attack of the fidgets.

His fingers abruptly stopped their beat and gripped the wheel. 'What's your name?'

'Pardon?'

'Your name.' He kept his eyes on the road ahead. 'I don't know what it is.'

'You don't know my name?' Stunned, Dani stared at him. 'How can you not know my name?'

'We never finished our introductions.' His high cheekbones were streaked with slashes of colour. 'I have a lot of employees.'

'Oh, and I was just one of the temps.' OK, so she was. But she hadn't been just one of them—he'd kissed the hell out of her. She'd *felt* him and he had her—*intimately*. Or did he do that with all the girls? Anger roared through her again— vicious, wild anger. 'You could have found out.'

'I don't use the HR files for personal reasons.'

'No, you just use the temps.'

He braked sharply at the traffic lights. 'I didn't use you and you know it.'

Dani shook her head, stupidly hurt by his admission. 'No, I don't.'

She wanted to get out of the car and away from him right this second. It was beyond humiliating—she'd gone to him because she had nowhere else to go for help, using her anger to mask the hope that he'd actually feel some kind of responsibility. Buried right beneath everything had been the teeny, tiny hope that he might have actually liked her. What a fool. The whole thing had been so meaningless for him that he hadn't even bothered to learn her name. He could have found out—his HR dragon or his oh-so-efficient PA could have told him. But he hadn't asked—he hadn't wanted to. So while she'd been blown away by that kiss, he hadn't given it a second thought, other than to be a little annoyed about the resulting clip—or perhaps amused was what he'd been. But the video didn't affect him the way it did her—all it did for him was enhance his reputation as some kind of playboy sex god. But for her it ruined everything—her prospects, her plans, *her* reputation. 'You know something, Mr Carlisle, I don't care how good a job you can offer me. I don't want it.'

'Look—'

'I'm serious. You can drop me at the corner.'

The locks in the car clicked on. She shot him a venomous look.

'I'll take you to the hostel.' He looked angry, which was so wrong because he was the one who had been insulting, not her.

They were almost at the hostel already—Dani recognised the landmarks. He must have intended to take her there anyway. So much for a conversation somewhere more relaxing—so much for the possibility of a different job.

She was out of the car as soon as he'd pulled over and released the locks, felt her tension yanking tighter when he got out of the car just as quick. 'You don't need to see me in.'

'The least I can do is see you safely home.' He glared at the hostel's sign, his frown saying all that he thought about her home—all that he thought about her.

Dani marched up the stairs ahead of him, wishing he'd get the hint and just leave. But he was right behind her as she crossed the floor.

'Excuse me,' the receptionist called out to her. 'Danielle Russo?'

Dani veered towards the desk. Alex got to the counter at the same time as her. So now he knew her name—way too late.

Dani lifted her brows at the woman behind the desk and managed an almost-smile—not able to trust that her voice wouldn't be razor sharp if she asked if there was a problem.

'We need you to pay for this week. It's nothing personal— but we have had trouble with people leaving without paying and then their credit-cards not working. And, er—' the receptionist looked at her notes '—we don't seem to have credit card details for you.'

That was because Dani knew all about credit cards not working—and, worse, being abused. 'I paid cash,' she mumbled.

'Great. Shall we settle it now, then?'

Dani swallowed. 'I already paid for last week.'

'I know.' She looked apologetic. 'But I now need payment for this week.'

Alex was like a statue next to her, listening to every word of the painful exchange. Could the day get any worse? Did he really have to be here to witness this last painful humiliation?

'Um.' Dani mumbled some more. 'I'm waiting on my pay before I can do the next week.'

'Oh.' The receptionist frowned and then suddenly smiled. 'Well, what about you pay up to tonight, then, and you can pay the rest tomorrow.'

'Sure.' Dani nodded. 'Thank you.' There was no pay tomorrow. All she had was in her bag—the two days' wages she'd got from the agency this morning. She felt her face on fire, felt the sweat trickling down her back as she handed over most of her last dollars.

Nightmare.

She turned and saw him watching her closely, his expression serious. Had he seen the lack of notes in her purse? Her anger spiked again—what was he going to do, pull out his fat wallet and hand over a couple of hundred to her? The humiliating thing was, much as she wanted to, she wouldn't be able to refuse. She hated being backed into a corner like this. While she needed help, her pride didn't want to take a thing from him. She wanted him to leave. Now. Bitter tears stung her eyes and she blinked them away, trying to build up her defences again—getting emotional only made things a million times worse. Getting emotional made you vulnerable.

'Thank you for dropping me back to the hostel,' she said fiercely. 'I'm sorry I bothered you at work. Let's just forget the whole thing, shall we?'

Alex watched her go—head high, shoulders back—but it was more of a run than a walk. He hesitated for half a second, then strode straight after her. Damn it, he couldn't just leave her so obviously on the skids. He walked into the dorm room she'd turned into. His skin crawled when he saw the state of it; what a dump.

'What are you doing in here?' She was standing by the bunks, her hands visibly shaking. As he glanced at her she screwed them into fists. No, she didn't want him to see her distress. He looked about the hideous room to give her a second, feeling like rubbish himself. Her pack was open on the bottom bunk. His eyes flicked over the gloriously huge bra poking out the top and quickly he turned his back on that. He glanced back at her—now she was watching him as if she wanted to beat the hell out of him.

OK, this was bad. Really bad. She was living in a dodgy part of town in a flea-infested hostel in a room with a bunch of strangers. And she was about to be turfed out of it. He felt terrible. He felt responsible. And this was the last thing he needed—he already had enough mess cluttering up his mind. So he had to do something—anything—to fix it. 'Danielle.'

Her eyes narrowed.

'I heard the receptionist.' He shrugged. It was a pretty name. He wished he'd known it sooner. 'Put your things together.'

'Pardon?'

'You can't stay here.' It just wasn't going to happen.

'Yes, I can. Look, I was wrong to interrupt you today. *I* made a mistake the other day. I can live with the consequences.'

'Well, I can't.' He took a step closer. 'Gather your things together and we'll find you someplace else to stay.'

'Where?'

He clamped his mouth shut. Yeah—where? Was he going to put her up in a hotel or something? For how long? Think, brain, think. Where were the solutions to problems that he usually found so easily? But he couldn't think because he was still seeing the lace edging of that pretty white bra and the play part of his head was imagining what it would look like on her. 'Someplace else.'

'I can't afford anywhere else.'

Yeah, and she couldn't afford here, either, could she? He could offer her money. Lots of money. Wouldn't that make it all go away? Why the hell hadn't he just written her a cheque in his office?

Because Alex hadn't got to the top without dotting 'i's and crossing 't's—Alex never left a job unfinished. He needed to make sure she really was back on her feet. She couldn't get a job—there were no jobs. He knew this—his HR department had got over a hundred applicants for the single permanent position they'd advertised. For her to have got the temp position meant her references and skills were brilliant. The personal issue between them had blown it. So he owed her.

But what made him determined to truly see for himself that she was OK was the expression he'd seen—the vulnerability in the elevator. In those brief moments when the façade had dropped, he'd seen the fear in her eyes. And he'd seen it again at the counter of the hostel. She was isolated and alone.

The protective male bit in him dominated the direction of his thoughts. 'Do you have any friends here?'

The answer was obvious and she didn't even bother voicing it.

'Do you know *anyone*?'

Her chin lifted. 'I only arrived in the country two weeks ago and got straight to work the minute I could. Sadly I didn't have the time to make friends there.' She got in a little dig.

Why was she in New Zealand anyway? He turned; there was time to find that out later. What mattered now was settling her in someplace else. Someplace safer. 'Let's go.'

'I'm not leaving here with you. I'm fine.' Her feet were firmly planted shoulder width apart; she looked as if she was about to declare that he'd have to carry her out forcibly.

And he felt like it. But instead of obeying the urge of his body, he softened his words with a smile. 'Face it, Danielle, you don't really have a choice. You're not getting paid tomorrow because you got paid when you left the agency. You could only pay for one more night here. You have no money, no friends to call on. And you're obviously not fine, because if you were you never would have been so worked up that you had to come and see me today.'

Her eyes were huge in her face now. He saw her blinking

fast a couple of times and gentled his tone even more. 'Get your things. I'll take you to a hotel or something.'

For another long moment he thought she was going to refuse. But then he saw her swallow and turn, bending to pull her pack from the bed. He moved to help her but was lanced through with her glare.

His lips twitched but he managed to bite back the smile as he froze. She had to accept his help anyway and she hated it. She'd hate him more if he showed his amusement. So he looked away, checking the cupboard beside her bed was bare. Just as he turned to go he caught sight of something under the bunk, and bent to see what it was. A little candle, deep red in colour and new—the tip of the wick was still white. He picked it up and sniffed. The fragrance was delectable. Edible.

'This yours?' He held it out as she turned, the pack now on her back.

Soft colour rose in her cheeks. Interesting.

'Yes,' she answered shortly and took it from him.

Alex watched her tuck it into the pocket of her handbag. So beneath the snappy defensiveness there was a feminine side—she liked pretty candles with sweet smells. The kind of scent he could handle in his sheets.

No, Alex.

His moment of irresponsibility in the lift last week had caused her trouble enough already. She might be attractive, but he wasn't going to mess around with her more. He'd see her right and then run far, far away. He had enough to deal with without lust fogging up his brain—and that was exactly what was happening every minute he was near her. The fog blurred everything—especially his reason. So the sooner he had her sorted, the better it would be, because he had far bigger issues to stomach.

He glanced at his watch, surprised to see how late in the afternoon it was. Lorenzo would be waiting for him. He might as well take her home and figure out what to do from there.

Dani watched the sky-high metal gates in front of them roll back and then Alex drove the car into the garage. Only once the engine and his seat belt were off did he look at her, brows lifting. 'Safe at last.'

Oh, yeah. Real safe. She listened as the heavy garage door sealed shut. So here she was in Fort Knox with the guy she barely knew but who had all but ravished her in the lift last week. And she'd let him. Really, really safe.

He was wearing that far-too-wide smile again. 'Come on, Danielle. Let's go sort this out.'

'This isn't a hotel.'

'No.'

'This is your house.'

'Yes.'

'This isn't a good idea.'

'Relax.' He led the way up the short flight of stairs. 'I want to find a solution to this mess just as much as you do. Here we can do that in privacy.'

'Is there really a job?'

'Danielle—'

'Dani,' she snapped, unable to bear hearing her full name a second longer. She hadn't been Danielle in years. She was Dani. Her tomboy name—keeping her sexless and uninteresting to her mother's boyfriends, until puberty had really hit and her body had let her down. Then she'd had to go for more forceful tactics.

'Dani,' he repeated, smile vanishing.

She regretted correcting him. When he said it with his

rounder New Zealand vowels it sounded so much smoother. The tingle went in her ears all the way down her centre to her toes—causing them to squirm restlessly in their boots.

'Everything OK?' Someone else spoke—with more than a hint of dryness.

Dani craned her head round Alex. There was another tall guy waiting for them at the top. So much for privacy.

'It will be.' Alex climbed the last of the stairs.

'It better be.' Dani followed him up into the room, determined to master her chaotic emotions. 'Who are you?'

'Lorenzo,' he answered as bluntly as she'd asked.

'Do you live here?' She couldn't keep the challenge out of her voice—it was the way she'd always hidden her fear.

A glance passed between the two men. Lorenzo took a step towards the stairs. 'I'm guessing we'll talk later.'

'No, I want you to meet Dani,' Alex said so smoothly that Lorenzo paused and looked. 'She's going to take over when Cara goes on maternity leave.'

Lorenzo's mouth opened, but then shut.

'Full-time position, of course, but starting from now,' Alex added.

Dani darted looks between Alex and Lorenzo—saw Lorenzo's eyes had widened slightly, but still he said nothing.

'You'll get Cara to show her what to do.' Alex was telling, not asking.

'Absolutely. No problem.' Lorenzo's impassivity shattered with a smile. 'And as Dani is obviously staying here with you, you can drop her to the warehouse tomorrow.'

Alex's eyes were the ones widening now.

'Talk more later, Alex,' Lorenzo said.

'Yep.' It was amazing sound could emerge from the mask his face had become.

Lorenzo looked at Dani and then at Alex again, his smile turning into a total smirk. 'Nice to meet you, Dani. See you tomorrow.'

CHAPTER FOUR

DANI waited 'til he'd gone down the stairs and she'd heard the door shut after him. Then she turned to Alex. 'What job?' She'd deal with the most palatable issue first.

'Administrator for the Whistle Fund.'

The charitable fund his company supported. Alex was on the board. She knew this from his fangirl at the water-cooler.

'Lorenzo is the chief exec. The organisation is based in his building. Cara, the current administrator, is pregnant and needs some help.'

'And it's a paid position? Full-time?' She'd always thought these kind of jobs were voluntary—wealthy wives doing some part-time hours for fun and fulfilment.

'Yes.'

Dani thought. 'I've done numbers more than admin.'

'Which is perfect, because this is all about dealing with money and there's a huge overlap in terms of dealing with systems for paperwork. And there's probably more variety. You'd be taking lots of calls, answering queries, sending out info packs, sorting the requests, updating the Web site. I'm sure you can manage a phone and talk nice to people.'

She'd started as a teller. She liked the interaction with the public—more so than the back-room dealing with the corporate banking she'd gone into.

'Cara really does need help.' His persuasion continued. 'You're good at your job. I'm sure you'll pick it up, no problem.'

'How do you know I'm good at my job when you didn't even know my name?' She couldn't resist sticking a pin in his smooth-talking bubble.

'We only recruit exceptional employees—even temporary workers have to be of Carlisle standard.'

Carlisle standard? Oh, he had an answer for everything. And what was the bet he had a standard in bed too? If it was anything like his kissing standard it wouldn't just be exceptional, it would be nothing short of spectacular. But it wasn't helpful to think about that now. She took a step back towards the stairs.

'Why don't you do a week's trial?' He was relentless, taking a step after her—not letting her increase her distance from him.

OK, so she really didn't have a choice. But she had to admit she was actually interested to see what it was like too. 'OK,' she answered, crossing her fingers that this wasn't a huge mistake. 'Thanks.'

He smiled then. 'Now that's sorted, come on through and have a drink.'

He was walking off before she could refuse. And she couldn't refuse, could she—couldn't be completely rude—not now he'd given her a job?

The town house was gorgeous—a traditional wooden villa on the outside but one that had been rebuilt on the inside. High ceilings and big windows let in lots of light. Neutral but warm colours made it welcoming. A huge painting hung on the wall above the fireplace. The lounge was big and the sofa comfortable-looking. But she didn't sit, instead she walked to the window and saw the last of the sun's light was turning the clouds a fiery orange. She was unfamiliar with the geography of Auckland, but somehow she'd expected a view of the city buildings, or perhaps the water. She wasn't expecting the verdant, lush garden. It was like a miniature forest. So gorgeously green in the middle of winter and so private.

'Can I get you a drink?'

She turned her back on the beauty of it. 'No, thanks.'

He didn't get himself one, either, just stood on the far side of the long, low coffee table by the sofa. 'Take a seat, Dani.'

'I don't feel comfortable about staying here.'

'Why not?'

She opened her mouth and then shut it again.

'You're no longer working for me. Technically Lorenzo will be your boss.' With wide-spread fingers, he ruffled through his hair, rubbing his head hard. He closed his eyes for a second. 'I'm sorry, OK?'

Oh, it was hours too late for the repentant-man act. She wasn't falling for it. 'Maybe next time you should try keeping your hormones in check. What was it all about anyway? Kiss-a-temp day?'

'You misunderstand.' His eyes shot open, lancing through her. 'I'm not sorry I kissed you. I'll never regret that experience. It would be an insult to you if I did.'

'Oh, please.' Too smooth. Way too smooth. And the sparkling humour in his unwavering gaze just made her want to tell him so. But, damn, her cheeks were burning—she must look like a totally floored teen. So embarrassing.

His scrutiny intensified. 'What I'm sorry about is the whole office watching, and the gossip.'

'I don't care about the gossip. People can think what they like—it makes no difference to me.'

His brows flickered but he didn't question. 'Fair enough,

but I care about it and I won't have either you or me on the line because of it. I'm sorry about what the agency did. This will make it right.' He sighed, jammed his hands in his pockets. 'Where's your family—in Australia?'

'I don't have any. My parents are dead,' she said baldly.

'I'm sorry.' His frown deepened.

Instantly she regretted telling him—she didn't want his pity, but more than that she didn't want to remember. The lump in her chest when she thought of her mother was like sharp, burning ice and she hurriedly turned her thoughts away from her. But not to her father—as far as she was concerned he'd never been alive to her. Instead she pushed the focus back onto Alex, remembering what she'd been told. 'Your father died last year.'

Silence. She'd hit a nerve. His frown disappeared as his face smoothed, then it shuttered completely into unreadable blandness. 'You're up on your research.'

'You were the number-one topic of conversation at the water-cooler.' She aimed for flippant, trying to cover the moment of awkwardness. 'I didn't even have to ask.'

A slight grin reappeared. 'But you were going to? You wanted to find out?'

'No. It was all thrust upon me.'

His low laughter refreshed the room, lightening everything—including her mood. She even grinned back.

He immediately pressed his argument home. 'Look, I'm hardly here. I travel a lot. It would be good to have someone minding the house. You can stay for a week or two and save some money to get into a place of your own. It's the simplest solution. We'll hardly see each other.'

Dani considered it. What was she so worried about—her unreal attraction to him? If he was away a lot, then she could control it, right? And it wasn't as if he were trying to pounce again. He might have said he didn't regret kissing her, but neither had he asked for another. It was a bit deflating, but it seemed all he felt for her now was a sense of responsibility—not unbridled lust. She wouldn't misinterpret his charm as meaning something more.

His brows lifted fractionally, as if he knew he'd won. 'So it's a deal.' He held out his hand.

Dani looked at it. Surely she had nothing to lose and everything to gain. She could work, not worry about a roof over her head and be able to find Eli.

But, like that day in the lift, her instinct was warning her again, that sense of impending danger. She ignored it and reached out. 'Thanks.'

The spark shot up her arm. His fingers tightened. And she realised her instinct had been bang on the money. She shouldn't have touched him. *He* was the danger—his attraction too magnetic. He made her body go on edge in an entirely new way.

'Don't you want to know, Dani?' The warmth from his whisper flooded her.

'Know what?' She beat the breathlessness with assertion.

'What would have happened if we hadn't been caught on camera? What would have been the next step?'

'There wouldn't have been a next step. I've already told you, it was a moment. Nothing more.'

'You're sure about that?' He kept hold of her hand but took the two steps around the coffee table between them. 'See, I think there would have been a next step, Dani. A very pleasurable one.'

Oh, hell. So it wasn't just her feeling it. But she held her ground. 'I'm sorry to disappoint you, Alex, but I'm not going to be your next lover.'

'No?' His eyes danced.

'No.' She smiled sweetly. 'I'm going to be your flatmate. And there's a rule about flatmates, isn't there?' *Don't screw the crew.*

His smile was reluctant but it was there. She took the chance to tug her hand from his. Even so, the victory was hollow. Now she knew she couldn't possibly stay here, for she'd lied—she desperately wanted to know what would have happened next. But she figured she could get him to change his mind and hustle her into a hotel pronto. 'Aren't I going to cramp your style?'

'How so?'

'Who did you go out with last Friday night?'

'No one.' He shrugged. 'I was in Sydney working.'

'OK.' Dani frowned. 'What about the one before that?'

His hesitation was telling.

'A woman. Obviously,' Dani said, her voice as melted-chocolate smooth as his had been before.

Slowly he nodded.

'And the Friday before that?' Dani enquired. 'A different woman, right?'

He squared his stance, facing her full on. 'Yes.'

'And you slept with them.' Still calm, determinedly not judging.

'No.'

That made her pause a moment. 'Kissed them goodnight, at least.'

'Yes.'

Yeah. She knew what his kisses were like. 'So isn't it going to be tricky for you to bring a woman home when you have me staying here?' She let a touch of taunt out then. She had to get him to realise sticking her in a hotel was a much better option. The prospect of staying in close confines with him made her feel giddy—she wasn't sure she could keep her need-to-shimmy urges under control.

'You know, you're right.' He had a devilish look on his face. 'It might be a bit weird to bring dates home while having you as my little flatmate here. But that's no problem.' He paused, and she swore she could see the wickedness rippling through the rest of him as he stepped closer. 'You can be my date while you're staying here.'

'What?'

'There are a few things I have to go to and, you're right, I like a companion. No reason why that can't be you.'

She opened her mouth but he put a finger on it.

'There isn't anyone else around right now anyway.' His green eyes bored into hers as he oh-so-unsubtly let her know he was available.

'Not this week, you mean.' So there damn well shouldn't be or he shouldn't have kissed her like that.

'So you can stay here and save, just for a week or two.' He ignored her hit. 'Until you're in a position to take a place of your own. Meantime I have a dinner to go to tomorrow night—very nice venue, black tie. Don't you love a little glamour?'

'No.' She threw him a dark look, trying to keep a grip on herself. This wasn't what she'd meant to happen. He hadn't even bothered to learn her name—she needed to keep that little fact up front and centre in her head.

'I thought all women did.'

'Not me.'

'Oh.' He smiled. 'I'll have to help you change your mind on that. Dances like this one can be a lot of fun.'

'I thought you said it was a dinner.'

'Followed by dancing.' He looked thoughtful. 'Have you

got something to wear?' He ignored her start of annoyance. 'We can go shopping tomorrow afternoon if you'd like.'

Go shopping? 'You don't need to *Pretty Woman* me, Alex,' she said sharply. 'I have something to wear.'

'Great, that's settled, then.' He turned away flashing a Cheshire Cat smile, then turned back just as quick. 'Oh…'

'What?' Rattled, she snapped—had she just agreed to go out with him tomorrow night? How had that happened?

'What about you?' With that too-bland expression he moved back into her space. 'Who did you go out with last Friday night?'

'I—' She blinked. No one, of course.

'What about the Friday before? Is there a boyfriend I ought to know about? I mean, you asked me, I can ask you, right? I don't want to put you in a difficult position as my escort.'

Escort was not a good word—the unpleasant connotation compounded with his offer to take her shopping pushed her defence button. She wasn't anybody's paid-for plaything. She'd prefer to be the player, not the toy.

'Of course you won't.' She lifted her chin and fired a shot at him. 'I don't do "boyfriends" as such, but I have a few joy boys around. I choose one to service me occasionally but we share nothing more than that. *Variety*,' she added with a conspiratorial whisper. 'You know.' She was quite sure he did know. Quite sure he had a whole variety line-up of lovers himself—only his wouldn't be imaginary.

'Occasionally?' His brows lifted. 'Only occasionally?' His smile was feral. 'No wonder you burned so hot in my arms.'

She opened her mouth to snap at him but this time he laid his whole hand across her mouth, leaning in to quiz her. 'You don't believe in romance?'

She pulled back from the sizzling touch. 'I don't believe

in romance, relationships or anything like that. I certainly don't believe in marriage.'

'A free woman?'

'Absolutely,' she declared. 'An independent one.' Her aim was to take only what she wanted when she wanted and leave the rest of the rubbish for others to suffer through. Except she'd not really managed it yet and now wasn't the time to start trying. She had something way more important to be focused on. It had taken her long enough to earn back the money her father had stolen, and truthfully she'd come over too soon—without all she should have. So she didn't need distractions now—not of any kind.

He stepped even closer, gleaming green eyes trained on her. 'Don't you believe it can happen, Dani? A look across a room? Love at first sight?'

'Never in a million years.' She straightened her shoulders. 'And you don't, either.' The man was a complete playboy. But he had every right to be—he had every necessary asset: the looks, the humour, the drive.

'No,' he agreed, looking her over, top to toe and back again so every inch of her skin was sizzling. 'Not love. But lust is another matter.' He tilted his head as if to study her from a different angle. 'Why are you breathing so hard? Something bothering you?'

'I don't like confined spaces.' Hell, he got to her.

'I know the house isn't huge, but it's not exactly tiny.'

It wasn't tiny at all. She stared into his green eyes. 'I don't like feeling trapped.'

'You're not trapped,' he said calmly, then moved fast, his arms hauling her to him. 'But now you are.'

She twisted in his embrace. 'Watch it, I've a black belt in Tae Kwon Do.'

'Really?'

His muscles tightened—catching her, stopping her. It felt appallingly good. She twisted again, only succeeded in pressing her breasts even harder against his chest. Her nipples screamed with sensitivity. 'OK, no. But I have done self-defence classes.' She tried to twist free one more time.

'Let me guess—practising against other women, right?'

Damn. She fought harder. But he must have had some kind of fighter training too. It couldn't just be his sheer strength stopping her. Oh, hell, the adrenalin surged through her—excitement, challenge, anticipation. She summoned her strength back up.

'I don't think you should do that again.' He grunted as she hit out with her leg.

'Why not?' Panting, she sent him a death look.

'Because all you're doing is turning me on.' Goaded, he pushed her from him. 'And you're turned on too. You're aching for it, just like I am.'

Breathless, she stared, mouth falling at his arrogant certainty. But standing with her feet planted shoulder-width apart, she felt it, the flood of juices that would make his entry slick, the softening within her. He was right, so right.

She bit down on her lips. Wanting and angrily not wanting to want. Her teeth seemed to sharpen. Every muscle primed. She could howl with the need.

'You want to fight for it? You like it fast and hard? 'Cause I can do that. I can do that right now,' he growled. 'But tell me, who is it you're really fighting, Dani? Is it me or is it yourself?'

She gasped. 'You arrogant jerk.'

'Yeah.' His laugh was rough. 'But it's just sex. It's just fun.' He walked towards her again. 'You already know how incredible we'd be.'

It was surprisingly easy to fell a full-grown man—but she did have the element of surprise. A quick kick with her leg tripped him and sent him to the floor. But he was faster—his hand catching her ankle before she could dodge back to a safe distance. He pulled. The breath knocked from her lungs as she thudded down on top of him. He rolled, spinning her over and pinning her half under him. He was heavy. Hard. The shiver ran through her whole body. His body flexed in response.

Their eyes met.

'I could beat you if I wanted to,' she said, wincing at her breathlessness.

'I'm sure you could. *If* you wanted to.' His hand swept down her side.

'Get off. You're heavy.' She wasn't in the least afraid, but she was desperate to deny the way her body was softening—the way her bones were melting with need.

'Oh…no…' he said slowly, brushing her hair from her eyes with gentle fingers before putting his hand on her hip. 'I don't want to.'

'I want you to.'

'Do you?' He stroked up the side of her body, his hand gently sweeping up to cup her breast, his thumb caressing the stiff peak. 'You don't want to do anything about this?'

She didn't play dumb and ask what he meant. Instead she chomped on the urge to arch her back so it would press her nipple harder against the palm of his hand. And she pleaded with her hips to stay still and not rock that little bit more into his hardness. She dug her fingers into the carpet. The heat was stifling—it wasn't the weight of him hindering her breathing, it was the searing temperature between them.

Their eyes held, vision intensifying. Every inch of her body loved the feel of him, but her head was hurting.

'It would be a really bad idea,' she whispered. She lowered her lashes so she wouldn't drown in his eyes and say something she'd regret. 'My life is complicated enough right now.'

There was a long moment of silence when they were utterly motionless, both straining against the delicious torture of temptation.

'Yeah,' finally he groaned. 'So is mine.' He rolled and stood in the one movement. Shook his head as he looked down at her. 'I'll stay away.' Then he walked—fast—as if to emphasise it. 'I'll get your bag.'

Dani scrambled to her feet as soon as he was gone. Smoothed her hands down her flaming cheeks, tried to get her grip back and shake off the stab of disappointment. Unbelievable. She'd been so close to surrendering everything just then. But she'd spoken the truth—her life was complicated enough. And messing around with a guy like Alex would only make that worse. Despite what she'd said, she wasn't a player. She needed to stay on the sidelines.

He returned a few minutes later, lugging her pack, didn't look at her as he spoke. 'I'll show you to your room.' He led the way up another flight of stairs, stopping at an open door.

'This is your bedroom. You have a bathroom through that door.' He nodded towards the far corner of the room.

'Where's your bedroom?'

The corner of his mouth tilted up. 'You want to see it?'

'No, I just want to ensure it's far, far from mine.' She was only half kidding.

'This is only a two-bedroom town house, sweetheart. Mine is just up those stairs there.'

So he'd be sleeping above her. She was not thinking the naughty about that.

'There's a pretty high-tech security system I switch on at

night,' he said. 'If you go outside, you'll set off all the alarms. Even the balcony.'

'Are you telling me I'm a prisoner in here?'

'No. I'm telling you that if you go outside, you'll set off all the alarms. If you want to go out you can, just call out to me first and I'll disarm them.'

She relaxed a smidge. 'I won't want to go out.'

'Great.'

He moved into her room and she followed, looking about at the light walls and rich coverings on the fantastically huge bed. She didn't expect him to just drop the bags and turn so that she nearly bumped into him.

They both made like statues.

Except on the inside Dani's vital organs were at war—her brain was shutting down while her heart was pumping faster than the pistons in a Formula One racing car.

When he was close like this all she could think about was kissing him again—and doing a whole lot more. *Why don't you?* The little imp whispered inside her head.

Dani looked into his widened green eyes, teetering on losing herself in their mesmerising depths. He was so close and so aware.

Why didn't she? Because it would be too easy. And Dani had never been one to take the easy option. She would never *be* the easy option—for all her tarty talk to him. A simple few minutes now would mean complicated mess later—that she did know. She was her mother's daughter—susceptible to over-emotionality and that spelt weakness. Time after time she'd seen her mother's softness used against her. And when Dani had finally opened up to someone, she'd been trodden over too. Independence and clear-headedness was all—she needed to reclaim both right now.

The defence Dani had learned was to challenge, to say something smart, even issue a sting. But only millimetres from Alex, it was taking everything she had to stay in control. That made her nervous—and in turn that increased her determination to succeed. Her body went even more rigid.

One, then two, long seconds passed. His mouth was clamped shut and his eyes narrowed. Then he laced his fingers together, put them on his head as if he were an apprehended offender, and stalked from the room.

CHAPTER FIVE

DANI dragged herself from bed—having got to sleep only when the birds started their pre-dawn 'say hello to each other' chatter. She tugged up the trousers of her flannelette pyjamas and thudded down the stairs in search of coffee.

Newspapers were scattered all over the breakfast table and the radio was blaring. Dani blinked, struggling to adjust to the light, all the activity and the smell of fresh cooking. Alex was dressed in another devastating suit, sitting at the table with a giant glass of juice and halfway through demolishing an omelette already.

He paused, his fork halfway to his mouth as he looked her over. Dani held her head high—OK, the pink-pig-stamped pjs were indefensible, but at least they weren't sexy.

'You want one?' he asked. 'Won't take me a minute to whip it up.'

'No, thanks.' She turned her back on his blistering brightness. The words *want one* and *whip it up* coming from his mouth made her thoughts go squirmingly naughty.

'Not a morning person?'

Not when the night had been so long and she hadn't had her necessary six solid hours and a couple more in the doze-zone. She hadn't been able to move on from the doze-zone.

Because the semi-conscious dreams she'd had there had been rampantly X-rated and out of control. So, no, she wasn't a *this* morning person.

He made a small movement and the radio went silent. 'What about cereal? There's a selection in the pantry there.'

'Got coffee?'

He stood. 'How strong?'

'As strong as you've got.'

Dani looked at the pantry while he pushed buttons and got the oversized coffee contraption working. The pantry was oversized too—not just a cupboard you opened and filled the shelves of, but a small room that you could actually walk into—complete with its own butler's sink and small bench space. But despite her wanting to explore all the interesting-looking packs of foodie things on the shelves the space was just that bit too confined for her to feel comfortable. She walked out and inhaled.

'Nothing you like the look of?' Alex noted her empty hands.

Dani picked up the steaming mug he'd put on the table for her and told herself that there were plenty of other things in the whole entire world to like the look of. Not just Alex Carlisle.

'My housekeeper will get whatever you like in for you— just leave a note on the fridge.'

'Housekeeper?'

He nodded. 'Cleans, launders, cooks meals and is utterly discreet.'

Dani sank into a chair. 'The last being the most important, huh?'

Alex's brows lifted. 'You definitely need food.'

Dani just took another deep swig from the mug and closed her eyes as she swallowed the burning brain fuel. When she returned to almost-alive land Alex was at work behind the bench. There was a popping sound and he put two halves of a hot toasted bagel on the plate in front of him. He spread a thick layer of cream cheese onto it and several strips of smoked salmon on top of that. He put the finished plate of perfection in front of her.

OK, so that was something else to like the look of.

He nudged the plate closer. 'It's for eating.'

'Yeah. Thanks.' And it tasted almost as good as she figured he would.

He sat in the chair next to her and reached for his glass of juice, pulling part of the newspaper closer to read. 'Do you want me to organise a stylist for tonight?'

'A *what*?' She nearly choked on the bit of bagel.

'You know, someone to fix your hair and make-up?'

He thought she needed someone to fix her hair and make-up? Why? Didn't she make 'Carlisle standard'? Dani shrivelled inside as his words sliced right through her superficial layer of confidence. So she wasn't good enough to be seen out with at one of his posh fundraisers? She wasn't pretty or polished enough? Hurt, she put the bagel down, her appetite all gone. 'Are you sure you want me to come with you tonight?' She shrivelled more—hoped he hadn't heard her insecure edge.

Alex turned quickly to look at her, a frown drawing his brows together. Dani didn't look back at him, couldn't, was too flattened by his offer.

'Dani,' he said deliberately. 'There's nothing I want more than for you to come with me tonight. But I did promise I'd go to the dinner. And I don't want an empty chair beside me.' He put his hand on hers to stop her leaving the table.

She ignored her sizzling skin and gave him a baleful look. 'That wasn't what I meant.'

'I know you didn't,' he said, the cheeky grin giving way to

an earnest expression. 'Look, my mother never used to leave the house without having checked her appearance with her stylist. It's just something I'm used to. Not a comment on the way you look.'

A personal stylist? Wow—rich people like him really lived in an alternative universe, didn't they? But she didn't want to get sucked into the fantasy and start thinking such things were normal. She didn't want to be sucked in by Alex Carlisle any more than she'd been since she first clapped eyes on him.

'Umm, I think I can manage. It's only hair, right?' She cleared her throat, trying to get rid of the wounded rasp. 'And my style you can't do a lot with.' It was so thick she had to have it cut regularly into a plain and simple bob. But it was well overdue now, her fringe annoyingly long and too unruly for her to risk trimming herself—another reason to earn money asap.

He brushed the stupidly long bit back with his free hand and smiled, his gaze dropping to her pink pyjamas. Her toes curled into the heated tiles beneath her feet. What was she doing without shoes? And what was he doing looking so fine in his dark suit so early? And so clean-shaven? It was too early for that—shouldn't he be tousled, shouldn't his eyes be shadowed and sleepy, shouldn't he be...in bed?

'I'd better get ready.' She jerked up. 'Don't want to be late on my first day.'

The warehouse was impressive. Turned out Lorenzo was some sort of wine god and there were pallets of cases everywhere. And a very flash reception area and even a tasting room. Not that Alex stopped to give her the guided tour.

'The office is on the first floor.' He headed straight up. 'Cara, this is Dani.'

The woman behind the desk gave Dani a wide smile. Dani

registered the russet-coloured cropped hair and the elfin features and sparkling eyes.

'I'll leave you to it.' Alex was crisp. 'Take care of her.'

Dani wasn't sure who he meant by that—but he was gone before she could check.

'It'll be great to have you onboard,' Cara said cheerfully. 'There's always way too much to do.'

There was too. Dani's head whirled as she followed Cara through the routine. The woman was a dynamo—full of energy, effervescence and unfailing good humour.

She took the seat beside her and shadowed her while Cara explained everything in minute detail. It was fascinating and full on. But there was one burning question Dani couldn't bring herself to ask—how pregnant was Cara? Because her tummy was really, really flat. In fact, her tummy was flatter than Dani's. But she wasn't going to go personal—not on her first day. She was just here to work and pick up the wages.

Alex checked his watch again. He'd been stuck behind his desk for hours—hadn't gone down to the floor. No point. She wasn't there.

He should be feeling great. The situation with Dani was resolved, right? Now he could concentrate on far more important matters—like figuring out what he was going to do, whether he had any real right to be the boss at the bank. But his brain was stuck on one track. If he so much as thought of her his body went rock-hard. The things he wanted to do…but he hadn't taken her to his home to jump her bones the minute he had the chance, except the ache in his body had made him make moves and he'd loved every moment of touch and tease between them.

So had she. She couldn't deny the heat in her gaze, the reaction of her body—and she hadn't tried to. But she didn't want to act on it. And that got him.

He could kind of understand it. Her life was messed up enough—and in large part because of him. So succumbing to the lust—seducing her—just wasn't on, even though he knew it wouldn't take much to make it happen. But while Alex liked to play, he wanted an equally enthusiastic playmate.

Until she stepped up to the plate, he was standing back.

And she was a flatmate now, right? He knew the rule as well as she did—*don't screw the crew*. The one everyone learnt while flatting at university. Alex didn't mess around at work, and he sure as hell wasn't messing with someone in his own home.

He really shouldn't have taken her back there.

His phone rang, he glanced at the caller ID and congratulated himself on programming Patrick's mobile number in, because, nope, he was not answering. Alex wasn't ready to talk to him—maybe wouldn't ever be. What did the man expect—that he could back walk into his life, say, 'Hey, by the way, I'm your father, let's be friends.' As far as Alex was concerned, Patrick could stay in Singapore, where he had his luxury pad, a zillion servants and even more women. And if his conscience had started to prick him, too bad. Alex had no intention of making it easy for him. He took in a deep breath. He was too angry and he'd really rather channel that energy elsewhere.

He toyed with his pen and wondered what she was doing. He didn't like not being able to check on her. But Lorenzo could. Alex tossed the pen down as he realised he didn't like that, either. Lorenzo was a good-looking guy. Lorenzo liked women. And they liked him more.

He picked up the phone. His buddy-suddenly-turned-nemesis answered after one ring.

'How's she doing?' Alex skipped the preliminaries.

'I don't know. Fine, I'm sure.'

Alex frowned and spun his chair to look out the window—he could see the warehouse in the distance. 'Haven't you been to check?'

'I've got work to do so, no, I haven't. Do you want me to put you through to her phone?'

'No.' Silence. But Alex couldn't let it go yet. 'Why haven't you been to check?'

'What do you think I am—stupid?' Lorenzo grumbled. 'I'm not going anywhere near my best friend's latest lover.'

'She's not my lover.'

'Only a matter of time. Minutes. A few hours at the most.' Lorenzo chuckled. 'Breathe easy, brother.'

Alex sighed, then puffed out a smidge of amusement. 'Sorry.' They had never competed over a woman—had never had to given they went for totally different types. And until this second Alex had thought he'd walk away from any woman who threatened to come between him and Lorenzo—no hesitation. But Dani was different. The lust he felt for her made him want to fight his closest friend—the need was that sharp. But it seemed Lorenzo knew him better than he knew himself and was keeping far, far away.

So he could breathe easy? Yeah, as if that were possible when he had temptation-on-legs living in his town house and a bad case of honour afflicting him.

For the first time in ages he left the office for lunch—wandered down to the little exclusive line of shops round the block—an idea bubbling at the back of his brain. He didn't bother going back up to the office, got the car and went to the warehouse early to pick her up instead. Lorenzo was on the phone and waved his hand towards the stairs.

He could hear her voice. Given that Cara finished up early

afternoon, he knew she was on a call. He hovered outside the door so he wouldn't interrupt her.

'But this is my brother. Doesn't that count for something?'

Oh, it was a personal call. Alex stilled completely. He shouldn't listen. He'd done it before and suffered—losing the last of his childhood innocence as he'd realised his mother was having an affair. He didn't know who the lover she'd been talking to was—hadn't registered the extent of it, certainly hadn't dreamed there'd be that direct implication for him. Not then. But it had been a bitter enough pill. He'd been so angry with her—disrespecting her so much that Samuel had sent him to boarding school. The blindness of the man he'd thought was his father—whom he'd loved as his father—had made Alex even angrier.

So given what he knew about listening in to other people's conversations, he should walk down the hall and give Dani some privacy now. But his feet wouldn't move.

'But our mother is dead. How can she file the request when she's dead?'

He heard her sigh.

'But how can I find him if I can't get the paperwork from you?'

Silence while whoever it was talked some more.

'I'm in Auckland—what if I came into the office?'

Whoever it was, he was letting her down. Alex couldn't stop bending forward a fraction so he could see her through the gap in the hinge of the door. Her head was bent, her fringe hiding her eyes. From her slump he guessed the answer she'd just got was another negative.

'Is there any other way I might be able to find him?' She listened for a while. 'I've already put messages up on the Internet.' She was silent as she listened, and clearly not happy. 'OK. I understand. Thank you for your time.'

She put the phone down and buried her face in her hands, elbows thumping onto the desk.

Alex straightened and counted to five before walking on the spot for a few paces and then opening the door. 'Are you ready to leave?'

Her head snapped up. 'Alex. I didn't know you were here.' A flush mounted in her cheeks. 'I was using the phone but it was a local call.'

'It's fine to use the phone.' He was dying to ask more but she stood quickly and became busy pulling on her jacket. OK, he'd bide his time—but he'd find out what the deal was. She didn't suit the defeated look.

She said nothing until they were belted into his car, but then she launched a hit. 'I thought you said Cara was pregnant.'

Alex winced. Yeah, he should have seen this one coming. 'She is.'

'Not exactly due next month, though, is she?'

'No.' More like seven or so months. Cara had told them a couple of weeks ago, too effervescent to keep the news to herself any longer. She'd bounced off the walls when she'd blabbed it, while her husband had been all teasing protectiveness—warning that she wasn't to work too hard. Ironic when he was the CEO of one of the country's biggest accountancy firms and worked dog hours as bad as both Alex and Lorenzo.

'She's had terrible morning sickness.' Alex said, amazed at his inventiveness. Then he panicked, knowing the way women talked to each other. 'But don't mention it. She's very private. She doesn't want us to think she can't cope.'

'Oh.' Dani nodded. 'Of course. And is that why she works part-time hours at the moment?'

'Yes.' Lying was allowed when it was to help someone, right?

* * *

'You nearly ready?' Alex hollered.

Dani gave herself one last despairing glance in the mirror and fully regretted declining the use of the stylist.

Style—of the Carlisle standard. Could it be bought? Fashioned from the rawest of material? The dress was good, she knew it was good—it fitted perfectly. But the body beneath wasn't perfect, and there was no glitz or glam to dazzle the eyes and blind them to those imperfect bits.

She turned her back on her image and walked down the stairs to the lounge. He wasn't there. She took the few steps into the kitchen. He had his back to her. His perfectly fitted, perfectly pressed suit gleamed blacker than ink and oozed expense. He looked lean and long and definitely strong—could his shoulders be any broader? Then he turned around.

It took several moments before she could drag her gaze all the way up his body to his face. Even so his mouth was still hanging open, still another beat before he shut it. The surprise written all over him stung. Had he really expected her to walk in wearing some ill-fitting off-the-rack budget-chain number?

She was so glad she'd packed it. She'd laughed at her mother for making it. Argued she'd have been better off making her some more work shirts and skirts. Her mother had always altered her clothes for her—her breasts were too ample and her shoulders too narrow for store-bought to sit right. But she'd wanted to make her a dress—'to look beautiful' in. She'd despaired of Dani's jeans and tee habit. Just as Dani had despaired of her mother's 'must have a man' complex.

'Where did you get it?' He swallowed.

'My mother made it.' She cleared her throat. 'She was a seamstress.'

'A very good one.'

'Yes.' It was as beautifully made as his suit, which frankly she couldn't bear to look at a second longer. But the sting from his shock had gone now and left the heat of relief. She pushed her hair behind her ear. 'Should we get going?'

He walked over to her. 'I have something for you.' He reached into his pocket. 'To keep that bit out of your eyes.' He uncurled his fingers.

She had a quick peek and resolutely looked back up at him. 'I'm not wearing that.' And she wasn't going to look at it again. Her retinas were suffering enough already—bright spots danced the rumba before her.

'It's just a hairclip.'

It wasn't just a clip. It was a very grown-up piece of art. She might not have money but she wasn't stupid. Those weren't zirconias or even crystals. Only diamonds sparkled like that. It was an iris, wrought in a fine gold setting, some petals studded with diamonds, others decorated with yellow stones and a long slender gold stem. It was so, so pretty. Exactly the sort of totally feminine thing she secretly adored. How could he have known that? She couldn't deny she was thrilled. But even so, she couldn't possibly wear it. 'Where did you get it?'

He tilted his hand so it caught more light.

'I've never seen a clip like that.'

'It's a brooch—I got them to convert it.'

'Got who?'

'The jeweller.'

Oh, no. Her instinct was right—and no way could she accept something so expensive. 'Alex, I—'

He moved so close she could smell him—fresh and citrussy and so yummy she had to shut her mouth to stop herself drooling over him. His hands were firm on her head as he swept her hair back and pressed the clip into place.

He didn't move away once it was done. His hands dropped but he stayed.

She looked up at him. His eyes were a vivid green and a small smile tweaked his lips—as if he knew how much she liked it. She shook her head but he spoke first, not giving her the chance to say no.

'It looks better on you than it would on me.'

Alex marched five paces away from her—putting the stainless-steel bench between them. Breathing space—he needed it *now*. But he couldn't stop staring. He'd seen many black evening dresses in his time. He'd seen them long, short, high cut, low cut, backless, strapless, sleeveless, braless, sequined, sparkly, matte, smooth, velvet, silk, satin. He'd seen them twirl and he'd seen them creased. He'd helped slide zips both up and down. And he'd seen many of them slither to the floor.

But he had never, ever seen a black dress like hers. It fitted so perfectly. Utterly emphasising her petite, hourglass frame—cupping her full breasts, hugging her deliciously narrow waist and sweeping over those curving hips. Her short bob was sleek and glossy and there was that lock that slipped from behind her ear and curled on her cheekbone and he'd just had to deal with it—because if he didn't he'd spend the night tempted to swish it back with his teeth. His trawl of the jewellery stores had paid off. Now the clip sparkled, but not half as much as her eyes.

She was stunning.

'We should get going.' He didn't recognise his own voice. Apparently he had laryngitis now.

Ten minutes later Alex looked for the fiftieth time from the road to her, his head clear of all the confusion that had fogged it for this past week. His focus was sharp—on one thing: getting close to Dani. The urge to conquer was all-consuming. Driving every other thought beyond the mountains and into the sea. Right now, having her was all that mattered and damn the stupid complications.

It was amazing how someone so small could inspire such a big reaction in him. Although she wasn't that small—not where it counted.

'You look beautiful.' Such a useless cliché. And not nearly enough. But he was incapable of more.

'Not as beautiful as you,' she said.

She might think she was being flippant, but he knew she actually meant it. He'd seen the way she'd looked at him—the way her attention clung, the way her brown eyes darkened even more when he moved closer. And he was determined to move closer still. The frustration was immense. If it hadn't been for them getting caught on camera he could have had her already—couldn't he? Taken her on a date and ended up in bed. Surely she wouldn't have resisted?

But in his bones he knew she would have. The look she'd given him as she'd left the lift? Terrified. Turned on, yes, but terrified too. Fortunately her head had been away from the camera because he wouldn't have been crowned an online Don Juan if those in the blogosphere had seen her expression then. In his office she'd said it was nothing—a moment. Frankly he just didn't believe that. Sarcasm was her favourite form of defence—it had taken him only minutes to learn that. So he wanted a real-life replay of the lift kiss to prove his point—that the spark didn't get better than the one between them.

He steered the car with one hand, curled the other in a fist on his thigh. He wasn't going to drink tonight—that would only inflame the heat coursing through his body. He was on the edge of control as it was. It would need only the smallest provocation to tip him over the edge. Alex had never been on an edge quite like this before and he didn't like feeling so close to it now. And Dani was nothing but provocative.

'Where is this thing anyway?' She fidgeted—running her fingers over the edge of her dress. He really wanted her to stop because he was watching and all he wanted was for it to be *his* fingers feeling the transition from smooth silk to soft skin.

'Sky City.' The laryngitis was back.

She turned sharply towards him. 'I can't, Alex.'

Her voice was so panicked he nearly drove into the gutter.

'I can't go up in that lift.' Her huge eyes were even bigger and *so* dark.

Oh, dear, he should have thought of that. But damned if he could be bothered climbing however many million flights of stairs it was to get to the top of the tower that overlooked the city. He was just going to have to help her through the thirty-second ordeal. And just like that he had a plan. 'It'll be OK. I'll help you.' It would be his pleasure to.

She said nothing more but he felt her tension mounting as they drew closer to the brightly lit building and turned into its basement car park.

He could see her breasts rising too quickly as they waited but she walked in, head high. She stood with her back against the wall of the lift. He followed her but didn't turn to face the door, just stood bang in front of her—only an inch between them.

'I'm getting a sense of *déjà vu*.' He looked her over with deliberate boldness.

'Don't even think about it,' she croaked.

Oh, yes, he totally wanted to distract her that way again.

Press her against the wall and kiss her senseless so she wound herself round him again. Was that all it had been for her? A way of escaping her stress about riding in an elevator?

Her chest was still rising abnormally fast, but he saw her nipples had peaked now too. So he had her a little distracted.

'You can't stop me thinking, Dani.' Unfortunately he couldn't stop himself thinking, either—and he was thinking about it all the time.

She flicked a look up over his shoulders, lost colour as the door slid shut. He couldn't stop her thoughts, either, but maybe he could get her even more distracted—to think about something other than her fear.

He lifted a finger, traced the full curve of her lips. She hadn't plastered them in thick lipstick, but they did have a shine to them. Very pretty, very full, totally kissable. The colour returned to her cheeks in a sweep.

'I told you not...' Her feeble whisper died away as he stepped closer.

He ran his fingers up her cheekbone, turning his hand to brush the back of his fingers on her soft skin. She had a sweetheart-shaped face. Those big brown eyes dominated it. Her nose he'd barely noticed because of her drown-you-deep eyes and then there was the lush mouth beneath. But now, as he stood so close, he saw there were two freckles—one off to the left of the bridge of her nose, and one right near the tip. The tip of his finger circled them. He was going to have to kiss them.

Yeah, she was sweetheart pretty all right, with a body soft and curvy and built to contrast with his hard one. And when she opened her mouth it was all sarcasm and sass. The combination had him caught tighter than a fly in a spider's web— and he wanted her to suck him dry.

Wide-eyed, she gazed back at him, her breathing growing

choppier—but he liked to think it wasn't all about being shut up in a lift. Maybe she was reading his mind. If she was, then she knew she had far more to worry about than any stupid lift.

He heard the doors slide. They were there.

He took her hand in his, tightening his grip when she'd have pulled it away. 'Time to have a ball, Dani.'

CHAPTER SIX

DANI was so hot she could barely breathe. All the people she'd met tonight must think she was an idiot. She'd hardly been able to talk. It had been full on introduction after introduction, conversation and speculation and adoration—of him. But he hadn't left her side. Had turned to her when people asked questions, included her in the answering, not speaking for her but supporting her as she'd quietly replied.

He was doing it deliberately—touching her, looking at her like that—making it feel as if they were the only two in the room when in reality they were surrounded by hundreds. It was obvious everyone thought they were together. Not surprising given he was acting as if they were. And like a mythical beast it uncoiled between them, flexing the kind of strength no human had a hope of beating. It was the one thing that would reduce even the most sensitive, erudite, highly evolved person to the animal they really were—*lust*.

They moved together on the dance floor—his eyes glinted, teasing as he drew her closer then spun her away again. Oh, he would have all the fancy dance moves, wouldn't he?

'I need a drink,' Dani begged, needing a breather from him more than anything.

He chuckled as if he knew and led her by the hand towards the bar, letting her have her little respite.

'Alex.'

Dani turned at the unfamiliar voice, at the urgency with which it had spoken. But just as quick she looked at Alex because his hand suddenly crushed hers—his grip had gone boa-constrictor tight.

He'd frozen. His ready smile wiped. He didn't even say hello to the man who'd threaded his way to where they stood. He was about an inch shorter than Alex and dressed in a suit that Dani recognised as made to order. Flecks of grey peppered his dark hair, but despite his age he was still a good-looking man—a hint of charisma in the smooth face, his smile practised.

'I hoped you'd be here tonight.' Yes, the smile was definitely practised, because his eyes were too watchful, betraying a hint of uncertainty. 'I've tried calling you.'

Alex didn't even blink.

The man shifted, glanced at Dani and offered her a wider version of the smile before his attention flicked back to Alex. 'Aren't you going to introduce me?'

The silence stretched. The awkwardness excruciating. What was the problem here? Didn't Alex want to introduce her? But instinctively she knew it was this man that he had the problem with, not her. And it was some problem—she'd never have guessed a master of people skills like Alex could be so impolite.

'Dani, this is Patrick. Patrick, this is Dani.' He finally spoke. No qualifiers, no descriptors, no other info. Just names. Totally different from how he'd spoken with any of the others they'd mingled with tonight. His face had gone totally mask-like. 'I didn't realise you were in New Zealand.'

'I thought it would be a good idea. I take it you've had the results back.'

'Yes.' Alex's mouth barely moved as he replied, his eyes like stones.

Dani felt goose bumps rise over every inch of her skin. Alex's voice was blowing a chill direct from Antarctica.

The two men stared at each other. Alex stood ramrod straight and still, unrelenting in his cold scrutiny.

'It would be good to talk.' Patrick shifted his feet, his tongue touching the corner of his lip.

Was that the faintest touch of a plea in his comment? Dani almost felt afraid—the undercurrents swirling between the men seemed dark and downright dangerous. *Alex* seemed dangerous. The aggression she could feel mounting in him was raw. And this silence was too horribly long.

'Not now.' Alex shattered it. Brutally dismissive. Unbelievably cold. Then he turned, practically dragging Dani away with him.

Dani swallowed and half skipped to keep up. Stunned by this facet of Alex she hadn't known existed. He went straight to the bar, ordered her a wine and himself a neat whisky. He knocked it back in one swallow. It was the first drop of alcohol he'd had all night. Dani sipped her wine slowly, wondering if he was going to have another, wondering what it was about the Patrick man that had him feeling so lethal. But he turned, looked her over, his eyes nothing but fire now.

'Dance with me.'

She couldn't refuse, her heart thudding as she felt the barely leashed emotion in him. He held her close—much closer than when they'd danced before. The music was loud, the tempo fast, but all the energy zinged from him— electrifying her nerves. And then she felt the change within him, from anger, to passion—but no less intense. He pulled her closer still, his hands firm on her body—moulding her to him. The way he moved was incredible, intoxicating, dizzying—indeed she stumbled.

He took her by the elbow and led her to a secluded table on the far side of the dance floor. He poured her a glass of water from the carafe on the table.

Dani took a sip of the cool liquid and asked before she lost the nerve. 'Who's Patrick?'

His eyes were dark, unreadable in the flashing lights from the dance floor. 'No one.'

She had another sip of water, unsurprised by his answer. It wasn't any of her business anyway. He pulled his chair closer, facing her rather than out to the floor. And then his hands disappeared.

'What are you doing?' She could hardly move her mouth enough to ask.

'Nothing.' Beneath the table his fingers were lightly caressing her knee—rubbing over the silk hem of her dress and onto her skin.

Nothing? Nothing like the lift?

His fingers moved higher.

'I'd have thought a high-society fundraising dinner wouldn't be the place for public displays of lust,' she choked. 'Aren't you too well bred for that?'

'Who said I was well bred?' His hand slid higher up her thigh, the touch suddenly far more insistent.

Dani gulped. 'I thought you were staying away.'

'Was I?'

'Stop it.'

Make me. He didn't say it. He didn't need to. He was so used to getting his way, wasn't he? He understood the power of his charm. The way people had fawned over him tonight proved it. He thought he could get away with anything.

And maybe he could.

But Dani was suddenly filled with the urge to better him—just the once. The thrill of the challenge was irresistible, and what better way to drive away the shadows in his eyes from his frosty encounter with Patrick?

'All right.' She turned towards him. 'If this is what you want.'

She lifted her hand to his face, ran her hand down his smooth jaw. Leaned closer and breathed in. She loved the light, crisp scent of his aftershave. She dropped her hand to his chest, feeling the beat of his heart and its acceleration, the heat of his skin burning through the shirt. Sizzling—that was Alex.

She moved her hand again, placed it lower—far higher up his thigh than his fingers had ventured up hers. She twisted her wrist, spreading her fingers, stroking his already rigid length, encircling it and then squeezing.

She was unable to stop her smile as he stopped breathing. His discomfort registered even more on his face. His mouth snapped shut, jaw went militarily square. She saw the ripple in his muscles as he struggled for control.

She leaned closer, her mouth a millimetre from his skin, and teased him some more. 'Dare you to walk across the dance floor now.'

His breath hissed out between his teeth as he jerked, flinging far back into his seat and out of her reach. No, he wasn't really into public displays at all, was he?

Triumphant, she met his eyes, her smile widening with the thrill of the dangerous line she was treading.

But then he moved. His grip on her upper arm was hard and he stood so fast that she stumbled as he hauled her up beside him. His other hand went around her waist, clamping her so she was just in front of him. He pressed his hot, hard body against her back. Insistent, he pushed her forward.

She walked. She had no choice. Right across the dance floor.

But he didn't release her once they were clear; instead he guided her out of the room completely, down a corridor, and left, down another corridor.

Halfway along that he swiftly turned her, his arms powerful as he pulled her close. He pressed her against him, one hand slid beneath the hem of her dress. Her knees sagged at the touch and he pushed her until her back hit the wall. But he kept pushing until his body was sealed hard to the length of hers. Save a scrap of satin, a whisper of silk and his strained trousers, they were as intimate as two people could physically be.

Her gasp rasped in her ears and her most feminine muscles clenched instinctively, the hungry ache down low unbearable.

'Don't play with me and think you can win.' His words dropped into her ear like sparks of wildfire—igniting frustration, temptation and anger. He felt so good against her. So incredibly good. She gazed at him, anticipation smothering any chance of thought.

'My turn to dare,' he taunted.

Her awareness surged to new heights, her body supersensitive.

'Kiss me.' He'd loosened his hold yet she couldn't escape, couldn't make herself push away the heat. Instead she wanted him closer again.

Pleasure and satisfaction—his promise of both beckoned her. His fingers stroked her thigh, inching higher, then higher, delicately tracing across her soft skin and sending ripples of sensation out to the rest of her body—especially those secret parts.

'Kiss me.' He flexed—closer—a minuscule movement with maximum impact.

Her lashes drooped as she studied him up close, no longer

conscious of anything else but him. He tilted his chin at her, just the way she had at him in the lift that day, and his lips twisted into that irresistible smile.

And she couldn't resist him. Not when he looked so good, smelt so good, felt so good. Her lips parted, her body going on instinct now, her brain defunct. All she could see was his mouth—almost parted, waiting—and the desire in his eyes. All she could hear was the thunder of her heart as it sent hot blood racing through her body.

As her head lifted, her lashes dropped, blocking everything so she could focus only on the sensation of his mouth against hers. Even so just the briefest touch overwhelmed her; she shivered. His whole body tensed. He lifted his hand from her back, tangling his fingers in her hair, keeping her close to him so she wouldn't break the contact of their lips. Not that she could. Not now, no. She threaded both her hands through his hair too, clinging, so eager for more than a taste of him. She moved her lips over his. He had full lips, firm and yet soft. She touched them with her tongue, tasting, then pushing closer, exploring the heat of his mouth. More. And then more still.

He let her dominate for a moment, but then rewarded her hungry searching with a deep thrust of his own. Involuntary spasms racked her as he held her close and plundered. Her fingers tightened in his hair as she tumbled headlong into his stormy passion.

The hand between her legs coasted higher, skimming across the satin of her knickers, making her squirm, making her wish she could arch against him freely. His hand spread wide against the back of her head, holding her even more firmly to him. She felt his groan vibrate through his whole body as he stroked her intimately. His fingers gently moved back and forth as he savoured the damp evidence of her desire for him—desire hurtling her to abandonment.

She opened deeper for him, the kiss almost savage now as the full power of their physical attraction was unleashed. She pressed against his chest, trying to please her painfully taut nipples with contact against his hard heat.

The high-pitched laughter and the tinging of glass on glass screeched over the roar in her ears. Her eyes snapped open, shattering the moment. Suddenly she was aware of where they were.

'Stop, Alex,' she panted against his mouth. She could see the sheen on his skin and fiercely suppressed the urge to lick the salty flavour of him.

His breath gusted across her face as he pulled back.

'Not here.' As close to a plea as she'd ever uttered. They were in a public space. A minute or two more of that kind of kissing and she was going to be coming loud and wild only a thin wall away from Auckland's most rich and famous. Her heart pounded so hard she thought it must be about to blow apart in her body. The physical need burned through to her bones. She tore her gaze from his, made herself look along the corridor— Oh, hell, someone had just walked past. They'd only have to turn their head to see them. Alex's broad body partially protected her privacy, but even so.

Lust had made her forget everything—who she was, where she was, and what she was supposed to be doing. A different kind of heat engulfed her.

Humiliation.

Dani refused to let desire turn her into such a mindless *slave*.

'Let's go.' Temptation personified murmured into her ear.

If she went with him this minute they'd end up in the back seat of his car, or in the loo on the way, or a cleaning cupboard, or down an alley, or something equally tacky but convenient. So she had to claw back her self-control fast because having sex with Alex wouldn't just be reckless, it would be dangerous. The feelings he aroused in her were too strong. She couldn't let herself drown in them. Her response wasn't just physical, it would be over-emotional too. All Alex was up for was a little playtime—she needed time out to get a grip first. 'Aren't you supposed to draw some prize or something?'

'Lorenzo can do it.'

'You can't let them down.' She pushed him away. He moved and she smoothed down the front of her dress in a quick gesture.

'It's your turn to dare,' he said too coolly, too confidently.

She shook her head. 'I'm all out of challenges.'

He chuckled. 'I don't believe that.' He stepped closer again. 'Maybe you just need some provocation.' He leant forward and kissed her again, his mouth seeking, demanding. She bit back the moan. He wasn't touching her anywhere else but she ached to ride him, to rock her hips back and forth and take him inside her. If they were alone she would do just that. Shed her clothes and his and have all of him hard and fast and right *now*.

She tore free of his kiss and gulped in air. But no matter how many breaths she took she still felt dizzy. She stared at him, shocked at the need still rampaging through her defences. So easily he had won this from her. So much for staying away—so much for either of them having self-control.

'What do you think about a truce?' She was panting too much for the question to come out as tart as she'd have liked.

He lifted his hand and ran the tip of his finger over her lips. She gasped again.

'We can delay a little longer if you like. But this is inevitable.'

She wanted to shake her head but it felt heavy and she

couldn't move it. Passion shone in his eyes, pleasure and satisfaction broadened his smile.

'We're flatmates,' she finally managed. 'We can be friends but we can't…' She trailed off as he laughed.

'Honey, we can't be friends. Not 'til we've burned this out.' He nudged her chin with his thumb. 'After that we can—I get on well with all my ex-lovers.'

Oh. Was that so? 'Regular Lothario, aren't you?' Dani drawled, sarcasm dripping.

'Well, you have your *joy* boys—right?' His smile had sharp edges. 'Nothing wrong with liking sex, Dani. It's natural.'

Slack jawed, she could no longer cope with his subtle-as-a-brick sensuality. Because the worst thing about it was that it made her body burn hotter. 'I need to freshen up.'

'Coward.'

How long was it possible to live with an Empire-State-Building-size erection? Alex wondered whether there was an entry in the Guinness Book of Records and knew with certainty that if there was, he was going to beat it.

'You're taking her home?'

'To her separate little bedroom, yes.'

Lorenzo laughed. 'That won't last long.'

Alex leant his shoulder against the wall. From here he could see when she exited the bathroom. 'It's complicated.'

'Yeah. The whole Internet movie, invent her a job, move her into your home kind of complicated.'

Alex shook his head. Lorenzo didn't know the half of it. He didn't know the whole I-just-found-out-who-my-father-really-is nightmare yet. And it was a nightmare. Alex swept a quick glance around the room, couldn't see the bastard. How dared Patrick just appear like that—what was he trying to do? What did he want? Well, whatever it was, he wasn't getting it.

That was really what was eating Alex alive, not some five-foot-nothing sexy piece of a woman. He sighed as the thought of Dani made his whole body ache with need. 'It was your dumb idea to move her in to my place.'

'Thought it might be convenient.' Lorenzo chuckled.

Alex shot him a filthy look and drained the last of his juice. OK, so she was eating him up too. But he could deal with lust, couldn't he? Wasn't he Alex Carlisle? Didn't he have a phone full of names and numbers of wannabe dates? If he wanted sex he could get it, no problem.

But he'd happily fling the thing in the harbour. Normally he did a few dates, a few laughs, never anything complicated and certainly not committed—a two-months sort of man, that was him. Women were for fun, nothing more—he was never having anything more. But now he wanted sex with only one woman. The scent of her incited an untapped depth of hunger in him. He didn't know how he was going to assuage it. There were so many options, so many fantasies swirling in his head all the damn time.

So much of it was the game, wasn't it? The hunt, the chase, the challenge she threw at him. Since when had he had to work for it like this—or to wait? Usually he didn't bother if someone was giving him the hard-to-get routine. He wasn't that desperate. But Dani was different. She didn't want a 'relationship'. Fantastic. But her determined denial of a fun fling bit him hard. This time the game was everything. Oh, yeah, he was getting off on every minute of it and doing everything he could to aggravate a response from her.

He straightened as he saw her appear. If he were to judge by the look on her face he wasn't getting any further with her tonight, but, judging by the tension in her body, he figured he had another shot. And he was damn well taking it.

Dani waited with him for the lift and focused on her breathing—the last of her Alex-induced heat doused by the fear of the few seconds to come. So stupid to be like this. But every time she got into a small space her stomach knotted and all the oxygen vanished. Every time she remembered the darkness, and the silence—the terrifying silence that had been shattered by that vicious thud.

Alex pulled her into the hideous rectangle. 'Look at me.' He pointed to his eyes. 'Look right here.'

She glared at him. Cross with his patronising attitude. 'Look, I'm not some mad cow and you're not some animal whisperer with a mesmerising gaze.'

'Dani.' He took her upper arms in his broad hands and gently shook her. 'You're totally a mad cow.'

'Yeah.' She barely registered her pathetic reply because he did have magical green eyes. They were twinkling right now and imparting some kind of secret message.

She stumbled as he let her go with an ironic murmur. 'Look at that—we're on the ground already.'

As they walked to his car the dark quiet night seemed to swallow them. The thick silence kept them company all the drive home.

She climbed the stairs. Her pulse stepping up a notch, and then another, then more in rapid succession until she was filled with more adrenalin than when she'd been frozen with fear in the cupboard that day.

He pressed buttons for the alarm system. She heard the keys land on the wood of the table and walked even faster, keen to get to her room, *alone*. He caught her arm, his hand sliding to her wrist. She stopped. He had to feel that galloping rhythm in her veins. She heard him step closer and fought to keep the feeling of fear. That would give her strength.

He kissed the nape of her neck, kept near enough for her to feel his breath warm her skin. 'When were you last serviced, sweetheart?' The smile was soft in his voice. 'Seems to me you're in need of a tune-up.'

Dani couldn't breathe, let alone answer. All the old fear dissolved—*she* was dissolving.

His laugh was low and sexy. 'You said about your men, Dani, but it's all a tale.'

'What makes you think that?'

'Because when it comes down to the moment, you hesitate.' He turned her to face him. 'You're not off having one-night stands all over the place or maintaining an assortment of lovers. You go so far, and, honestly, it's not even that far. Then you stop.'

All talk and no action, huh? OK, so there might be some truth in that. Not that she'd admit to it.

'I'm even starting to wonder if you're a virgin,' he teased.

She choked. OK, so she didn't have anywhere near the kind of experience she'd implied, but she wasn't that. She looked at the third button down on his shirt and assumed a bored tone. 'Maybe I'm just not that into you.'

'Oh, but you are.' He bent so it wasn't his buttons she saw but his smile—the one that lit up his whole face. 'Want me to prove it to you?'

His pursuit was in earnest now. She could see the determination, the seriousness in his eyes, feel it in every deliberate touch. He'd said that they were inevitable. And if she were honest she'd have to agree. So why was she bothering with the fight? Why not give in?

Because she didn't want to be his latest prize. Sure, he was compelling, charming. But he was also competitive, driven to win. She suspected he could be ruthless about that. He'd been born to succeed and obviously thrived on it. And right now *she* was the challenge—but that was all she was. She felt like a bug in the path of a steamroller. And there was that innate part of her that always fought—not to be the statistic, not to do the expected, never to give up or give in.

But most of all she didn't want to open herself up. Because she had the feeling that Alex would take more than she intended to give. She liked to be in control of her emotions— but she couldn't see herself keeping that control in his arms. Not when he made her feel like some mindless nympho with just one kiss and a pet or two. So, even in the face of the impossible, she made her stand.

'Actually I'll pass, Alex.' She walked to the relative safety of the doorway. Then she went for the flick-off. 'You know, you're right, it has been a while. I found my servicemen to be a little lacking. But, you know, a girl can do so much better for herself.' She fluttered her fingers up past her breast, to her mouth, and watched his slightly stunned expression widen even more. 'Infinitely more reliable. Satisfying.' She ran the tip of her index finger across her lower lip, let her tongue touch it briefly. 'I can take care of my needs myself. I don't need anyone else.'

CHAPTER SEVEN

HEAVY-HEADED and grumpy, Dani dragged herself from bed more frustrated than a sex addict trapped in solitary for three years. Because that was exactly what she was, wasn't it? Some kind of sad addict—craving for his touch, his kiss. It was just because it had been ages, right? That was why her hips were so keen to wriggle now. But her hips had never wanted to wriggle as bad as this.

She imprisoned them in her most conservative black skirt and topped it with a pale blue blouse. Thick black opaque tights helped keep her legs warm and hidden and her wedge-heeled shoes gave her some help in the height department—stilettos weren't something her ex-tomboy self could walk in.

She brushed her hair, took care applying her usual light layer of make-up. Armour. She needed conservative today.

She stared at the finished result in the mirror and sighed. The frustration was evident on her face—her increased pallor, the shadows under her eyes. Hell, she was letting him mess with her looks. Not good. Was she becoming as much of a victim as her mother? Letting a man upset the life she was trying so hard to get on track?

Maybe, she should just have sex with him and be done with it. She wanted to—*how* she wanted to. And wasn't she over-analysing the whole thing? Wasn't she overstating the effect he had on her? Wasn't it just because she hadn't had sex in eons? Couldn't he be exactly the kind of fling she'd said she did—routine 'maintenance'. No emotion. No complication. Just fun—it was just sex, after all. And once done, it was done. Why, then they could be *friends*.

That was how he did it, right? He'd said it was *just sex, just fun*. Surely if she went in eyes wide-open, she wouldn't make the mistake of making more of it. Surely with this awareness, she could stay in control?

She walked down the stairs into the kitchen. Got halfway to the pantry before she finally looked at him and stopped—impaled by his intense stare. Long moments disappeared into a vortex while he somehow looked over every inch of her outfit yet held her eyes captive with his.

Her nipples tightened; so did the muscles in her womb. It wasn't going away. And it was only getting worse.

Owl-like, she closed her eyes and moved her head down, opening her eyes again, she saw her shirt and skirt. She hadn't realised it, but it was the exact outfit she'd been wearing that day in the lift. OK, maybe she had realised but had been in denial. The look in his eyes had told her he remembered too.

'Have a good night?' he asked way too intensely. 'Enjoy playing by yourself in that big bed?'

Oh, yeah, her hollow words came back to haunt her. What a joke that had been. She'd shifted round restlessly the whole night. She wanted only one thing—his body filling hers. She frowned.

He leaned back against the bench and ran his hand up his chest to his heart, drawing *her* attention to *his* fine physique displayed in his crisp white shirt. 'Don't ruin my fantasy now.' He tilted his head, studied her with half-closed eyes and a smile born of wickedness. 'You know I'd love to watch.'

'Pervert.' But she felt the blush covering her skin. Even worse a ripple of excitement stirred in her belly. She couldn't really *want* like this, could she?

She moved. The pantry. Cereal. Breakfast. Then work. But her blood pounded, deafening her. She'd had enough of this starvation. She went into the small room and tried to find some food—what had happened to his host act? Why hadn't he made her breakfast?

She heard a sound, glanced behind her, his body filled the frame of the doorway into this tiny space.

Ragged-breathed, butter-fingered, trembling—she couldn't even pour the cereal.

'Is it the small space? That's what's upsetting you so much?'

So he'd noticed—hard not to when she'd dropped the box of crunchy clusters twice already.

Her mouth was dry. The swallow hurt. 'No.'

'Then why are you so on edge?'

She spun on her toes to face him, now he stood a mere whisper away. 'You know why.'

He held her gaze as he had only minutes before. The green of his eyes disappeared in the darkness as his pupils swelled.

She was fascinated. And suddenly she was decided. She was determined—in control. 'If we do this,' she said firmly, 'then you're with no one else while I'm with you.'

His eyes flashed fire. 'Do you really think it necessary to make that clear?'

'You kiss complete strangers in elevators. Of course it's necessary.'

'Yeah, well, you admit to spreading your legs like margarine for a whole *variety* of men. So no other lovers for you, either.'

She adopted a faux crushed look, gave an equally faux sigh. 'It'll be hard. But I guess I can find the discipline somehow.'

He lifted his hand and waved his palm at her. 'I can help you with discipline if you want, honey.'

Her jaw dropped. 'Don't you dare.'

His low laughter sent waves of want pulsing from her belly outwards.

'It's *my* turn to dare.' She wrested back the lead.

He sobered instantly. 'What do you want me to do?'

Her answer was short. Explicit. And very, very naughty.

'Now?' He was already moving.

'Yes.'

'Here?'

'Just hurry up.' She reached for him with both hands, mouth open.

Ravenous.

He met her more than halfway. The pressure of his lips bruised but still it wasn't close enough. She mewled into his mouth and pushed her whole body closer. And what had begun that day in the lift surged forward, continuing at break-neck speed towards the only possible conclusion. She rubbed against him, so eager to explore him, to have his thighs between hers, to have his hands there too, his mouth and most of all his rock-hard penis. Everything, all at once. Right now.

He moved, kissing her cheek, her neck, down to her chest, pulling the shirt aside so he could access skin. She fumbled with buttons, cursing when they wouldn't undo as fast as she needed them to. She grabbed his hair and yanked, bringing his mouth back to hers. She gasped for air when she could and dived straight back into the heat of his kisses, the need burning her up. She arched against him, her hips writhing round and round in a mad rhythm.

Now. She wanted him there now.

He ripped his lips from hers. Swore. 'I don't want to stop.'

'Hell, no, *don't*.' Feverish, she raked her hands down his back, urging him closer.

'Contraception,' he cursed. 'I don't want to screw up this situation even more.'

'I'm covered.' She nipped his mouth angrily. 'I'm never having an unplanned pregnancy. Get on with it.'

Still he paused. 'I've never want—'

'Me, either.'

Passion spiralled higher. Never had she wanted a man to be inside her the way she wanted him. She worked fast, desperate to get her hands on his bare skin. Feral, crazed. Fabric tore and buttons burst.

Her fingers curled into his hard muscles, not just testing their strength, but provoking a forceful response with her sharp little nails. She wanted him—his body, his strength, his absolute attention.

Now.

Alex had never had such animal sex, ever. Usually he was courteous, making sure his partner was well satisfied before allowing his own release. It was frivolous, frisky, carefree. This was anything but. This felt like a battle to the death. He seized her round the waist as he had that day, pleasure rippling through his muscles as they exerted, lifting her up and pinning her back against the wall. Now he could press against her. Now he could have her.

She was still fighting like a wildcat—wanting him with an aggression that matched his. Tearing his shirt free of his trousers, she pulled at the buttons. Busy fighting for what she wanted while he was fighting to get what he wanted—her naked.

It was a mess. She was wearing tights and neither of them

could get them off her. In the end he got them as far down as her calves and then stepped over the stretchy Lycra so she could loop her legs around his waist. Her skirt was hitched up, her torn blouse hanging half open. He spared a half-second to suck a nipple into his mouth, bra and all. Her gasp felled him. He simply shredded her knickers. Oh, she was wet, and smelled so good and moved even better against the fingers he used to test her—clamping on them, promising insane pleasure.

Ready. So ready.

He moved. Suddenly, finally, thrust into her.

His heart seized.

The world fell away as he looked into her eyes, unable to move, unable to think, unable to believe how good he felt. How good *she* felt.

She too was frozen, her lips parted. In jagged bursts she released the breath she'd been holding. The moans that came with it were the sound of pure bliss.

It surged into him. Like a burst dam, emotion flooded him. Her fingers curled into his hair at the same moment. Wide eyed, shaking, she put her lips to his. Kissing him—the kind of soul-searing kiss that would have had him on his knees if he weren't suddenly imbued with the ability to handle super-human sensations. Sensations so raw he thought he'd die silently screaming with the pleasure.

At last their movements matched. They worked together, locking into the dance so deeply now. She met his hard thrusts with forceful ones of her own. Taking him further, her legs curled tighter around him. Her mouth was open, lips full and swollen as she panted, and then moaned with delight. Her sounds matched the rhythm of their bucking hips. He too was grunting in time with each pound, half crazed with the way she

made his body sing. Trying harder and harder to get closer—
to her, and to the blinding peak that was just out of reach.

He saw her bite down on her lips, her face screw tighter in
agony as ecstasy approached. She was flushed with pleasure
and that curling lock of hair flopped on the side of her face.

She was beautiful. Born for this. As was he. Her neck
arched as she threw her head back and he couldn't resist the
vulnerability of the soft skin.

Her scream sliced through his skin and bone, piercing right
into his marrow. And instinct took over, driving his body.
Surging harder, faster, seeing her ride the whole of the crest
before he lost it entirely. A guttural shout ripped from him—
hurting his throat, echoing relentlessly in the small room.

He kept his eyes closed. He felt the trickles down his face,
his back. How the hell had they got so sweaty in what had surely
been only a few minutes? He didn't think he'd ever catch his
breath. With one hand he gripped the edge of the shelf behind
her, trying to keep control, keep his mind conscious as the
blackness threatened to trap him completely. The overwhelming feeling, that post-orgasmic relief, had him trembling.

Trembling?

Intense didn't cover it. His lungs burned as he strove to get
more air in. At last he looked down at her. She looked shocked
and she couldn't wipe her expression in time to hide it from
him. But as he watched she shut it down; he saw the defensiveness veil her from him. All it did was make his body stir—
made him want to hold her close and do all kinds of things with
his hands and mouth. Because then she couldn't hide from
him—not when it was like this between them. And what she
hadn't been able to hide just then had satisfied him even more.

Out of control. She'd been as out of control as him.

Thank goodness for that.

* * *

Dani summoned her last crumb of energy and pushed him away. She stumbled in the attempt to untangle her legs from his and he hopped free, pulling up his boxers and trousers, wiping the sweat from his brow with a broad palm.

Dani's limbs shook. She needed to get out of here. Not because she was stuck in a small space, hell, she hadn't known where she was for the last few minutes—couldn't have cared less. But she was in a far more scary zone now. All that mattered was getting away from him—quickly, so she could pull herself together again. Else she was going to launch herself back into his arms and beg for more—beg for everything.

Sex was sex? Fun? Meaningless?

That hadn't been either.

That had been the most intense experience of her life. So wild. So wonderful. So scarily insane.

He grabbed her by the wrist as she made it to the doorway. 'We should talk, Dani.'

Um. Why? She didn't want a post-mortem on that moment. She wanted to wrap it up in tissue and put it pride of place in her memory chest.

'Not necessary.' She aimed for casual, struggled to walk in a dignified way given the remnants of her knickers and tights were down round her ankles and her shoes were still on. 'I have a job to get to,' she said shakily. 'So do you.' She yanked off one shoe and freed her foot from the tights.

'Work can wait.'

'I'm not walking in an hour late because I slept with the boss.' Actually she really ought to forget it. Go to a hypnotist and have the memory erased or something.

'I'm not your boss.'

'Semantics.' She raced to her room. 'I'll be ten minutes.'

She took twenty and that was still nowhere near long enough for her to recover. She was going to need a few centuries for that. Wow oh wow oh wow.

Who ever knew it could be like that? No wonder the man was so popular—and so confident.

He was ready and waiting downstairs, hair still drying from its obvious dunking in the shower. She looked away, heat flooding her. She didn't want to think about him naked in the shower.

'Dani—'

'Let's not, Alex,' she almost pleaded as she clipped down the stairs to the garage. 'You were right, it was inevitable. But we've done it now.'

'You think that's done?' He laughed. 'You've got to be kidding.'

Not at all. Not doing it again would be the most sensible thing by *far*. She was too inexperienced to play with a champ like him. 'Can we get going? It's only my second day on the job.'

He slammed the door and fired the engine. 'We're not done.'

'I'm not going to argue with you, Alex.'

'Good, because I'm right and you know it.'

She reached forward and turned the volume of the radio up and made a point of staring out of the side window.

Stupid, so completely stupid.

She'd known it, hadn't she? Her instincts had been bang on. Now her body was screaming chaos—wanting to cling but wanting to run just as much. Getting close to him was like volunteering to abseil into a live volcano—an adrenalin rush like no other, but with a high chance of incineration.

'Why are you in New Zealand, Dani? Are you looking for someone—your brother?'

Dani whipped round to look at him—how did he know that?

'I heard you on the phone last night,' he said bluntly.

The stitches holding the hurt in her heart ripped. That was her most private business, her greatest treasure, and she didn't want anyone—not even him—invading the preciousness of it. 'You shouldn't eavesdrop on private conversations.'

'I might be able to help.'

How? Did he have access to all those secret files? She couldn't breathe. Most certainly couldn't speak. Just stared back out of the window.

'Look, you don't have to tell me if you don't want to,' he said softly, 'but I know a really good private investigator.'

'What do you need a PI for?' she asked, surprised.

'Every family has its secrets, Dani.' His smile twisted.

'But not every family uses a PI to find them out.'

He went quiet as he turned into the car park in the front of Lorenzo's warehouse. She knew he was waiting but she'd never told a soul about Eli. He wasn't her secret, he was her mother's.

Finally he shrugged and switched off the engine. 'The offer is there.'

'I'll think about it,' she lied out of politeness. She wasn't sharing that with him—way too personal. 'Thanks,' she added as an afterthought.

He'd got out too, walked round to her side of the car, suddenly looking fiery. 'Do you have to wear those shirts?'

'What's wrong with my shirts?' They were beautifully fitted, hand-stitched in parts, and conservative. 'They're not too tight.' Not like some of the numbers she'd seen around his office.

'They *hint*.'

Hint? She frowned at a small noise. 'Are you grinding your teeth?'

'Now I know what's underneath…'

She looked at him as his voice trailed off, her gaze colliding with his. Longing tumbled over her and her legs went new-foal wobbly—she was feeling desperate for him again already? 'I'll dig out my caftan later.'

'Don't bother, I'll still see your curves.'

He claimed her hand with a 'don't even try to stop me' grip. So she didn't try, because the need in her body for some kind of touch was too strong.

'What are you doing?' And why did she have to be so breathless around him?

'Proving a point.'

But the last word never made it out because he pressed his lips to hers, his body pushing her back against the car, his hands sweeping over her. Dani's body both melted and went bowstring taut. So much for sex snapping the tension.

Alex lifted his head and smiled. She was flushed, soft in his arms and unbearably tempting. 'You'd better go in, sweetheart. You don't want to be late, do you?'

He laughed as she gave him a glare. Then he got back in his car and gunned it.

Sweet, mindless sex. Hours and hours of hard, physical, frisky distraction. That was what he needed and all he wanted. It was the one thing guaranteed to take his mind off his nightmarish family crisis. Images from last night flashed in his head—the shock he'd felt when he'd seen him: Patrick. He'd stared at him, searching for the familiar in his features. Hating himself for not having seen it before. Hating the man more for the years of lies.

Alex had worked and worked and worked for years—and for what? He had no right to the name, his mother had had no right to raise him thinking he did. No right to instil in him the sense of *duty* that had meant he'd never considered any other option—that his life had become the business.

He couldn't believe the extent of the deceit. Couldn't bear to think of the betrayal. It made him glad Samuel was dead—glad he'd never know the truth. Because it really sucked.

So Alex deserved some fun, didn't he? On tap in his own house. He wasn't going to let any stupid regrets take hold of Dani. He knew she was full of it—there weren't any joy boys. But he'd been blowing the hot stuff too—wasn't the total playboy he'd let her believe. Sure, he'd had a rampant phase for a few years there, but he'd matured. Only the occasional date had made it to first base, let alone third, recently, hardly any home runs. OK, he'd got bored.

But he wasn't bored now.

He'd help her with her search if she'd let him. He wanted her to get the answers she needed—he knew all too well how horrible it was not to have those answers. And while she might not want a relationship she was a touch romantic—with her pretty candles and lacy underwear—so he'd do some romancing. Because he wasn't letting her deny them the physical fling that he was sure would make them both feel fantastic, and let him forget everything else. Even if only for a while.

Cara was at her desk, her smile sly. Dani glanced out of her window—yeah, it overlooked the car park. OK, so that was embarrassing. Thank goodness Cara was too well bred to comment on anything so personal. There was a part of Dani that would have loved to share her anxiety and excitement—to have a good girly chat about it as she would have done with her mother or her old schoolmates. But she'd lost touch with those friends when her mother was so sick and her father had made it so much worse. Now her mother had gone and Dani didn't know Cara anywhere near well enough to confide.

Instead she got on with her work—sneaking time to post a

question on one of the adoption boards. She'd left messages on a reunion site for him but had no reply. What could she do next given she was unable to request his full file from the authorities?

And after Cara left in the early afternoon, Dani went back online. She wasn't into the whole online social networking thing. Even less so since she'd starred in a downloadable clip of her own. But right now she was a glutton for punishment. She typed in his name. And hers. Found the elevator kiss clip. Winced at the number of hits it had received and blushed beet red when she read some of the comments. People needed to get their own lives. She quickly logged back into the message board, hoping someone might have an answer for her. There was only one.

If he hasn't replied to the ads, there's not much else you can do without professional help. Hire a PI.

CHAPTER EIGHT

'ABOUT this morning.' Dani finally broached the subject.

'Yes?'

Dani glanced sideways at Alex, a touch apprehensive. He looked uncharacteristically stern, had been quiet on the drive home. 'I'm not sure we should repeat it.'

'Dani, be honest.' He served up something from the slow cooker his housekeeper had filled while they were at work. 'It was mind-blowing and you want to do it again as much as I do.'

'I don't want to screw up this situation even more.' She quoted his words back at him.

'Sleeping together isn't going to do that.' He reached for another plate and ladled food onto that too. 'You've made it clear you don't want a relationship. Well, neither do I. This is just sex. Just fun. Just for now.'

Bed buddies? That was all he wanted, wasn't it? The scenario she'd used to tease him with was the exact one he wanted from her—nothing more. While she'd known that, hearing him say it aloud made her heart beat horribly— skipping beats here and there.

He put the plate down, and the spoon, moved around the bench—and all the while didn't take his eyes off her.

'You don't want to eat?' Her pulse hammered in her ears.

'Not food.'

He was going to prove a point again, wasn't he? 'Alex—'

He leant close, touching her only with his lips. It was all he needed to do. Her lashes lowered as she felt the sensations wash over her. He was right—*mind-blowing*. She stepped forward, melted into his arms. Without breaking the kiss he lifted her, carried her up the stairs. And she was happy to let him carry her wherever so long as he kept on kissing her like that. The desire to be with him dominated everything.

He set her on her feet in his bedroom. 'Sweetheart.' He smiled as he set about stripping her, muttering more beneath his breath as her body was exposed to him. She was as keen to see him—grappled with the buttons on his shirt until he growled and got rid of it himself. When they were finally naked they stared at each other. His smile faded as he raked her body with his hot gaze. She shivered as she took in his beauty—the sculpted shoulders, defined muscles, the fine scattering of hair on his chest that arrowed down below his belly button, drawing her attention to his straining erection—his physique was sheer perfection and deep inside her a primal readying was occurring. She wanted him absolutely.

Their eyes met. His were fiery. Dani instinctively dampened her lips with her tongue and saw him tense even more. It was going to be explosive again. Good.

And with a suddenness that stole her breath he moved, tumbling her back onto the bed, lunging after her. As his body collided with hers there was instant friction, instant heat. He was so strong. She kissed him hungrily, those last little doubts in her head toppling like sandcastles in the tide. Sure it could be simple. It could just be sex.

His kiss was hot, his body strong. His lips and tongue probed, his hands swept over her shoulders, down her arms until his fingers clasped hers. He broke the kiss and smiled at her. He lifted her arms, placing one then the other above her head. He gazed into her eyes, at her lips, at her breasts. He shook his head slightly.

'So beautiful, Dani.' He shifted his hold on her, freeing one of his hands but keeping her wrists pinioned above her head by the other. He moved onto his side, one thigh still weighting hers but baring her body to his view.

He smiled as he gazed down her length again. And then his fingers followed his sightline. Coasting lightly down her body, caressing, teasing down her neck, her breasts, circling her belly button and then lower over her stomach, lower still…

Dani shifted restlessly, breathing faster.

'What?' he murmured in her ear. 'What do you want?'

She arched her spine in response, aching to feel all of him against her again. His fingers teased, twirling in her hot, wet space. She was so close to tipping over the edge—but it wasn't what she wanted. It wasn't all she wanted. She moaned, unable to stop the sound of pure frustration.

'Isn't this enough?' His words tickled her ear. 'Don't I just let my fingers do the walking, hmm? Isn't that what you do? Isn't this all you need? Better than a man, more reliable? Satisfying?'

She was so *unsatisfied*. 'Alex.' Even as she complained she tried to snuggle closer, wanting more of his body against her.

'So tell me, then, what you really want.' His fingers didn't stop teasing and she was beside herself. The ache widened inside; her body yearned to cushion his. To have him imprinted on her. *Inside* her.

But he didn't alter the slow, teasing touches—just kept them the same—keeping her right on the edge and not letting her go over.

She moved again, grinding into his hand, trying to force a

harder, faster stroke, but he just chuckled and kept it the same maddening torture.

The heat overwhelmed her. 'You want me to spell it out for you?'

'Yes.'

She whispered it in his ear—the same words she'd used this morning. The ones that had made him move so wickedly.

He rolled right on top of her, his knees pushing her legs further apart, and she nearly fainted with the blissful anticipation of it. His thighs were heavy, strong. She hooked her feet back over his calves. Tangling with him was irresistible. And he was so close, she could feel the head of his erection pressing against her. She only had to lift her hips the slightest and she'd have him. But he looked down at her, his eyes dark, and lifted his hips away—just enough.

His chest was squashing hers but she didn't mind. In fact, she loved the weight and the hardness of it—loved the feeling of being trapped beneath him. She arched, seeking. 'Alex.'

'What?' He pressed kisses to her neck, his body warming hers, his hand cupping, clasping.

'Don't tease me.'

'Who says I'm teasing?' His eyes glinted. 'Sex as good as this doesn't happen that often. You have to admit that.'

She looked up at him. Surprised into silence. So this was off the charts for him too? Her excitement ratcheted an impossible degree higher.

His whole body flexed. He knew—he'd felt the tremor of response in her body. He lifted, repositioned, pressed even harder against her. 'You know how incredible this is, Dani.'

He thrust home and every last thought fled in the warmth of feeling that engulfed her.

'Tell me how it feels,' he asked, teeth gritted, body rigid.

She was so aware of his strength. The strength she now had inside her—barely leashed, about to burst through her. But it didn't frighten her. All the fear she'd had bottled inside for years had vanished in the instant he'd taken her, chased away by the absolute feeling of *rightness*.

'Good.' She managed to breathe—unable to be anything but honest. 'So good. So good.' So much better than good.

He released her wrists. She swept her hands over his back, tracing the muscles, and then stretched to clasp his shoulders, her fingers spread wide. She arched up to him—loving the heat and weight and power of him.

Staying slow wasn't something either of them could manage. The ability to form words faded, sighs sounded instead. Faster they moved. Pushing closer, rotating so the friction grew unbearable. And yet he had just enough discipline—changing the angle, watching her face, waiting those few minutes until she could no longer hold back. Her body went taut, every cell seizing, her breath caught for an endless moment. And then she convulsed—shuddering with the spasms of delight that ravaged through her.

His grip broke, his body freed to move as fast and hard as it craved to, his hands holding her so close and his groan gorgeously rough in her ears.

When she opened her eyes it was morning already and she was alone. Maybe she'd somehow staggered down to her own room during the night? How would she know? All she could remember was the way they'd moved together—how many times had it been? She blinked, shifting the all-too-delicious images from her head, and focused. No, this wasn't the spare room. This was his room. She slipped out of the bed gingerly, then made a dash for her bedroom. Saw it wasn't yet seven. Wow. He did rise early.

She showered, trying to soothe her still hypersensitive skin, and dressed. By the time she got to the kitchen he was in place—breakfast half eaten. He stood as soon as she appeared.

'I've got an omelette for you ready to go.'

'I can't eat a rich breakfast.'

'You need sustenance. You didn't get much sleep last night.'

Well, he'd had even less. 'What time did you get up?'

'I get up at five.'

'*Why?*' Madness. Especially on a Saturday.

His phone beeped and he flashed a grin. 'There are bankers awake in all twenty-four hours of the day. And people always want their questions answered *now*.'

Really? It was all work? She pointed at his phone. 'You just set this up to try to impress me. Make me think you're an amazingly committed worker.'

'You don't think I am?'

Of course she did. But she couldn't resist teasing him. 'First impressions, Alex. First time I saw you, you were wandering around the office like a butterfly—stopping to chat and smile and make the place pretty while the worker ants got it all done for you.'

He didn't seem remotely offended, just sent a lecherous look over her body. 'Want to know my first impression of you?'

'No.'

'Chicken.'

'I'm not biting.'

'No, that was my first impression of you. A little scaredy cat in the lift.'

She tilted her chin and called him on it. 'You'd been staring at me for days before the lift incident. That wasn't your first impression.'

His smile widened. 'My very first impression I can't say aloud. It wouldn't be gentlemanly.'

She flushed.

'And, no, that impression hasn't changed. In fact, it's been enhanced.' He gave her a playful pat on the rear. 'Now hurry up and eat—we've got to go help Lorenzo.'

Dani was sorely tempted to slap him back, but she suspected she'd end up beneath him if she did that and her body needed a couple of hours' recovery time first. 'Help him with what?'

'You'll see.'

Ten minutes later Dani watched out of the window as they drove out of the inner-city flash-apartment zone, through a commercial area and eventually into a much poorer residential area. 'How do you know each other?'

'Lorenzo?'

'Yeah.' They seemed an odd mix. Alex was so the outgoing charming kind whereas Lorenzo was definitely the silent brooder.

'We were at school together. Became friends there and have been ever since.'

So it was just the boys' network thing. 'And you set up the charity together?'

'Lorenzo had the idea but didn't want to be the public eye so much. He collared me for most of that. I wanted to support him.'

'Why did he want to do it?'

Alex sent her a quick glance. 'Lorenzo didn't have a great upbringing. He wants to help kids in a similar position.'

How not so great an upbringing? 'But you were at the same school?' Somehow she imagined Alex had gone to some exclusive number that cost lots of money and she suspected that when he said Lorenzo's upbringing hadn't been so great, he meant it had been lacking—in every way.

'Boarding school, yes. Lorenzo was a scholarship kid.'

'Boarding?' Dani lifted her brows. Alex was an only child

whose parents had lived in the biggest city in New Zealand—
there were posh private schools practically on their doorstep.

'It was one of those boys' own schools out in the country—
lots of physical endurance stuff to keep us out of trouble.'

'Don't tell me you got into trouble, Alex,' she teased.

His grin was twisted. 'Why do you think my mother
sent me there?'

She didn't really believe him—this was Alex, the straight-
up finance boss. But while he might be grinning, there was
an edge of bitterness too—she wanted to ask more but he
pulled the car to the kerb. 'Here we are.'

Dani took in the scene—the tools, the wood, the sign on
the building. They were building a new fence for a playgroup?

'I'm happy to dig the last couple of holes for the side
fence.' Alex slammed the door.

Lorenzo looked up from where he stood in the back of the
truck, tossing out implements. 'You got energy to burn?'

'And then some.'

Dani stepped out of the car. OK, what was her role here?

'You mind raking the leaves, Dani?' Alex glanced over
from where he was already picking up a spade.

'Sure.' She wasn't work-shy. Good thing too because it
took her over an hour to rake up all the leaves from the paths
and heap them into the green waste wheelie bins. Then she
swept and pulled a few weeds. By then she was burning to
make a cutting comment or two because this wasn't exactly
her idea of Saturday-morning fun.

'Where are the cameras?' She stood alongside the fence
line Alex was digging the post holes for. 'Don't you want your
charity bit to be recorded for publicity?'

'This is just a little job we're doing on the quiet. We save
the cameras for the big set pieces like the dinner the other

night.' Alex leaned on the spade and drawled, 'When we're looking our handsomest.'

Dani could argue that one. Sure, he was to die for in a tux, but in faded old jeans and a tee shirt that was now clinging to his sweaty torso, well, hell. Officially it might be autumn, but as far as she was concerned it was hotter than Hades.

He was obviously used to a bit of physical work—could handle a spade and a wheelbarrow. But she couldn't sit here and watch him all day lugging wood and digging and looking way too manly. And it looked as if they were going to be doing this *all* day. Lorenzo had put up the horizontals on the front fence—where the posts had already been concreted in.

She picked up the bag of nails and interrupted Alex again. 'Give me a hammer.'

'Pardon?'

'A hammer.'

'I'm not sure that's such a good idea.' Alex stood back from his work. 'You've got such precious fingers, very little thumbs.'

'Lucky, aren't I? Means they're easy to miss,' she said smartly. 'What makes you think a girl can't hammer in a few nails?'

She'd done all the DIY in the little flat her mother and she had rented—well, as much of it as she could without doing worse damage. Plumbing was beyond her, but nailing up a few fence palings was a cinch. She went to the end of the fence and got started.

Alex had dug the last of the holes for the back fence and he and Lorenzo concreted the poles in. They'd obviously worked together a lot. And she wasn't noticing how good Alex looked grubby.

Finally they stopped for food. Alex magicked a hamper from in the boot of his car. Dani stared at the yummy pottles he was finding forks for.

He noticed her salivating, and his grin was too cocky. 'I know a great deli.'

'How come you two are so good at this?'

'Summers working on a farm. Fence post after fence post.' Alex handed her a pottle of pasta salad and a fork.

He'd spent his summers working? She was pleasantly surprised—would have thought a richer-than-rich playboy prince like him would have been off gallivanting round the globe every semester break. She looked at the perfectly straight fence posts. Nope, he was definitely experienced with this.

As soon as she filled the pit that was her stomach she turned her back and got on with her section. Banging in the nails was a rewarding way to burn off some of her energy. It was accruing again, in giant tubfuls—the desire to be with him.

'What makes *you* so good at this?'

She jumped. He was standing right beside her, tracing his finger along the palings where she'd hammered the nails in a neat row.

'Necessity.'

His brows lifted. 'Is there nothing you can't do all on your own, Dani?'

'Not a thing.' She slung the hammer back into the tool box, glanced up to see a frown on his face. 'What?'

He brushed the backs of his fingers along her jaw, slid them up to sweep that annoying bit of fringe back. 'Are you sure about that?'

His tone was different—loaded with meaning. He wasn't teasing her. It wasn't a reference to the way he'd played with her in bed last night. His eyes held none of that heat; instead it was all seriousness, all concern.

Eli.

Her heart started thundering. If she asked Alex to help, it would happen. He would find him. And wasn't that what she wanted more than anything in the world? Suddenly she was scared. Really, really scared of what she might find. And too scared not to search. She watched, distracted, as Alex and Lorenzo loaded the rest of the gear on the truck, then all three stood for a moment and admired the pristine fence.

Alex shot Lorenzo a look. 'Tempted?'

'Like you wouldn't believe.'

Alex laughed. 'Bad boy. Come back for a drink instead.'

Dani saw Lorenzo glance from Alex to her and then back to Alex. 'Not today, thanks.'

Once they were in the car she just had to ask. 'What was he tempted to do?'

Alex grinned. 'Renz liked to tag as a teen.'

'Graffiti?' Dani's brows lifted. 'Did you help him get on the straight and narrow?'

'Are you kidding?' Alex laughed. 'I got him the paint.'

He disappeared upstairs when they got home. Dani's body had seized up in the car; it was all she could do to hobble to the kitchen. She got ice-cold water from the fridge and carefully sat on a stool.

'Tired?'

Warm fingers slid beneath her tee shirt and walked up her spine.

'Yes.'

'Come on.' He sounded husky.

Heaven help her, she thought she might be too tired even to manage that. He chuckled and picked her up, easily loping up the stairs with her. He went straight through his bedroom to the en-suite bathroom adjacent to it.

'Oh.' She blinked.

There were candles lit everywhere—tons of them, all different sizes, but all that gorgeous deep red, and her favourite berrylicious scent. Out of the window the autumnal sky was closing in, a blue-grey that darkened with every beat of her heart.

'Alex...' She looked up at him, registered his slightly smug smile, and his arms tightened. She put on a pout and shook her head. 'Don't think this is going to get you any extra points.'

'I don't need any more points.' He grinned and then tipped her into the bath, clothes and all. She went right under and emerged with a splutter, sending fluffy white bubbles everywhere. She knelt up and looked at him, watched as he yanked his shirt off his head. Sinking back into the delicious, almost-too-hot water, she melted as he scuffed off his jeans. Heaven.

He laughed as she sighed, stepped into the bath behind her. Oh, yes. He didn't need any more points. She turned to face him and he pulled her close, the tips of his fingers making patterns with the bubbles on her skin. 'Wet tee shirt.' His eyes gleamed. 'Nice.'

'You're a gentleman and a rogue, Alex Carlisle.'

He blew some of the bubbles from her arm. 'What makes you say that?'

'You do this—' she waved a froth-covered hand at the flickering candles that cast a warm glow in the room '—set it up so beautifully and then you dunk me in fully clothed.'

He leaned back, water streaming over his bronzed body emphasising the lean, hard muscles, and his brows flicked up and down. 'Irresistible impulse.'

'Succumb to them often, do you?'

'Around you. Yes.'

She gazed at him, experiencing a rather irresistible impulse of her own as his silky-smooth words washed over her with that undertone of laughter as the chaser.

Utterly irresistible.

She rose to her knees, leant forward and gave him a gentle kiss on the cheek. 'Thank you.'

Lifting far enough away to focus, she saw a curious expression in his eyes.

'I'm glad you like it,' he murmured.

'You remembered the candle from the hostel.'

He nodded.

'You're very good with details.'

The curve of his mouth deepened.

She leant closer to him again, her voice merely a hot breath by his ear. 'What else are you good at?'

He inclined his head just that touch so his faintly stubbled jaw brushed her cheek. 'You sure you want to find out?'

'Absolutely.'

What felt like hours later she was finally naked and her muscles utterly slack, her legs floating in front of her as she used Alex like a lilo. She didn't think she'd ever felt so relaxed. The tiredness swamped her—the long months of hard work and heartbreak as she'd cared for her slowly dying mother were finally taking their toll. The devastation at her father's callous abuse of them. What kind of person stole at a time like that?

Dani would give anything to have her back. Just anything. But there was nothing she could do. Except the one last thing she'd asked. Maybe she could bring peace to her mother's final rest—and peace for herself.

She was too tired, too desperate, not to take the help Alex had offered. Her pride in her independence had to be shelved. 'What you said yesterday…'

'About the investigator?'

She felt the reverberations in his chest as he spoke—even as softly as he had—and felt reassured by the solid strength of him.

'Yes.'

His wide palms stroked down her upper arms. 'You don't have to tell me about it. I can just make the appointment for you.'

She smiled sadly. He was offering her privacy, offering her help, but she wanted to share it now—it was a burden that had got too heavy for her, but that would be nothing to him. 'My mother had a son eight years before she had me. Here in New Zealand. She named him Eli. She adopted him out.'

'And you want to find him.'

She nodded. 'We've never met. He doesn't know I exist. I only found out about him just before she died. I only have the vaguest details and I've tried, but I can't get anywhere.'

'You don't have any other family, do you?'

She shook her head—none that she recognised.

'The PI will help.' Alex sounded all CEO certain. 'We'll call him tonight.'

'It's Saturday.'

'They work all hours.'

Like him. Unless he was in party mode. 'Shouldn't you be going out somewhere?'

'Nowhere else I'd rather be than here.'

Dani rested her head back on his chest and smiled at his hot-chocolate-smooth words—he always had the right answers, didn't he? But now, having told him about her search, she felt her exhaustion quadruple. She closed her eyes.

'Don't worry, Dani.' She heard him from a distance. 'We'll find him for you.'

CHAPTER NINE

DANI looked up at Alex's deep sigh.

He'd laid his cutlery down and his smile curved lopsidedly. 'We have to go out tonight.'

'We do?' She nearly choked on her last mouthful. He'd picked her up from work bang on time, spun her in his arms the minute they got to the top of the stairs of his house, kissed her while walking them through to the kitchen and made the most of the big bench. When they'd finally come up for air and done their clothes back up, they'd sat down to dinner. All she wanted to do now was fall into bed—and play some more.

Yesterday had been divine—according to Alex the 'day of rest' meant no getting out of bed all day. In between the ferocious sex they'd dozed, she'd read the newspapers, he tapped on his laptop and they'd snacked on whatever they could find in the fridge. She was still hot from it—and exhausted in equal measure.

'Drinks with the charity divas. It won't take long but I need to put in an appearance.'

'I don't, though.'

'Yes, you do, you're the newest employee and they're all

very keen to meet you. Besides, you're my excuse to leave early. You'll have a headache.'

'What? No way. You can have your own headache.' She watched him clear the plates. 'Do we have to dress up?' She didn't want to take up his offer to buy her some clothes—an offer he'd repeated in the guise of a loan—but the fact was, apart from a few work skirts and shirts and her one little black dress, it was jeans and tee and that was it.

'Casual is fine.'

But after a quick shower she put on one of her quality cotton work shirts, tucking it into her jeans and securing them with a belt. She pulled on her boots instead of the trainers she preferred to jog round in when she was doing 'casual'. Her casual and his casual were two quite different things. As a last touch she slid in the clip he'd given her the night of the dance. There were a couple of other women in jeans, Dani noted when they got there, but their jeans were designer.

It was a much smaller gathering than the dinner had been, much more informal and much more intimidating. The dinner had been too busy and too loud for any real in-depth conversation with anyone. This was more like appearing in front of a selection panel for an elite club. She was sure she was being judged—and that she was failing.

Alex held her hand and she was grateful for that because, beneath the tastefully mascaraed lashes, she was getting a few scarily close looks. The princesses of society all seemed to have gathered together and now they inspected her with barely veiled curiosity. She made her head stay up high; she would not drop it and stare at the floor. But she was nothing like them—she didn't have the breeding, the elite education, the looks, definitely not the wardrobe. His fingers gripped hers tighter and she sensed him looking at her.

She met the look and murmured softly in his ear, 'How many of the women in this room have you slept with?'

'Not even a tenth of how many you're thinking.' He lifted her hand to his chest, pressing it against the fine merino sweater so she could feel the steady beat of his heart, and grinned broadly at her. 'Not feeling insecure, are you?'

'Oh, no.' Hers was going machine-gun–style.

He grinned. 'They just want to get to know you.'

More like they just wanted her out of the way so they could get to him. Now she understood why his arrogance was so innate. People thought he was wonderful—they just about bowed and scraped as he made his way across the room. And now they were doing the same for her—granting her a kind of power just because of her perceived association with him. Except for her they had sharp eyes, even sharper smiles. She didn't fit in and they knew it.

She looked around desperately as Alex chatted to an older couple. Another jeans-clad woman stood across the room, alone and on the outer. The thoughts so readable on her face mirrored the ones inside Dani—she wanted to get the hell out of there.

Dani murmured an 'excuse me' and walked towards her, ignoring Alex's movement to keep her close.

'Hello,' Dani introduced herself to the woman. 'I'm Dani.'

'Sara.' The woman smiled shyly. 'It's my first time.'

'Me too.' Dani gave her a look and both their smiles went wider. 'What brings you here?'

'I'm representing one of the charities the fund is considering supporting. I'm doing a presentation at next week's board meeting and they invited me along tonight so I could meet some of the board members. To break the ice.'

Well, the ice was shatterproof in some corners of the room.

'Tell me about your charity.' Dani grinned. 'You can practise on me.'

It was so nice to talk about someone and something else for five minutes. Dani was tired of smiling and 'mmming' and 'ahhing' and trying not to give her secrets away. They took a drink from a passing waiter and bonded.

Every so often Alex would glance across to her and she saw the keen question in his eye—not so much an 'are you OK?' kind of caring question, but a 'what are you up to?' keen observance. She turned her back on him and made herself relax. Another charity worker joined them, then another, and they found chairs and talked about their projects.

'How's your head, Dani?' Alex bobbed down behind her seat and enquired—all seeming solicitude.

'It's fine.' She smiled brightly, deliberately missing the message in his eyes. 'Honestly, that delicious dinner really seemed to do the trick. I feel so much better than I did an hour or so ago.'

She turned back to Sara and the other women sitting beside her and smiled. 'So tell me more.'

Sara's cheeks were deep pink as she looked from Dani to Alex and back again. 'Are you sure you have time?'

'I have all the time in the world.' Dani looked up and smiled sweetly at the tall man towering beside her. 'Don't I?'

'Of course.' His smile was set charm, then he walked off.

Dani beamed at Sara, savouring the moment—she did like to tease him.

Another half-hour passed and she was engrossed in conversation. Well, almost engrossed—her Alex-radar was as on as ever. She was aware of him watching her almost stalker-like. And she lifted her head when he approached again—with unmistakable purpose.

'I'm very sorry to interrupt, Dani—' Alex broke through the circle of chairs and held his hand out to her '—but it really is time for us to go.'

'You haven't met Sara—'

'Alex Carlisle.' Alex immediately turned and took Sara's hand instead. Shaking it briefly. Then he wrapped his arm around Dani's shoulders and literally hauled her to her feet.

'I'm sorry I've talked at you all evening.' Sara stood too.

'Not at all,' Dani reassured her with a genuine grin. 'I really enjoyed hearing about it.'

He didn't drag the goodbyes to the hostess and Dani was so amused by his impatience she was able to rise above the cool nods she got from some of the queens.

Outside they walked to where he'd parked.

'You meant it, didn't you?' Alex unlocked the car.

'Meant what?'

'That you enjoyed hearing about Sara's work.'

Dani slid into the seat. 'So what if I did?'

His smile broadened. 'And you can be so nice to people. So social.'

'I'm house-trained too,' she said witheringly. 'Isn't that an advantage?'

His smile gave way to laughter then.

'Well, really, Alex, what did you think—that I'd sit there sullen and stupid all night?'

'No, but nor did I expect you to have half the room hanging on your every word and have them falling over each other to talk to you.'

'That wasn't me,' she said acidly. 'That was my status. Walking in with Alex Carlisle, I couldn't be anything but a success.'

'Why do you insist on hiding behind a wall of sarcasm

from even the vaguest compliment?' He accelerated. 'Dani, it was you. I've seen far more famous women, far more supposedly *important* women, fail to have anything like that effect on a group like that. You charmed them.'

'I didn't. I just talked to them.' Dani fidgeted with the side seam of her jeans. 'Why were you in such a rush to leave, anyway?'

'I want you.'

OK, that was to the point and something of a relief given the lust she was grappling with. Even so, she couldn't resist a tease. 'But I have a headache, *remember*?'

Alex dragged himself away from her warm, sleepy body, showered and dressed. Made himself a nuclear-strength coffee and forced the bitterness down his throat. He needed the caffeine hit. He powered up the computer on the desk overlooking the garden, then checked his phone. There were five messages waiting. He scrolled and then stilled. One was from Patrick, which he ignored. One was from the investigator.

Alex didn't care how early it was, he was paying the man enough to be able to call him any time—even two hours before dawn. The guy was impressively lucid considering he'd just been woken—but there wasn't much to report. Nothing on Dani's brother. Not good enough.

'Where else can you look? There must be something, right?'

He was increasingly determined to find him for her. The investigator explained the problem—when searching the birth records, Dani's mother's name wasn't coming up anywhere, which meant that at the time of her son's adoption the original birth certificate was sealed. So, without a court order, the only person who can access the full details on the certificate is that child himself—no one else, not even his sister. The in

vestigator needed to find him through other means. He asked
if Alex knew any more details.

'No. I don't have more details—no date, no photo, no nothing. There can't have been that many babies adopted out that
year. Check the ones before and after. Just find him.' He
jabbed the end button and tossed it in the bench. Damn.

A faint sound alerted him. Whirling round, he saw her—
in the doorway, her wide eyes searching his, so full of fearful
hope. Alex winced. He wasn't big on bursting bubbles for people. And so he did it quick—less painful that way, right?

'There's nothing yet, sorry, Dani. It's not looking good.'

For a moment she did nothing, the shock etched on her
face. She believed he could help, didn't she? Frustration
burned hotter inside him. He wanted to be able to. He wanted
to smooth away that pinched look—to sweep the pain from
her eyes. He moved. But she did too—turning her back to him.

'I'm going to make breakfast.' She opened the fridge.
'Pizza. Sounds weird, I know, but it's the only thing I can
cook. You've got ready-made bases in here. I saw them the
other day. Spinach and egg. Some people think it's gross but
I love it.'

Alex said nothing, just stood on the other side of the bench
and watched her sudden burst of busyness. She put the bases,
spinach, eggs and cheese down. Found his biggest knife.

'Do you have pasta sauce? I need some pasta sauce.'

Hell, she looked tired. And suddenly he too felt exhausted.
Maybe they should both just go back to bed—to sleep.

By now she had the board. The green leaves were under
the guillotine.

'Dani.' He risked life and limb and put his hand on hers.
'We'll do everything to find him for you, I promise. Everything.'
He applied more pressure to his grip. 'You can trust me, OK?'

'Sure.' The knife hit the board.

Bang, bang, bang.

No more talking. She wouldn't look at him. She wasn't going to let him in on it—her disappointment, her fear, her hurt. And that made him almost as disappointed himself.

His phone beeped again and he wanted to chuck it in the waste-disposal unit. He wanted to help her. Wanted her to have the success that he hadn't—to find the happiness she wanted. Instead he was rendered useless.

When he looked up from tapping out a message she'd abandoned the spinach. 'I don't feel like pizza anymore.' She put the knife down. 'What a mess.'

'The housekeeper will take care of it.'

But she wasn't talking about that mess and he knew it.

Her shoulders slumped. 'I'm sorry the search is taking up your time, Alex. I know you have more important things to be doing.'

Was that defeat he'd just heard from her? He saw the way her fingers trembled as she tucked her hair behind her ear. Well, that wasn't right. He wanted the strong, sassy Dani back.

'You mean, you think I actually do important things?' He tried to tease her out. 'I thought I was only about swanning around and seducing the nearest available woman.'

'OK, I admit that when you've done your seducing for the day you might put some effort into your work, as well.'

Clearly she was not herself.

'Why, thank you.' He walked to her side of the bench, determined to bring the sparkle back to her eyes. 'But you're mistaken about something.'

'I am?' She finally looked at him. 'What?'

'I'm never done with seducing for the day.' He smiled down at her. Then his smile stuttered as he saw how the pain came from right inside her, her big brown eyes dulled with sorrow and uncertainty.

He wound his arms around her and pulled her close for a plain old-fashioned hug, tempering the desire that surged every time he got within three feet of her, pressing her head into his shoulder so he didn't have to see that hurt anymore, because somehow it hurt him. And he wanted to pretend he really was helping somehow.

'It's going to be OK, Dani.' It was all he could think of to say. And it wasn't enough. He couldn't guarantee her anything, but in this moment it didn't stop him trying.

Dani figured she must be the worst temp ever. She hadn't been paying any attention to what Cara had been saying. All she could think about was the news Alex had relayed. The disappointment was overwhelming. *Nothing.* No leads—no possibilities. She might never find Eli. She might never get to tell him how sorry their mother was—how she'd thought of him every day—how she'd wanted to love him. Dani might never find her family. The thoughts cut her heart. She had to focus on something else—like answering letters or inputting numbers. But futility drummed a relentless beat—she wasn't going to do it; she wasn't going to be able to do it for her mother.

And the follow-on questions grew louder and louder in her head—if she wasn't going to find her brother, why was she still here? How much longer did she give Alex's PI to find him? How much longer would she let herself be with Alex?

For the first question the answer was easy—they had to have more time. She hadn't packed up and moved countries to give up after only a few weeks. She wouldn't let them stop. Somewhere someone must be able to help—surely they'd find him eventually.

As for Alex, he was just part of the deal, wasn't he? The physical favour. Hardly—she mocked herself. No way was it 'just sex' and uncomplicated—it already was complicated for her. Half her heart was his. And he hadn't asked for it. How she wished he would.

'Did the meeting run late last night?'

She finally heard Cara. 'Oh. Not too bad, no.'

'Oh.' Cara smiled. 'You seem a little tired today. Distracted.'

Dani felt her cheeks warm. 'I'm sorry.'

'It's OK,' Cara said. 'There's not much to do today anyway.'

Dani's mobile rang.

'I'll send a taxi to pick you up this afternoon.' Alex got straight to the point. 'I have a thing I have to go to. I forgot to mention it this morning.'

'Sure. No problem.' So he didn't need his 'date' for this one. Dani battled against feeling disappointed but lost. Nor could she control the feeling of concern from rising—he'd sounded tired, which was unusual. She wished she could see him—to read his expression—because something had definitely been off.

Silly. She reminded herself with hard words—she wasn't his mother, or his girl, not even a friend. She was his flatmate with fringe benefits. That was all.

'That was Alex?' Cara asked.

Dani nodded, knew her colour was rising.

'Gorgeous, isn't he?' Cara sparkled. 'He and Lorenzo are the most eligible bachelors in town—and not because of their bank balances or bodies. Although—' she looked coy '—I don't know that Alex is going to be a bachelor for much longer.'

Dani looked at Cara with great concern. 'Can I get you a cup of tea or some cold water?' Pregnancy was making the poor woman delusional.

Alone in his house, she found some ready-made soup in the fridge, ate it while standing. She sloped up to bed early. But despite feeling exhausted she couldn't sleep. She went back downstairs and curled up on the sofa—but she couldn't settle into a book, decide on a telly channel, or choose a movie. It was the tone she kept hearing—that discordant note in his voice when he'd rung. She couldn't sleep until she'd seen him.

She heard the gates and the garage door. He wasn't nearly as late as she'd thought he'd be. She listened to his slow, heavy tread on the stairs and waited. He appeared in the doorway and shock rippled through her. She sat up. 'What's wrong?'

He looked awful—his face all shadows and angles. And as he stepped further into the room she saw the shadows were darkened by something else—pain. He looked at her, his expression so tortured that the vulnerability struck a knife in her heart. She couldn't believe this wreck of a man was Alex. Usually full of such vitality. She'd never thought he could look so destroyed.

'Tell me.' She needed to know. She needed to help.

But he was silent.

Her cheeks heated. He didn't want to tell her. Was she overstepping the mark? Too bad. She reverted to blunt speak. 'You look awful.'

A little puff of air escaped him and he flopped onto the sofa beside her. He closed his eyes, his brows knitting. Then suddenly he spoke. 'I had a meeting with my father.'

Dani blinked. That she hadn't expected. 'But—'

'Samuel Carlisle wasn't my father.'

Oh—Dani thought it but no sound came out of her mouth. Instead she sat utterly still. And waited.

'I always knew my parents weren't that happy. It wasn't fights all the time or anything. It was just…chilly. Then I heard my mother one day on the phone. I was only twelve but I wasn't naive. It was an argument with her lover. I walked in to where she was and she hung up straight away. I asked her and she denied it, tried to laugh it off. But I knew. And I never told Samuel because I knew it would freak him.'

He went silent. 'After that I went to boarding school. I was still close to Samuel, but not her. I went to university, went into the business. Then Da…' he paused '…*Samuel* got sick. He needed a donor. She didn't want me to be tested—said I was too young. But I did it anyway. The blood work came through. I'm a really rare type. I looked it up, and Samuel's— had them checked. There was no way he could be my father.'

Dani bit down on her lips as she watched his pallor increase.

'I confronted her—she admitted it but begged me not to tell him. To him I was his only child. It would kill him.' He sighed. 'So I didn't, of course. But I wanted to know the truth. She wouldn't say—said his name was irrelevant. Nothing more than a sperm donation. Insisted Samuel was my real father.'

'And wasn't he?' Dani asked softly. 'In every way that counted?'

He turned his head and looked at her. 'I had the right to know. Samuel had the right to know.'

That was true. She nodded—she understood the need to know.

'She died before she ever told me who my father really was. I could never ask Samuel. So I thought I'd never find out. Samuel lived for a few more years—desperately sick, desperate to see the bank succeed. So I made it succeed.'

The silence was long. And eventually Dani prompted him. 'And then he died.

'And almost a year to the day I got the call.'

Dani's mind searched for the answer and then made the stabbing guess. 'Patrick.'

'So obvious now, isn't it?' His smile was faint and bitter. 'He was their best man, can you believe that? He used to be like an uncle—always around when I was a kid. Now I know why. After she died he moved to Singapore—for business, apparently. He's been there since. Never married. He insists the affair ended years before, but how can I believe a word he says? And now he wants a *relationship*.' He turned and stared at Dani. 'How can you have a relationship with someone when they've done nothing but lie to you all your life?'

He screwed his face up. 'How could they? It could have been found out so much sooner if I'd ever been seriously sick. She ran the risk of it for years. But she never said anything. All my life I had the Carlisle duty drummed into me.' His anger mounted. 'The bank. The business. It was my destiny—rammed into me.'

'What else would you have done?'

'I've no idea. I never seriously thought about it. It just was. Even Patrick advised me to go into it—when he was doing his honorary uncle bit.'

'But you're good at your job, Alex. You enjoy it. No one could work the kind of hours you do if they didn't enjoy it.'

'You think? What about all those people who work two, three, four jobs just to get food on the table? It's about necessity, Dani. And it was necessary for me. Samuel was sick—he was dying and the company hit the skids. I had to turn it round—rescue it while he was alive to see it saved. I had to prove to everyone that I was good enough to do it—that I deserved to be the boss, not just because I was his heir. I did it all for him. For her. And she'd lied to me. For years and years she lied.'

Betrayal. It hurt so much when a parent let you down. Dani understood that too.

He shook his head. 'My whole life has been a lie, Dani.'

She looked at the tension etched into his face and took his hand in hers. 'When did he call?'

'Thursday, almost two weeks ago.'

The day before he'd kissed her. Now she understood why he had. He'd been having a rough time and gone for a moment of fun. And, boy, had he got a whole lot more than he'd bargained for. Poor Alex.

His anger rippled out again. 'I insisted on tests. But it's true.' His fingers tightened unbearably on hers but she held in the wince, knowing he wasn't aware of his strength. 'Why should I have anything to do with him?'

'People lie for all sorts of reasons, Alex. I'm not saying it's right, but maybe you need to ask what those reasons might be.'

'There's no excuse.'

'People lie to protect—sometimes themselves, sure, but sometimes to protect others too. Maybe they lied to protect you. They didn't want to hurt you.'

'Protect me from what? Not knowing hurt more, Dani.' He lifted his hands from her and looked at them. 'I used to wonder if she'd been raped.'

'Alex.' Her heart wrenched and she grabbed his hands again with both of hers and pulled them to her chest. Of course he'd have worried about the worst. Afraid of what his mother's secrecy might have meant.

He looked at her, tormented. 'And they let me wonder. Worry. For nothing. I can't forgive them for that.' The deepest hurt poured out. 'He's despicable, Dani. I don't want anything to do with him. I can't believe he's my father. I don't want to be related to him.'

She had to reach out to him. She had to help somehow, because she understood that hatred—and the underlying fear that the badness might come through his blood.

'I've lied to you too, Alex,' she said quietly. It wasn't even a lie that would affect him, yet she felt terrible for it. Even more so as she felt him freeze. 'I told you my parents were dead,' she said quickly. 'And my mum is but my father isn't.'

Silent, he stared at her.

She breathed in and then said it. The one thing she tried never to think about. 'He's in jail.'

'Oh—'

'As far as I'm concerned he died the day he came to see Mum when she was dying of cancer and conned the last of her life savings from her.' Dani spoke fast, stopping his interruption. She wasn't telling him this to get his sympathy, but so he'd grasp what she wanted him to learn. 'He's a crook, Alex. A conman—theft, fraud, you name it, he's done it. The kind of lowlife who preys on the sick and dying.' She hated him, hated the way her heart raced and her skin went cold when she thought of him. 'He wandered in and out of our lives—between sentences, between better options. He'd come and sweet talk his way back to Mum, saying he was changed. Always lies. Right up to the end, he stole from her. He has no conscience, no empathy, nothing.' And she'd wanted to believe him too, hadn't she? Every time. So not only had he stolen from her mother, he'd stolen from her too—taken her credit card and maxed it out. She let go of Alex's hand to push back the sweep of her fringe. 'His blood runs through my veins, Alex, but I'm not like him,' she said fiercely. 'I'm not anything like him.' She spoke faster, insistent. 'It doesn't matter who your biological parents are. You're still you. You're not him. You'll never be him.'

Alex just kept staring at her. 'Is it that easy to accept, Dani?'

'No,' she said honestly. 'But you have to. We're unique, right? It's our experiences that shape us, not just our DNA.'

'Yeah.' His smile was a shadow of its usual self, but at least it appeared. For all of a second. Then he went serious again. 'Wow.' He paused. 'Thanks for telling me.'

She scrunched deeper into the sofa. 'I don't like to think about him.'

'No.' He'd gone pale again, staring at the low coffee table in front of them, looking too tired to move.

'I guess you have to decide whether you want anything to do with Patrick,' she said softly.

Alex shook his head slowly. 'I don't want to know him.'

'That's OK, Alex.' She smiled at him a little sadly. 'You don't have to.' She held his hand, her heart aching for the hurt in his. 'Your phone hasn't beeped.' It must be a record.

He jerked. 'Oh, I turned it off. I'd better check it.'

'Give it to me.'

Their eyes met. Silently he handed it to her. She didn't look at it, most certainly didn't switch it on. She put it on the arm of the sofa.

Two disappointed people. Couldn't they forget the past for a few hours? Abandon the search for answers? Just breathe and let rest soothe the aches they both had. She reached forward and unlaced his shoes. 'You're tired. You need to get some sleep.'

Neither of them had had a decent night's sleep all week. She took his hand and stood, tugged until he drew his feet in and stood too. She let him up the stairs—past her landing and on up to his bedroom. She undid his tie, his buttons on his shirt, his trousers, slid them from his body. 'Lie down.'

He got into the bed. 'I want you to stay.'

'I am.' In her pink-pig pjs she joined him.

'I—'

'Just go to sleep, Alex.' She put her arms around him. Hugged him close. Cared for him.

CHAPTER TEN

ALEX didn't want to move—couldn't. Way too content. Dani lay beside him, curling into him, warming him more comfortably than the softest wool blanket. And now nothing else did matter. Because just resting together like this was so complete. The questions faded, the need for answers, and the bitterness disappeared the way wisps of clouds did beneath the heat of the sun—just, like, that.

All that he needed right now was right here.

In the early morning he looked across at her. Still asleep, she looked so beautiful. He'd never seen anyone so beautiful. And he wanted to see her happy. He wanted to see her have some fun—and not just *that* kind of fun. His heart leapt up, somersaulted, and bellyflopped back into his chest. He was *interested*—in her and everything about her. The caring she'd shown last night had melted something inside him. Her telling him that about her father…he knew that had been hard. He knew how private she was, how protective. But she'd done it because she'd thought it might help him. And it had in more ways than she'd expect. It had made him see clearer—see *her* clearer. Now he needed to know even more. He needed to know everything—why she was so alone and what she hoped would happen when she found her brother.

He slipped out of bed. First he had to shower and get down to the office so he could make plans. But some of the peace from last night remained in his system. He felt freer somehow—less angsty about Patrick. He couldn't even think his relaxed state was from fantastic sex—they hadn't even had sex last night. Sharing a trouble—was it as simple as that? He glanced back to the sweet dreamer in his bed. No. It wasn't that simple. Not at all.

Alex appeared just before lunchtime, wearing jeans and tee. Dani stared—shouldn't he be at work?

'Come on.' He grinned. 'We're bunking.'

She gestured to the pile of letters in the tray on her desk. 'I can't.'

'Cara won't mind, will you, Cara?' He magnified the impact of his smile with a wink.

'Course not. Go on, Dani.'

'Where are we going?' she asked as soon as they were out of earshot.

He led her to his car. 'I realised that you've only been in New Zealand a couple of weeks and all you've done is work. You haven't had much fun.'

He was certainly in a play mood. She looked sideways at him—he was a different person from the tired, hurt man she'd seen last night. Now he was all colour and charm again. Her heart lifted and the smile bubbled out of her. 'So what we are doing?'

'It's a surprise.'

Dani felt excitement tingle in her tummy. So much for keeping her life free from getting more complicated. Complicated wasn't anywhere near enough of a description of her life—especially her *feelings* now.

'I brought your jeans and trainers. You might want to get changed.'

She wriggled in the passenger seat of his car, slipping off her skirt, laughing at his all too frequent glances towards her. 'Concentrate on the road!'

He pulled up near a big sports field. There were a couple of buses already stopped on the side of the road; the sound of people chattering carried through the trees.

'It's a rec afternoon for one of the Whistle Fund's beneficiary schools. They need some help with the kids.' He sent her an embarrassed kind of glance. 'Not that great a surprise, I guess. You up for it?'

She looked ahead through the trees to the football fields where orange cones were being set up and kids in trackies and trainers milled in a kind of amorphous mass. 'Sure, I like exercise.'

'I know.' His grin was pure shark.

She turned and went faux school marm on him in retaliation. 'But aren't you going to get behind with your work?'

'I can catch up tonight.'

And he would—the man worked round the clock. 'Admit it.' She poked him in the ribs with her finger.

'What?'

'You love it. There's nothing else you enjoy more than your wheeling and dealing. You're a banking and business geek. And you'd be lost without it.'

His eyes slid sideways. 'OK, I like it.'

'No.' She maintained her authoritarian tone. 'You *love* it.' He did—she'd *seen* him at work. He was happy there.

'OK, I love it.' He sighed and smiled at the same time. 'But I also like bunking now and then too.'

Yeah, but being the head of the family bank was his natural home—whether he was bloodstock or not. He was good at it too. They walked over to where the few adults were being sorted by the whistle-wearing coach. 'Skills and drills first, then games later.'

The kids were broken up into groups of eight and they worked them out—practising passes, forward and back, running games, short drills, team building.

Dani laughed—working her group while surreptitiously watching Alex work his crew just alongside her. His time at his 'boys' own outdoors' school was evident and it was equally clear he must work out a lot still—but then she knew that already.

She wasn't totally useless herself—she'd enjoyed her self-defence classes and working out at the gym. She might be on the curvy side, but that didn't mean she wasn't fit. She jumped up and caught a ball someone accidentally lobbed into the middle of her kids.

'Good catch,' Alex murmured. 'Nice to see a woman who isn't afraid of balls.'

'I *like* playing with them,' she answered, all soft sass and an oh-so-innocent smile.

He chuckled, shaking his head at their lame innuendo. She giggled too and got on with exercising her group for the best part of an hour—catching his eye too often and sharing that smile.

But the best bit was when the games of touch rugby began. A lightweight version of the thump-you-to-the-ground national sport—only in this you disarmed your opponent with a touch, not a tackle. Dani shouted encouragement to the kids whom she'd helped drill. Another hour slipped by until there was a grand winning team. Alex strolled over to where she was standing, applauding them with her gang.

'The winners want to play the leaders,' he said. 'You keen?'

'Absolutely.'

Some of the kids weren't that little and Dani felt her competitive spirit kick in. She looked along the field at Alex. They were on the same team. It was a nice feeling.

The game was fast, fun. Early on she got the ball, passed it straight to him and watched him run—all sleek speed and power. The try was easily scored.

The kids stood no chance against him.

At the end of it Dani asked him, 'You wouldn't let them win?'

Alex laughed and shook his head. 'It's good to learn how to lose. Besides, they wouldn't respect us if we didn't play an honest, hard-out game.'

He was right, of course. Except Dani wasn't sure he'd ever had to learn how to lose. She walked with him to where the coach was looking harassed. Now it was all over, some of the kids were tired and heading towards cranky.

'We'll load the shed,' Alex said. 'You guys head back. It'll be easier if Dani and I do it when you're all gone.'

The coach hesitated for all of half a second. 'Thanks.' He immediately started rounding everyone up—ordering them back to the buses.

'Bye, Alex.' One of the young players from his group hovered near.

'See ya.' Alex grinned and waved before turning to gather more of the gear and head towards the shed.

Dani looked at the young teen, saw how her round eyes swallowed Alex whole, how the colour swept into her cheeks before she turned and ran away. Dani smiled; she knew just how overwhelmed the poor girl felt.

'I'll repack the shed, you hand the stuff through to me.' Alex was already in there.

'Thanks.' She didn't fancy the job of being inside that windowless shack.

They worked quickly—Dani stacking the cones and

tossing the balls through to him. It took no time in the space and silence the rowdy kids had left. She waited outside the door while he put the remaining items away.

'Why do you feel trapped in enclosed spaces?' he asked from inside the shed. 'What happened?'

She spun the last ball between her hands. It wasn't a small space putting her on edge now.

'Tell me.' He stuck his head out of the door. 'Something happened, right? You got a fright some time.'

It was a long time ago and she tried never to think about it. 'It was nothing. I was an idiot.'

'What was nothing?'

No one but her mother knew what had happened that day. No one but him, of course. 'I'm not telling.'

He took the ball from her. 'Why not?'

'Because it was nothing.'

'It obviously was *not*,' he said with feeling, tossing the ball home. He shut the door and fixed the padlock, then moved to tower over her. 'Look, if you don't tell me, I'll hold you on the brink of orgasm for so long you won't be able to walk for three weeks because your body will be so sore from the strain of wanting it, but not getting it.'

She couldn't help but giggle at that. 'Sounds great—when do we start?'

'Tell me.'

Dani sighed. So he wasn't going to give up. Well, she'd give him the abridged version. 'I locked myself in a cupboard when I was fourteen. Was stuck in there for ages.' She forced another laugh—but it was too high-pitched.

'Why on earth did you do that?'

OK, so here was the not-so-fun part. She hesitated and felt him lean closer to her.

'Dani...' A very gentle warning.

'My mother's boyfriend came round. She was at work. She used to give her boyfriends a key,' Dani blurted—sooner said, sooner forgotten. 'I didn't like the way he looked at me.'

'So you hid from him?'

'He came into the house and called my name—he must have known Mum was at work so I went into my wardrobe. I heard him come into my room. He poked around everything. I was too scared to move. He stayed for ages. Until I couldn't tell if he was still there or not.'

All she'd been able to hear was the pounding of her heart. And her ears had hurt with the effort she'd had them under—waiting for the tiniest sound, terrified he was lurking just on the other side of the door and was going to smash it open at any moment.

And she'd been right.

'What happened?'

'He tried to break down the door.' Dani flinched, lost back in the memory of it. Barely aware she'd answered.

'*What?*'

Heart galloping, she turned to stare at Alex. Her body trembling with remembered shock. 'He knew I was there. He knew. And he waited and waited and waited until he got sick of waiting. And then he smashed the door.'

Alex swore. 'What did you do?'

'At first I couldn't do anything. I just couldn't move and I thought he was going to, to...but then the scream came out. I screamed and screamed.' But that moment—that infinite moment when she'd been unable to make a noise—had been the root of nightmares for years after.

'Did he get you? Did he hurt you?'

She shook her head. A couple of bruises from a couple of punches was nothing on what she could have suffered. 'The neighbour came over, she banged on the door and threatened to call the cops. He shoved her out of the way and ran off.'

'Did you go to the police?'

'No.' They'd been too scared for that. 'We changed the locks. Then we moved. But it wasn't that long before she gave the key to another one—he was different, of course.' Dani started to walk across the field. 'I did those self-defence classes. I got quite good.' Or she'd thought she had. Fortunately she hadn't had to test it out.

Alex was quiet. 'But you still get freaked in small spaces.'

'Silly, isn't it?' She laughed—still too high-pitched. 'Happened years ago. I should be over it by now. I mean, it was nothing. It wasn't that bad. What a wimp.'

'Don't.' He took her hand and stopped walking. 'Don't try to minimise it.'

Dani shut up at the touch of his fingers on hers, but it took a long time before she could bring herself to look at him.

'You must have been really scared.'

'I couldn't breathe,' Dani answered almost unconsciously.

'He was going to hurt you.' Alex's face hardened. 'He did hurt you.'

She shook her head. 'No. He didn't.'

'He did,' Alex said quietly. 'Maybe not as bad as he could have, as he wanted to, but he did hurt you.'

She had no answer to that.

'Your mum had lots of boyfriends.' Alex stated the obvious.

So? Dani's hackles rose and she pulled her hand away, instinctively wanting to karate chop him in the neck. Instead she took a second to breathe—and heard the way in which he'd spoken. He wasn't judging. He wasn't even asking. It was a plain statement of fact—nothing more. And so she nodded. 'And every time she thought she'd found the One.' Then she shook her head. 'There isn't a One. She was so naive—such a romantic fool. She let them walk all over her because she thought she loved them and she wanted them to love her. I won't be such a fool.'

'Not every guy wants to take advantage, Dani.'

'No?' She turned to face him. 'He was still taking advantage right up 'til the day she died.'

'Your dad?'

'Yeah.' Always he returned like a damn boomerang. How her mother could take him back time after time she never knew. He was—amongst other things—a convicted fraudster, how could she possibly believe a word he said? But Dani did know why—because she had wanted to believe him too. She'd wanted him to love her—he was her *father*.

Instead he used them both.

'You and your mum were close, huh?'

'For a lot of the time it was just the two of us.' Those were the best times. When her mother wasn't bending herself into any shape the new guy wanted—trying to please him, to keep him, to make him love her. She'd never seemed to feel able to just be herself. Because she was loveable. Her mother had been a fun, generous, wonderful woman. But she'd also been co-dependent, believing it was impossible to be happy if she didn't have a man.

'So you decided to have your joy boys rather than relationships? Is that what happened?'

She wrinkled her nose. She should never have made that lot up.

'How many were there, really?' He bent to look into her eyes, his own glinting.

'What is this? You going on *Mastermind* and your topic of choice is the scintillating life of Dani Russo?'

He chuckled. 'I'm betting one. Two at the most. *Boyfriends.*'

'You think you're so smart,' she grumbled. 'What is it you really want to know, Alex? You think one broke my heart? Put me off men?'

'Maybe,' he answered calmly. 'I want to know who and how.'

'I haven't been put off completely,' she said brazenly. 'I wouldn't be sleeping with you if I had.' She turned and started to run. 'Race you to the car!'

She had a good head start, but she knew he was fast. As she ran ahead of him the old memories flashed faster than her feet. Yes, she'd had a boyfriend. After almost making it through her teens without becoming a statistic as her mum had, she'd finally fallen for one of the neighbourhood guys—the older brother of another of her employer's cadets. He'd pursued her so hard and so sweetly—or so she'd believed. Only she'd been determinedly single for so long she hadn't known she'd become a sport to the gang of them—the ultimate challenge. It had taken him six months of occasional dates, but he'd won a crate of beer for being the one to bed her. He'd bragged and betrayed her intimate secrets.

She'd been such a naive idiot it was embarrassing and she didn't want to tell Alex a thing about that one. What was she doing going all Oprah-sofa-open anyway? He'd heard more than enough already.

He overtook her in the last five metres to the car—easily striding out, and she knew he'd been holding back to let her think she could win. She leant against the door, trying to catch her breath back. But it was impossible. She couldn't touch the bottom of this pool they were swimming in anymore. She was way out of her depth. She didn't want them to just be bed buddies. She didn't want this ever to end.

So she was just like every other woman who'd slept with him—once bitten, his forever. That was why all his old flames stayed friends with him—because their hope sprang eternal, that he'd go back to them. And she couldn't blame any of them. Because when he turned his full attentiveness on?

All-consuming delight.

She shivered. Was this the feeling that had made her mother act so stupidly time and time again? To get so stuck on someone that she became blind to all those glaringly obvious faults?

Except what were Alex's faults again?

Oh, that was right. He didn't want a *relationship*. He just liked sex. And she was merely his current playmate. But what about last night? It hadn't been a night of pure physical pleasure and release. It hadn't been that at all. It had been much more. There'd been no physical intimacy, but total emotional honesty. She'd opened up to him, cared for him—shown him. But hadn't he opened up to her too? She couldn't help hoping he had—because although he didn't know it, last night he'd got that last little pocket of her heart too.

'Let's go to the movies.' Alex hadn't been to the movies in years. It'd be like a date—following on from the afternoon in the park. He was still smiling about the sight of her running ahead of him and the basic instinct that had risen in him—driving him to overtake her. Really he'd just wanted to catch her close, for he was still feeling vicious about what had happened to her years before. He could hardly bear to think about it.

They went home to shower and change, then went to a pizza restaurant where she had one of her egg-and-spinach numbers. Then the movie.

If he'd hoped that taking her to a spooky thriller would have her pouncing into his lap halfway through, he'd have been disappointed. But as it was he'd have been disappointed if she *had*. No way was his wannabe street fighter going to be scared by some movie. No, it was the more subtle things that set her on edge. Like him calling her Danielle.

'It's such a pretty name.' He spread his hands peaceably when she glared at him across the table at the café after, her forkful of cake suspended mid-air.

'I prefer Dani.'

'Dani like a boy?'

Her chin tilted.

Yeah, that was it. As if an abbreviation of her pretty name could possibly desexualise her. She was the ultimate in feminine—soft and curvy, short and sweet—though she'd probably kill him if he said so. But he understood why she'd wanted to hide from the succession of men in her mother's life, why she made out as if she were Ms Aggressive Man Eater— she didn't trust people. And who could blame her? Hell, he knew how hard it was to trust—and Dani had every reason to be as wary as him. Like him she'd been betrayed by someone she should have been able to trust completely—a parent.

But if he'd decided to be some kind of a chivalrous gent, planning to take the time to woo her—to win her trust and then win her completely—he supposed he shouldn't take her to bed tonight. He should just kiss her softly good-night—hold her close and then gently break away. Bide his time and all that. But Alex hadn't conquered the finance markets by being slow. Alex won by seeing opportunities and seizing them.

And this was one advantage he knew he had and he was going to play it for all he was worth. Besides, he just couldn't help himself.

Once inside the door he turned her into his arms. But as he kissed her, a whole new depth of feeling arose. Really, he could kiss her for hours and instantly resolved to. He loved the promise of everything that he felt when he was with her—the feeling of such rightness. He didn't want to sleep with anyone else. But much more importantly than that, he wanted to see her happy. Hell, how he wanted that for her.

CHAPTER ELEVEN

DANI pushed back so she could look at Alex. Really look at him. He said nothing, but he met her gaze—unwaveringly, openly, devastatingly. She couldn't speak, couldn't move, could only stare at the warmth, the promise of absolutely everything in his eyes.

He moved to kiss her again, so slowly, with almost unbearable restraint. The gentleness seemed to flay her skin raw. Slow kisses, kisses that grew deeper and deeper still. Kisses that—she suddenly realised—were filled with infinite tenderness.

She started to shake.

His hands smoothed down her arms, settled on her waist and gently pulled her closer.

'We have all night,' he murmured, kissing her eyelids closed.

He made her feel as if they had forever.

Dani moved uncontrollably, absolutely undone by his slow sweetness. He kissed her, kept kissing her—raining them all over her face and neck and shoulders and breasts and returning, always returning to her mouth, for such intimate, deep caresses. She met him with the infinite, yearning need of her own. Her hands lifted. She too needed to touch, to caress, to *care*. She found him so beautiful.

They moved slowly, working their way upstairs. No words

interfered with the beautiful bliss of the moment—the magic between them too powerful to allow anything but truth in their actions.

Eventually, as inevitably as the sun set in the evening sky, their passion rose. Touches grew firmer, faster as their breathing roughened. The emotion that made her cling to him wasn't just born of a need deep in her belly, but from the core of her heart too: to be close—to be one.

And then they were. Their hands laced, bodies intertwined, breath mingling as she met his gaze in wonder. She heard his choked cry and felt the way he muttered her name. She never knew what she said in response—whether it was words or just the pure sound of an all emotional ecstasy that seemed to endlessly pour from her.

Long moments later he rolled, taking her with him so she sprawled over his broad chest, locking her in his arms so she was kept warm and snug and safe. Yet somehow she still felt as if she were flying. As if she'd been freed—able to soar higher and further than she'd ever dreamed was possible.

He drew the sheet up to cover them, his hand drawing gentle circles on her back, soothing her still-too-sensitive skin. Slowly her breathing regulated, matching the gentle rise and fall of his chest. Her muscles softened as she relaxed completely and his arms tightened just that little more. Utterly at peace, she slept.

Alex heard the beep of his phone. It was in his trousers, which had been shed halfway down the stairs. He thought about ignoring it. Except the workaholic in him couldn't. Carefully, he slipped out from beneath his sleeping sweetheart. The query took only a minute to deal with. From habit he flicked through the rest of the messages that had landed while he'd been so utterly lost in Dani. He paused as he saw the number. Quietly he went down into the study, locked the door and dialled. The investigator answered on the second ring.

'Tell me everything.'

Almost an hour later he put the phone down. Stared out of the window at the dark garden and tried to take it in. Tried to decide what the hell he was going to do about it. How on earth was he going to tell her?

He didn't want to. He just didn't want to.

He'd never thought of himself as a coward before, but right now he knew he was. Dani didn't want to be lonely anymore, did she? Sure, she said she didn't want relationships, didn't want a lover, but she wanted a family. That was why she wanted to find her brother. He shifted in his chair. Yeah. There it was. That flicker of jealousy. Her brother would have had more of a claim on her than Alex did. She wanted that kind of relationship, not any other. So stupid, so wrong of him to feel jealous of that. And why did he?

Because he wanted her himself. He wanted his own relationship with her.

But not like this. It didn't have to be one or the other. She should have had both. She should have had everything.

It was the one thing he knew would make her crumble. And he couldn't bear to be the one to destroy her hopes. She'd waited for so long, wanted for so long. But it wasn't to be. And he was going to have to tell her.

He really didn't want to.

And, yeah, there was that other selfish reason too, wasn't there—why he wasn't waking her, telling her right now as he should be?

He didn't want her to leave.

Once she knew, she'd walk out of his life. He knew it in

his bones. While she might be beginning to open up, it wasn't enough yet. He hadn't had enough time to build the kind of bridge he'd never before built, that he knew she hadn't built, and he was afraid of losing her.

So he wouldn't do it. Not yet. He'd wait for the morning. Besides—the lab tests hadn't come in. He could justify the delay then—sure he could. He'd wait until he had all the proof.

And then he'd tell her.

He walked back up the stairs, stared at the little lump she made in his bed. She stirred slightly as he slipped in beside her. He gently wrapped his arms around her, stroking her hair, soothing her back into sleep.

But the future pressed heavy on his heart. He wished like hell it had been different. It was too awful that he had Patrick wanting to mend fences with him, but that Dani was to have nothing—when she wanted and he didn't. She deserved so much more. He waited, watched as the sky lightened and wished he could make a bargain with either a god or a demon to trade her loss over to him. Hoped against hopelessness—prayed that in the darkness she would turn to him.

When she woke the sun was streaming in, and when she saw he was still there beside her, her colour mounted. She almost looked shy. 'Shouldn't you be up already answering a million messages or something?'

Alex managed a small smile. She wasn't happy with him staying in bed with her? His tough cookie felt uneasy when he spent so much time with her. Too bad, because he was about to spend a whole lot more. No matter what, he was determined to stick with her through this.

She was like a little wild cat. If you stretched out a hand to caress her you might get scratched. Even though inside she was yearning for that little bit of love, her first instinct was to defend. Because she couldn't be sure you weren't going to hurt her.

Alex figured he could handle a few surface scratches. It was worth it because when she did relax she was the softest, sweetest playmate—with that hint of snap-your-head-off danger. His whole point of focus had shifted. No longer was this about a spot of play in a time of stress. It was all about her.

Trust took time, though. And he didn't have a lot of time. He had to make quick progress—and he'd make the most of any advantage he had to do it.

He swallowed the guilt and reached for her—surely it would be worth it. He wanted her to have the day—not to know just yet. A few more hours until there was certainty. Then he'd tell her.

Dani couldn't put last night out of her head—the way they'd been together, the way he'd held her, so close and right through 'til the sun shone high and bright through the window. And the way he looked at her...

Oh, she was so under his spell, and dreaming of that ending common to all fairytales—the happy-ever-after one.

When she slid into his car after work he leaned over and kissed her—another of those kisses that combined the sweetest tenderness with the most sultry passion. She smiled at him, her heart in her throat, in her eyes, beating its message loud in her ears. Surely he must see and hear it and feel it too? He took her hand in his as he drove them home. She didn't think she'd ever felt so happy.

'It's a play premiere, right?' She checked on the plan as she changed.

He nodded.

She smoothed down her black dress. She was going to

have to go shopping soon—another outing in this number and she'd be letting Alex down.

His phone rang again.

'You better be sure to switch that off in the theatre.'

'Vibrate,' he muttered, looking at the screen and turning away to take the call.

Dani finished combing her hair and leant closer to the mirror to carefully slide in the hairclip and then do her lippy.

'Dani.'

She looked up to see his reflection, struck by the new note in his voice. The tux was gorgeous. But his face was ashen.

'Alex?' She spun to face him.

'I have to tell you something.'

Whatever it was, it wasn't going to be good. He looked worse than when he'd told her about Patrick. Only this wasn't about him, this was about her. She knew because of the way he was looking at her—as if he didn't want to.

'You've found him.'

'Yes.'

She almost couldn't bear to ask. He was looking so solemn. Why? What was wrong? What had happened? 'Why are you looking so serious?' She couldn't do anything more than whisper.

'Because it's not what you wanted, Dani.'

She couldn't breathe. 'He doesn't want to meet me?'

'No.' Alex pushed out a long breath. 'He's dead, Dani.'

'*What?*' She couldn't move. 'He's what?'

'His name was Jack Parker. He got adopted into a really nice family. Did fine at school. He was going into the family business—working with his father.'

'What happened?' She needed to know: how, when— dead? Had he really said *dead*?

'A car accident. It wasn't his fault—he was in the wrong place, at the wrong time.'

'He was killed.' She was staring, unblinking, but didn't know what she was seeing.

'He was in a coma for a couple of days and then he died. It was five years ago.'

Dani's heart just stopped. All of her stopped. *Five years ago?* He'd died before their mother. He'd died before Dani had even known about him.

'Dani?'

She forced herself to swallow. It seemed like a huge action, her whole body involved in the effort. She blinked. Alex was right in front of her, his hand outstretched as if he was about to take her arm. She turned away and forced in a long, controlled breath. 'That's great he found a family.'

'Yeah, they seem really nice,' Alex said quietly. 'They offered to meet with you, if you'd like. They have photos they'd share, would talk to you about him.'

Dani bent her head. 'I don't think that would be a good idea.'

'Dani—'

'I know now. That's all that matters. It's finished.'

'No, it isn't. It's only just started.'

Dani closed her eyes. No. She didn't want to think on this anymore. Not right now. She didn't want to take it in.

Jack Parker.

She pushed the name away—didn't want him to become real; it would only heighten the loss. What she needed now was oblivion. And she'd make the most of the opiate she had right here. She turned back to Alex, didn't look into his eyes, just looked at his broad chest. In her mind's eye she could see the muscles beneath the suit—he was the perfect instrument of pleasure. Even now she could see his whole body tense.

'Dani, you need—'

'Action.' She walked towards him.

'No, you need to talk. To me.'

'No.' She shook her head, and pressed against him. 'I need action. That's all.'

He caught her hands before she could even try to tease him into play. Damn. She could be mindless in less than a minute if only he'd touch her.

'This is too important. Dani. No.' His grip on her wrists eased, his thumbs stroking. 'It's OK to grieve, Dani.'

No, it wasn't. She didn't want to cry. She didn't want to feel anything—she just wanted to forget.

Because if she didn't forget it—and soon—she'd want to lean on Alex and cry. Dani never cried, certainly not in front of anyone. She drew on the iron will she'd built up inside her over the last year. She was not going to be weak—she was not going to let it out. She didn't want to be that vulnerable. Her heart hurt too much already. And if she acknowledged it, it would hurt more—she couldn't bear to be hurt more.

'There's nothing to grieve. I never even met him.' She denied it all. 'I wanted to know. Now I do.'

'No, you wanted family. You wanted someone.'

She shook her head. 'I don't need anyone.'

'Dani,' he admonished gently.

She stood still, fighting the gaping wound inside, determined to stop the hurt gushing out of her. She couldn't cope if it did. She couldn't let this become *real*. But she couldn't stop that last little thread of hope uncurling. 'You're sure. I mean, there's no doubt, is there? It's definitely him?'

'The DNA test proved it.'

'The DNA test?' Stunned, she pulled her wrists free and stared at him. 'What DNA test?'

There was no hiding the guilt in his face now.

'You did a DNA test without my knowing?' Her voice rose up into screech territory. 'How the hell did you do that—take a pubic hair or something?' She felt that violated.

'Dani.' He took her shoulders firmly.

'Did you dig up his grave?' Raw feeling surged through her veins—the kind of feeling that gave her the strength she needed right now—*anger*. 'How long have you known?' He had to have known something to get the tests done. 'Why didn't you tell me you thought you'd found him sooner?' Yes, it was easy to be angry. So easy to be furiously angry with Alex.

'I didn't want to get your hopes up until it was certain. I didn't want to hurt you.'

Well, right now she wanted to hurt him. 'So last night you knew.'

'I found out late last night. But I only got the lab confirmation in that call just now.'

She hardly heard him. So it had been pity that had driven his tenderness this morning. 'You're a bastard, Alex. You're such a bastard.'

'I know.'

'Oh, please.' She turned on him, striking out in her agony. 'You're still upset about your parentage? Come on, Alex, get over it.' She hurt so much and she wanted to hurt him more.

'Dani—' His fingers were painfully tight on her shoulders now and she was sure he was about to bodily chuck her out. And she'd be glad. She wanted everything to end.

But all he did was say softly, 'You're not taking it out on me.'

Alex badly wanted to take her in his arms, wanted to kiss her to stop the hurtful words. Like a trapped, wounded animal, she thought the only way to escape was to attack.

But he didn't draw her closer. Instead he stiffened his arms, holding her away so he could read her expression.

What he wanted was for her to lower her guard again and let him in. He ached to comfort her. She was so obviously devastated, but she was denying everything.

'You're right,' she said. 'Sorry.'

He watched, helpless, as she shut down—freezing him out completely. His fingers instinctively pressed harder into her bones—as if it were some way to bring her back to him—but she didn't even flinch. It was as if she were turning to marble before his eyes—a version of herself but with her beauty, her vitality, sucked out.

It crushed him. Already she was gone. And whatever closeness or intimacy he thought they'd been building over the last few days was revealed to be the sham it was. She trusted him no more than she had on day one. She was no less afraid.

Her brown eyes were almost black, like bottomless holes in a face too pale to be well. His heart contracted. 'Dani—'

'I'm going to…check my lipstick.' She twisted away and he let her go.

'You've just done your lipstick.' Her wretched lipstick was on the table. She was running away—not facing what he'd told her.

'We have this play to go to, don't we?' She picked up the lipstick and reapplied.

'No, I'll cancel—'

'There's no need to do that.' She carefully replaced the lid.

No. She wasn't one to crumble, was she? She denied all the way—refused to admit to weakness, hurt or need. But it would come out some time—it just had to. And he was damn sure he was going to be there when it did. He sighed. OK, maybe a little distraction might help. An hour or two in a theatre might give her a chance to think. No way would she concentrate on the play—her mind would wander.

And he was getting nowhere with her now and he didn't want her packing her bags in the next five minutes, which she'd probably do if they stayed at home. 'Are you sure you're up to it?'

'Of course I am.' She shoved her feet into her shoes.

Yeah, of course she was. Alex stuffed his fists into his pockets. 'Then let's go.'

It was a living hell. Ten minutes into it Alex was ready to leave. Dani was doing her zombie impression beside him. He covered her hand with his, hers was freezing. A trickle of dread slid down his spine and his eyes hurt from trying to read her expression in the dim light.

'Let's go,' he murmured in her ear as soon as the curtain went down on the first act.

Deathly pale now, she swayed as she stood. Was the shock wearing off and the reality hitting her? He wished she'd talk to him. He needed to get her home so he could make her talk to him.

'I'm just going to freshen up.'

In other words go put on her armour. She'd run away for a few minutes and try to pull herself together. Except she was so on edge he didn't think it was going to work this time. The sooner he got her home, the better. He'd hold her close, just hold her in his arms and cradle her until those tears came. She needed it. Hell, *he* needed it.

Dani blindly followed Alex to the car. Trying really hard not to think. But her brain was screaming—she had to run, she had to hide from this truth. 'I'm going back to Australia,' she said as he drove home.

'Not yet, Dani. You've had a shock—you need time to take it in.' His eyes were dark.

'I want to move out.'

'You don't want to talk?' He looked at her searchingly. 'Don't you think we both could do with a little comfort right now? Some companionship? At the very least, aren't we friends?'

His words thickened the ice around her heart. He'd said they couldn't be friends. And they couldn't. He was much more than that to her. 'You have other friends. You have Lorenzo.'

'I haven't told him about my father. I haven't told anyone but you.'

A tiny bird fluttered its wings, wanting to fly in her heart. Silly to be so moved by that one little comment and its implication of intimacy, of trust. Surely she couldn't trust it—it was just that she'd been there at the time when he'd needed to share. She couldn't believe it was anything more than that. She couldn't believe in anything right now. 'I really want to go, Alex.'

'Not tonight.'

Dully, she supposed he was right. Where would she go? It wasn't practical. He was so generous, wasn't he? But she didn't want any more of his tender pity. 'OK, but I need to be alone.'

He swallowed. 'Sure.'

'I promised Sara I'd go to the meeting on Monday. I said I'd be there when she delivered her presentation. I'll go after that.' It was all she could think. She couldn't let her down.

She'd let her mother down.

When they reached the house, she took far too much care undoing her seat belt but he didn't even move. When she looked at him he was staring at the garage wall, his face so expressionless she wondered if he'd even heard her. She slipped out of the car and suddenly picked up speed. She'd meant it. She needed tonight to be alone to lock away her demons.

But he moved faster, grabbing her hand as she got to the lounge. She stopped. Eyes closed, she kept her back to him. 'Don't—'

His fingers squeezed hard.

'You know where I am if you need me.' His voice was so husky it shattered her. She swayed, holding on by the last thread.

But he let her hand go and walked past her, going straight up the stairs, not looking back.

She stared at nothing as he disappeared, utterly unable to move. She couldn't let herself need him.

Hours later she stumbled to the kitchen, poured a glass of iced water and didn't look at the tray on the table she knew was meant for her.

'You're staying home today.' He walked up to her and touched her nose with a light finger. 'You're tired.'

So was he, but he was in his suit and ready to go. She was no less capable than him. 'I can go.'

'Stay home, Dani. You need to.' He was gone before she could reply.

She sipped the icy water and glanced at the plates he'd prepared for her—fruit salad, a bagel, juice. Then she saw the file on the other side. She didn't need to open it to know what it was—the information from the private investigator. Alex had left it deliberately for sure. She stared at it as if it were more terrifying than an armed intruder.

Jack Parker.

Could she bear to know any more than that?

She perched on the edge of one of the dining chairs. Pulled the folder towards her. She turned the cover, read the words. Dates, school—it was like a CV. How could someone's life be reduced to a couple of A4 pages?

She turned the next page and stopped.

Photos. A baby, a boy, a youth. Brown eyes. Brown hair. Like hers. So much like hers.

She slammed the file shut. Pain burning her inside out. She couldn't do it. Couldn't bear to see what she'd lost before she'd even been able to find it. Couldn't bear to face the fact that she'd failed her mother.

She stood. Ran. She wasn't going to sit here and mope all day. There was work to be done at the Whistle Fund. She wasn't going to let Cara down.

Cara looked up when she walked in, a surprised smile brightening her face. 'I didn't expect to see you today. Alex called to say you weren't feeling well.'

'Just a slight headache,' Dani covered. 'Gosh, if you can work with morning sickness then I can manage a mild headache.'

Cara laughed. 'I haven't had a single bout of morning sickness. Been eating like a horse from the moment I got pregnant.'

Dani sat sharply. 'You haven't been sick at all?'

She watched Cara shake her head. Saw how her eyes sparkled, and her skin glowed. This was a woman for whom pregnancy was a piece of cake. Painful realisation dawned. 'You don't really need me here, do you?'

'Well…' Cara blushed '…there's always too much work to do. I mean, usually we get other volunteers, but now we have you…'

Dani rubbed her head and felt the icy sweat beading on her brow. 'Do you do this voluntarily?'

'They insist on paying me something, but I give it back to them by buying lots of tickets to whatever they've got going. I, um…' she was blushing even harder '…I don't really need to work.' She said it as if it were something to be ashamed of.

Dani forced a smile to reassure her. But inside she was trying to process the info that should have been blindingly obvious before now. How could she not have worked this out already? Cara was a nominally paid volunteer, working part-time hours. Whereas she was getting paid top temp dollar—full-time.

But it wasn't the charity paying her wages at all. It was Alex. And *she* was the charity. She cringed. The whole thing was a charade. He'd felt bad about what had happened, and this was him taking care of it. He'd said duty to the Carlisle business had been instilled in him from birth. But his sense of duty extended in all areas of his life too. And when he'd played a part in her life being stuffed up, he'd taken every step to help. Duty—not desire.

And now pity.

While he might have wanted to play with her for a bit, she bet he hadn't meant for it to turn into this almighty mess. For she wasn't Alex Carlisle standard—she wasn't like those princesses at the charity—like Cara. She couldn't even begin to compare.

'Cara, I'm really sorry, but my head actually is a bit bad.' Dani stood.

'Oh, do you want me to—?'

'I'll be fine. I'll just go home again.'

Except there was no home, was there?

She raced to her room as soon as she got back into his house. It only took moments to throw her belongings into her pack. But she'd barely started tugging on the zip when she heard the garage door.

He was up the stairs with Superman speed.

'Lorenzo called.' He walked into the middle of her room. 'Cara said you'd come to work and then gone again almost immediately. She was worried.' He looked at her bag. When he spoke again, his voice was colder than ice. 'Were you going to leave a note?'

'Yes.'

'Written it yet?'

'No.'

'So tell me.'

'There's no need for me to stay anymore. I've found out all I needed to.'

'What about Sara and the meeting?'

'She doesn't need me. She probably won't even notice I'm not there. And *Cara* doesn't need me, does she?' she said bitterly.

His mouth tightened. 'What about me?'

'You don't need me, either.' And in another week he'd have someone else in her place.

'What if I told you I did?' He stepped closer. 'What if I told you I wanted you to stay? Would you?'

She shook her head. Not trusting her voice. For how long would he want her—how long 'til they became 'just friends'. She couldn't do that.

'What if I said we have something special?'

'What we have is good sex. That's all.'

'So you're just going to run away? From me? From this?'

He threw Jack's file at her.

She turned away as the pages scattered on the floor. 'I don't want it.' Her voice broke. 'I don't want…'

'Don't want what?'

She turned back. 'To stay.'

He walked right into her space. 'I won't let you go.'

'You can't stop me.' She pushed past him and picked up her bag.

'You think you're so tough. But you're not. You're scared. You're that total chicken.'

So what if he was right? So what if she was dying inside? She wasn't going to hurt herself more by lingering in an affair that had no future. She couldn't handle any more of the agony burning her through now. 'I told you from the start I don't do relationships.'

'What the hell do you think we've been doing? We've been living together, being together, *making love* together—that's not a relationship?'

'We didn't make love. We had no-strings, uncomplicated sex!' How could he say otherwise? It was him feeling bad for her—his caretaker duty on full steam ahead—but she wasn't his new pity project. 'We were flatmates trading favours—nothing more than that. Not a relationship.'

'That's ridiculous. What is it going to take, Dani?' He gripped her arm. 'When are you going to face up to your fears? When are you going to let yourself trust someone? When are you going to let someone in? Because until you do, you're going to be alone and lonely.'

'Alone is exactly what I want to be.' Alone meant there'd be no more loss. No more crippling heartache. She yanked her arm free and raced down the stairs.

'I want you to stay.' He kept pace. 'I want you.'

She ran to the front door.

'Did you hear what I said, Dani? I want you.'

Yeah, but the want wouldn't last—the want would die. Everything else had been based on him feeling responsible, feeling guilty, feeling pity. None of which would last, either. So she turned, faced him down. 'Well, I don't want you.'

'Liar. You want me just as much as I want you. You can't say no to me.'

'No!' she shouted. 'I'm saying it now. I don't want you.'

And it wasn't all a lie. For she didn't. She didn't want him like this.

CHAPTER TWELVE

'You have to get out of this office, Alex.'

'You'll just have to manage alone tonight, Renz. I'm sure you can handle it.'

Lorenzo had his hands on his hips. 'It'll be a good night.'

'Are we going to settle this the old way?' A hard out physical battle might just be the thing. At least it might wear him out enough to crash.

'I couldn't do it to you,' Lorenzo grumbled. 'The way you look, I'd knock you out first punch. Haven't you been sleeping at all?'

Three days. Three long, lonely, bloody miserable days that had dra-a-aged. No, he hadn't slept at all. In his head that row played over and over and over—preventing any kind of wind-down of body or mind.

Could he have been more lovelorn teen? Throwing the most desperate lines at her—'I won't let you go'—what, like he was going to imprison her?

He wished he could have.

Damn, it still hurt.

She wouldn't give them a chance. She wouldn't let him in.

'Have you heard from her?'

'No.'

'Do you know where she is?'

'Yes.' He'd had someone track her from the moment she'd left—as awful as that was. He'd never used a private investigator in his life before, but in the last month he'd spent more on one than a footballer's wife spent on botox for a year. 'But that's not the point.' He wanted her to come back. He wanted *her* to want to. But it looked as if that wasn't going to happen.

Lorenzo stared at him, his eyes darker than the moonless night. 'You're not going after her?'

'No.'

Alex sat in the silence after Lorenzo had gone. Eventually acknowledged to himself that he'd lied to his friend. Another lie—this time to try to stop himself from hurting. It hadn't worked. He could wait another day, maybe two, but then he had to go after her. He didn't know what he was going to do when he got to her, but somehow he would win. He checked his phone again, saw the little icon flashing. There'd been many messages now, and he'd ignored every one. But he couldn't ignore it anymore—had to have closure on something at least.

'Alex?' Patrick answered right away, sounded surprised.

'Yeah, ah, sorry I haven't got back to you sooner.' Alex grimaced, what was *he* doing apologising? A spurt of irritation heated him, driving his words. 'Look, I had a great father. He was fantastic. I don't need another.'

Samuel had been there for him, had loved him. He truly was his dad and Alex wasn't going to let anyone take that from either of them.

There was a pause. Patrick cleared his throat. 'I understand.'

Elbow on his desk, Alex shut his eyes and massaged round them with thumb and middle finger. Was that edge of disappointment genuine?

Yeah, he thought it was—it resonated with the disappointment deep in his own bones. 'But maybe, um…' his voice failed '…maybe I could do with a friend.'

He didn't really know if it was going to be possible. It was a huge chasm between them, a pit of bad history miles wide. But he'd learned from Dani: things were never black-and-white and, hell, it was so hard to tell someone you loved something that was going to hurt them. Every instinct was to protect, as his mother had wanted to protect both him and Samuel—he could acknowledge that now. It didn't make it right, but he understood why people sometimes lied. And he so badly wanted to be given another chance, surely he could offer one himself.

'That would be great, Alex,' Patrick said quietly. 'Thanks.'

'I thought you'd have been on a plane back to Oz days ago.'

Dani looked up from where she was staring at the bowl of sugar sachets in the café down by the waterfront. Lorenzo. Looking as unreadable as ever. Although his vibe was definitely one of disapproval.

'I am. Tomorrow.' She was working up to it. But there'd been one last thing she'd had to do first. Now even that was done.

'Then you need to go and see him today.'

Dani shook her head. 'He was doing me a favour because he felt bad about the video thing. He felt responsible. That's all it was.' He was doing what he thought he should. His sense of duty had driven him. And with all the stress he was under, things had got confused. But she was as right for him as an electric blanket was right for a snowman. She'd wanted to get out before he woke up to that fact. She just couldn't handle the heartache.

'Look, I've known Alex a long time and I've never known him to do something he doesn't want to. He's a smart guy—

he knows what he's doing,' Lorenzo said. 'I've never known him to move a woman in with him. He could have put you up in a hotel. He could have given you some money and walked away.'

'He's too meticulous to have done that. He wanted to be sure I was OK.'

'No. The Alex I know would never have taken a woman to his home in that situation for fear she'd get the wrong impression. He's always been very careful not to lead anyone on.'

Yeah, she knew that—for him it was 'just sex, just fun'.

'But it seems you've got the totally wrong impression anyway.' Lorenzo pulled out the chair beside her and sat. 'I don't like to see my friend hurting. Seems to me you're not that happy, either.'

Dani shook her head. For her it hadn't been just sex. It had been everything. Deep inside her that flicker of hope had refused to be snuffed. Lorenzo's words made it burn brighter than the sun. It took her three minutes to summon up courage to ask him. 'Do you think he meant it?'

'I think you need to ask him that yourself.'

Her heart thudded, more adrenalin flooding her than that time she'd been too scared to even blink. Could she ask him?

It was then that she realised just how brave her mother had been—to take the chance, to want to believe, every time. Even if it meant her heart might get squished. She'd always tried; she'd always taken the risk.

Dani had fought so long to be strong. To be independent. But now she saw she hadn't been at all. She was exactly what Alex had said—a coward. Had he been right about other things too?

She thought about Jack—his life had ended way before it should have. Her mother had died too young too. So she had to take the chance—she had to do it for them—she had to be brave and take life's risks on.

Dani turned to Lorenzo. 'Can I ask a favour?'

Alex worked late again. Left a message for his housekeeper to leave his dinner in the fridge; he'd microwave it later. The little he could be bothered eating tasted no good anyway. After nine, he walked out onto the balcony off his office, not caring about how cold and dark it was out there. Just needed the chill wind to whistle into his ears and blank out the angry voice yelling at him. His angry voice—berating himself for screwing it up so royally. And then the smaller voice wondered how on earth he was going to fix it. Nothing could stop the thoughts. Nothing numbed the pain from the knives twisting inside.

Eventually the freezing air bit hard enough to send him back indoors. He walked faster when he heard his mobile ringing. He picked it up just before it went to the answering machine. 'What?'

'Where the hell have you been?' Lorenzo bellowed.

Alex's brows rose and he held the phone a little from his ear. 'For a walk.'

'Without your *phone*?' Lorenzo never sounded emotional and here he was practically screeching at him.

Alex iced up inside, as well as out. 'What is it?'

'She called me. Wanted to set it up. But she's been there for ages.'

'Been where?' Damn it, couldn't Lorenzo make sense?

'Look at your computer—I sent you the link. You're supposed to be slaving at your desk, not getting fresh flipping air.'

Alex clicked the link and watched as the live webcast came on. No way.

'You'd better get moving, Alex. She's been waiting fifteen minutes already. She probably thinks you aren't coming.'

Alex swore. 'Why the hell is she in the lift?'

'It was her idea.'

Alex chucked the phone and ran.

Whichever daytime TV shrink it was who said confronting your fears was the way to free yourself needed to see a shrink themselves, because Dani was so not getting over her fears right now. Not any of them. In fact, they were worsening with every passing second. She had visions of herself riding up and down in the elevator for days—slowly starving, leaving only a skeleton for the security men to discover in ten months' time. Never mind the reality that only tomorrow people would arrive for work and find her there—a complete saddo but still alive. No, right now she'd rather indulge in the total drama girl-lost-in-lift-for-ever nightmare.

And when Alex found out he'd wince, hadn't realised he'd hurt her so much—he hadn't meant to, of course…thought she'd understood it was just an *arrangement*. Bed buddies and all that.

Because he hadn't meant it. He didn't want her.

If he did, he'd be here already.

She wiped her eye quickly, outraged that the tear had actually escaped her brimming rims. She never cried. Never, never, never.

Only now there was another tear. And another, and they wouldn't stop.

She turned her back to the damn camera and fished in her pocket. Double damn. No hanky, no tissue. Never necessary because she never cried. So she had to swish them away with her fingers again and sniff.

Ugh.

Now her fingers had black smudges on them because the mascara she'd applied with such excited care was running everywhere.

Great.

The lift wasn't even going up and down anymore. She couldn't be bothered getting up to press the buttons. Instead she just scrunched down, her back against the wall, her feet tucked underneath her. Lorenzo would probably take pity on her some time soon and come and tell her to give up and get out.

Yeah, it had happened. The lift was going up again. She buried her face in her hands, not wanting to see him. Beyond humiliated, beyond scared, she breathed short and fast, trying to hold back the wail that wanted release. If only she could ease the pain.

Large hands grasped her wrists and pulled hard, hauling her out of the lift.

'Can you breathe? Can you breathe, Dani?'

Alex. Oh, God, it was Alex. She could hardly see him through the tears streaming, but she felt his heat, his strength. She heard him.

'You're crying.' He sounded shocked. 'It's OK, honey, you're not in there anymore. You're out of there.' His hands rubbed over her back, pulling her hard against his strong frame. Oh, he was so warm. 'You're safe, Dani. You're safe.'

She hiccupped. He thought she was upset because she'd been in the lift? 'That's…that's not why I'm crying.'

His hands slowed on her back, relaxing the pressure, and she was able to pull away enough to tilt her head and look him in the eyes. 'I thought you weren't coming.'

For a moment she watched as he froze completely—his gaze boring into her. Then she couldn't bear it anymore and buried her face back in his chest. Too bad if he cared—his shirt was getting a soaking. But his arms clamped around her again—this time so hard she almost couldn't breathe.

'You lied to me.' He spoke softly, not relaxing his hold even a fraction.

'You lied to me too.' She closed her eyes but the tears still slipped beneath her lids. 'I guess the question is why did we lie?'

He slid his hand up her back, threading his fingers into the hair at the nape of her neck, angling her head so she felt his breath skim over her skin.

'I didn't tell you about finding out about your brother sooner for two reasons,' he said, his mouth millimetres from her ear. 'One, because I didn't want to hurt you—I knew you'd be upset. And two, I didn't want us to be over. I thought you'd leave as soon as you found out. I've been such an idiot, Dani. I thought we were just a fling. But we're not. We're forever. And I couldn't get that through to you before you left.'

He moved even closer, the warmth of his body melting hers so she leaned into him. His lips brushed her skin now—making her feel every word, as well as hear them.

'I know you don't believe in romance. You don't believe in love at first sight. But I sure as hell believe in lust at first sight. That's how it was between us. The chemistry just flared. You know that. I thought I was acting crazy because I'd found out about Patrick and needing you was a weird kind of release. But the fact is I'm just not in control about how I feel about you. Haven't been from the moment I laid eyes on you. And the more I got to know you, the more I felt for you, the more I wanted you. Barbs and all.'

'What do you mean, barbs?' She sniffed.

'I mean, the cold war concrete-wall, razor-wire, rooftop-sniper defence system you've got going.' His chest moved as he chuckled. 'But it's not going to work, Dani. Want to know why?'

She moved her head—a shake or a nod, not even she knew which it was.

'Because I love you. And I'm thinking maybe you love me too.'

'You think?' Her voice wobbled.

'You're here,' he said huskily. 'You've come back to me.'

She had. She nodded for certain then, her fingers curling into his arms, unashamedly clinging to him.

'When I'm with you, I'm happier than I have ever been,' Alex muttered. 'You light up my world. It's that simple.'

For a long moment Dani couldn't speak. But when she started she found it was easy. 'I lied to you because I was scared. I told you I didn't want you because I was scared about the strength of my feelings for you. And I was scared you didn't feel the same.' She took a shaky breath. 'I didn't want you thinking you were stuck with me. I didn't want to be the charity case that trapped you. I didn't want you to be with me out of pity.'

'Dani,' he groaned. 'I care about you. I want to take care of you. That's what people who love each other do. That's love, that's family. That's going to be our family. We've both been alone too long, Dani. You said you don't believe in re-lationships, but why were you looking for your brother? What did you hope to find when you found him if not some kind of a relationship? If not some family to love and be loved by?'

Tears flooded her eyes again. 'And I wanted to tell him how sorry she was. I promised her I would.'

'Oh, Dani.' He framed her face with gentle palms. 'Maybe she's found him now, huh? Maybe she's been able to tell him herself.'

'I hope so.' She breathed in courage. 'But you're right, Alex. I wanted to find him for me too. I don't know what I hoped for, really. But I was lonely. I wanted to find someone safe.'

'I'm the safest bet there is, Dani. Don't you know? I've the best credit rating you can get.' He smiled, joking just a little. 'Safer than any other finance company. Or any other man. Loving someone, wanting to care, isn't a weakness. Opening up takes strength. And you're the strongest person I've ever met.'

'I'm not. You were right before. I'm a coward,' she whispered. 'But I don't want to be anymore.' She drew in a shaky breath. 'I went to Jack's grave.'

'Dani.' He locked her in a bear hug. 'Alone?'

The tears streamed down her face as he cradled her.

'It's OK. It's OK.' She tried to say it so she'd believe it, but he shushed her. And at that she let all that was in her heart out—her sorrow, loneliness, and her love. Crying until the tears finally ran dry. And he just waited, just held her.

Neither of them alone now.

Long minutes later he brushed her silly fringe back behind her ear. 'I can't believe you were waiting in the lift.'

'I wanted to prove I could face my fears.'

'Tell you what, when we get home I'll shut us both in a cupboard and show you such a good time you'll never be afraid of small spaces again, OK?'

Oh, how that smile melted her. 'It might take more than one therapy session to cure me of the phobia.'

'Maybe.' He nodded solemnly. 'But we can only try, right? We face the fears together. Dani, you're determined, you're self-reliant, you're independent. I love how you fight your corner. But your corner is my corner too. From here on in we're on the same team, darling. We're building a life together.'

'Oh.' She swept her hand down his chest, totally floored by his flattery and feeling the need for some light, sarcastic relief. 'So it wasn't my boobs that caught your eye?'

He laughed, a wicked look lighting up his face. 'OK, so

they were the first thing I noticed. You guessed that already. But I took in the rest of you too—you're beautiful. I love the whole package that is you.'

She really was Carlisle standard? She was crazy pleased and her confidence blossomed. 'It's OK.' She moved sassily. 'You can like my boobs. I like your butt.'

'Oh, you do?'

'And your shoulders. And you have fantastic hands.'

'Yeah?'

'They're big enough to hold me.' She took his hand and placed it beneath her breast. He immediately spread his fingers, pushing up a little to take her weight, his thumb seeking her taut peak. Oh, that was what she wanted. 'There isn't a security camera in here, is there?'

'No.' His eyes dropped to her chest.

'The security guard isn't about to do his rounds?'

'He should be on the desk downstairs. I'll lock the door in case.' Alex backed her up against it. 'He knows I've been working late this week.'

She watched him watch her body respond to the simple, slow movement of his fingers. His eyes were hooded, pupils huge. His breathing more audible, but she was panting already. 'Please,' she whispered.

His gaze flicked up to hers. 'Please what?'

'Love me.'

His smile made her whole body heat with desire so sweet she almost couldn't bear it. And she believed it. Finally she truly believed it. 'Oh, Alex.' Overcome, she sobbed.

He kissed her. 'I do love you.'

His mouth was pure heaven. Filling her with pleasure and heat and she kissed him back with all her heart. Nothing held back. She pressed against him, needing to show him, to make him understand all that he meant to her. She threw her arms around his neck—loving him.

He was shaking, his hands moving fast. Somehow they did it, somehow not breaking that most sacred, searing kiss they moved enough to touch where they needed to touch, to become one, to feel the ecstasy that they could feel only with each other.

'I love you,' she breathed. 'I love this.'

Her legs wrapped around him as they had that day in the lift, her body rapturously absorbed his and the power surged between them. Like a flash of lightning it hit—so fast—her body shuddering as he cried out.

Afterwards he growled, practically flattening her against the door, his breathing rapid, his sweat dripping. 'How does it keep getting better?'

It was her turn to smile—that loving smile of total certainty.

He pushed away from her enough to gaze at her, ran his finger down her jaw and pushed that hair behind her ear again. 'You know, I have something for you.' A brief tease of a kiss before he pulled his trousers up and put his hand in his pocket. 'I've been carrying it forever, waiting to be able to give it to you.'

The solitaire was tear-shaped; it gleamed rather than sparkled—as if it was full of the sweetest promise. But what she loved even more was the setting, the thin gold and the pretty engraving on the band. It was unusual. And quite, quite girly. And inside she loved girly. So pretty. Just the thing she would have chosen for herself—not that she'd ever contemplated diamond engagement rings before. He held the ring on an angle so she could see the words etched on the inside.

Alex loves Dani.

Her silly eyes were watering again. But she went bold. 'It might get lonely being the only ring on that finger.'

'Oh, I already have a mate for it. A very pretty band. And I have a date for when I'm going to give it to you.'

'A date?'

'In just a couple of weeks, actually.'

'Alex,' she teased. 'Have you been organising?'

'Sure have. Everything.' He caught her hand. 'You can't muck up my plans now. I've got it all perfectly under control.'

'You've always got the answers, haven't you? Just the way you like it.' She watched as the ring slid down.

'Yeah, but it's been hell waiting for you, Dani.'

'I'm sorry.' She was. Her emotions still so raw she felt terrible for doing that.

He laughed then and pulled her close. 'It's OK. You have the rest of your life to make it up to me.'

'Yes.' She snuggled into his embrace and felt the magic between them healing her. 'I do.'

Her Not-So-Secret Diary

ANNE OLIVER

When not teaching or writing, **Anne Oliver** loves nothing more than escaping into a book. She keeps a box of tissues handy—her favourite stories are intense, passionate, against-all-odds romances. Eight years ago she began creating her own characters in paranormal and time-travel adventures, before turning to contemporary romance. Other interests include quilting, astronomy, all things Scottish, and eating anything she doesn't have to cook. Sharing her characters' journeys with readers all over the world is a privilege...and a dream come true. Anne lives in Adelaide, South Australia, and has two adult children. Visit her website at www.anne-oliver.com. She loves to hear from readers. E-mail her at anne@anne-oliver.com.

To old cats and favourite places in the sun.
Miss you, Cleo.
Thanks to Kathy, Linda, Sharon and Lynn
for your advice on all things PA,
and to Meg for her valued insight and suggestions.

CHAPTER ONE

OH...THE things the man could do... He was the most creative lover she'd ever had. She'd enjoyed a few but this one was the flame on her Flaming Sambuca. Slithering lower, Sophie Buchanan licked the lingering flavour of blackberries and cream from her lips. As sweet as it was, she was done with dessert.

The silk sheets slid cool and smooth against her skin, the perfect foil for his hard, hot weight as she arched her body beneath him. Wanting more. Wanting everything. And she told him what that was. Every glorious detail.

Then she sighed as he set about fulfilling those requests, starting at her ear lobe and working his way down.

His mouth was warm, wet and wicked, suckling at her neck, laving her collarbone and sending goose bumps from the roots of her hair right down to the tips of her toes and every throbbing place in between. His thumbs, lightly calloused, chafed her sensitised flesh as he tweaked her nipples until...oh...bliss... she was in heaven.

'There's more,' his gravel and whisky voice promised.

She hummed her approval, absorbing the scent and texture of his skin against hers while his hands continued their erotic journey.

Wanting to absorb the feel of his flesh through her fingertips, she slid her fingers slowly down his spine, touching every vertebra in turn, pressing her thumbs into the hard muscle on either side. She was rewarded with a harsh groan that tickled her ear and told her he was enjoying it as much as she.

Then he touched her some more. Everywhere. Everywhere at once. His fingers sought, found and satisfied all her secret places. Ripples of pleasure flowed through her veins like liquid gold—his expertise knew no bounds and it seemed his only desire was to bring her pleasure.

And he did, in *every* way. *Jared…* The name rippled through her mind like silken ribbons in a tropical breeze.

He smiled, traced her mouth with a finger then with his tongue, and she smiled too, before indulging in the most sumptuous of kisses. He tasted rich and dark, like the blackberries and cream they'd shared, and ever-so-slightly dangerous, which was okay, since she knew she was perfectly safe with him.

Yes… Perfection.

He kneed her thighs apart then slid inside her with agonisingly exquisite slowness. It was as if the world forgot to turn. As if it were coming to a stop. And perhaps it was. Perhaps it had ceased to exist, because it seemed it was only the two of them in a sparkling cocoon of everlasting velvet night.

And then…

She heard a moan, as if her voice came from somewhere else, and her eyes slid open, the darkness alive and glowing with wonder, the tidal wave of her climax still crashing around her. She lay a moment listening to the sound of her elevated breathing while her body slowly floated back to earth.

And reality.

She touched her still tingling lips, realised she was still smiling. And why wouldn't she be? Oh…my…goodness.

As her eyes adjusted to night's soft glow through her living-room window, she saw the Gold Coast's languid summer's evening had sprinkled the indigo sky with silver dust.

A dream. And the best sex she'd never had.

Yet even though his image remained tantalisingly vague, she could still taste him on her tongue. Which was as fanciful as it was true, she knew, but that didn't make it any less sumptuous. As dream lovers went he was a five-star keeper. Which, all things considered, was a shame because why weren't there any men out there in the real world to compare?

She shook her head against the cushion. It didn't matter if there were a zillion comparable men beating a path to her door, she wasn't interested. She didn't need—or want—a real man in her life ever again. Not after Glen. He'd destroyed what they had and left her feeling less than a woman. Her dream lovers suited her just fine. Dream lovers were all about you and your wants and they didn't let you down.

Best of all, they were safe.

Her laptop lay on the coffee table, its tiny power light winking in the dimness. Rousing herself, she switched on the reading lamp. *Every luscious detail, before the glory fades.*

Even though she no longer attended counselling sessions, the dream journal she still kept was on her night-stand, so she dragged the computer onto her lap, created a dream folder, flexed her fingers...

His name was Jared, and this dream hottie could scorch her sheets any time he wanted... The words flowed onto the screen, tantalising her all over again. She reread the document, flushing hot as she did so. *Whew*, it was like reading one of those steamy romance novels. What would her counsellor have made of it?

Then her fingers stalled above the keyboard. *Jared?* Her heart thumped once and a jolt of heat arrowed through her body. She didn't know anyone by that name... Unless she counted Jared Sanderson—and it couldn't be him. How could you have the hots for a guy you'd never met, let alone seen up close? Pam's boss. And since her friend was off work sick and Sophie was temping for her, that made him *her* boss for the next day or so.

A shivery sensation shot through her body, making the tiny hairs on the back of her neck and down her arms stand up. A glimpse of dark cropped hair and a snowy white shirt stretched tight over impossibly broad shoulders when she'd arrived at the office of J Sanderson Property Investments and Refurbishments this morning…

She shook the image away. Big boss Jared had been too busy or simply too rude to bother introducing himself to his lowly temporary PA before heading out for the rest of the day.

It wasn't *him*, she told herself firmly. The name had stuck in her mind, that was all. Not to mention that stunning physique… And tall and dark had always been her thing…

No. If he *had* hit her sweet spot on some subconscious level and it had manifested in her dreams, it didn't matter since he'd *never know.*

So it wasn't a problem. Not a problem at all. Nor was she going to allow this particular dream lover to erode the competent professional image she'd worked so hard for. She'd come to Surfers to bury past hurts, to begin a new life.

Professional. It reminded her that she'd not yet emailed the file Pam had asked her to edit before forwarding to the office. Switching to email, she entered the address Pam had supplied and began a brief accompanying note. *Dear Jared…*

She paused. Typing those words redefined the image and rekindled the smouldering heat in her lower body to life again. She fanned a hand in front of her face, a smile tugging at her mouth despite herself. Where the heck was that professionalism?

She deleted the words, then shook her fingers in front of her for a few seconds, pursed her lips and began again. *Mr Sanderson…* Much better. *Please find the Lygon and Partners report attached for your approval. Regards, Sophie Buchanan for Pam Albright.*

She attached Pam's revised document, pressed Send, then closed her computer and the lamp and headed to her bedroom through the shadows. She settled back against the pillows with a sigh. Maybe she'd get lucky some more.

She'd barely closed her eyes when something sharp and hot and possibly terminal lodged dead centre in her chest, and they snapped wide open again. She couldn't have... She *Could Not*.

Jackknifing up, she stumbled back to the living room and her laptop and stabbed the On button. Her fingers twitched with impatience while the little computer took its sweet time powering up. For heaven's sake, could it load any slower?

When her email screen appeared she scrolled to her Sent Items folder and...her breath stopped. Her heart stopped. Everything stopped. *Oh. My. God.*

Her dream file was this very minute awaiting Jared Sanderson's approval.

Her heart restarted and hysterical laughter bubbled up her throat as she quickly attached the correct document and resent. Did the man have a sense of humour? According to Pam, no, he didn't, and her mouth twisted as she blew out a breath.

Even if he did see the humour in the situation, what she'd written was so shockingly...well, shocking. The worst, the very worst of it, was his name was in there. Only his first name, but that was more than enough... She was never ever going to put her sexy dreams in writing again.

The swipe card they'd given her didn't operate the building's front door so there was no point going to the office now to try and delete it. Which meant she'd have to wait till someone opened up in the morning to get into the office. Seven o'clock at the earliest.

With a groan, she let her head fall back and gazed at the ceiling. But she didn't see it. All she saw was the look on the man's face when he opened her email.

She was so dead.

He was an uncle. Jared strolled into his living room just after 10:00 p.m. with two glasses and a bottle of the best Aussie Chardonnay. A niece. Arabella Fleur. Cute as a cupcake, with a mop of dark hair, big eyes and a rosebud mouth. Fingers and toes all accounted for. The grin he'd been wearing since Crystal had delivered her firstborn this afternoon seemed to be permanently carved into his cheeks.

His youngest sister Melissa was home already; he could hear the shower running. Setting the bottle and glasses on the coffee table, he sat on the sofa and checked his phone for messages and the day's office emails. He gave most only a cursory glance. Pam would have phoned with anything urgent.

Sophie Buchanan. The unfamiliar name popped up with a reference to the Lygon report. Ah…now he remembered Pam had gone home sick yesterday. Crystal's nine-fifteen call this morning informing him she was in labour ten days early and that Ian's flight wasn't due in from Sydney for another hour had pushed everything and everyone out of his mind. Sophie must be the temp Pam had organised.

'Hey, Liss?' he called when he heard movement in the hall-way. 'Get your butt in here. We've got some celebrating to do.' He popped the cork and filled the glasses as Melissa appeared in the doorway, wrapped in her robe, her red hair damp about her face.

'Ooh, lovely.' She wasted no time padding across the room and taking the proffered glass.

'Special occasion, *Auntie* Melissa.'

She grinned, clinked her glass to his but remained standing. 'Welcome to the world, Arabella Fleur.' She sipped then said, 'She's got your ears. Nice and flat.'

He tasted the wine, then grinned back, chuffed with the idea that some tiny part of him at least was immortal. 'You think?'

'I do. This is nice.' Another sip, followed by a long, slow swallow. Her brows arched over her aquamarine eyes as she glanced at the label. 'But I still prefer the French variety.'

The bubbles fizzed on his tongue as he studied her. Their father's death had left the three of them orphans. He'd been eighteen, Crystal thirteen, Melissa just six. She'd never known their mother, who'd died when she was two weeks old. When had that little girl become this sophisticated young woman? Too sophisticated. 'You're not supposed to be experienced enough to know the difference.'

'Oh, *pul-lease*, I'm nearly eighteen.' She swung away. 'You sound like a father.'

Her accusation took the shine off. Twelve years ago Jared had taken on the role and responsibilities of both parents. And he didn't regret it for a minute. But sometimes…

'Maybe,' he acknowledged. 'But I won't apologise for it. I love you, Lissa, and that's never going to change.'

'I know.' Her voice softened and she shook her head. 'But sometimes…'

Yeah. Raising Lissa had been the most challenging experience of his life. And he had a feeling the hardest part wasn't done yet. The letting-go part.

'Speaking of fathers…and babies and all…' Twirling her glass, she pinned him with the same intense gaze. 'When are you going to find some poor girl who's willing to put up with your conservative ways and start a family of your own?' *And let me get on with my life,* her eyes said.

To avoid her familiar rant, he picked up his phone again, flicked through his messages once more. 'No hurry. I still have you to look out for.'

She made a noise at the back of her throat. 'You were my age when Dad died. When are you going to get it into your head that I'm an adult, w—'

'Not for another three weeks, you're not.'

'And another thing,' she steamrolled ahead. 'I've been…'

What the…? He blinked, refocused, Melissa's protests fading into the background somewhere. *His name was Jared, and this dream hottie could scorch her sheets any time he wanted—*

'Something wrong?'

'What?' He tore his eyes away momentarily to glimpse

Melissa staring at him. He shook his head, whether in denial or to clear it, he didn't know. 'It's nothing.' Nothing he wanted to share, least of all with his baby sister who'd just accused him of being conservative. *My snakeskin-print G-string melted away beneath the heat of his hand and my thighs fell apart as he—* Whoa.

He threw back a mouthful of the bubbly but the liquid did little to soothe his suddenly very dry, very tight throat. He set the glass down with a clunk.

'Bad news?'

'Not exactly…' Though what *exactly* this was, he didn't know. Yet. But he intended finding out.

'So, as I was saying, I've been giving it some thought, and—'

'Sorry, Liss, I'm going to have to deal with this,' he said, rising. He caught the frustration in her eyes but he couldn't give her his full attention until he'd resolved the hot little matter currently burning a hole in his palm. 'We'll talk later, okay?'

He headed straight for his study and booted up his computer. Drummed his fingers on the desk. The attachment was titled with today's date. No reference to Lygon.

He swiped his palms over day-old stubble, clicked the file open. The text flashed onto the screen. It was pink. Wild, colourful and erotic. Despite himself, he felt a smile tug the corner of his mouth. The more he read, the hotter it became.

The hotter *he* became.

He shifted on his chair to ease a growing pressure beneath the front of his trousers. The scene was so vivid he could almost feel the silky smoothness of her inner thighs, the budded nipple against his palm, her sultry heat as he plunged inside her.

When he'd finished, most of his blood had pooled in his lap. He leaned back, rolled tensed shoulders and shook his head to clear the images. He'd had no idea words alone could turn a man rock hard in less than a minute.

Man, he really needed to get laid.

Sophie Buchanan. Had he met her? He didn't recognise the name, but then he didn't always remember the names of women he'd slept with a few months after the fact. And it *had* been that long. His business and family made sure of that.

Snakeskin print. He grinned to himself. He'd definitely remember snakeskin. And he was pretty sure he'd have remembered that kinky position... Was it even anatomically possible? He was damn well willing to give it his best shot—given the opportunity...

So...Sophie Buchanan must have attached the wrong document to her email. Didn't stop him sending it to his printer. Should he ignore it tomorrow? Mention it to her? Tempting to watch her reaction, but, professionally speaking, in his place of business? Probably not.

She'd sent it thirty minutes ago, he noted. Had she been in bed? In her snakeskin G-string, perhaps. Lust hazed his vision, sweat slicked his palms, his brow, the back of his neck.

Steady, he ordered himself. Then another thought occurred to him. Was this some kind of set-up? Perhaps it was her intention to get him hot and bothered. What if she'd deliberately set out to seduce him? Looking for a more permanent position in his company via his bed. Disgust left a nasty taste in his mouth. Equally distasteful was the thought that she was attracted to his wealth and prepared to do anything to savour some of it.

The printer shot out the first page. That was when he noticed the minuscule print in the footer: *dreamdiary.*

A dream. Scanning the page, he nodded slowly and his smile returned. Okay, that made sense. Some woman's dream fantasy...and he'd been the star attraction. His smile widened to an all-out grin.

What did this woman look like? Masses of unruly wheat-blonde hair. A wickedly clever mouth. Overinflated breasts with large pink nipples. Sexy, supple and spontaneous. Sophie.

Still grinning, he folded the two steaming pages, tucked them in his pocket.

He was looking forward to tomorrow morning.

* * *

From her car parked nearby, Sophie stared through the windscreen of her Mazda hatch. The tall building's glass façade seemed to glint with power and authority in the early morning sunshine. The offices of J Sanderson Property Investments and Refurbishments occupied the top two floors.

Just the thought of what she had to do had her heart pounding into her throat, her fingers white-knuckled on the steering wheel. *He won't be there. Please don't let him be there.* She'd set his agenda yesterday and knew he had a breakfast meeting in Coolangatta, a thirty-minute drive away. He wasn't due at the office until 10:00 a.m.

Which didn't mean squat. In Sophie's experience bosses never did the expected.

She drew in a deep fortifying breath. *Get this over with.* Gripping her bag, she climbed out into the already balmy, salt-scented air, smoothed her fade-into-the-background beige knee-length skirt and headed for the building.

A few people were out on their morning jog along the wide stretch of beach, a soft aqua sea foamed along its edge. Not a suit or briefcase in sight. She checked her watch. Two minutes to seven. She'd not slept a wink, worrying about Jared Sanderson's reaction if he saw her email before she could delete it. If he hadn't already checked his emails from home, that was.

Don't even think about it.

Pam had complained the man never knew when to stop. Sophie's stomach dipped suddenly as if weighted down with a bag of that wet sand beyond, and she quickened her steps.

At the entrance, she fiddled with the collar of her white blouse, ensuring all but the top button was secure. She'd scrunched her thick long hair into a clasp at the back of her head.

She smiled a good morning to the security guy unlocking the door as she withdrew her swipe card from the pocket in the side of her bag and kept moving—not too fast so as to draw attention to herself—to the elevators.

A moment later she stepped out into the hushed Sanderson offices. Quickly skirting the main reception area, she crossed the oblique sun-striped carpet to Pam's desk, then slipped her handbag into the desk drawer.

The room was empty, still and so quiet she could hear the ocean's eternal shoosh beyond the thick glass windows. And the guilty echo of her pulse.

The swipe card gave her access to the Inner Sanctum but she'd not had a reason to enter yesterday. Today, however... Pushing the door open, she registered nothing beyond the scent of leather and electronics as she swooped on the only thing that mattered right now. His desk was L-shaped and the computer was positioned against the wall, which meant if he turned up she'd see him to her left.

She switched the machine on. Waited on a knife's edge. Because her legs were shaky, she barely hesitated before she sat down on his wide leather chair and rolled it forward. The faint fragrance of sandalwood met her nostrils, a heart-stopping reminder that this was a gross invasion of his privacy. She tapped in the password Pam had given her. The email icon appeared, she clicked on it, waiting, barely breathing while the messages rolled down the screen. *There.* Her email. Flagged as unread.

A noise, part sob, part laugh, mostly relief, escaped her as with two swift clicks she deleted the email permanently. Done. Simple.

She leaned back, blew out a long slow breath while her heart continued to thump like crazy against her ribs. I.T. security never audited executive email. Did they?

She would *not* think about that now. She hit the keyboard and brought his day's agenda up on screen. All she had to do was slip back to her desk and no one would—

'Good morning.' The deep masculine voice steamrolled over her senses like steel wrapped in black velvet.

She couldn't have leapt out of the chair quicker if she'd been shot at. Her mind scrambled for words—any words—but to her mortification all that came out was the sound of air rushing past her tonsils.

She got an impression of height, power and stunning sexuality while a pair of enigmatic olive-green eyes studied her. And her stomach dropped to her professional, low-heeled, slingback shoes.

'Ms Buchanan, I presume?'

CHAPTER TWO

How long had he been standing there?

'Yes… Ah… Sophie…' she managed, two stuttering heart-beats later. 'Sophie Buchanan.'

And, oh…he was *gorgeous*, from the sun-bleached tips of his dark brown hair to that clean-shaven jaw that looked strong enough to crack rocks on. From the pressed white shirt and charcoal tie to the fresh sandalwood soap scent winding through her senses. She didn't dare let her gaze wander down the rest of him.

He was the kind of man that made you momentarily forget your own name because you were too busy drawing breath and taking in the view.

For heaven's sake, you could be in serious trouble here, girl. Focus. She dragged the scattered remnants of her business self together. 'Good morning…Mr Sanderson…I was just…I've brought your agenda…up.' Then, as if she hadn't just been hacking into his computer without his knowledge, she walked smartly around from behind his desk, stuck out her hand. Smiled. And, for once, thanked the genes that had bestowed her with a five-feet-ten height advantage—but still it wasn't enough because this man was at least six feet two. 'I'm looking forward to working with you today.'

His firm unyielding palm met hers—an instant zap—and she had to force herself not to think about the way he'd palmed her breasts in her dream last night.

Because nothing surer, this *was* that guy.

And that was bad. Very bad. She didn't *want* her dream lover spilling into her working life and she needed every day's employment she could get. How was she going to face him all day today and not remember how it felt to be made mad, passionate and sizzling love to? And more importantly, not to let it show?

At least he didn't know. He couldn't… Or did he? One corner of his mouth stretched into some semblance of a smile but the eyes…there was a lot going on behind those shadowed green eyes…

'Call me Jared,' he said, still imprisoning her hand within his large firm grip. 'We keep things informal around here.'

Yes, very informal. Smile still frozen in place, she tugged her fingers from his grasp, clasped her tingling hand at her side and reminded herself that he hadn't bothered to introduce himself yesterday. 'Right. Jared—' She practically bit off the word and pressed her lips together. She had *not* just moaned his name the way she had last night, but guilty heat streaked into her cheeks anyway. He was only speaking to her now because she was in his office.

To delete an email from his computer.

The screen of which he was studying, brows lowered. Against her will, her eyes flicked there too, to make sure the file hadn't somehow popped up again. When she looked back at him he was studying her with that same inscrutable expression.

He seemed to shake it away and said, 'I apologise for missing you yesterday, I had to rush off. My sister went into labour and her husband was unavoidably detained. I trust Mimi looked after you?'

The receptionist. 'Yes, she did.' Sophie instantly forgave him for yesterday's lapse. How many guys were so involved with their sisters that they'd rush off to be with them during labour? Unlike her brother, who'd not contacted her since he'd escaped the hell that was their home and moved to Melbourne years ago.

'Did everything go okay?' she said, relieved to have something other than that dreaded email and the sexual buzz that seemed to surround them to focus on. 'What did she have?'

His eyes warmed and, oh, my, he had the most disarmingly crooked grin that kind of creased his left cheek and threatened to buckle her knees.

'Everything went great.' If he'd been the father he couldn't have sounded more delighted. 'It's a girl. Arabella. Three and a half kilos or seven pounds seven ounces in the old money.'

'Wonderful. Lovely name.' She paused. 'So I guess you were busy last night, then. Celebrating?' *Far too busy to catch up on boring old matters such as emails from the office.*

He looked at her with an unsettling directness, as if he'd heard her thoughts. Indeed, as if he knew what she'd been enjoying last night, with him. And more of that blood pumped into her cheeks.

He smiled again, that warmth back in his eyes. 'Melissa and I had a champagne or two.'

Melissa? He was involved. Sophie felt as if something had jabbed her skin and left her deflating piece by piece. She had to force her shoulders back and stand straight. Pam hadn't let her in on that little snippet. She'd told her he didn't have time for relationships, his family took precedence, that women were way down on his list, and, no, he wasn't gay.

Sophie reminded herself quickly and sternly that it made no difference. In fact it was good. Great. Men were off her agenda for life. And she was going overseas in three weeks and five days.

She lifted her chin to demonstrate a confidence she was far from feeling. 'I won't hold you up. I know you have an eight a.m. meeting in Coolangatta.' Thank heavens. She could—

'No rush,' he said in that steel and velvet voice that both startled and enticed.

'I...' She watched the way the muscles in his back shifted beneath the smooth white cotton as he sank into his plush leather chair. Held her breath and waited for her heart to stop while she watched his long tanned fingers work the keyboard and… *Oh, dear…* Remembered those clever fingers working on her body… The sensation peppered her skin with instant goose-bumps.

She shook the fantasy away. More important to worry about how long he'd been watching her at his desk and what he'd seen. From her position, she saw him click off his agenda and bring up his emails. Her stomach tightened. Oh, *no.*

'Wouldn't want to miss anything important…' He glanced sideways at her, although how a glance could scour your eyes for every secret you'd ever kept and last for eternity—

Prickly heat climbed up her neck and her hand rose unsteadily to play with the button at her throat. 'I'll let you get on with it,' she said, backing away before he decided to open his Deleted Items folder and flash her private thoughts onto the screen and…she'd just die of embarrassment. No, no, she reminded her stunned self, she'd deleted it permanently. She was off the hook—

'What's this?' He stilled, leaning closer to the screen, blocking Sophie's view and her heart jumped into her mouth again. 'This is your work, I take it?' He turned slowly towards her. His eyes seemed darker and there was a gleam there that she was sure hadn't been there before.

She found herself backing away from his powerful gaze as if pushed by some physical force. Her hands alternately fluttered and clenched in front of her. 'I can…explain…'

'No need.' He leaned back in his chair, a slow smile touching his lips. 'I left it with Pam but I see you've finished it. Everything looks to be in order, you can email it today.'

The Lygon report. A sigh escaped her lips, instantly bitten off when she caught him still watching her, eyes darker than she'd thought. She straightened. 'I'll get right on it.'

'This afternoon will be soon enough.' He glanced back at the screen, then said, 'Nothing else here that can't wait.'

He rose and she almost sagged with relief. Her legs were like jelly and she really, really wanted to escape to her desk and regroup.

But before she could propel herself forward—rather, backward and away—he opened his briefcase, pulled out a few files. 'Since you're here and obviously enthusiastic to get on with the day, I'd like you to come with me.'

'Me?' *To Coolangatta? With him?* Her breath caught. 'But...'

He looked up sharply. 'Is that a problem?'

Uh oh. A temporary PA's golden rule: do not irritate the boss no matter how short your stay is. 'No. Not at all. Absolutely.' She shook her head, then nodded. Her head spun.

'Good.' His eyes pinned hers so directly, so intensely, she felt as if she were being probed, naked, with twin lasers.

She flicked at her collar, lifted her blouse away from her skin, sticky now despite her morning shower, and flashed him a smile. 'I'll leave a note for Mimi.'

'Fine.' He blinked, then seemed to shake his head, the movement abrupt, and frowned at his watch. 'Better make that call from the car on the way.' He handed Sophie the files without looking at her. 'These need mailing this afternoon.' His voice was clipped as he snapped his case shut. 'Bring Pam's laptop, you can familiarise yourself with the project before we get there. Coffee— Forget it, we don't have time.'

'No worries.' *This* was more like the Jared Sanderson Pam had talked about. Complained about. Adjusting the files in her arms, she swung around to carry them to her desk. 'I'll meet you downstairs in two minutes...'

But he was already out of the door, leaving that spicy fragrance in his wake.

Jared tossed his briefcase and suit jacket onto the back seat of his new pride and joy, his BMW hard-topped convertible, and blew out a strained breath. Took off his cufflinks, slid them into his trouser pocket and rolled his sleeves up—something he never did before meeting a new client. He was a professional and he dressed like one. Every day. He liked routine, the predictability of it.

There was nothing routine about this morning.

Nor was Sophie Buchanan, dream-weaver, what he'd expected. Unlike the brazen and over-endowed vision he'd imagined, she was tall, slim and understated. She wasn't his usual blonde; her hair was the colour of a mid-winter's night. Smooth and sleek and shiny.

He hadn't missed her fragrance on the air when she'd all but leapt off his chair. Not the expensive perfume most women he knew wore, but something light and sparkly, like fresh fruit and summer.

And all he'd been able to see when they'd made eye contact was the disturbing image of her sprawled over his bed wearing nothing but a blackberry-stained smile and dangling a sliver of snakeskin from one finger. It had taken considerable restraint not to yank her against him and find out if the reality was as good as the fantasy she'd described.

She'd deleted the email.

He'd seen the nerves, read the body language and was confident it had been a genuine mistake, not some scheme she'd devised to get his attention.

The devil of it was it *had* got his attention, and in a big way. Just looking at her and knowing what she'd been dreaming had given him a hard-on and he was still feeling its effects. Not a professional image. And knowing all those intimate details, how was he going to deal with having her right outside his office all day?

So why had he asked her to accompany him to Coolangatta? He couldn't resist the smile. Maybe because she was here already and his PA usually accompanied him? The smile teased his lips into a full-on grin. Maybe he wasn't going to change his routine just because Pam was unavailable?

And maybe he wanted to find out more about Sophie

Buchanan. Like why this woman had dreamed sexy dreams about him when they hadn't even met. The trick would be not mixing business and pleasure.

She exited the building, sunshine sparking off her ebony hair as she searched his car out. Unlike her fantasy, her dress code was wishy-washy conservative, but a gust of wind blew the fabric of her blouse against her body, outlining a low-cut bra and subtle yet teasing curves. He leaned across the seat and shoved open the passenger door, slid on his sunglasses and fiddled with his GPS while he waited—hardly courteous, but it was preferable to the alternative of letting her see how she'd affected him.

How her *creative writing* had affected him.

So he wouldn't let the way he'd noticed her hips undulate provocatively as she crossed the car park—not to mention those long tanned legs beneath her fitted skirt—distract his thoughts from the upcoming meeting.

She dropped into the passenger seat as if those spectacular legs were about to give out and he grinned to himself. Dying to know if he knew, wasn't she? But she wasn't asking, and he wasn't telling.

'Been temping long?' he asked as he swung out of the car park.

'A few years. But not for much longer.' He noted she wasted no time opening the laptop.

'Why's that?'

She tapped keys, her attention riveted to the screen. 'I'm going to the UK next month.'

'Oh? Working or sightseeing?'

'Both, I hope.'

'Anything lined up there?'

'Work-wise, not yet. I'll take it as it comes.'

They were cruising south along the Gold Coast Highway, negotiating the morning peak-hour traffic, and he wondered for a moment how it would feel to take off across the globe with no responsibilities and only oneself to think about.

'We'll be meeting with the building's owner and the architect to discuss the project brief,' he informed her. 'You'll find the info in the file labelled CoolCm20. Familiarise yourself with it and be prepared to add to it later.'

They followed the bitumen past Burleigh Heads and crossed the bridge where a glimpse of turquoise water met white sand lined with Norfolk pines. Salty air with a whiff of motor fumes blew through the open window, but at this time of day he preferred the fresh morning breeze to air conditioning.

'So your company offers clients advice on refurbishment projects,' she said, looking up from the file a short time later.

He nodded, checking his rear-view mirror before changing lanes. 'Not only advice. We prepare a complete project brief. Should he or she wish to proceed, we initiate contracts and manage the project to completion.' He glanced her way. 'So you and Pam know each other?'

She nodded. 'We go back a long way. As a matter of fact, we're still neighbours in the same apartment complex.'

'You're from Newcastle too, then.'

'Yes. I moved up here four years ago.'

'With family?'

She shook her head and looked away towards the side window.

'Boyfriend? Partner?' he asked, glancing her way again when she didn't elaborate. He saw her shoulders tense, her jaw tighten.

'I needed a change of scenery,' was all she said.

Obviously it wasn't only the scenery she'd wanted to change. Someone had hurt her. None of his business, Jared told himself. He didn't need to know her life history. He was only interested in the Sophie who was sitting beside him right now. The one who smelled as fresh as the morning and dreamed about him.

He couldn't help the smile that threatened to give him away every time he thought about it. The idea of this quietly professional woman playing out those erotic fantasies with him had grasped him firmly between his thighs and wasn't about to let go.

Unless he did something about it…

Change of scenery. If only it had been that simple. Sophie refocused her gaze on the safety of the computer screen. How could she have stayed in Newcastle knowing she might bump into Glen and his new lover—his new *pregnant* lover? Which was inevitable given their mutual friends and working environments. She hadn't wanted their pitying glances and platitudes so she'd moved to the Gold Coast and taken a business course.

But recurring childhood nightmares had continued to hound her, screwing with her life, making her ill until she'd had no alternative but to seek professional help. Her counsellor had suggested a dream diary and they'd used it to work through her emotional issues. Her abused childhood, her failure as a woman. Even the fact that she'd sought help was still, to her, a failure.

She'd come a long way since arriving in Surfers but the past still haunted her at the oddest times. A word tossed out and she was back in her childhood purgatory, her disastrous marriage. Nightmares were few and far between these days but she still recorded her dreams. A security thing, she supposed.

At least Jared had taken the hint and not pursued further conversation as the car sped south. It gave her a moment to shake off the bad. The bad was gone, over, done, she reminded herself. As Roma had told her at her final session, *good times ahead.* And that was what it was all about, right? Refocusing on the present, Sophie resumed her attention to the upcoming meeting.

She reread the document on the screen for the umpteenth time. She couldn't remember a darn word. It was as if her mind had shut out everything except her awareness of the man beside her. Right now his forearm relaxed on the steering wheel. Suntanned, sprinkled with dark hair and sporting an expensive-looking watch, ropes of sinew shifting as he swung out from behind a truck and changed lanes.

She jerked her eyes back to the screen. This infatuation, or whatever it was, was not going to get her paid at the end of the day. She reminded herself he was unavailable. Involved with someone else. Focused on family and his high-flying career. And most important: she wasn't interested in getting involved.

It should have been easy to push it aside and if it hadn't been for that stupid dream this whole attraction thing never would have happened. Would it?

'No special guy, then?'

The question asked in that deep voice jerked her out of her self-talk and put her immediately on the defensive. She focused her gaze on the road ahead. 'I don't see how having a man in my life is relevant to my ability to do my job.'

He was silent for a beat, as if considering her snarky response. Then he said, 'I generally find women in steady relationships make for more stable employees.'

'Only women?' How sexist was that? But she didn't say it. She'd done enough damage in the past twelve hours. She just wanted to do her job with a minimum of fuss and attention and get paid at the end of the day. Then she never had to see him again.

'Rest assured, I have a strong and committed work ethic, Mr Sanderson—Jared. And while we're on the topic, how about women in *no* relationship?'

And why the heck had she said that? Was her subconscious *trying* to get her into trouble?

With smooth efficiency, he overtook a shiny red Porsche. 'Which category do you fall into?'

'Does it matter?'

'It might.'

A sharp excitement stabbed through her, followed closely by one of anger. She forgot her decision not to look at him. His profile—his very strong, very masculine profile—betrayed no clue as to what he was thinking. 'What do you mean "it might"?'

What about Melissa? Did he think she'd forgotten? Not noticed? No matter how gorgeous his looks, no matter what she'd fantasised, she did *not* play the other woman. She knew how it felt to be left for someone else.

'I need to know whether you're expected home this evening,' he continued as they neared their destination. 'I missed work yesterday, which means we'll need to work late tonight to catch up.'

'Oh.' The barely audible word escaped her lips as the implication sank in. Just him and her alone in his office. To catch up on *work*. How ridiculously foolish and pathetic she was, to have assumed he'd had something more on his mind.

'No one's expecting me. I live alone.' She hoped her face wasn't as pink as it felt. Still, it wouldn't have mattered since he didn't even glance her way.

'You don't have other plans, I hope.'

'No.' And from his tone she rather gathered that she'd have had to cancel if she had. Pam had warned her the man was work-driven and focused and expected the same of his staff.

'Which reminds me...' He indicated his phone on the console between them while he adjusted his earpiece. 'Get Melissa for me, please. She's on speed dial.'

'Melissa.' Her stomach dipped, clenched, but she did as he requested, then turned away and watched the scenery slip by. High-rise apartments and businesses interspersed with strips of green and pandanus trees and now glimpses of blue sea. She wouldn't allow herself to feel uncomfortable.

'Lissa, hi, it's me. I won't be home for tea, I'm working back.' Brisk and to the point. Pause. 'I don't have time to talk about that now, Liss. I have someone with me.' He lifted his sunglasses to rub the bridge of his nose. 'Later. And tell Cryssie I'll call by the hospital tomorrow for sure. Yeah. Bye.'

Sophie couldn't pretend she hadn't heard the conversation. The way that smooth tone had roughened with something that sounded close to exasperation.

'My sister,' he muttered.

A tiny shiver danced down her spine and she remained motionless a moment, lips pressed together to stop the smile threatening at the corners of her mouth and trying not to feel ridiculously...what? Pleased? Excited? Delighted?

She shouldn't be feeling any of those things.

Leather creaked as he shifted in his seat. She saw the movement from the corner of her eye, saw him glance at her as he exhaled an impatient breath through his nostrils. 'I fail to see the humour. Ever tried reasoning with a seventeen-year-old girl?'

Her smile bubbled over into a laugh and she glanced his way. Clenched jaw. Hands a little tight on the steering wheel. Speedo a little high as they cruised along the esplanade and into Coolangatta. 'Can't say I have. But I've been one, so I can tell you it does get better.'

He made some non-committal noise as he pulled to a stop outside a four-storey apartment block and switched off the ignition. 'It can be a challenge at times.'

He spoke as if he were Melissa's parent rather than her brother. Or maybe it was just that brothers were never meant to get along with their sisters. Yet she knew that wasn't true. The dysfunctional household she'd been brought up in had tainted and distorted her perception of family life and love.

'Do you have siblings?' His voice interrupted her thoughts.

'A brother. In Melbourne.'

Somewhat surprised by her instant switch from bright and chirpy to gloom and doom, Jared reached for his jacket on the back seat. 'You're not close?'

She followed his lead, gathering her bag and laptop. 'I haven't seen him in years, so no.' She peered through the windscreen at the nondescript grey building behind a cyclone fence. 'This is the place?'

'Yep.'

Jared had been itching to get another good look at her since they'd left Surfers but the traffic had been snarly and required his full attention. Now he took a moment. The brandy-coloured eyes had lost that desperation he'd seen in his office and he doubted the hint of blush on her high wide cheekbones was make-up—more likely her natural colour. And her lips... they were something else. Full, luscious-looking and caramel glossed...they promised to taste as sweet...

Damn it, not now.

He reminded himself this wasn't a date, ordered his unruly body to cooperate and forced his attention to the building in front of them while he rolled down his sleeves. 'You have to think potential, Sophie.'

He'd made his fortune by seeing possibilities and making them happen. He'd been a millionaire at twenty-seven because he dared to dream and didn't let others tell him it wasn't possible.

'I'm afraid I'm not very imaginative.'

His gaze swung back to her just as she turned to him with a stunned tell-me-I-didn't-say-that expression and their gazes locked and for a beat out of time the spectre of that dream fantasy smouldered in the tiny space between them. 'I don't believe that for a moment.'

'Believe it,' she muttered, and, pushing out of the car, she started walking.

He shrugged into his jacket, grabbed his briefcase from the back seat and caught up with her along the path. Without further comment she accompanied him to the main door where they met the owner, Sam Trent, and Ben Harbison, an architect who'd worked with Jared on several projects. After a briefing in Sam's office, they spent half an hour inspecting the premises while Sophie took notes. For the remainder of the meeting, she worked unobtrusively at one end of the table, the only sound the quiet click of her keyboard.

Unobtrusive? For the second time in as many minutes Jared looked up from the plans in front of him, his gaze unerringly finding Sophie. Focused on her task, she wasn't giving him a second's glance.

How did she manage cool concentration when he couldn't? Her fast, efficient fingers with their clear-varnished nails were the cause of the clicking and Jared couldn't stop thinking about them being fast and efficient in other ways, as she'd described in her dream. And whenever the breeze wafted through the open window, it wasn't the sea air but her fragrance that floated to his nostrils.

The meeting wrapped up at nine-fifteen. He was glad his ten o'clock appointment didn't require his PA. And his eleven-fifteen would keep him busy until lunch. Only the afternoon to get through, he thought, watching the little hollows behind her knees she bent over to retrieve her bag from the floor.

Swinging his gaze away, he focused on Sam's conversation while he stuffed a couple of files into his briefcase. Reminded himself again that he didn't get involved with employees.

However, a couple of hours of working back this evening would clear yesterday's clutter and when the work was finished Sophie's two-day fill-in for Pam would be over. She would no longer be in his employ…

CHAPTER THREE

'YOUR ten o'clock cancelled,' Sophie informed Jared as they walked to the car.

A hunger fist clenched around her stomach. She hadn't had time for breakfast. And she'd refused Sam's offer for refreshment because she hadn't been sure she'd keep it down she was so uptight, and had stuck to her bottled water. 'He'll ring back this afternoon and reschedule.'

Jared aimed the remote at the car and the alarm blipped. 'In that case, I'd like to make another stop before we head back.'

She'd been hoping for some time and space back at the office. Alone at her desk. She didn't want to be anywhere near him, inhaling his scent, listening to his voice and wondering... This on-the-edge-of-the-seat feeling that Jared might have read her diary was killing her. In a way it was almost worse than knowing. At least if she knew, she could make some attempt to deal with it. But she wasn't going to risk asking.

It was a beautiful day with the sky's blue dome reflecting on the sea. Ridges of surf scrolled along the sand, already dotted with beach-goers. Right now Sophie wished she were one of them. No boss to stress over, just a day of relaxation stretched out to enjoy. Or better still, to be one of the gulls wheeling high and low over the ocean.

As she watched Jared open the boot she reminded herself she'd be as free as those gulls in just under four weeks. He dropped his gear in, motioned her to do the same with Pam's laptop. He shrugged out of his jacket once more, then to her surprise he yanked off his tie and tossed it in the boot with the rest of his stuff, and said, 'What do you say to fish and chips?'

Now? What was wrong with muesli and fruit and a nice hot coffee? 'It's only nine-twenty—'

'First off, do you like fish and chips? And I'm not talking the fast-food skinny-mini deals but the old-fashioned crisp on the outside, soft in the middle and wrapped in butcher paper kind.'

'I do, but—'

'So forget the office—and the boss—for an hour and take a break. I know a little seafood shop here that's open early. They do take-away cappuccino too, if you need your caffeine fix.'

Forget the office? Take a break? She'd barely done an hour's work. Forgetting the boss wasn't going to happen and fish and chips at nine-thirty on a weekday?

Was this happy-looking, suddenly smiling man the same man Pam said was all work and no play? There had to be a catch.

'O-k-ay.' She smiled back, blinded by that knee-weakening crease. It really should be registered as a deadly weapon.

One block back from the esplanade and a few moments' walk brought them to a row of shops. They passed a bakery and its rich scent of coffee and fresh bread. Sophie slowed her steps, all but drooling at the window selection, but then Jared laid a casual hand on her shoulder.

She jumped at the startling contact as he steered her past the shop with barely there persuasion. It seemed an easy relaxed gesture, except that she was super aware of the slight pressure of his fingers on her collarbone, like a low-grade current tickling her flesh. Aware also of the sun-warmed fragrances of clean cotton and masculine skin surrounding her.

As if he knew she'd been about to forgo chips in ten minutes in favour of a sticky bun *right now*, he dipped his head and said, 'It'll be worth the wait.' His voice was lazy and layered with all the richness of the Black Forest gateau she'd just salivated over.

'Is that a promise?' She heard her own voice echo that same tone and her suddenly dry tongue cleaved to the roof of her mouth. Her heart rate accelerated as she turned and looked up at him. They *were* talking food, weren't they?

His expression revealed nothing...but had his eyes gone darker? 'You can tell me afterwards.'

'Right.' His eyes *were* darker. And up close she noticed the distinctive olive green was ringed with a fine rim of navy. She also noticed they'd stopped walking. He was still touching her and her flesh was still tingling.

She hitched her bag higher so that his hand slid away, and resumed walking, but he was close enough so that their arms bumped, a too-delicious friction of firm flesh, crisp shirt and masculine hair.

A moment later he slowed again, this time outside a bright shop called The Baby Tree with teddies spilling out of prams and the cutest little baby outfits suspended from colourful chains. 'Come on. Help me choose something for my new niece. Thirty seconds. What do you think—a teddy or that fluffy red kangaroo?'

For one trembly moment of indecision Sophie stared at the pretty window and the pair of tiny overalls covered in roses with a matching sunhat. The rainbow selection of lace booties. And yearned.

Then the familiar chill that accompanied such visions swirled through her heart and she shivered in the balmy air. She hadn't set foot in a baby shop since— In a long time.

'I'm not really a baby person.' She spun away from the window and gazed at the shop across the street, but didn't see it. 'Don't let me stop you, though.' Without looking at him, she dredged up a smile from somewhere and pasted it on her lips, while groping in her bag for her sunglasses. Hoping she looked more careless and indifferent than she felt, she waved in the direction they'd been heading. 'I'll go ahead and order.'

She slid on the glasses, turned and walked. *One foot in front of the other.* Her smile dropped from her lips and she was conscious of the residual sweaty palms and heavy heartbeat. Of all the shops he could have chosen, he'd stopped at The Baby Tree.

It had caught her off guard. With most of her friends down the coast in Newcastle, over the past four years it had been easy to avoid the baby trap. Pam was seriously single and Sophie's focus was her upcoming overseas trip. *Not* making babies and playing happy families.

Those things hadn't worked for her.

She'd be ready next time he pulled that trick. Next time? She coughed out a half-laugh. Hardly. After today she wouldn't have to see Jared Sanderson again. She kept her eyes peeled for the fish shop, but she hadn't gone farther than a couple of metres along the footpath when he caught up.

He fell into step beside her. 'Hey.'

His tone was bland and she couldn't decide if he was annoyed or concerned. Please, God, anything but concern. She could deal with annoyance, indifference, even anger, but concern... Concern could weaken her resistance, leaving her vulnerable. Again. She refused to allow anyone too close. Giving your love, your trust, yourself to someone else only brought heartbreak. She'd learned that lesson too.

Jared must have caught the vibes; he'd put at least an arm span between them and guilt pierced the self-preservation she normally surrounded herself with. 'I really don't mind. She's your sister... If you want to—'

'No big deal, I'll do it later. We're here.' He stopped at the next wide glass door and pushed it open, the air-conditioned swirl mingling with the aroma of hot fat.

'Rico. *Buongiorno.*'

'*Buongiorno.*' The rotund swarthy man beaming at Jared as

if he was some long-lost friend looked to be in his late forties. He also looked as if he'd been dining on his own menu for a good many of those years. 'Didn't expect to see you down this way today.'

'Had a spare hour.'

'And you haven't come alone.' He shone his beam on Sophie.

'Rico, meet Sophie. Sophie, Rico. A serve of your best chips to go, please, my friend. And a cappuccino for my hard-working colleague here.'

'Very happy to make your acquaintance, Sophie.' Rico winked at her as he scooped chips into a wire basket, lowered it into the fryer. 'If this man doesn't treat you right, I have a brother. Has his own seafood restaurant in Broadbeach. He's single and better looking.'

Sophie shoved her sunglasses on top of her head. She glanced at Jared, caught him looking at her and didn't quite smother her grin. 'I'll keep it in mind.'

'Get Jared to take you there for dinner one night.'

She jerked her gaze back to Rico. 'Oh…no. I'm…we're not… dating.'

His thick black brows rose, then a look of pure devilment danced in his dark eyes. 'Why not?'

'I'm just temping at Jared's office for the day…' Why had she said the D word, for heaven's sake? Rico had no doubt meant a business dinner. But it had just burst out…and, oh, she wished the floor would open up and swallow her.

'Don't listen to him, Sophie,' Jared said, his voice tinged with amusement, and to Rico, 'Did you go over those figures with Enzo yet?'

And just what had Jared meant by that look he'd given Rico? To her relief, he seemed to have forgotten she was there already. To keep from feeling like a spare part and to give them some privacy since they were discussing business, she crossed to one of the little round tables by the window, sat down and flicked through a well-thumbed women's magazine.

Anything to keep from looking at him. Or admiring the cut to the trousers that showcased long legs and firm butt and imagining… *No.* Frowning, she forced herself to refocus on the latest celebrity break-up.

Her eyes remained on the page but her mind worked as the guys talked. The familiarity and bond between the two was obvious. Jared hadn't taken an hour out of his day to 'forget about the office' and entertain her. He'd used the opportunity to catch up with Rico and make it seem as if he were doing Sophie a favour at the same time. Very clever.

'Bring your coffee,' he said, dragging her out of her contemplation, 'and let's go see the beach.'

They took their white paper-wrapped package to the esplanade and sat on a bench overlooking the sand. The sea's *boom-dump* vibrated through the soles of her feet. The gulls swooped in noisily from nowhere the moment Sophie unwrapped the shared snack. She took a chip, broke it open, popped a piece in her mouth. Then she threw the other half to the birds to watch them squawk and squabble while she sipped at her much anticipated frothy cappuccino.

'You're right, they're yummy,' she said, reaching for another while carefully avoiding Jared's fingers. She hadn't eaten chips this good since she couldn't remember when.

'Haven't done this in a while,' Jared said, popping the top on his can of soda.

'Probably just as well. Salt, fat, calories. Too much of a good thing…'

Sophie watched, mesmerised as he downed his cola in deep slow swallows that made his Adam's apple bob amazingly. He lifted his lips from the can a moment and smiled, eyes twinkling. 'You can never have too much of a good thing, Sophie.'

Oh, the way he said that, all luscious and low as if he was talking about sex. And drawing her attention to his lips, wet with the cola...and they'd be cool and sweet...

Not going there.

She plucked another fat, fragrant chip, slid it between her lips and, closing her eyes, savoured every drop of excess. If she couldn't have sex, at least she could eat. 'So...' Licking the salt from her fingers, she opened her eyes once more to find him still watching her. More precisely, watching her mouth. 'That's your opinion and you're sticking to it.'

'A good thing is only a good thing for as long as you enjoy it.'

Glen had lived by that code too, Sophie remembered. She drained her coffee to mask the sudden bitterness in her mouth. 'Then what? You discard it for another passing fancy?'

'If it's not bringing you pleasure, then yeah.'

Her fingers tightened around the polystyrene cup. 'Sounds totally self-absorbed to me.'

He laughed. 'Probably. And why not? So long as it's not hurting anyone else...'

'Exactly.' She relented. Okay, maybe he didn't include relationships in that particular philosophy. It seemed he genuinely cared about people. Rico. His sisters. Even Pam. He was one of the good guys after all. And mega rich, mega gorgeous, mega motivated.

She noticed his gaze had turned speculative and probing. Something glimmered in the green depths and her heart skipped a beat. Did he read minds as well? Looking away, she took aim and tossed her empty cup neatly into the trash can.

'What about your favourites list? What can't you have too much of, Sophie?'

You. Naked. Inside me.

Her skin warmed, prickled, and she swore every internal organ turned to mush. She felt like an over-ripe peach, ready to be plucked, split apart and plundered. Gloriously and within an inch of her life.

Liquid heat gathered between her thighs and she bit the inside of her lip. Had she just accused *him* of being self-absorbed? Behind her sunglasses she met his unshielded gaze and reminded herself of what she really wanted these days. 'Wealth,' she said, reaching for the bottled water in her bag. She sucked it down with a vengeance. 'And independence.'

He looked surprised, as if he'd expected her to say something indulgent or female, like chocolate or shoes. A crease dug a groove between his brows. 'Sounds a little sad and lonely.'

'Why?' Annoyed with his response, she tipped her bottle in his direction. 'You don't strike me as lonely. Or sad. You've obviously worked towards those same goals all your life, and by all accounts you've succeeded better than most.' Which made him a hypocrite or sexist or both. 'So don't tell me you're not happy with your success.'

'That goes without saying and I assume you're talking financial success. But mostly I'm happy because I don't allow myself to think any other way. Doesn't mean I don't have my disappointments.'

Not knowing how to respond, she nodded as she reached for another chip. With his wealth and charisma, she'd not thought of Jared as a man to experience setbacks. Which was totally naïve of her. Everyone had setbacks. It was how one dealt with them.

He gave the impression that he was powerful enough to accomplish whatever he wanted, but she knew nothing of his background or what obstacles he'd overcome to get to where he was.

Before she could form a question around that, he said, 'I take it family and kids figure somewhere in all that wealth and independence.'

A few years ago Sophie's answer would have been an un-equivocal yes. Despite the emotional trauma she'd experienced

growing up in a family where booze and violence were the
norm, she'd always believed it could be different for her. All
those years of growing up with her collection of dolls and
romantic ever afters, but now...

Reality check.

For the second time in less than an hour a reminder that her
female body had let her down in the baby-making department.
Which was hardly relevant since she had no intention of getting serious with a man, ever again. Still, it was failure and
she chugged on her water bottle to take a moment to compose
herself.

She pushed herself up from the bench, grateful for her sunglasses shield. 'Not me.' She laughed, turning seaward and
throwing her hands wide. 'Why tie yourself down with kids
when you can travel the world? Do what you choose when you
choose. Live life the way you want.' She turned to him and
nodded. 'Yes, I'm completely and unashamedly selfish. I admit
it.'

Shading his forehead with a hand, Jared studied her through
eyes squinted against the beach's glare. Hard to tell if she was
being completely truthful because he couldn't read her eyes
behind her sunglasses. Thanks to her, he'd left his own damn
sunglasses in the car. She'd thrown him off course last night
with her dream, and twelve hours later nothing had changed.

'Good for you,' he said, crushing the empty chip wrapper
and standing too. 'I like an honest woman who's not afraid to
say what she means.'

Why not take her at her word? he decided. He had no reason
not to. So she admitted she was selfish—didn't matter to him
in the great scheme of things. Besides, he had a feeling she
wasn't as self-absorbed as she let on. He picked up his empty
cola can and headed for the bin. 'It's time to make a move.'

At least she was upfront about what she wanted, he mused
as they drove back to Surfers. Rico was right—Sophie was a

beautiful woman. And red hot to boot. He'd not had a woman in too long, which was why his skin felt as if it were on fire and he couldn't for the life of him, get her out of his head. Beautiful. Single. Living in the moment.

Bianca had been the same, he remembered, with her wild sensual beauty and Bohemian lifestyle. God only knew why— when he thought about it with the wisdom of five years more maturity—but he'd fancied himself in love and had asked her to marry him.

But Bianca had refused to accept twelve-year-old Melissa as part of the deal. Something Jared didn't compromise on was Melissa's well-being, so it had been bye-bye Bianca.

After he'd picked up the pieces of his heart and fitted them back together, he'd realised he and Bianca would never have made it work in the long term.

But circumstances were different now. Melissa was more or less independent even if she did still live at home. So…if he and Sophie got together… From the outset he knew Sophie wasn't going to be long term. She was going overseas, so there was no possibility of anything serious developing between them.

Not that he could ever get serious with a happy wanderer who didn't like kids. He wasn't looking for marriage right now, but when he settled down he wanted a woman who held the same values he did. A lifetime commitment to family. Sharing, trust. And children.

But that wasn't now.

A few weeks with no-strings Sophie wouldn't be a hardship. Wouldn't be a hardship at all… He just had to seduce Sophie a little, tempt her with a taste of her own desires, her private fantasies… He ran a hand around the back of his neck, shifted on the seat as his blood pumped a little faster around his body. Then a smile touched his lips. Who knew her desires better than him? Who better than Jared to make those fantasies a reality?

CHAPTER FOUR

MEETINGS took up the rest of the morning. In the afternoon Jared escorted a millionaire businessman from Dubai and his entourage on a tour of inspection of a dozen complexes and resorts. Negotiations followed over a late lunch in one of Surfers Paradise's top restaurants.

He'd left Sophie an overflowing outbox and several reports to edit, file, print, mail.

Jared would be the first to acknowledge that Pam was a brilliant PA. She knew her stuff, was ruthlessly efficient, indispensable, in fact, and he'd hate to lose her. But he had to admit that behind her desk she tended to merge into the background.

Not Sophie Buchanan.

On his return at five-thirty, before he reached his office he could smell that sparkling fresh fragrance that had been spinning inside his head all day, making him think inappropriate thoughts. Taking his focus away from work.

Instead of concentrating on ways to convince Najeeb Assad that transforming an aging condominium building into a slice of paradise was a sound business decision, Jared had been visualising Sophie astride him on his office chair, her fragrant skin glowing with a sheen of sweat while she rode him hard and fast…

To Jared's relief, Mr Assad had concurred with his suggestions for renovation, but it could easily have gone the other way—and that concerned him. Jared had never allowed himself or his work to be sidetracked by a woman before.

It reinforced his belief that it was an idiot boss who got personally involved with his employees. So he afforded Sophie only a brief acknowledgement on his way through late in the afternoon, issuing a practical, 'Can I see you in my office with those reports you worked on yesterday in thirty minutes, please?'

Blowing out a breath, he dropped into his chair. With Pam due back tomorrow, he needed to go over yesterday's work with Sophie. But in a couple of hours he could loosen up and enjoy getting to know her better. On a more personal level.

Meanwhile he pulled out this afternoon's paperwork, skimmed it before setting it aside and working through the day's emails. From his position he couldn't see her beyond his door, but he could hear her moving around, the sounds of her desk drawer opening, closing.

Five minutes before she was due, the quick *rat-a-tat* had him half rising as he looked up from his screen. The smile already on his lips stalled… 'Lissa. Hi. I wasn't expecting you.'

Her brows rose. 'Clearly. You look stunned. Rabbit-caught-in-headlights stunned. So who *were* you expecting?' Not anticipating an answer, she crossed the room, set a bag of Chinese takeout in front of him. 'I was on my way home and remembered you said you were working late. Extra Special Fried Rice from the Lotus Pearl. See, I do care about you.'

Its spicy aroma steamed through the plastic carry bag. He wondered if he could extend it to two. 'Thanks, Liss, that's very thoughtful of you and I appreciate it, but I'm not working alone tonight.'

'Didn't you say Pam was off sick? Ah-h-h…' He'd never seen that knowing, womanly expression on his baby sister's face and it threw him for a loop. 'You mean that attractive long-legged brunette in the staffroom lounge making café lattes—for *two*.' Her grin widened—irritatingly so. '*That* kind of working late.'

'No, Liss.' Resisting the temptation to rub the back of his

neck, he pushed out of his seat and grabbed a folder on his bookshelf. 'That's *not* it.'

'I believe you.' She pressed her lips together but the sparkle of humour in her eyes betrayed her. Rising up on tiptoe, she pecked his cheek and murmured, 'Don't work too hard. Or too late.'

Sophie stopped dead outside Jared's door, a café latte in each hand. The sight of the petite but gorgeous Titian-haired female kissing his jaw had her stomach knotting in a strange way. So his almost-flirty conversation this morning had been her imagination. The imagination she'd told him she didn't have.

Her imagination was working just fine now.

As she watched the redhead turn towards the door, Sophie's inner turmoil grew. The girl must be at least a decade younger than him.

And Sophie could cast stones? Hadn't Sophie been years younger than Glen? So young, too young. Too young to know the dangers of falling for the wrong type of man. All she'd wanted was an escape, to feel safe, to belong with someone. To matter. Instead, she'd jumped from one disaster into another.

Before Sophie could analyse her way out of the instant over-reaction, the girl caught sight of her and smiled. 'Hi.' Her aquamarine eyes sparked with feminine curiosity and friendly interest and Sophie couldn't help but like her even though her stomach was tied in double knots.

'I'm sorry,' she murmured. 'I'll come back.'

Jared looked up, bright eyes finding hers. 'No, it's okay, come in. Melissa, this is Sophie.'

Sophie propelled herself towards Jared's desk with a breathy kind of, 'Hi.'

He leaned across and rescued the listing lattes from her stiff fingers. 'Liss brought some fried rice by.'

'That was kind.' Ridiculously relieved for the second time today, Sophie smiled back, her gaze darting between the two but finding no resemblance. Charm and charisma obviously ran in the family, however. 'Pleased to meet you, Melissa.'

'Likewise.' Her voice practically bounced with enthusiasm as she stepped back. 'I'll leave you two to get on with whatever...' With a glance at her brother, she swung her bag onto her shoulder, then smiled at Sophie on her way out. 'Get Jared to bring you over some time.'

'Ah...hmm. Bye for now.'

Was there some sort of conspiracy going on? She could have reiterated that she was temping for the day, that they weren't dating, but she'd been there, said that, this morning. Now hot, flustered and empty-handed, she made an abrupt about-turn as Melissa passed, murmuring, 'I'll just get those reports...'

When she reached her desk, she pressed both palms on its smooth cool surface and took a deep calming breath. Closed her eyes a moment and listened to the muted office sounds as the few staff still remaining closed down computers or chatted outside the elevator bank.

Why was everyone so interested in Jared's social life? More incredible and disturbing were suggestions that she be involved. The fact that he shared a place with his sister surprised her. Surely a man like him would have his own apartment and want to do his own no-doubt-frequent 'entertaining' without a kid sister around, even if said sister was practically an adult?

Sophie didn't care what Pam said, a man with that much sex appeal must have women falling over themselves to get his attention. Pam had meant the workplace, where he was by all accounts legendary for his strict workplace ethics.

And this was the workplace.

Ergo, anything remotely flirty or sexual was off-limits.

Their quick trip to Coolangatta this morning had been a time-out away from the office, Sophie reasoned, hence a little more relaxed. A teensy bit flirty even. But since they'd been back around mid-morning he'd certainly been all business, barely noticing her except to slide some paperwork across her desk to be mailed just before he disappeared around lunchtime for the rest of the day.

Satisfied—and relieved—that the next couple of hours would be no different, she'd lifted the documents and files she'd organised for the evening's session off her desk and turned... to find Jared watching her from the doorway.

And looking anything but business.

The sun had set but the high-rise office was still bathed in the sky's ruddy reflection, painting his skin a swarthy bronze, contrasting with his shirt, which glowed like a white-hot coal. Against the files, her fingers twitched with the itch to stroke his skin and discover if it was as warm and firm as it looked.

As it had felt in her dream.

Sophie inwardly moaned that if she hadn't dreamt about him she wouldn't be having these totally inappropriate thoughts. She prided herself on being a professional. She did *not* gaze at her boss as if she wanted to lick her way up the side of his throat, over his prominent Adam's apple, along his firm afternoon-shadowed jaw to that luscious-looking mouth...

She barely refrained from darting her tongue out to moisten her newly glossed lips courtesy of the quick pit-stop in the Ladies. Which would be a disaster since Jared's gaze seemed to be focused on them with what looked like impatience. Probably waiting for her to explain why she'd been taking so long with the files.

'I do love sunsets, don't you?' she said into the loaded silence and hefted the documents higher against her chest as a kind of barrier.

'Yes. Especially when it's shared with a nice bottle of wine and good company.' He didn't so much as glance towards the window.

'Shall we get started, then?' *No,* she wailed silently as soon as she voiced the words. That came out wrong. Particularly since he was still looking at her lips and she was still drooling over that dusky jaw.

He walked towards her and didn't stop until he was one skinny latte away from her personal space. She didn't move. Just breathed in the scent of his shirt—a day's work mingled with man.

His gaze rose from her lips to meet hers and she realised the one thing she hadn't noticed in her dream was his eyes. That unusual blend of olive and navy. The creases that fanned out from the corners and the long, long eyelashes. How his irises took on the colour of the sunset…or was that gleam she saw there now something else? Speculation? Attraction?

An intimate knowledge of the contents of her diary?

She shivered, caught between desire and dread, but then he reached out, relieved her of the files, thank goodness, because the shiver had spread to her limbs.

If he noticed, he hid it well, suggesting, 'How about that coffee first before it gets cold?'

Rubbing her fingers over the goose-bumps on her upper arms, she murmured, 'Good idea.' The tone in his voice brought everything back to a business level and Sophie forced thoughts of her diary away. 'I hope you like latte—I asked Mimi and she said she thought you did.'

He nodded. 'Anything with caffeine will be welcome around now.'

She followed him into his office, pulled up a chair in front of the paperwork, curled her fingers around her mug for something to grip. To avoid any personal questions or to fill the silence in this strange electrified atmosphere that had sprung up in the past few moments, she asked, 'So…does Melissa have your keen business acumen?'

Jared sat too, drawing his mug close with both hands. 'If she does, she's keeping it to herself. At the moment she's studying design. For her it's all about colour and taking her inspiration from the environment. She's very talented, if I do say so myself.' He smiled. 'A big brother's prerogative.'

Was it? she thought darkly. Hers hadn't thought so. 'Your parents must be very proud of all their children.'

'Our parents are dead.' The dispassionate way he said it sent a chill down her spine.

'Oh…I…' She trailed off, sensing that beneath the utter lack of emotion on his face there was sorrow and anger he no doubt didn't want to share with his temporary employee. 'I'm sorry,' she muttered and immediately could have bitten off her tongue for that tired cliché.

He looked at her as if he'd heard that platitude one time too many, then brought the mug to his lips and swallowed. 'It was a long time ago.'

She should leave it there but she couldn't. She wanted to know more about this man who'd obviously been more than just a brother to his sisters. And now she knew why. He'd taken on a responsibility few other guys would have been willing to do. 'Was…it an accident?'

He shook his head, a faraway look in his eyes. 'Mum died two weeks after Lissa was born. Liss turns eighteen in three weeks.' Then it was as if a winter wind swept over his gaze. 'Dad was killed driving under the influence twelve years ago.' His voice turned brisk and he rose. 'And if we don't eat this rice now the aroma's going to be a distraction.' His quick glance her way told her they had enough distraction to deal with already. 'We can share while we get down to business.'

So he'd changed his mind about a sociable coffee break. Sophie knew it was because the conversation had hit an exposed nerve. She opened the nearest file.

They sipped on their lattes and dipped their forks into the fluffy rice mixture while she brought him up to speed. Rather, he drank and ate while she talked. Which was fine because it helped calm her.

He was a courteous listener, focused on the work spread before them and what she was saying. Putting her at ease. He even asked her opinion on a couple of major proposals he was considering.

Temping wasn't the most satisfying of jobs, but today, thanks to her boss, she felt as if she'd made a contribution. He'd made her feel welcome, and, more importantly, she felt valued as an employee, even if it was temporary.

'We'll call it a day.' He closed the folder they'd been working on.

'Already?' She glanced up, noticing the sky had turned black and the glitter of city lights twinkled below. Where had the time gone?

'It's after eight. That's enough. I'll take it from here.'

She glanced at her watch, incredulous, and gave a half-laugh as she rose. 'You know the old saying about time flying.'

'Thanks for your competent help over the past couple of days.'

Then he smiled. With genuine warmth. And, oh, my, was he drop-dead gorgeous or what? And not only that. How many of the people she'd worked for over the past couple of years had bothered to acknowledge her efforts? She couldn't help but smile back as she met his eyes. 'It's been a pleasure.'

She realised she was still smiling when his eyes turned dark, his pupils expanding till they almost touched that rim of navy. Hotter, spreading warmth over her skin, and she got that he was thinking of pleasure too.

Warning bells clanged in her ears, echoing in the tiny part of her brain that wasn't focused on the pleasure she had no doubt he could provide. She needed to leave. Now. Before something happened that changed…everything. 'If there's nothing else, I'll say goodnight…'

He didn't reply and a shivery sensation swept through her. She stepped away from the chair and through the doorway, then grabbed her bag from the drawer in Pam's desk. With only the reflection off adjacent high-rises, the glow from Jared's office and a security light at one end of the bank of elevators, the entire floor was cloaked in semi-darkness.

The back of her neck prickling—*he hadn't said goodnight so what might that mean?*—she set a brisk pace past the deserted office cubicles. Her pulse rate stepped up and she had to force herself not to break into a run. She was short of breath by the time she pressed the button to summon the lift.

'Wait up, Sophie.' His voice was nowhere near far enough away. 'Where are you parked? I'll walk you to your car.'

She scowled up at the floor numbers as the lift approached from the ground floor with what seemed like agonising slowness. She knew she'd never make sanctuary before he reached her and she said, 'A couple of spaces away from where we parked this morning. I'll be fine,' over her shoulder.

'I'm sure you will but it won't hurt to make sure.'

I wouldn't count on it. The lift doors opened on a cushion of air and she stepped inside. So did Jared. The doors closed, silence and intimacy surrounded them and their eyes met again.

Her feet moved towards the back of the lift, but her gaze remained locked with his and she realised this wasn't just about last night's dream or whether he'd read her dirty diary or not. The glimpse of promised pleasure she saw in his eyes was real—and would have consequences.

She didn't want a man unless he was the kind that faded with dawn. And yet, standing here within Jared's aura and being bathed in his gaze was a naked sensation of heat and desire and imminent surrender, stripping away not only clothing, but denials and reasons.

Beneath her blouse, her skin felt slick, tight. Her blood turned syrupy and throbbed through her veins to a place deep down in her belly and she wanted him with every female cell in her body.

Stupido.

She closed her eyes to lessen the impact. It didn't work

because now her senses focused even more acutely on her body's reaction and her surroundings. She could smell his scent in the confined space and, with all external sound extinguished, she could almost hear him breathing. Worse, she could almost hear him thinking.

'Sophie…'

Her eyes snapped open and were immediately drawn again to his as if there were some kind of force at work. 'Did you press the button?' she asked, and heard her words come out high-pitched and breathless. 'How come the lift's not moving?' And how come she hadn't noticed that? She leaned against the wall. Were they *stuck* in here?

His gaze glittered with something like amusement. One elbow and forearm was casually propped against the lift wall. 'You're not claustrophobic, are you?'

No, they weren't stuck…at least the lift wasn't. 'I don't think so.' Except that the walls seemed to be closing in, or maybe it was Jared's height, the breadth of his shoulders that made it seem that way. And the air…she dragged it in slow and deep… she couldn't seem to find enough.

'Good. Because work's over for the day. In fact your short tour of duty at Sandersons is over.'

Still a little breathless, but a lot relieved, she nodded. *Over. Good.*

His eyes didn't reflect his body's lazy stance. There was alertness and heat in the amusement now, too. Not so good.

He seemed to consider, then spoke slowly. 'So now maybe it's time to confess that I've been thinking about you all day.'

Her heart skipped a beat then pounded so loudly she was sure he'd hear it knocking against her ribs. But did he mean he'd been thinking about her or that cursed diary entry? She glared at him. 'Me? You don't even know me.'

'I know I'd like to.'

'Then you'd learn that I don't get involved with my employers on a personal level.'

'I don't do office flings either. This…thing…whatever it is, is a first for me.' He leaned closer. 'I told you, work's over. We clocked off a good five minutes ago. Correct?'

The warm scent of his skin had her sucking her breath in deeper when she should be exhaling and backing away. 'Yes.' She swallowed. 'But…'

'No "but". I'm attracted to you, Sophie.' He ran a fore-finger lightly down the side of her face. 'And the attraction's mutual.'

Blood rushed to the spot on her cheek like iron filings to a magnet. Even when he removed his hand the hot tingly feeling remained and she heard herself asking, '*What* have you been thinking?'

'I've been thinking about how your hair would look if I just unclasped it…'

She couldn't move, could only stand there and let him do it while goose-bumps chased over her body. She had no idea where the clasp vanished to. Was only aware of the weight of her hair tumbling over his arm, then she felt the soothing—*soothing?*—touch of his fingers against the back of her scalp. She didn't feel the least bit soothed and she barely resisted arching against his hand and sighing with pleasure.

She could feel his breath against her face as he leaned closer, could see the faint sheen of damp on his brow, above his lip. And there was no mistaking the arousal smouldering in his eyes.

Her mouth went dry, her heart rate sped up. This wasn't supposed to happen. Never with her boss. And with this man, Jared Sanderson? Not in real life. The paradox was that he might have well and truly brought her undone last night but she'd only met him today.

She was in too deep, too fast. She dragged her gaze from his. 'I should go…' Since he wasn't inclined to shift, she slid a hand past his midriff in search of the control panel behind him.

A subtle but swift move on his part brought her palm into

contact with a hard wall of muscled torso instead. Trapped. Yet his arm was still propping up the wall while the other one played loosely with her hair. He was making no attempt to keep her there and she was shocked and furious with herself for not trying harder to leave. Couldn't she see where this was heading?

She could—that was the problem. And he knew it.

'You've been thinking about me, too.' He caught her hand, held it in a relaxed grip.

'No.'

His thumb whisked over knuckles. 'Admit it, Sophie.'

She made one final, albeit half-hearted, attempt to pull away, but his gaze held hers and he lifted her hand to his chest. His heart thumped strong and deep. 'You've been wondering about our first kiss all day,' he continued in that low seductive tone. 'Like when…' Still massaging the base of her scalp, he leaned in, touched warm, firm lips to hers. *Oh, my.* 'And where…' Heat flowed like honey as he slid the tip of his tongue over her bottom lip. 'And how…'

His mouth moved over hers once more and her lips parted at his gentle coaxing. It perturbed her how easily she let him persuade her, then he released her fingers so that both his hands cupped the back of her skull and she stopped analysing and simply enjoyed the moment.

He slid his tongue against hers. She tasted the sweetness of the coffee they'd drunk, the saltiness of the rice. He made a rough sound that seemed to come from deep in his chest and she sensed the slow smouldering edge of impatience.

Oh, the *'how'*. The slide of his hands over her shoulder blades and all the way down her spine reminding her of her dream. Shifting closer, tucking her against him and, oh…*how* she could feel the hard ridge of his desire.

She leaned into the deepening kiss, wrapping her arms around his neck and momentarily forgetting everything but

Jared. She wanted more. More of that heat, that taste and that rock-hard body against hers. A kiss to build a dream on…

Or a dream to build a kiss on?

No. No. No. She didn't need this complication. She needed to focus on her goals. Her trip. Nothing and no one was going to get in her way. She made one last-ditch effort. 'I need to go,' she snapped out, and reached for the lift panel.

CHAPTER FIVE

'WAIT.' Jared moved like lightning, positioning himself in front of the control panel for the second time. Sophie opened her mouth to argue but he spoke over her. 'There's no need to rush off.'

'You don't think?'

Her voice held a slight edge—hysteria or humour? He didn't know her well enough to be sure. She closed her eyes on a soft groan that sounded suspiciously like surrender. His body clenched at the sound and he wondered if she made that noise when she had sex. And just for a moment, looking at her—head tipped back, throat exposed, eyes shut—he could imagine... When she opened them again they were wide and dark gold and...well, simply irresistible.

He reached out to let his fingers glide through the midnight silken waterfall over her shoulders. 'I think you should give it further serious consideration before you decide,' he murmured, bringing her hair to his nose and inhaling the soft herbal fragrance.

Eyes fused with his, she stepped away and he followed until he had her against the elevator wall. He wasn't backing off unless she told him to...and she wasn't saying anything at all. In fact, whatever it was that was flaring to life between them now was as much from her as it was from him.

He caught both her hands, raised them level with her head, and, with her wrists against the wall, he slid his hands over hers. Palm to palm where heat met heat. Still watching her face, he drifted his fingers down. Slowly, so that he could absorb every tiny line and ridge in her palms, then lower still to the rapid beat of her pulse at her wrists.

Enclosing her hands in his, he worked his thumbs deep into her palms—lazy circles, over and over, then slid his fingers between hers, a slow, sinuous rhythm. An erotic imitation of how their bodies would move together when he got her into bed. He saw her gaze widen, her pupils dilate. He leaned close to linger at her mouth, just enough to remind himself of her taste—

'You!' Her whole body stiffening, she reared back. She yanked her hands away, rubbing at her wrists as if they'd been bound. Her eyes flashed hellfire while the air inside the elevator seemed to plummet. 'You—'

'Sophie. Calm down.' He hesitated then reached out but she shrugged him off.

'Don't. Just don't.'

He blew out a slow breath. The hand massage was a dead giveaway. He'd intended it to be because the charade was over. It was time she knew he knew.

'You...*read* it.' Her voice gathered intensity like a low-pressure system crossing the coast. 'Not the first couple of lines, oh, no, you didn't stop when you realised it wasn't meant for you. *You read the whole freaking chapter!*'

'I couldn't put it down. I'm sorry. I should've told you this morning.'

'Yes, you should have.'

'Would it have made a difference?'

'Yes. No.' She shook her head. 'I don't know. How the hell should I know?'

'So...it was a fantasy or a daydream?' he ventured aloud. 'Or a real dream?'

Heat streamed up Sophie's neck. 'Of course it was a real dream! Why on earth would I fantasise about you? I don't even know you.'

Those amused eyes twinkled down at her. 'We seemed to know each other fairly well.' He smiled.

Sophie squirmed. *Thank you so much for pointing that out.* 'I've been recording my dreams for years,' she struggled on. She didn't tell him about her counselling sessions. None of his business. 'They bring forward stuff from our unconscious, help us understand ourselves better. It was nothing to do with *you,* per se.'

He tilted his head and his voice was low when he said, 'What do you think it meant, then?'

She'd done some of her own research. Dream theorists might say she wasn't getting enough love in her life. And they'd be right. That eating in dreams, particularly fruits, like luscious juicy blackberries for instance, were associated with sexuality.

Yep, sexual frustration. Right again. And she was hardly going to tell Mr Sanderson any of that. Nor was she about to tell him she'd never had a dream quite like it. 'I'm at a complete loss,' she said tightly.

'Erotic dream or not, that's some attraction we've got going here. You feel it too. Come on, Sophie, admit it. I'm not letting you out of this lift until you do.'

'Okay. I feel it. It was…good. But it was just a momentary indulgence.'

'Momentary?' When she didn't answer, he said, 'I want to see you again. Away from the office. And believe me, it won't be momentary.'

Her heart battered against her ribcage and the hot flush already invading her body intensified. Oh, the way he said that, the desire in his eyes—for her. But she had to think of practicalities. Nothing was going to persuade her from the goals she'd set for herself. Not even Jared Sanderson. Especially Jared Sanderson because she had a feeling he could change those goalposts to suit himself. 'I'm going overseas, I don't want to start something—'

'Honey, it's already started.'

'That doesn't—'

Her phone's cheerful jangle cut her off. *Salvation.* She pulled the offending item from her bag and answered, turning away from Jared as she did so.

'Sophie, it's Pam. I'm glad I caught you. Can you cover for me for a few more days?'

'Sure.' *Uh-oh.* Definitely *unsure*, but she couldn't tell Pam that right now. She'd need to find a replacement herself. 'You're still not well? Have you seen a doctor?'

'You'll never guess, I've got chicken pox.'

'No way.'

'Discovered the spots a few hours ago, the doctor confirmed it.'

'You poor thing. I'll call in on my way home. Is there anything I can get you?'

'Thanks, but there's no need. I'm going to switch off my phone and sleep. Oh, and I tried phoning Jared before I called you but his mobile's not answering.'

Of course it wasn't. Pam sounded perplexed about that, as if it was completely out of character. And it probably was if he was as dedicated to his work as Pam said.

'Don't worry, I'll let him know.' She rubbed at her temple. 'I'll talk to you tomorrow. Ring me if you need anything, no matter what time. Day or night.'

Sophie disconnected but remained facing the back of the lift. She didn't want the sight of Jared distracting her any more than she wanted to be the one who'd distracted him. The memory of the past few minutes burned in her blood. Her lips still tingled with his taste. Her entire body felt as if it were smouldering. How could she possibly cover for Pam now? But that extra income would have come in so handy.

Hearing the tightness in her voice as she disconnected, Jared touched Sophie's shoulder. 'What's wrong? Anything I can do?' None of his business, but he had to ask. He knew what it was like to deal with family crises.

'That was Pam.' Slipping the phone in her bag, she turned, her expression taut, shoulders rigid.

'And…?' he prompted when she just stared at him as if he'd turned into some kind of monster.

'She's got chicken pox.'

'*Chicken pox?* Do adults even catch chicken pox?'

'They can. Sometimes.'

Before he'd finished saying, 'That's unfortunate,' his mind was already leaping ahead. Sophie. At his beck and call for a week…but not in his bed as he'd anticipated. He didn't fool around with his staff.

'Pam tried to contact you just now,' she continued in a voice devoid of that husky passion he'd heard earlier. 'I told her I'd let her know.' She hesitated before saying, 'Under the circumstances I'll arrange for someone to cover for her.'

'No. I want you.' His body, already pumped, hardened further. He fought it down. *Hang on a damn minute.* They were talking business hours here. 'I need a PA and you need the work.' When she didn't reply he pressed on. 'Couldn't you use the extra spending money?'

'Yes, but—'

'So I'll see you here bright and early in the morning. Sophie, you're a professional, you can do it. Think of London. That side trip to Paris.'

'I wasn't planning a side trip to Paris.'

'Everyone plans a side trip to Paris.'

'Not me.' She chewed her lip a moment. 'I want to see Rome. And maybe Florence.' Stepping sideways, she stabbed the elevator button…and this time he let her.

The quiet click of gears was the only sound in the rapidly descending lift but the residual crackle of sexual energy sparking off the walls was deafening.

'Okay…' she murmured finally. 'We'll give it a try.'

He watched her refusing to look at him. It wouldn't work if they didn't talk about it. 'You don't want to resolve this unfinished business first?'

'There's nothing to resolve,' she said, tight-lipped. 'As for unfinished, as of now, what just happened here didn't happen. And I'd like my hair clasp back, please.'

He withdrew the tortoiseshell clasp from his pocket, handed it to her. 'Your idea's not going to work, you know.'

She shot him a look while she twisted her hair into a rope, jammed it haphazardly into the clasp. 'It will. I'm your employee. Everything changes. We've acknowledged...the whatever it is. Now we can ignore it and—'

'It'll go away?'

'Exactly.'

They exited the lift. The front doors opened and they stepped out into a muggy evening swamped with humidity and the *brzzz* of night insects.

'You really think so?'

'I *know* so.'

'I like your optimism.'

She turned left and headed for her car, her heels clicking a brisk rhythm on the pavement. 'What's more, I have every confidence in your ability to do the same.' She keyed the remote and a dark-coloured hatch's lights winked. 'We're both professionals.'

Professional. With the star-spattered sky stretched over a calm ocean and a woman he'd just been enjoying getting up close and personal with beside him, professional was as far from Jared's mind as that distant Pacific horizon.

She came to an abrupt stop beside her car, yanked open the door and tossed her bag across the seat all in rapid succession. 'Goodnight.'

Strands of hair she hadn't managed to contain in her clasp moved in the breeze. She still had that just kissed look. Plump lips, overbright eyes, breathing a little too fast.

The salty tropical evening was made for loving and for once he didn't want professional. If she'd been a date, he'd have been working that top buttonhole in her blouse right now. Hell no, he'd have had her naked already and moaning for more—after all, he knew what she liked, didn't he?

He fisted his hands in his pockets. *Cool it.* 'Okay. We'll try it your way.' He schooled his voice to neutral. 'So goodnight, Sophie, and thanks for working back, I appreciate it. Is that friendly-formal enough for you?'

She nodded once. It amused him to note that she actually looked disappointed he hadn't pushed his luck and kissed her again. Not that she'd want him to know he'd noticed. Her slim dark brows pulled down as she climbed into the car. 'You're welcome. Goodnight.'

'See you in the morning.' He shut her car door and watched till she pulled out of the car park. He let her go because she was still stinging with the knowledge that he'd read her dream. But he didn't care how determined she was to deny their attraction, tomorrow after hours they were going to talk about it. And then he'd inform her that his business plans for Noosa next week were already set and they included his PA.

Sophie checked the rear-vision mirror to ensure Jared wasn't following her, then pulled over to the side of the road. She switched off the ignition, let her head fall back on the seat and closed her eyes. *Oh. My. God.*

She blew out a shuddering breath. She'd managed to keep it together, but now that she could fall apart in private her whole body trembled. Darts of what felt like electric shocks tingled through her limbs and over her skin.

He'd made love to her hands exactly the way she'd told him to in her dream. The only difference with tonight's scenario was that they hadn't used her Secret Sensation moisturiser or done it naked and horizontal on some fluffy mat that didn't exist—at least it didn't in her house.

And he'd know that too.

She slammed her palms over and over against her temples. He'd read her diary entry. He'd known, damn him, and he'd said nothing all day. He'd probably watched her when she wasn't looking and imagined all the things she'd written... She could quite easily kill him and with no conscience at all. In fact, when she pulled herself together again she still might.

He kissed like a dream.

And, oh, that was *so-o-o* not funny. She sighed, remembering the luscious feel of his lips on hers, how she'd lost all willpower, wound her arms around his neck and practically sucked his face off.

He'd let her make a complete fool of herself. No, she'd done that on her own by sending the wrong email. She should have come clean with him first thing this morning and got it out of the way. Instead of hoping he hadn't read it. Of course he'd have read it. What normal red-blooded guy in his sexual prime would stop at the first couple of lines?

Since he'd asked her to stay on and she'd agreed, changing her mind and phoning the office in the morning wasn't an option. Her pride wouldn't allow it and an extra week's pay would be more than welcome. She considered herself a responsible employee. She didn't let people down, particularly Pam, the one person who'd been there for Sophie when she'd needed support.

But this thing with Pam's boss couldn't continue. It would affect their working relationship and her ability to do her job. Tomorrow she'd inform Jared she'd do her best to cover for Pam but that outside office hours she wanted nothing whatsoever to do with him.

After a practically sleepless but mercifully dream-free night of trying not to think of the mess her life had become, Sophie spent the morning filing and typing up reports that had been accumulating in Pam's inbox. She'd beaten Jared to the office by ten minutes, organised his agenda for the day and greeted him all cool, smooth politeness on his arrival. He'd been no less courteous, with hardly more than a flicker in his eye to remind her of last night.

But that single flicker was the killer.

It was more than hot enough to set her cheeks aglow and remind her that beyond these walls she wasn't going to get involved with him. She'd needed to excuse herself and make a dash to the bathroom to pat cold water on her face with a tissue and think calming thoughts.

Jared was in the town centre somewhere busy with appointments all morning and this afternoon he was driving into the Gold Coast Hinterland. Good. He hadn't asked her to come with him. Even better. Instead, he'd left her with a further list of proposals and phone calls to follow up. *Those* she could manage.

Then just before midday the helium balloons arrived. A dozen heart-shaped pink foil balloons tied to a small pink and white striped box.

'This can't be right,' Sophie told the uniformed delivery girl who was touting the arrangement in front of her desk.

'I was told to bring them over here.' She glanced in Mimi's direction, shrugged, then set them on Sophie's desk with a smile. 'Have a nice day.'

'And you.' Sophie's smile felt brittle and, inside, her anger built like a tropical storm. Ignoring the attached envelope, she picked up the whole thing, carried it into Jared's office and dumped it in front of his computer screen.

She scowled, its pretty, cheerful presence only infuriating her further. After his assurance to the contrary, how *dare* he bring their attraction and what had happened between them last night into office hours? And so publicly. She couldn't believe it.

And yet…something deep down, something she'd almost

forgotten how to feel, let alone respond to, fluttered around the region of her heart.

She shoved it down deeper. A solitary lunch in the fresh air would be a timely and welcome distraction so she took her sandwiches to the beach, a few minutes' walk away.

She'd been back at her desk twenty minutes when she heard Jared's voice. He was too far away for her to hear what he was saying but the relaxed delivery in those deep sexy tones sent her pulse into overdrive.

Suddenly she wished she hadn't been so hasty with the balloons and, since she'd not read the note, she didn't know what to accuse him of... She pushed out of her chair. If she could just duck back into his office and undo...

She swore inwardly. Too late, he was coming this way. With his sister. Her heart pounding, she grabbed a file she'd set aside to take down to Accounting on the floor below. Now seemed like a good time...

'Sophie.' He slowed as he passed her desk on his way to his office. 'Any problems this morning?' The expression in his eyes told her he wasn't only referring to computer glitches and client complaints.

'No.'

The denial sounded like a sharpened icicle, and he blinked in surprise. So she smiled—for Melissa's benefit. 'Everything's fine.'

Jared paused, then must have decided whatever he was going to say could wait, nodded and kept walking.

Sophie turned to his sister, glad of an excuse to look away. 'Hello, Melissa.'

'Hi. You must think I have nothing better to do than hang around my brother.' She grinned. 'I assure you nothing's further from the truth. But he's giving me a lift back to uni after we've been to the hospital.'

'Right, let's go.' Jared reappeared, briefcase in one hand, balloons in the other.

'Oh, they're gorgeous, she'll love them.' Melissa reached out and ran a hand over the foil ribbons.

Sophie stared. Uh-huh. *R-i-g-h-t...* The balloons were for the new arrival. How stupid and naïve of her to presume and she'd presumed so wrongly. She wished they'd leave now so that she could have her third—or was it her fourth?—hysterical breakdown.

But Melissa was in no hurry. 'I want to show Sophie the baby bracelet first. We're going to put it in the little box with the balloons.'

Jared's phone buzzed. He muttered, 'Liss, Sophie looks like she's busy,' as he pulled it from his pocket.

'It'll only take a minute.' Melissa pulled a little packet from her bag, opened it and poured the contents into Sophie's palm. 'Isn't it precious?'

Sophie stared at the delicate gold links, the tiny heart clasp with Arabella's name engraved on it. Beautiful. But not nearly as precious as the tiny new life it was named for.

'It's the sweetest thing,' she agreed, forcing a smile and returning the bracelet to Melissa. 'Crystal will love it and so will Arabella when she's old enough.'

Jared was still talking as he walked back into his office and closed the door. Sophie grabbed the opportunity to escape further face-to-face contact and waved her folder. 'If you'll excuse me, I was just on my way down to Accounts...enjoy your visit to the hospital.'

She walked swiftly towards the elevators, then changed her mind and veered towards the stairs. She didn't want to have to wait for the lift and risk sharing it with them, especially with last night's memories still steaming up the walls.

In Accounts she took her time delivering the folder. Introducing herself to George, the balding fifty-something head honcho. Waiting while he fumbled through the mess on his desk for a report to take upstairs to Jared. Long enough to give Jared and Melissa time to leave the building. But in case they hadn't, she decided returning the way she'd come was the safest option.

CHAPTER SIX

TEN minutes later Jared disconnected and exited his office to find Lissa balanced on the corner of Sophie's desk, fiddling with the balloon ties. Sophie was nowhere to be seen.

He must have frowned because Lissa smiled as if she knew something she shouldn't and said, 'She went downstairs,' then glanced at her watch. 'We need to—'

'Did she say anything to you?' he demanded before he could rein in his impatience. Professional communication with his PA was key and Sophie was avoiding him.

Lissa raised her brows. 'Like what? Come to think of it, she did look kind of flustered. Did you upset her?'

'No. Wait in the car.' He tossed her the keys and headed for the elevator.

'She took the stairs,' he heard Lissa call behind him. 'Don't be long, I've got a class…'

The smell of cool musty concrete invaded his nostrils as he yanked open the door to the stairwell. It swung shut with a hollow boom, cutting off Lissa's voice.

He started down, taking the steps two at a time. He needed an assistant who could put personal issues aside during office hours and work with him. He didn't have time for this game of denial she seemed to be playing.

He heard the door on the floor below open, close. Peering over the railing, he saw Sophie starting up. Slowly, as if she didn't have an afternoon's work awaiting her.

As if she was making sure he'd left before she made her reappearance.

A file she was holding slipped and she grabbed at it, giving him a peek of cleavage. Smooth, dusky, *inviting* cleavage. He ran a tongue over his teeth. She wore a conservative dress the colour of watermelon. Square neckline, straight skirt, wide emerald-green belt.

His body hardened as he remembered last night. The taste of her skin, her sexy little moan as he'd tucked her against him. The way her eyes had clashed with his when she'd felt his erection. She'd been all-the-way with him. Willing, wanting, desperate. Until Pam had rung.

She was still interested. If he'd found another temp he could have been seeing Sophie socially this evening. He'd not been thinking straight when he'd talked her into staying on as his PA. He'd just wanted to see her again and the sooner, the better.

Okay, she was a current employee, but not for long. A few days, then nothing was stopping them acting on that attraction for however long it lasted. She was off overseas indefinitely in a matter of weeks, which suited him fine—he was nowhere near ready for anything long term. And obviously she didn't want serious either at this point.

Perfect. Well, almost.

So they were going to clear this up. Now. As he descended she glanced up and caught sight of him. He watched the dismay cross her gaze. Watched her stop and try to compose herself.

'Sophie.'

'Jared.' She jiggled the folders she held tighter against her bosom. 'Do you want to go over these figures from George before I file them?'

'No. That's what I pay you for.' He stopped two steps above her, then sat down on the concrete so that they were eye to eye. 'Last night you said you were a professional.'

Her eyes widened. 'And I am.'

'You're avoiding me.'

'No. I'm busy.' Then her gaze turned worried. 'Oh. Since you were on your way out I figured I'd—'

'I don't have time for this, Sophie, and nor do you. We need to do something about it.' He wanted to touch her so badly he had to fist his hands at his sides. 'Whatever you're doing tonight, cancel it.'

'I can't. Not tonight.'

He narrowed his eyes while trying to read hers. 'Can't or won't?'

'I'm spending the night with Pam.' Her lips firmed and her eyes flashed a defiant topaz. 'She's family to me and she's ill and on her own. So call me unprofessional or sack me on the spot but an understanding boss knows which comes first.'

Yes, he knew. He had to admire her for standing up for herself. 'Okay.' Rising and stepping down to her level, he breathed out his frustration. Slowly. 'Tomorrow night, then.'

She took her time responding, as if trying to come up with another excuse. He decided to let her off the hook for now and said, 'Listen, why don't you finish here early today since you worked back last night? Buy some flowers from the staff at the florist around the corner on your way. You'd know what Pam likes. Put it on my business account.'

Her tensed shoulders softened. 'Okay. Thanks. Pam'll love that.' A smile lit up her whole face and reflected in her gold-flecked eyes. It brought a glow to the moment. It made him think of the sun dancing on a sapphire sea. It made him forget he was her boss and this was his place of work.

'Summer,' he murmured. Heat. Bared, bronzed bodies. Playtime and passion. He wanted it all with Sophie Buchanan.

The images his mind seemed determined to conjure up both startled and aroused. He breathed in sharply and his nostrils filled with her familiar fresh scent. Her smile faded as they continued to stare at each other. His heart pounded like a fist on a drum. Her shoulders tensed up again and she gripped the metal banister with her free hand, the other clutching at the files.

'Hey...' Seriously aiming for detached, he grinned, then... somehow...his thumb was sliding along her lower lip. 'Relax, I'm not going to ravish you on the stairwell no matter how hard you beg.'

She didn't smile or move a muscle, didn't react in any way. A block of wood. His inappropriate touch and humour drained away, leaving him feeling confused, unsteady and...damn *exposed*... What the hell was wrong with him? With his body already rock hard, he shifted closer, desperate for one taste of that generous mouth, just one...

She didn't move away. She didn't resist as he leaned in and the instant their lips met her whole being seemed to sigh with satisfaction. He knew because he felt the same way. Her mouth, so warm, so soft, so rich. So right. His body tightened further.

The sound of the upstairs door opening echoed in the stairwell. He reacted instantly. *What in hell was he doing? This wasn't so right, this was all wrong.* His hands instinctively rose to Sophie's shoulders—to steady her, that was all—but she shot backwards, still grasping the files, wide eyes flashing with accusation.

'Jared?' an impatient voice called. 'Are you down there? Some of us haven't got all day...'

'Be there in a jiff, Liss.' His voice reverberated off the walls.

He heard a strangled sound coming from Sophie, who was shooting upwards like a rocket and already a few stairs above him. She turned, looked down on him and whispered fiercely, 'That's what happens when you don't stick to the rules.'

He was uncomfortably aware of the tent in his trousers. Sophie would be too. And Melissa, if she noticed. And Melissa would be bound to notice. He ground his teeth. *Sisters.* He threw out a hand, snapped his fingers. 'Give me the files, Sophie.'

She passed them down to him with…was that a hint of smoky humour mingled with the agitation in her eyes? 'I'll let Melissa know you'll be right along,' she said, and resumed her ascent.

'Tell her I'll meet her in the car park. And check the agenda for next Wednesday and familiarise yourself with the details,' he informed her retreating back, trying to get some sort of business rapport going between them again.

'Next Wednesday?'

'I've left you an email.'

'I'll get right on it.'

The door above swung shut. He drew in a ragged breath and tried to bring his wayward body under some sort of control. He couldn't believe what he'd just done. During office hours. With his PA, for pity's sake. What an ass.

His professional self had never done anything remotely like it. Never been tempted. Sophie Buchanan was the first. The one-off.

When he'd kissed her last night he'd not anticipated she'd still be his PA today. He reassured himself that in less than a month everything would be back to normal.

Who was he kidding? He shook his head as he made his way upstairs. Somehow he doubted anything would be the same, ever again.

Noosa? They were going to Noosa. Sophie stared at the email Jared had forwarded moments ago while she'd been downstairs. Her and him, together for the three-hour journey past Brisbane and on to the northern Sunshine Coast. And staying at some fancy address on the Noosa River. Alone.

No way.

She reached for the office phone, but before she could make a connection it buzzed. To curb her impatience she fixed a smile in place. 'Sanderson Property Investments, Sophie Buchanan speaking, how may I help you?'

'Miz Buchanan.' Jared's voice. With not a hint of the husky heat it had exuded moments ago. Just deep and calm like a high mountain lake.

Unlike her. Her pulse, which had barely settled, raced again. He'd kissed her senseless and just like that, now he was being all business? She heard a car's horn in the background. Right, of course he was all business because he was in the car with Melissa, who was no doubt listening in on every word. *Now who's playing games?*

'*Mr* Sanderson.' She leaned back in her chair, tapping her fingernails on the desk and studying the photo of Noosa's riverside luxury home on her computer screen. 'What can I do for you?'

Should have rephrased that. A shiver shimmied down her spine and she swore that amazing sexual tension they seemed to have between them spun through the air, as if he were standing right behind her. Leaning down, his breath hot against her ear—

'You've read the email, I presume?'

She jolted upright. 'Yes.' Brief hiatus where neither spoke. Did he expect her to back out now? Moreover, did she *want* to back out now? The refusal on the tip of her tongue melted away. 'I'll be ready,' she said.

'Excellent.'

No way could she interpret the nuance of that single word.

'We've a busy schedule ahead of us,' he continued, 'and I want to familiarise you with a few details before we leave on Wednesday. I'll be in Brisbane on Monday and Tuesday, so we'll discuss it over dinner tomorrow evening.'

She opened her mouth to argue, closed it. So it was a business dinner now. How cunning. And when he put it that way how could she refuse? 'Very well. Restaurants…' She flipped through Pam's list on the desk. 'Do you have a preference?'

'I'll make the reservations this time. We'll make it seven, I'll pick you up on the way.'

Nuh-uh, that sounded too much like a date and the panicky feeling fluttered back. 'I—'

'Until tomorrow, then. Bye for now.'

The line went dead.

'Fill me in on the latest lunchroom gossip,' Pam said while they ate the home-made chicken soup and hot crusty bread Sophie had brought upstairs.

Pam was a brunette with short bouncy hair, abundant curves and dark expressive eyes. Right now those eyes begged for news from the outside.

'I'm just the temp, remember. I'm not privy to gossip.'

'But you must have heard something—any sordid little tidbit that'll brighten up my miserable, itchy and scratch-filled day will do.'

'Oh, you poor thing.' Sophie looked at her blister-covered friend across the table and almost felt itchy herself. 'Are you sure there's not anything I can get you?'

'Thanks, but I'm fully medicated for the moment. Especially with the gorgeous flowers you brought. Jared really is a darling.' She smiled at the bunch of yellow roses on the coffee table. 'Come on, Sophie.'

She wanted to get this thing with Jared out in the open with someone and Pam was the only person she was close enough and trusted enough to confide in. 'Are you sure you're up to hearing it? You don't need to go and relieve that itching some more in a cool cornflower bath?'

Pam's eyes brightened considerably. 'You *have* heard something. Out with it. Now.'

'Okay, but don't blame me if your itch turns feral. It may take a while and you have to promise not to tell.'

Leaning her elbows on the table, Pam settled in. 'Promise.'

'It started two nights ago when I emailed your report to Jared, only it wasn't your report that I emailed…'

When Sophie had finished, Pam sat back and stared at her. 'Oh, *cringe*… You're genuine. If I hadn't heard it from you I'd never have believed it.'

'I can hardly believe it myself. And yeah, the cringe factor for this particular blunder surpasses all previous records.'

'Agreed.' Pam's slow smile had a hint of wicked humour about it. 'You and Jared together. It's kind of…I'm not sure yet, let me think on it.'

'Not too deeply, please.' Sophie felt her cheeks heat and dared herself to hold Pam's gaze. 'And let me point out we're not *together* together.'

But after that moment on the stairs this afternoon… When he'd touched her lips with that very tanned, very sexy and no doubt very experienced thumb, it had been all she could do not to open her mouth and take it inside. To wrap her tongue around it and taste him.

Then he'd swooped in and kissed her. He'd tasted rich, dark, hot. But it hadn't been long enough. Not nearly long enough. She pressed her lips together. Hard.

And now…now there was next Wednesday… *Business* trip, she reminded herself.

'There's never been a whiff of scandal around Jared.' Pam interrupted Sophie's thoughts. 'But if they see you the way you are now…all pink and flustered-looking…I wonder who'll be the first to start the rumour mill?'

Sophie glared at her. 'Not you. You promised.'

Pam made a zipping movement with her thumb and forefinger. 'My lips are sealed.'

'Tell me what I should know about this upcoming trip to Noosa. I only found out about it this afternoon. By *email*.' The funny feeling she'd got in her stomach back at the office unfurled again and started to flap.

'We were going to Noosa to consult with a few clients and look at property,' Pam said.

'*And* staying overnight,' Sophie continued.

'Two nights actually.' Pam smiled as if they were co-conspirators in a secret, and that funny sensation flapped some more.

'What if I don't want to go?'

'Are you seriously thinking of refusing?'

'I—'

'Because if you are, you'd better organise someone else pronto.' Pam sounded surprisingly aggrieved. 'This trip's important to Jared.' She stared hard at Sophie. 'I know I go on about him but, honestly, he's one of the good guys. Think of England. Spending money, Soph.'

Rome, Florence. The Colosseum. Michelangelo's David. 'Thinking, thinking. Still doesn't make it a good idea.'

Sophie realised she wasn't focusing on the professional aspect. She was temping for Pam and Pam had wangled this job for her instead of going through the agency as she was supposed to. She couldn't let her down. 'Just my thoughts spinning, Pam. Of course I'm going.'

Pam's expression relaxed. 'Don't worry, the accommodation's a luxury waterfront home on Noosa River. Five bedrooms, four bathrooms, spa, pool.'

'I've been looking at the info.'

'So you'll know there's plenty of room to stay out of each other's way if that's what you want... Is that what you want, Sophie?'

Sophie evaded the question with one of her own. 'Why not a couple of rooms in a hotel?'

'Because Jared wants to refurbish a place here in Surfers that he's purchased for himself. He saw this one available for short-term rent on the net and liked some of the ideas. And it makes a change from hotels. Lighten up, work might actually be fun for a change. For both of you.'

Oh, Sophie had no doubts about that. None at all. But when they came back she could see the word *Complication* looming on the horizon, even if Pam was back at work by then. 'Okay, tell me more. What's he like out of office hours?'

Pam studied her through very perceptive eyes. Too perceptive. 'He's turned up at staff functions with gorgeous sophisticates—always blonde—but never the same one twice. Does that answer your question?'

Sophie shrugged as if it didn't matter. 'I reckon so.' It *didn't* matter, she told herself. She frowned, annoyed. It was no concern of hers how many women he had. Then she remembered Jared's words. *A good thing is only a good thing for as long as you enjoy it.* 'So he's commitment phobic.'

Pam pursed her lips. 'I'd say it's more like work-focused.'

Sophie *hmphed*. She'd reserve judgment on that for now.

'Career and family are his life,' Pam went on. 'He fought for and won guardianship of Crystal and Melissa when he was only eighteen. That was twelve years ago and he's done a brilliant job all while expanding a now very lucrative and successful business.'

Oh. Sophie tried not to be impressed with his dedication and commitment. It didn't extend to his relationships with the opposite sex. Again she tried not to compare him with her ex-husband but she couldn't help it. Glen had loved women. Lots of women.

All behind Sophie's back.

And it seemed both men preferred blondes.

Superficial beings, men. A timely reminder and one she intended keeping uppermost in her mind for the next few days. Weeks. And even when she boarded that big shiny jet and headed for the other side of the world she would remember.

Superficial suited her purposes too. Superficial was safe.

She thought about that later, lying in bed and staring at the ceiling while the tropical breeze did nothing to cool her overheated body. Overheated because she couldn't stop thinking about Jared. In that *superficial* way.

He made her hot. From his tanned skin and toned body to the way he looked at her with those intense eyes the colour of smouldering olive leaves.

Then there were his lips. Firm and full and fabulous. The way he'd used them to kiss her. Talk about weapons of mass seduction. Her temperature rose another degree just thinking about it. She wanted those lips against hers again. She wanted them on other parts of her body—the way they'd worshipped her in her dream.

Rolling over, she squeezed her pillow and bunched it beneath her head. Why was this happening *now* when she was leaving Australia indefinitely?

She'd never been kissed by a man like Jared, certainly never involved with one. It was an all-new experience. A cocktail of power and authority with a twist of devilish wit and charm, to be served hot in a dark grey suit. Enticing, irresistible.

Possibly lethal.

But even though Pam the PA certified him all work and no play, Sophie knew Pam her friend considered him the quintessential good bloke.

Not so superficial.

Not so safe after all.

CHAPTER SEVEN

THE workload Jared gave Sophie on Friday was so heavy she barely had time to go to the Ladies, let alone think of him in any other way than her slave-driver boss.

She didn't have time to think of him at all actually. She worked her butt off all morning without a coffee break, and by lunch she'd cleared most of the paperwork. She stretched in her chair, wiggled her fingers, satisfied with her efforts, then reached beneath her desk and pulled out her lunch box.

'These need filing, please.'

Jared dumped another pile of manila folders on her desk. She realised he'd hardly have noticed if Pam had come back early and was sitting in this chair instead of Sophie.

'Right away.' She watched him not looking at her as he walked past.

He turned back just when she thought he wasn't going to acknowledge her in any way and said, 'And see if you can dig up the hard copy of the works schedule for the Carson Richardson project from last month, ASAP, client wants alterations as of yesterday.'

Resigned, Sophie slid her lunch box back into her bag. 'I'll get right on it.'

He checked his watch. 'I'll be back at two, if you can have it ready for me by then.'

* * *

'For heaven's sake, Sophie, you haven't stopped all morning,' Mimi said at one-thirty. 'You *are* permitted a lunch break. Take one.'

She did. She ate her honey and walnut sandwiches in the lunchroom and washed it down with a coffee all in under ten minutes. No way was she going to let Jared see that she wasn't up to the job. She could handle anything he threw at her. In fact, she wondered if he was testing her, just to see how she performed under pressure. Why, she had no idea. It wasn't as if she'd be a regular here.

The rest of the day kept up the same frenetic pace. In one way it was good because it took her mind off the man and the evening ahead. Mostly.

The business dinner, she reminded herself as she responded to an email enquiry.

Five-thirty rolled by. Five forty-five. Sophie had plenty of work still to keep her busy but she really needed to know the details for tonight. Since he hadn't mentioned it again, neither had she.

Jared and a client were still in his office. With the door closed. The ebb and flow of a tense-sounding conversation warned her it wasn't a good time to interrupt. Was she to assume the arrangement still stood?

The door opened and both men walked out.

'Sophie. What are you still doing here? It's almost six.'

'I needed to finalise a few details.' *Like where to meet you tonight?* But she could hardly ask that in front of a client and give the impression it was business. Not with the flush she could already feel creeping up her neck.

She smiled blandly at his client, then busied herself tidying her desk. 'I'm just on my way home now.' Not that Jared heard; he was already walking away. She clicked off the screen and closed down the computer.

A moment later, Jared returned from seeing the guy to the elevator. 'You're still here.'

'You noticed,' she said with asperity and immediately regretted it. She reached for her bag. It was the sort of jealous female response you might give a lover and wasn't what she'd meant, in addition to being totally inappropriate in the workplace.

He stared at her a full ten seconds with those intense green eyes. She had him speechless. A first. Then he said, 'You're still on for tonight, I hope,' and something in his gaze sharpened.

She felt its effects right down to her toes. 'Why wouldn't I be?'

'So you're one of those quick dressers, are you? That'll be a first.'

'Not particularly,' she said, trying for nonchalant, but that flick of his eyes over her body as he'd spoken had felt like a flame thrower. 'You haven't told me where to meet you.'

'I told you yesterday I'm picking you up at seven.' The tone of command with a dash of impatience.

'I said I'd meet you there...wherever.'

'No. You didn't.'

He was right, she realised. He'd cut her off when she'd tried to ask. With a little resigned inward sigh, she slung her bag over her shoulder. She didn't have time to argue and she knew she wouldn't win this one. She also knew it wasn't all business, so she asked, 'What's the dress code for this place you've chosen?'

'How does casually elegant sound?'

'Fine.'

'Pacific Gold apartments...?'

'Unit 213.'

'Make it seven-fifteen.'

Humour snuck in and she arched a brow. 'We agreed on seven. You saying you can't be ready in fifty-five minutes?'

He didn't reply but his eyes flashed a challenge.

She shook her head once. 'Seven o'clock.' She turned away quick smart and headed towards the lift, praying, praying, he didn't follow. She simply couldn't handle another trip in the elevator with him right now.

Jared drove home only a touch above the speed limit and jumped in the shower. He didn't have time to think about the tight sensation in his chest, nor to acknowledge the sense of anticipation he hadn't felt since his teenage years. Which was just as well.

Moments later he ran his fingers through his damp hair. Quick shave, splash of subtle cologne at the last minute. He threw on dark chinos and an open-necked oatmeal linen shirt. No tie. *Casual* business dinner. One that might lead to a more relaxed after-dinner coffee somewhere?

He was walking to the front door at the same time as Melissa, also dressed for a night out.

'Wow.' Looking him up and down, she sniffed the air. 'Is that a new cologne?'

'You and Crystal gave it to me last Christmas.' He just hadn't had an occasion to wear it. 'And it's a business dinner, Liss.'

'I certainly hope so—I heard you arrange it in the car. You wouldn't win any dates with that austere approach...' She studied him some more, met his eyes with a cryptic look. 'You don't *look* business... Are you going to be late home?'

'I don't know, Liss,' he said, annoyed and running late. She was asking *him* that question? 'Why?'

'Just letting you know I'll be out late too,' she said, walking to the door ahead of him. 'I'm meeting friends for burgers then we're going clubbing later.'

'Don't get into a vehicle with anyone who's been drinking.'

He was checking for his wallet but he could almost see her eyes rolling up as she walked down the garden path when he heard, 'No, Daddy.'

* * *

He made it to the front door of Sophie's apartment with two minutes to spare.

The door opened as he was about to knock and he was looking straight into those eyes, touched with humour now. 'What took you so long?' she said.

'No points for being early?'

Her warm brandy eyes weren't the only things attracting his attention. His gaze dipped. She was wearing a slim white knee-length dress. A complicated series of straps pulled the bodice into a bunch of fabric just below her collarbone and tied behind her neck, leaving her shoulders bare. Stunning smooth shoulders that gleamed like honey in the amber light behind her.

So she hadn't gone with strictly business either.

Half-moon earrings the colour of limes dangled on gold thread. She wore a matching bracelet. She reminded him of a tropical milkshake cocktail, long and cool and inviting. Too inviting. He wished they could just dine in. On each other.

'I'll grab a jacket.' She hesitated before asking, 'Do you want to come in for a moment?'

Come in? His groin tightened. *More than you know and for a lot longer than a minute.* He cleared his throat. 'Maybe later.'

She disappeared while he counted the various species of tropical flora on the other side of the balcony that formed a courtyard within the apartment block, and thought about penguins and Antarctica and ice-cold beer.

When she pulled the door closed, mercifully he had himself pretty much under control. 'I hope you like seafood.'

'Love it.' She led the way. They took the stairs down. Three flights. 'I try to keep fit.'

She didn't need to explain; it was obvious the elevator was a problem for her. He thought of telling her so. It would be ridiculous if they couldn't even manage an elevator together, but he also wanted to make it to the restaurant with a dinner partner. He wanted her at ease with him. It was vital to have her comfortable in their working relationship. Or any kind of relationship.

The journey took ten minutes. On the way Jared stuck to the usual and asked about her working day. They pulled up outside Enzo's Seafood and Grill and were shown to a corner table overlooking the beach where a few tiny lights winked on the dark strip of ocean.

With the fine weather this evening, the windows had been removed, allowing the balmy tropical evening in and giving the impression they were outside. On the decking a string of party lights and a couple of flaring bamboo torches provided a warm ambience.

After they'd ordered, for the first time all day, Sophie forced herself to relax. To enjoy the experience of dining with a gorgeous man at a classy restaurant and converse on a variety of non-threatening topics. The latest in local entertainment, the real estate market. The pros and cons of living in a high-profile tourist destination.

The champagne he'd ordered was perfection—cold and fruity and fizzy. Her prawn and avocado cocktail tasted fresh and sweet. On the table, the tiny tea light inside its ruby glass cube seemed to draw them closer. Way too intimate for a business dinner but *business* wasn't what this was about. Had never been what this was about. She knew it. He knew it.

While she waited for him to initiate the discussion on the supposed reason they were here, she took another sip of wine and let the bubbles tickle her nostrils and dance on her tongue. She'd not seen Jared in anything other than business attire and this more relaxed Jared was no less stunning.

He'd taken the short time he'd had to shave and to splash on something that made her want to lean forward and breathe him in. But she wouldn't want to stop at breathing... To avoid the temptation, she reached for her napkin, pressed it to her lips and leaned back.

'Good evening, Jared.' A good-looking Italian appeared at their table. Black hair and eyes, and a roguish smile, which was currently directed at Sophie. 'And to your lovely dinner companion tonight.'

Jared grinned at him then at Sophie. 'Enzo. I'd like you to meet Sophie Buchanan. She's filling in for my PA for a few days.' He turned to Sophie. 'Enzo's Rico's brother.'

'Ah, yes, the best fish and chips in Coolangatta. I remember. Pleased to meet you, Enzo.'

He smiled at her again, all smooth Italian charisma. 'We're very busy tonight or I'd stay and chat. Charmed to meet you, Sophie. Come back another time, meanwhile have a pleasant evening.'

Sophie smiled back. 'Thank you.'

They'd decided on a shared seafood platter; a variety of oysters, salt and pepper calamari, grilled prawns and tempura garfish, served with a crisp rocket salad drizzled with a lemon olive oil dressing.

Conversation ceased while Sophie, who'd eaten nothing all day but her sandwich several hours ago, savoured every delicious mouthful and made each one count. How often did she get to eat at such a pricey restaurant? The answer was never.

While she tucked in, she noticed Jared's attack on the sumptuous food was just as enthusiastic. She asked, and discovered he'd skipped lunch too. Watching him eat was as much a treat as watching him work. He gave both tasks the same enthusiasm and undivided attention and she knew with a quiet certainty that rippled through her feminine places that he'd give the same to a lover.

'Dessert?' Jared asked a while later when the main dishes had been cleared away and she'd more or less calmed down, for the moment at least.

'Yes, please.'

'Allow me to order for both of us.' He motioned the waiter.

'As long as it's loaded with calories.'

He smiled at her then referred to the menu, indicated his choice. 'For two, please.' A corner of his mouth tipped up. 'I guarantee you'll like it.'

A short time later, she stared at the plate the waiter had set between them. She felt the colour rising up her neck, bleeding into her cheeks, and thanked the little red tea light on their table for its camouflaging effect.

Italian blackberry Frangelico torte, she was informed. With a mountain of whipped cream.

Blackberries and cream…well, it was an obvious choice, wasn't it? Bolstered by a couple of glasses of bubbly, she met Jared's eyes across the table. Amusement flashed back at her.

In spite of herself, she couldn't help the wry little twist of her lips. 'And here's Pam telling me you don't have a sense of humour.'

He leaned back in his chair. 'Pam said that?'

She toyed with the stem of her wine glass and ventured, 'Maybe it's her way of saying you should loosen up some.'

He cocked his head as if the notion was absurd. 'And what do you think?'

'From what I've seen in the office today, she may have a point. Then again, there's this other side she obviously hasn't seen that kind of balances everything out.'

His lips curved. 'You're talking about my sharp wit and immeasurable charm.'

'Naturally.'

His smile widened to a grin for a split second, but then it faded and something other than humour stole into his eyes. Something darker, harder, more ruthless. He was silent a moment, staring into space. 'I run a multimillion-dollar company, Sophie. It's my life's ambition, my reason to get up in the morning, my passion.' He picked up his dessert spoon and drew circles on the heavy white cloth. 'Sometimes I forget that employees have priorities other than their nine-to-five job at Sanderson's.'

Sophie nodded. There was a sense of remoteness about him. As if he was used to distancing himself from the rest of the world. She picked her way carefully, watching his expression as she said, 'She also mentioned Crystal and Melissa and how you've been brilliant with them.'

His distance remained, his expression shut down. A barrier she couldn't cross. 'The business is the reason I've been able to afford to give my sisters something of what they've missed out on over the past twelve years. Enough about that. We've more interesting matters to discuss.'

His relaxed convivial demeanour returned as if he'd flicked a switch. How did he do that? she wondered. How could he turn his emotions off so easily and so completely? She only wished she had the same ability.

She finished the remainder of her wine while she studied the mouth-watering layers of hazelnut sponge, white chocolate and blackberry coulis in front of them.

'I ordered this concoction for a reason.'

'I can see that.' She was tempted to ask if he was going to feed it to her and watch her moan in pleasure. After all they both knew how the story went... She pressed her tingling lips together. Thank heavens they were in a public place because she was appalled to think how easily she'd let him seduce her if they were somewhere more private.

But as she watched him dip his spoon into the cake, add cream and lift it towards her mouth it was like falling into a hypnotic state.

Especially when he murmured, 'Open up, Sophie,' in that deep silky sexy timbre that made her think of dark chocolate... and a different set of circumstances when he might say those words.

He was thinking the same thing because his eyes seemed to take on a smoky gleam as he leaned closer, offering the spoon.

Her heart stopped, thumped once then pounded out a fast

rhythm and her mouth fell open of its own volition. He slid the cake between her lips. Smooth, slow, slippery. She couldn't look away—it was as if he held her captive. She sucked the delicious mouthful from the spoon. He'd engineered this sneaky... whatever-it-was...and she'd played right into his subversion.

'What's the verdict?' he asked.

'It's nice,' she managed. It wasn't only her tongue; every part of her was out of kilter. She gave herself a mental shake and made every attempt to pull herself together.

'*Nice?* Is that the best you can do?'

'Right now?' she snapped out—but quietly. 'Yes, it is.'

He grinned slowly. Using the same spoon, he scooped up another morsel and popped it into his own mouth. Still watching her. Still with that smoky gleam in his eyes.

She picked up her own spoon. 'Remember where we are.'

'And the reason we're here.'

She watched him through narrowed eyes while she ate. When she'd almost finished, she said, 'This dessert wasn't on the menu, was it? You ordered it specially.'

'It was worth it, don't you agree?'

'Your business dinner's a fake and we both know it.' She scooped up a final mouthful, then sat back and crossed her arms.

'No,' he said slowly, as if talking to a child. 'We do need to discuss Noosa.'

Suddenly it was decision time and she wasn't sure she knew the right answer. Or if he was even going to ask the question. 'I plan to spend the upcoming weekend familiarising myself wi—'

'I'm talking about after hours.' He cut her off with an impatient flick of his hand and his gaze pinned hers. 'And we both know it.'

Her words echoed back to her. At the same time, his eyes promised all manner of tempting after-hours delights and her insides flipped like a stack of pancakes. Beneath the table she twisted her hands together. 'Go ahead and talk.'

'Make no mistake, Noosa's been on the agenda a while.'

She nodded, knowing it was important to him that she understood he hadn't planned the whole thing to seduce her. 'Pam told me.'

'The way I see it, this is the perfect opportunity to explore this attraction we have. Get it out of our systems. Move on.'

Attraction. Physical, sexual. Mutual. She was still overawed with the knowledge that this dream of a guy was interested in her. For however long it took to 'move on'.

Was she game enough to go along with this? Experienced enough? To play it casual, have great sex—and it would be great sex with Jared Sanderson—then fly away to the other side of the world? She was leaving in three weeks and nothing and no one was going to stop her. So many ifs. Dream lovers were much less complicated.

But looking at the real man there *was* no comparison.

'If you're worried about repercussions,' he said, 'Pam'll probably be back at her desk by the time we return.' We can continue to see each other if we both decide that's what we still want.

'And your overseas plans won't be a problem,' he continued. 'We both know up front how it's going to be.'

Like a New Year sky-show, she thought. An explosion of sparks, heat and energy, over almost before it starts. And very terminal. Sky-shows also left an inevitable trail of cold ashy destruction as a reminder.

'So this…' she untangled her fingers, laid her palms flat on the table '…this…what we're going to "explore"…is a fling.'

He must have heard the doubt in her voice because he leaned across the table and covered the backs of her hands lightly with his—not soothing or reassuring so much as enticing. It sparkled all the way up her arms to her shoulders.

'You're not comfortable with that, are you?' he said. 'It's only a word, Sophie.'

'A word which conjures up other words like self-indulgence and irresponsibility.' *A good thing is only a good thing for as long as you enjoy it.*

He nodded slowly. 'So call it whatever you like.'

'A short term relationship,' she said. 'At least the word relationship implies a certain commitment, no matter how short-lived it may be. Don't worry,' she hurried on, 'I'm not looking for long term any more than you are.'

He looked at her kind of funny and she couldn't remember if he'd told her he wasn't looking for long term or whether she'd just assumed it. Of course he wasn't looking for more, she told herself, still holding his unreadable gaze. He didn't date the same woman for more than a few weeks.

She didn't date, period.

And yet, with Jared, even knowing all that, she felt...different somehow. Apart from being sexy he was a nice guy. Genuine. The kind of guy you could *maybe* trust. Maybe.

Turning her hands over so that his hard palms abraded her ultrasensitive ones, he laced his fingers through hers and his gaze seemed to reach down deep inside her to some unexplored place she'd never known existed. Maybe she was ready to take a chance on some fun with a guy. And since he'd enjoyed some fun at her expense, wouldn't it be kind of fun to tease this workaholic back just a little?

'So what do you say, are you with me?'

She just smiled a flirty smile and said, 'Tell you what, how about we have our coffee at my place?'

CHAPTER EIGHT

JARED leaned on Sophie's balcony and watched the palm fronds move lazily in the allotment across the street. A car-chase movie wailed from an open window in an apartment somewhere below. High-density living in apartments where the walls were thinner than cardboard wasn't for him. Then again, nowadays he could afford to be selective.

He knew Sophie's answer. Was one hundred and ten per cent certain. Didn't know why he'd asked the question. The question he was more interested in finding out the answer to right now was when did this short-term relationship start?

The brief drive back to her apartment had been…intense. Inside the car the tension had been so tight it had been almost explosive. Like sitting on a bunch of live wires.

Or maybe that had just been him.

She'd invited him into her cramped but cheerful living room with its hotchpotch mix of furniture and colour. Mostly maroon, cream and forest green with slashes of peach in the furnishings. She'd switched on a muted lamp then slid the balcony's full-length glass door open to catch the night breezes and invited him to make himself comfortable. He'd nearly laughed aloud at that and chosen the balcony, thankful for its cool camouflaging darkness.

She'd firmly refused his offer of help. Presumably, and some-what to his relief, she'd wanted to make the coffees herself.

He turned as she set two steaming aromatic mugs on her patio table in front of the open doorway. A muted gold light from the lamp spilled onto the balcony, leaving the far end with its potted palm draped in purple shadows.

'I'm afraid there's no such luxury as a cappuccino maker here. I…' She trailed off as she looked at him, and stood perfectly still.

Which gave him time to drink her in. Who needed coffee? She was glowing and beautiful and warmed his insides as no cappuccino could. She smelled of flowers in full bloom and hot velvet nights. Summer. No, he didn't want coffee. He'd waited all evening to reacquaint himself with her taste.

But before he could make his move she pulled the clasp from her hair and shook it free. An invitation if ever he saw one. He watched, transfixed, as the shiny black silk slithered loosely over her shoulders and down her back. The air between them smouldered with desire. With intent.

He wasn't aware that he'd crossed to her but here she was, an erratic pulse-beat away. In the half-light her skin was creamy smooth, her lips ripe and full, her eyes huge and aware. Then his fingers were skimming her jaw, angling her chin towards him. Up close he could pick out the subtle fragrance of sun-drenched petunias.

His heart seemed to stutter, his throat dried up. Right now he had no words to tell her how gorgeous she looked, how desirable. How much he wanted her. He lowered his mouth to hers.

Her body softened instantly against his, allowing him to pull her closer, to slide his hands beneath her hair and over her bare shoulders, down her spine to where the top of her dress fitted just below her shoulder blades.

She shifted with a moan that vibrated through his senses and settled in his throbbing groin. Her arms slid up and around his neck as she fitted herself against him. Her breasts rubbed against his chest. Her legs tangled with his. The smouldering heat threatened to spontaneously combust them both right where they stood.

And then, on the little table, his phone buzzed.

He almost lifted his head but suddenly something inside him rebelled. Years of putting everyone else first. Being there. Taking charge. He tightened his hold. Always-on-hand Jared was, at this moment—and for however many moments it might take—unavailable. With his fingers splayed against her back, he pressed her nearer, as if that might make the noise disappear.

But Sophie wasn't of the same mind. She drew back breathless, her hands still on his shoulders, and looked up at him. 'You want to get that?' she murmured.

'No.' No way. No. Not in a million years. 'It'll go to voicemail.'

The offensive sound ceased. He slid a finger along her collarbone, turned on just watching her lick her lips, wet from their kiss. 'Now…where were we…?' Putting her arms back in place around his neck, he nibbled at her mouth, *not* thinking about whether whoever-it-was had left a message and whether it might be important.

But, no matter how hard he tried, the moment was spoiled. He wanted to howl. Years of owning a business, and, more importantly, being there for his younger siblings, made it impossible to disregard the phone no matter how badly he wanted to make it with Sophie.

And he could already feel her cooling off. There was a tiny tremor of tension that hadn't been there before, as if she'd suddenly realised where this had been heading and come to her senses.

He only wished he felt as cool.

With a sigh he touched his forehead to hers. 'I'm going to have to see who that is first so I can ignore them guilt-free.'

She drew back. 'Timing,' she said, nodding as if she knew what she was talking about. 'Maybe it's a good thing it happened after all.'

'How can it be a good thing?' he muttered, stalking to the table. He swiped up the phone. One missed call from Lissa.

His pulse spiked in a different way when he remembered she'd gone out tonight. She'd left a message…

'Um, hi, Jared. Are you coming home any time soon? This is real dumb and I'm sorry and all, but I've locked myself out of Fort Knox. Any chance you can swing by and let me in?'

He closed his eyes and prayed for patience and understanding. Because right now he didn't have much of either.

'Is everything okay?' Sophie's soft voice reminding him of what might have been.

He opened his eyes but he turned away, didn't look at her. 'Melissa's managed to lock herself out,' he clipped, already returning her call.

Melissa answered on the first ring. 'Jared. Good, you got my message. Um…did I disturb you?'

He unclenched his teeth before they cracked. 'Why didn't your friends wait with you?' And why so early? She didn't usually stroll home till three. He fisted his free hand against his trousers and tried to maintain an outwardly calm and composed façade.

'I've got a headache so I caught a cab home and it was gone before I realised I'd forgotten my keys,' she said. 'I didn't notice because I left first and wasn't the one who locked the door tonight—you were. Sorry, are you…busy? I can—'

'Stay right there. I'll be home in ten minutes.' He swung around to Sophie. He wasn't going to make it with her tonight. 'Lissa's not feeling well, I have to go.'

'Yeah, you do.'

'I'm sorry about the coffee. I'll ring you.' He paused on his way to the front door to look back at her. She was still watching him with that wide expressive and slightly stunned gaze. 'What are you doing this weekend?' He realised he'd never asked his PA that question in quite that tone nor with the same interest and expectation.

The rush of surprised excitement in her eyes was quickly doused. 'I'm going to keep Pam company since she can't go out in public. I've got chick flicks, calamine lotion, chocolate ripple ice cream and a book of cryptic crosswords.'

He had to grin at the cosy scenario. 'Sounds like you've got all bases covered there.' So Sophie was the kind of person who was willing to put her weekend on hold for a friend. She knew what he was offering but she'd turned him down because she was needed elsewhere. Putting her needs aside. *Not so selfish as you profess, are you, Sophie Buchanan?*

He understood all too well. He also knew she understood why he had to leave now. He opened the front door, stepped onto the common balcony. 'I'll be in Brisbane first thing Monday morning and back late Tuesday.'

Sophie caught up with him, curled her hand around the door. 'Have a successful trip.'

He nodded briefly. 'Any problems, ring me.' His tone sounded brusque to his own ears as he turned abruptly away. Abrupt because he had to force himself not to touch her again. Because if he kissed her goodnight, he'd not want to stop at one and Liss was waiting and it was well past midnight.

Sophie was glad to have something to do over the weekend. During the day, Pam's companionship took her focus away from Jared. It was a different story at night when she lay on hot sheets and her body itched and burned so that she had to wonder if she was coming down with chicken pox too.

She watched the stars track across the night sky. She knew she and Jared would have ended up in bed if he hadn't been called away. Overwhelmed by the burning tension between them on her balcony and his obvious intention to take things further, she'd let her hair down. Literally.

She'd never played the seductress role but with Jared... well...it was different... And there'd been just enough wine in her system to loosen her up and free that inner woman she'd denied for so long.

Maybe he was the best thing to ever happen to her.

No. She shook her head against her pillow. She couldn't allow herself to think that. *Would not.* She had to keep her focus on her future. *Hers.* She was going overseas. Her goal, her life. He was just that fling she'd fantasised about.

'Yes, *fling*,' she declared into the darkness. And, as she'd stated to him on her opinion of flings, it was going to be self-indulgent and irresponsible. *And risky,* a little voice whispered.

But didn't she deserve one self-absorbed, giddy and reckless performance before she turned thirty? Only two years away.

She pushed away the melancholy thought that by that age she'd always expected to be happily married with her boisterous brood of three kids and assorted pets.

Circumstances changed, expectations changed accordingly.

Back at the office on Monday morning there was a mountain of work and preparation to be done before Wednesday. She shook her head when she reread the report she'd written, jabbed the delete key and started over. It seemed that every two minutes Jared popped into her mind. His name, the way he kissed, something he'd said, making her flustered and forgetful and somehow rendering her incapable of stringing together a coherent sentence, let alone transferring it to the computer.

What was this? There didn't seem to be any room in her mind for anything else but him. Nothing like it had ever happened to her before. Not with Glen, and he'd been the only man she'd dated seriously and she'd married him at eighteen.

Jared phoned on Tuesday afternoon to make final arrangements for their trip. Because she hadn't been expecting to hear his voice, her heart did a stop-start and her pulse *rat-a-tat-tatted*. He made her feel like a ditsy teenager, self-conscious and giggly.

She couldn't wait to see him again. Since when had she felt that way? It was dangerously like missing someone. Nowadays she made sure her happiness didn't depend on other people. So how was it possible? And she'd only known him a few days.

And then it was Wednesday.

Jared was picking her up soon after lunch, which gave Sophie time to ransack her bag and cull unnecessaries. To add an extra jacket. At the last minute she fretted over today's choice of attire. Casual or business? She eventually decided on something comfortable yet feminine. She was changing her monotone white trousers and blouse for a more vibrant silky knit dress when he knocked.

Her heart jumped into her mouth at the commanding sound. He was early again. She'd wanted to be super relaxed and in control when he arrived and she was anything but.

She sucked in a deep calming breath before opening the door. 'Hi.' Her voice still came out more breathless than she would have liked.

'Hi, yourself.'

His eyes met hers and seemed to brighten to the colour of moss. She raised a hand to the door jamb. There really was something about that creased cheek that made her weak at the knees and tipped her off-centre. Which was why her gaze took a quick southern slide...

And *ooh, yeah*...what Jared did for a pair of jeans. Dark denim faded in all the right places and tight where it counted.

She dragged her gaze up—and over a blinding white Ralph Lauren polo shirt with Sanderson's logo screen-printed in navy over one solid-looking pectoral. Top two buttons undone, a few wisps of dark masculine hair, prominent Adam's apple, a tiny C-shaped scar where maybe he'd nicked himself shaving once upon a time...

'Nice dress,' he said, and she realised while she'd been eyeing him up he'd been returning the favour. 'Orange suits you.'

'Orange.' She screwed up her nose and clucked her tongue—

such a common and inadequate word for such a beautiful colour. 'Stormy sunrise.'

'Even better.' He grinned. Another blinding moment. Then his grin sobered a bit and his eyes took on a sexy silvery glint as he reached for her rolling suitcase at her side. 'Maybe we'll see one of those together in the next couple of days.'

'Oh?' she replied, casually ignoring his meaning as she locked her door. 'Did they forecast bad weather?'

'Blue skies all the way.' He smiled, then headed for the elevator.

She followed him inside the lift without comment. Ridiculous not to now when they'd already shared more than just air and were about to get even closer in the next couple of days.

A moment later she settled into his luxury convertible for the three-hour drive. It was, as Jared had promised, blue skies, and a lovely day to be on the road rather than stuck inside an office somewhere.

Before they turned onto the Pacific Motorway, which would take them past Brisbane and on to the Sunshine Coast, Jared asked, 'Do you mind if we call in at Crystal's place on the way?'

The question seemed to come out of the blue and jolted Sophie right out of her comfort zone. 'No, of course not. Is she okay?'

'Fine. She came home from hospital on Saturday and Ian took a few days off, but it's her first day on her own with the bub and Ian's working late tonight to catch up. She asked if I'd drop by.'

'If you ask me, I think Jared just wants another look at his niece.' Sophie smiled his way and saw his mouth kick up at the edge.

They pulled up outside a cream brick home surrounded by several palms and a high fence. 'I'll just wait here…' She didn't want to intrude, nor did she want to see a newborn baby and experience the associated emotions that went with it.

He turned in his seat to face her. A puzzled frown puckered his brow. 'Crystal's expecting to meet you. I told her we couldn't stay long.'

'You told her about me?'

'I told her my temporary PA was accompanying me to Noosa, yeah.'

Oh. Of course. A tinge of embarrassment stung her cheeks and she smiled casually to cover it, glad she was wearing her sunglasses. 'This is a family time...I mean there's a million things she'll be catching up on—sleep, or feeding...'

'She's not. I spoke to her just before I picked you up.' He tossed his sunglasses on the dash and swung open his door. 'Come on, five minutes.'

Sophie followed. What else could she do? She didn't want to see the baby, or, worse, to be asked if she wanted a hold. And she just knew neither of them would understand. They would think her rude. Still, she could be lucky. New babies slept a lot. Didn't they? Sometimes.

Tension snapped her spine straight all the way to the door, where they were greeted by a gorgeous golden retriever who raced around from the side of the house.

'Meet Goldie.' Jared ruffled the dog's fur. 'Hello, girl.' Her eyes drooled adoration up at him as he caught the expressive face in his hands, and was rewarded with a sloppy kiss.

'Oh, isn't she beautiful?' Sophie crouched beside Jared to join in the petting. 'Do you have pets?'

'No. Our much-loved and ancient Betsy died a few years back. I'm too busy to train a new puppy and now that Lissa's home less and less...it wouldn't be fair on the dog.'

But Sophie saw the fleeting shadow that crossed his gaze before his sister opened the door.

'Great meeting you, Sophie.' A remarkably hassle-free-looking Crystal led the way to her kitchen. 'I've heard a lot about you.'

Sophie looked to Jared, who shrugged his shoulders and

blamed Lissa. He set the bag of supplies on a table crammed at one end with baby products and a florist's arrangement of pink blooms that were starting to wilt, then promptly disappeared down a hallway, presumably to see his niece.

Unlike Melissa, who shared no apparent familial traits with Jared, Crystal was the feminine epitome of her brother. Same tall, dark, green-eyed attractiveness. And looking amazing considering she'd given birth only a week ago.

They chatted a few moments while Crystal unloaded an unlikely selection of disposable nappies, pâté and crackers and a fresh pineapple from Jared's eco-bag. She was as easy-going as Melissa. Both sisters obviously thought the world of Jared and seemed to be ever-so-subtly interested in Sophie's life.

Sophie was starting to relax and think that it was about time they got moving when Crystal said, 'You have to meet Arabella before you go.'

Oh. Sophie bit the inside of her lip. 'I wouldn't want to disturb...'

But Crystal was already leading the way and the last thing Sophie wanted to do was offend the new mother in any way, shape or form. These days she was experienced at masking her feelings. No one would know that inside where it was just her, her heart was still crying over her once-in-a-million miracle that had never had a chance.

Sophie could smell the baby's room from the end of the hall. It streamed through her senses. The lovely soft scent of powder and silky skin and newness. Crystal showed her into the room and Sophie made a valiant attempt to lose the melancholy.

Jared was leaning over the bassinet, stroking the infant's cheek. And *he* was the one making goo-goo noises. He turned when they entered, his expression full of pride and pleasure. 'She's just waking up.' He looked to his sister. 'May I?'

Crystal set a pile of baby clothes on the blanket box. 'Go right ahead. Just remember the clean nappy by your left arm's included in part of the picking-up ritual.'

'Fine by me.'

Somewhere a phone rang. 'I'll just get that,' she said and left the room.

Sophie watched Jared pick his niece up with infinite tenderness and care, cradling her fuzzy-topped head in his palm. The rest of her fitted snug along the length of his forearm.

'There you are, princess.' There was a smile and love in his voice as he tucked her closer. 'Uncle Jared's got you, you lucky girl, you.' Princess chewed on her fist while unfocused eyes of an indefinable colour stared up at him.

Sophie had never seen anything more beautiful or more powerful than the sight of this tiny fragile infant against Jared's tanned, hard and muscular arms. It was one of those life-affirming moments and the pity of it was that she didn't think uncle noticed.

Made for fatherhood. The fleeting thought skimmed the edge of her consciousness. She'd heard people talking about a woman being made to be a mother but had never applied the parenthood tag to a male. But yes, she thought, watching the muscles in his arms twist and bunch as he adjusted his hold, that was what he was. His arms were as capable of holding babies as they'd be accomplished at holding a woman.

Her heart swelled and blossomed and seemed to open up like the petals of a flower.

Because right here, right now, she was falling for him.

It wasn't his looks or wealth or charm, they were just side benefits. No, it was much more basic and simple than that. It was his underlying goodness, his empathy for others, his honesty. Core values she shared.

One day he'd make some woman very happy. His wife, the mother of his children would never want for anything. But it wouldn't be Sophie. It *couldn't* be Sophie.

His eyes looked unexpectedly her way, catching her watching him. Catching her thoughts? She hoped not, and drew herself up, eyeballing him boldly, daring him to take issue with them.

But he only said, 'Want a hold?'

At first she was afraid her voice wouldn't work, but luckily her 'not today,' didn't carry the emotion she held inside. She forced a laugh to cover the wretched awkwardness. 'I'd probably drop her or something.'

'No, you wouldn't.' He stared at her a moment, eyes slightly narrowed. She could see the questions shuffling behind his eyes.

'Babies and I don't hit it off.' She shrugged carelessly. 'They take one look at me and it's waterworks.'

'Not with Arabella, she's too young yet.' He kissed her nose. 'Aren't you, sweetheart?' But to Sophie's relief he didn't pursue her protest, preferring to talk some more *ga-ga* to his niece. He lowered the infant onto the change table and managed the nappy-change process with the same skill and confidence he used to conduct a business meeting.

And, oh… Rather than detract from Jared's powerful masculinity, the child he tended simply added another dimension to the already multifaceted man she was coming to know. Her legs almost sagged beneath her and something rolled over in her chest. She was, without a doubt, looking at a picture-perfect poster for the sexiest man alive.

She turned away.

She needed to remember a couple of important things. One. Jared wasn't a one-woman man. Second, she was leaving Australia. And top of the list, she reminded herself a man who loved kids this much could never be the man for her.

No man could.

CHAPTER NINE

SINCE Sophie had never travelled up this way and seemed so enraptured with the passing scenery, Jared let her indulge in relative silence, pointing out places of interest on the way.

One thing was certain, she wasn't looking for home and family. He'd seen the almost panicked look in her eyes when he'd asked her if she wanted to hold Arabella. He drummed his fingers lightly on the steering wheel as Brisbane's hazy skyline came into view in the distance.

She was the most skittish woman around babies he'd ever seen. She'd shown zero interest in the baby shop in Coolangatta. Too much so, in fact. Had only met Arabella because basic courtesy required it. She'd admitted she had no interest in tying herself down with kids.

Like someone else he'd known. Bianca had kept her no-kids policy to herself until she'd discovered Jared intended Melissa to be a part of their lives after they married. Bianca might have reconsidered his proposal but he knew it would never have worked in the long run. He'd counted himself lucky he'd found out before he'd made a commitment. No second chances.

At least with Sophie he knew everything up front. Short term was all they were looking for. When it happened, his children would be wanted and loved by both parents. But settling down was years into the future. The years he should have been out drinking till dawn and getting laid had been spent being a responsible guardian to his sisters, and he had some catching up to do.

He was looking forward to doing some of that catching up with Sophie these next couple of days.

'Spectacular, don't you agree?'

Jared's voice somewhere behind her, plush velvet stroking over her shoulders and down her back.

'Very.' Sophie stood in the middle of the room, not knowing where to look first. This palatial riverfront home was *their* home for the next couple of days. And nights.

It was the ever-present thoughts about those nights that had her nerves twitching and her hormones bouncing like lottery balls on a Saturday night. She quashed them quickly, focusing on the here and now. It was more than spectacular, it was over-the-top dazzling.

White-tiled flooring and furniture flowed outwards in all directions, giving the impression it went on for ever. A few touches of blue and lime green in the cushions or decorative art invoked a cool sense of peace and tranquillity. Extending out from the patio was a private jetty where one could moor their luxury yacht, and on the other side of the river in the reddening haze of sunset she could see other multimillion-dollar homes.

Turn to the right and she could see the master bedroom and its snowy white king-size bed reflected in the turquoise infinity pool off the main living area. Floor-to-ceiling sliding glass doors in both rooms virtually allowed one to swim to the bedroom if one so desired.

Of course they'd taken separate bedrooms. One had to act the part of a PA to begin with at least and she still needed some privacy at this point in their relationship.

Right now her thoughts were on the upcoming business dinner in a little over an hour and she needed to turn herself into the professional Jared expected. She didn't have time for the heat she saw in his eyes that promised to make them late.

'I'm…ah…going to jump in the shower.'

His eyes darkened. 'Do you need your back scrubbed?'

Her blood warmed, her skin tingled. He hadn't moved a muscle but Sophie had the impression he'd come closer. She had no doubt he was well skilled in scrubbing backs, making fast, furious love and getting to his meetings on time.

Not her... At least she didn't *think* so. 'Do you want this new client on your books?' she said, turning away before she decided to test the theory for herself. She headed for the refuge of her en-suite bathroom.

She felt the smile in his voice when, from behind her, he said, 'If you change your mind just give a yell.'

Her lips curved. 'If you hear me yell you have my full permission to come right on in and to hell with being professionally punctual,' she tossed over her shoulder as she walked away.

As refuges went it was a marble palace—all white with gold fittings, fernery spilling from hanging pots and warm downlights that turned her paler-than-average skin colour—especially the parts not normally exposed—a flattering honey tone. She twisted her hair up and clasped it on top of her head.

Setting the water to moderately hot, she stepped beneath the spray. Under the circumstances she really didn't need hot, but when it came to her shower she was a creature of habit...

A squelchy squirming sensation beneath her toes had her jumping back and glancing down. She saw a centipede—longer and thicker than her middle finger—its hideous body writhing in the shower stall at her feet. *And they bite...*

But it was the way it thrashed about that had the blood-curdling scream springing from her lips while her fingers scrabbled for the shower-screen door. *Get out! Get out!*

'What's wrong?' Loud knocking on the door. 'Sophie?'

'Get it out!' Through the glass enclosure, she was aware of Jared bursting into the room but her eyes were pinned to the sight inches from her toes while she struggled to open the door. She finally got the door to slide and all but fell out of the

shower, backing up as far away as she could. 'That…*that*…' It was all she could get past her constricted throat.

Shutting the water off, Jared reached for the wooden handled back scrub hanging beneath the shower head and she screwed her eyes shut…

Water trickled down her cooling body as she clasped her arms around her and heard a series of loud knocks. A convulsive shiver shuddered down her spine. 'Oh, *God.*' She didn't want to know how he'd done it, only that he had. 'Is it dead? Is it gone?'

'It's dead.' She heard the toilet flush. 'And now it's gone.'

A tortured sigh escaped her lips. Only then did she take it all in. She was naked. He wore jeans, nothing else. She slid her eyes to his, willing him to do the same.

To his gentlemanly credit, his gaze remained locked with hers. Not even a flicker of a glance where it shouldn't go. He reached for a towel on the rail beside him, passed it to her.

'Thanks.' She grabbed it and pulled it in front of herself. Shivering. With cold or relief or excitement? 'Just so you know, I'm not one of those squealy women,' she felt compelled to point out. 'Normally. But those…' She shuddered again.

'Okay.' He didn't move a muscle. But there was a flicker of movement at one corner of his mouth saying maybe he believed her, maybe not.

'I'm going to get back in there now,' she said, as much to herself as to him. Then another flesh-crawling thought… 'You don't think it came up the drain, do you? What if it has a mate somewhere…'

'I don't know. Maybe you should let me stay here and make sure.' There was a roguish light in those eyes, a hint of the devil in his chivalrous words. He reached into the stall and switched the water back on for her.

Then—and she didn't know what demon possessed her… yes she did and his name was Jared Sanderson—she tossed the towel on the floor and stepped under the water. 'Maybe I should.' Her heart was hammering, her blood coursing hotly through her veins. *Take a chance, be that sensual woman you want to be.* Knowing she was starting something she might not be able to stop, keeping her back to him, she dangled her soap-filled sponge-on-a-string over one shoulder. 'And maybe I should let you be useful and wash my back while you wait.'

She felt him take the sponge and, oh, that first glide across her shoulders was warm, slow and reassuringly impersonal. Another pass, this time down her spine, stopping at her waist. Then pressure at the base of her neck.

She inhaled sharply. 'That's not my sponge...'

'No.'

Thumbs. Working tensed muscles in her neck. Then hands. Slick, soapy hands that began at her nape and slid across her shoulders. Down either side of her spine and over the curve of her waist, fingers both tantalisingly close to the sides of her breasts and frustratingly far away.

And she maybe shouldn't have let him start... Her breathing grew heavy. So did her breasts—heavy and tight and full. She wanted to turn around and let him give them the same slow, slick attention.

His hands slid lower and cupped her bottom. Her feminine core grew hot, her breaths quickened. But when his thumbs dipped between her butt cheeks, then lightly down the backs of her thighs, her legs sagged and she braced her hands on the tiles in front of her for support. *'Jared.'*

'Right here, honey,' he murmured, his lips so close she could feel his breath hot on her ear. He'd stepped into the shower— she could smell the wet denim—but the only part of him in contact with her were his hands.

And what contact.

'This was a bad idea...' She gasped when his exploration grew bolder, his fingers delved deeper. Too deep. Not nearly deep enough...

'You don't really think that,' he assured her.

'Oh. Yes. I. Do.' She was so breathless she couldn't seem to get out more than one word at a time between shallow gulps of air.

'So you want me to stop...' His hands moved away.

'Yes. *No*,' she moaned.

She heard his soft chuckle, then sent up a prayer of thanks when his newly soaped-up hands skimmed her waist and came around to cup her breasts. Holding their weight in his palms, he massaged and teased, swirling his fingertips around her tight nipples and sending sensation spiralling to her core and lower, between her thighs.

Steam billowed and swirled around them like an intimate cloak. Just the two of them in their own private steam bath. The water pelting her now oversensitised body felt like hot hailstones and sounded harsh in the stall's confines.

She squirmed as the ache between her legs intensified. Moving her legs farther apart, she arched her back and begged him silently to, 'Touch me.'

She hadn't realised she'd spoken aloud but her whispered plea sounded harsh and desperate in the humid air and not like her at all. And then one of his hands was between her thighs, fingernails cruising along her slippery cleft, the fingers of his other hand rolling a nipple, teasing it into almost unbearable hardness.

'Like this?' he whispered against her ear and plunged his fingers inside her. He withdrew them slowly, drawing out the wetness along her sensitised flesh and making her moan some more.

Her legs trembled like stalks of wheat in a rain storm. She leaned her forehead against the cool tiles as well as her hands. 'Yes.' *Exactly like that.*

He repeated his exquisite torture. And again. Over and over, each thrust of his fingers more erotic, more persuasive. His lips nuzzled her neck then bit gently, possessively, and his voice was thick with arousal when he said, 'You're so hot. So deliciously wet.'

His explicit words, the skilful way he touched her, as if he'd known her body for years, the sound of his voice against her ear sent her soaring up, up, up. Over the silky precipice on a low heartfelt cry, her body convulsing around his fingers.

'Oh. *Wow*,' she whispered when she'd got her breath back. His hands trailed over her thighs, then away.

But when she finally turned, she saw nothing but steam and a trail of water across the tiles. He was gone.

Like a dream.

How did you walk into a room to face *your boss* as if you hadn't just been given the most intense orgasm of your life? Sophie wondered as she stared at her reflection in the bedroom mirror. She adjusted the collar on the cream dress and asked herself how did you face that boss, the one who'd given you that orgasm, over a business dinner as if your private parts weren't still on fire and already aching for more?

Grabbing her jacket and purse from the chair, she headed for the living room. She was about to find out.

He was wearing a charcoal suit and baby-blue pinstriped shirt with matching blue tie and watching the local news on the ginormous flat-screen TV on the wall. His short hair was still damp and his fresh foresty scent drifted in the warm air.

His gaze flicked to hers across the expanse of tiled floor. Dark, hungry, slightly desperate. As if he wanted to eat her alive and wanted nothing to do with her at the same time. And she could hardly blame him. As earth-shattering as her climax had been, it hadn't exactly been a mutually shared and satisfying experience.

'Hi,' she said, since he didn't seem inclined to speak.

He looked her up and down, then his eyes lingered on her bare legs and she saw his jaw clench.

'Is it too short? It's too short.' She should have gone for the mid-calf green instead of the above-the-knee. Thoughtless under the circumstances. 'I'll ch—'

'It's not too short.' He cleared the huskiness from his throat and a little of the tension eased from his features. 'It's fine just the way it is. You look lovely.'

'Thanks. So do you. Well, not *lovely* exactly,' she babbled on. 'More smart, savvy businessman.'

'I'm not sure how smart and savvy this businessman's going to be this evening.' Flicking off the TV with the remote, he crossed to her, curled hard fingers around her upper arms. 'I didn't play it too damn smart back there in the bathroom.' His olive-green eyes turned to unreadable slate and he dropped his hold as if he'd been stung.

Her cheeks burned, sparks shot through her bloodstream. Her body was already clamouring for an encore of his sexpertise and *he regretted it*?

Jared clamped his jaw shut. She looked like a fantasy in that nude-coloured dress and black shoes. And if he stood here a microsecond longer looking into those molten amber eyes and knowing he was responsible for putting the heat in them, he'd lose his tenuous hold on control and his *smart savvy business* reputation really would be a memory. Turning away, he strode to the door. 'Let's go.'

The deal was in the bag. Jared already knew. The groundwork had been done over the past month and tonight was more of a social event.

Sophie was the perfect PA and partner. She involved Trent's wife Tania in girl talk, leaving him free to discuss plans and possibilities with Trent, but was eerily able to switch to business when he needed her to. She'd obviously swotted up on the information over the weekend because she was conversant and up-to-date with the project.

It had been a terminally long dinner, but Trent was meeting

them tomorrow to show them over the property and sign off on the deal.

But then their hosts wanted to show them a little local hospitality and it was on to the newest supper club to listen to the latest jazz/blues trio over a cheese and wine nightcap.

It was torture sitting so close to Sophie that he could smell the soap she'd used—the soap he'd used, actually—and not being able to touch her the way he wanted to. Not as a boss but as something more. For the short time they had before she left he wanted to know Sophie better. A lot better.

A couple of times their thighs had bumped beneath the table and their eyes connected—a brief clash of heat—before she shifted position and resumed conversation. With Tania, with Trent. Not him. Since this was business, *his* business, there was nothing he could do about it now, and she knew it. She was driving him mad. Payback, no doubt, for the way he'd left the situation hanging on their way out this evening when he'd dropped her arms as if she had some terminal infectious disease.

He had a few ideas for payback himself.

It was nearly midnight before they said their goodnights to the clients. The journey back to their accommodation took less than five minutes. During that time Sophie went into PA mode with tomorrow's plans. A meeting at ten to discuss a new project, a couple of client follow-ups, signing the deal with Trent…

He knew it backwards; he'd given her the instructions for the damn schedule in the first place.

He pressed the remote and the security door rolled up, rolled down as he drove through and parked undercover at the side of the house. He killed the engine. Unclicked his seat belt with unnecessary force. 'That's enough.' She stopped speaking immediately. 'Your PA duties are over for the evening.'

'Okay.' She chewed on her lip a moment, then turned to face him, disengaged her own seat belt.

He couldn't read her eyes in the dimness. 'Sophie. Honey.' He caressed the side of her face. Noticed his fingers all but trembled. 'You misunderstood me earlier when I said what happened in the bathroom wasn't a smart move.'

She tilted her head to one side, as if to say 'go on'.

He caught her face between his hands. 'If I'd touched you again I'd've had you on the floor with that dress up around your ears before you could blink and we'd never have made it to dinner.'

She gave a tiny gasp and her fingers worked at the neckline of her dress.

He shook his head. 'If that sounded crude, I apologise. You've been driving me to distraction all evening. All week. I'm going crazy. Do you know how hard it's been all evening? Watching you and not being able to touch you?'

'No. I can't begin to imagine...' a corner of her mouth kicked up, a smile that spread to her cheeks and twinkled into her eyes as she looked pointedly down at his swollen crotch '...how hard. But if you take me indoors maybe you can show me.'

He sat back and watched her gaze heat as she reached for his tie, slid it through her fingers. 'And for the record I'd really, really like for you to have me on the floor. Dress around my ears and all. It's a personal fantasy of mine.'

'Be sure you know what you're asking.' His voice came out rough-edged, harsh in the car's close confines as he ripped off his tie.

She shook her head. 'I know exactly what.'

CHAPTER TEN

A QUIVER of excitement thrummed through Sophie as Jared gripped her upper arms and pulled her against him. His mouth crashed down on hers, demanding. His fingers plucked at her nipples through her dress, arousing. His breath was harsh and fast and hot against her cheek and she shivered in anticipation.

This wasn't the charming, focused entrepreneur she'd spent the evening with. Nor was he the suave and skilled and generous lover who'd sent her into ecstasy in the shower earlier. That man had been a man in control.

This man was not and the knowledge that Sophie was the woman to bring out this wild, desperate side sang through her body like fine wine. Feminine power. She'd never experienced it, and it felt amazing. Her blood frizzled beneath her skin wherever he took those impatient hands and clever mouth.

Quick as a snap he had the zip in her dress shirring down her back. His mouth was hot and wet on her neck as he slipped the dress off her shoulders. 'I want you...'

'Yes...' she breathed, quivering at the edge of desperation she heard in his voice.

Quick deft fingers plunged beneath the edge of her bra to tweak her already hard nipples into throbbing points of lust. He yanked the bra cups down. 'I want you *now*.' His urgency sent hot shivers down her spine.

Closing her eyes, she arched her aching breasts upwards. 'Yes. Right now.'

And she would have let him take her right then, right there in the car with the squeak and smell of leather, the gearstick between them like some secondary phallus, but he was out of the car, opening her door, pulling her out.

He tugged her to the front of the car, somehow losing her dress on the way, and splayed her across the slippery smooth bonnet to feast on her semi-exposed breasts like some primeval starving animal.

The heat of the car's engine warmed her back and buttocks, cool damp air caressed her décolletage. A hard thigh nudged her legs apart, one hand shot between them and up to find the edge of her panties.

And, oh, that first flick of his fingers over damp cotton… She sucked in a gasp as the small but electric sensation bolted to her core.

'Sophie…' It was a growl, as strong and dangerous as any predator, and she trembled, not with fear but with desire. Excitement. Anticipation.

One tug and his fingers twisted beneath her panties. He stroked her once, twice, then plunged inside. Her inner muscles quivered and clenched around his fingers.

Their gazes clashed. She stared in wonder, in awe. All trace of civilised gone, just primal aroused male. She could see it smoulder behind his night-darkened eyes, could feel it in the heat coming off his body in waves, could smell the musky scent of arousal on his skin.

And the long, hard and demanding ridge of masculinity against her thigh.

She wanted it inside her. She wanted him stretching her, invading her, filling her. *Ful*filling her. Yanking the annoying clasp from her hair, she shook her hair free, aware of the feminine nature of her action and revelling in it. 'Yes…*now*,' she ordered, leaning back on her elbows, spreading her legs wider for him and rocking against his hand.

With a sharp, ripping sound her panties were gone, tossed

away, leaving her fully exposed to Jared's hot eyes. There was a stunned moment of stillness from both of them. Then the want, the impatience.

'Now, now, now.' The fevered chant beat through her blood, keeping time with her frantic pulse.

Jared's fingers were so unsteady he could barely unzip his trousers. She didn't want finesse, neither did he. He could have given her words—how alluring she looked in starlight with her hair tumbled over her shoulders, her eyes hot for him, her dusky nipples glistening from his mouth, but she didn't want romantic words, neither did he.

Now, now, now.

The flames in his gut leapt higher at the husky sound of her ragged demand on the still evening air. She didn't want slow, neither did he.

Sliding his hands beneath her arms, he reached behind her back, flicked the catch on her bra. She pulled it off and sent it sailing behind her with an abandon that surprised him almost as much as it seemed to surprise her. She might have tossed her stilettos the same way but he shook his head. 'The shoes stay.'

He freed himself from his boxers while he muttered, 'Protection.'

She stared into his eyes for a beat longer than he expected before she said, 'Got it covered.'

Praise be to heaven for that.

No more waiting, no time to think. He plunged into her hot slippery sex in one swift glide. He knew it was only physical but the groan that erupted seemed to come from the very depths of his being.

Clamping her legs around his waist, she answered with a low keening sound of her own and latched onto his shoulders, her fingernails digging hard into his flesh. He relished the exquisite pain, returning the favour with lips and tongue and teeth on the delicate fragrant skin beneath her jaw.

She was the sweet new temptation of a spring morning, the sultry seductress of summer's heat. And wherever he led, she kept pace with him. To places of hot, dark pleasures and whirling dervishes and erotic delights.

He told himself it was all need and greed and speed yet... for an infinitesimal hiatus, there was a lifetime in her eyes. But there was no time to puzzle it, less to wonder. He drove faster, harder, until he heard her cry out as she came, the wonder of it as he lost himself inside her.

For a long moment he rested his head on her breast, listening to her heart's rapid pounding, his own heart beating in his ears while they both came down to earth. What had just happened here? Was this intensity normal? Surely it hadn't been so long he'd forgotten what it was like?

'You okay?' he murmured, moving his lips over her skin. He looked into her eyes.

She blinked at him. 'Mm-mm.' It was a lazy, satisfied sound. 'I reckon so.'

'I think I can just about feel my legs again. What say we find somewhere a little more comfortable?' Without waiting for an answer he carried her across the patio and inside.

He set her on her feet in front of the white leather couch and stared at her. With only the underwater lights from the pool beyond the window to lend them light, awe and...something more...filled him.

She was a picture of perfection. Her lips were ripe, full, thoroughly kissed, her eyes wide and soulful, her long bare legs, dainty feet crammed in the sexiest pair of shoes he'd ever seen. Who was this dishevelled Sophie with her hair a tangled dark halo, her nipples pinched in the cool air? 'Are you cold?'

Sophie looked into his eyes and wondered who this woman was that she'd suddenly become. And how could she be cold bathed in all that stunning heat? She shook her head. 'But there is a problem here.'

He frowned. 'What?'

'I'm the only one naked. Hardly seems fair.'

A slow smile touched his lips. 'You're probably right.'

Her gaze drifted down his dishevelled torso. His shirt was crushed, his trousers hung open and low on his hips. She reached for his top shirt button. 'My turn, I think.'

She worked the rest of his buttons, then she was dragging the shirt aside so she could see if her dream lived up to the reality. To splay her hands over hard, bronzed skin sprinkled with dark hair. 'So hot,' she murmured, then leaned forward to press a kiss over his heart and feel the strong beat beneath her lips.

Still stroking his skin with its hard muscle beneath, she flicked her tongue around a tight male nipple. A tingle of salt, a whiff of masculine soap, the unique scent that was Jared. Sliding her hands over his shoulders, she eased the shirt off his arms. The immediate urgency over for the next few moments at least, she continued her journey of exploration in a leisurely, indulgent fashion.

Enjoying her newly discovered feminine power, she tugged the waistband lower and ordered, 'Everything off. Now.'

'Bossy little creature, aren't you?' he murmured, voice tinged with amusement.

When he'd obliged, she took a moment to admire the view. Gorgeous. Perfect. She had to touch. So many places. So many textures. He reigned over Michelangelo's David any day... *Venice, Rome.*

Her joy in the moment slipped a little. Soon she'd be far from here and this would be a memory. And it could never be anything more with him. This afternoon with baby Arabella had confirmed she'd never be the woman for Jared.

Oh, but what if she could? Rather than meet his gaze, she pressed her lips to his chest. What if he didn't care that she couldn't have kids? What if he could love her for who she was and it would be enough?

Love? She yanked herself back. Whatever was she thinking?

'Regrets?'

'Oh, no.' Now she met his eyes. 'No. I was thinking, that's all.'

'Sad thoughts.' He slid his arms around her and held her close. And his skin when it touched hers was like fire, intensely arousing yet quietly comforting at the same time.

'I've seen that look in your eyes already today,' he murmured, his words muffled against her hair.

'No.' She had to be more careful. Keep her guard up around him. She mustn't let him see. It was all about good times for the next couple of weeks. She wouldn't let herself think beyond that. 'You imagine too much.'

And she kissed his chin and smiled into those perceptive eyes. Her fingers busied themselves lower down and she saw his gaze change from concern to arousal and felt him stir to life again in her hands. She blinked and ran a thumb over the silky tip. 'Already?'

He grinned. 'Just give me a few minutes.'

She wondered how long it had been since he'd been with a woman.

She let him tug her down onto the wide leather couch. They lay close in companionable silence for a moment, staring up at the underwater light from the pool reflecting on the ceiling. Somewhere across the water drifted the distant sound of wind chimes.

'Tell me about him.'

She frowned in the darkness. Just when she thought he'd forgotten about it… 'Who?'

'The guy from your home town. The reason you left.'

'How do you…?' She trailed off. That first day on the way to Coolangatta she'd talked about a 'change of scenery' and avoided mentioning him because it was none of Jared's business. But Jared was the kind of guy who made you want to share. 'That would be my ex-husband.'

She felt him shift, felt his gaze on her. 'You were married?'

She kept her eyes focused on the ceiling. 'For five years.'

'When?'

'We split up five years ago.'

'You must have been ridiculously young when you got married.'

The words hurt. And angered. 'I was eighteen and maybe it seems ridiculous to you but I had my reasons. Don't presume to know me, because you don't.' And just as ridiculous were the tears that stung the backs of her eyes.

He immediately rolled towards her, then up onto an elbow, and looked deep down into her eyes. Further. All the way to her scarred heart. 'Hey...' he said softly. 'That's me being an insensitive jerk. I had no right to say that and I apologise.' He pressed a chaste warm kiss on her lips.

She stared up at him, seeing genuine concern. Because he was that kind of guy. He'd been blunt but he hadn't meant to hurt her. He'd just touched a particularly sensitive nerve. 'Apology accepted.'

He dipped his head so that his brow touched hers. 'It's just that I think of Lissa at eighteen. If she— Well.' He blew out a slow breath.

'Maybe you're too protective,' Sophie said carefully. 'Big brothers are like that sometimes.'

'What about your brother?'

'No.' She tried to remember the last time she'd seen him and couldn't. 'Corey's one of the exceptions.'

'So this man you married and divorced still puts clouds in your eyes. He still has the power to hurt you.'

'No.' She shook her head. 'How can a man who means nothing to you hold that kind of power? He has another woman, a young son and another baby on the way. He's happy. I'm happy,' she finished, determined, as much to convince herself as to convince Jared. If Glen was unfaithful to his current wife, Sophie didn't know about it. Didn't care.

'Do you want to tell me why you married him?'

'Because I was ridiculously young?' She gave a half-smile, forgiving Jared, and he reached for her nearest hand, twined his fingers with hers and somehow the story flowed like the river outside while she lay in his arms. She'd never shared her past. Only Pam knew her story, but sharing it with Jared felt natural, like lifting a burden off her shoulders. And it was almost as seductive as sex.

'My parents drank a lot and fought more. Dad was in and out of work. Violence was the norm. Corey was out of there by the time he was sixteen.

'But when *I* was sixteen Mum was involved in a major car accident and I stayed on to help. That lasted about eighteen months but eventually I couldn't stand the arguments and the booze any longer.

'I'd met Glen a few months earlier. He was ten years older than me and we were both working in hospitality. He seemed a good-natured guy and, looking back now, I guess I saw him as a substitute father.' A safe haven. A way out. 'One day we walked into a register office and just did it. When I informed my parents, they told me I was nothing but a disappointment, no better than my brother. Then they cracked open a cheap bottle of wine and began to drink themselves into their regular oblivion. I never saw them again.'

Jared gathered her to him. For a long moment he offered no words, just a hug as sweet and comfortable as it was uncomplicated.

'I send them Christmas and birthday cards with a cheque when I can afford it. They cash the cheques without fail but I've never heard boo from them. So I don't go back. I don't want to.'

He squeezed her hand. They both knew the money was wasted. 'So…you keep a dream diary,' he prompted, switching to a less painful topic a moment later.

'Yes.' Her pulse skipped a beat and she swivelled to face him. How did he know?

'I saw it on your bed when I left you in the shower. Hard to miss with the bright neon scrawl on the cover. Relax, Sophie, I didn't read it. I would never invade your privacy that way.'

'Okay.' She blew out a breath. Silence filled the tiny space between them and in those quiet heartbeats she trusted him with the truth. 'I used to have nightmares. My counsellor suggested it way back and it's become a routine.'

She felt the warmth of his understanding flow over her. 'Do you still have bad dreams?'

'Not so much now.' It occurred to her suddenly that she'd not made an entry since Saturday morning.

'Am I in there?' His voice turned playful.

She shoved at his arm. 'You know you are.'

'How many times?'

She grinned. 'Not telling.'

'What about fantasies, do you write them down too?'

'No. They're entirely different.'

'Tell me a fantasy.'

'I…can't.'

'Sure you can.'

'You'll laugh. Or think I'm awful.'

'I promise I won't do either.'

She snuggled nearer. 'I've always imagined making love in the open. Under the stars. I've never done it outside.'

'Never?'

She shook her head, then looked at him in the semi-darkness. 'You?'

The curve of his lips and the twinkle in his eyes pronounced him guilty but he didn't answer, just lifted her off the couch and carried her to his bed.

* * *

Jared's body clock woke him daily at precisely five-thirty a.m. no matter what time he'd gone to bed. Another of those predictable patterns that made up his life. He was also one of those people many either envied or hated for his ability to rise and shine the moment his eyes opened. He habitually swam for thirty minutes then breakfasted on oranges or pineapple, two eggs and strong black coffee.

But it had been a very long time since he'd woken with a woman lying beside him.

And that woman was currently dead to the world. And no wonder—he'd kept her awake most of the night. He'd not been able to get enough of her. Her sweet taste, her summer fragrance, her silken hair rippling over his body in black waves when she was on top. The moans she made when she came... and there'd been a few, he thought with a smile.

He wondered how long it had been since she'd been with a man.

She shifted in her sleep, a tiny smile touched the corner of her mouth as if she was dreaming. Of him and the things he'd done to her through the night, perhaps. The things they'd done to each other.

His erection hardened, throbbed, almost to the point of pain while he continued to watch her. But it was more than the physical. And that bothered him. Healthy lust was all well and good, but this...almost desperate need— *Scratch that thought.* Good grief, he was *not* desperate. But he'd never experienced anything quite like the way it was with Sophie. Alarming was what it was.

Sophie was moving on, and that was best for both of them. He reminded himself he went for outdoorsy girls—personal trainers rather than personal assistants.

And yet... He frowned, trying to make sense of it. They'd both agreed it was short term, so what the heck was the problem?

He needed space. Hardly daring to breathe, he backed off the bed and padded outside to where the pool's mirrored surface reflected the waning night.

Away from temptation. Better. He rubbed chilled arms then slid silently beneath the water. Cold water rushed past his ears as he torpedoed forward, feet and legs working economically. There *was no problem*, he assured himself as he broke the surface halfway down the pool's length.

Deliberately blanking his mind, he sliced through the water, concentrating on his body. The pull of his muscles, the drag of air into his lungs, the taste of chlorine on his lips. After some time, more relaxed and to keep himself that way, he mentally rehearsed the day ahead. They didn't have to be anywhere until their appointment at Brett Cameron's office.

Brett was refurbishing an apartment block in Noosa Heads overlooking the ocean. He'd used Jared's services for one of his resorts in nearby Mooloolaba. A man with a well-known business reputation and seemingly limitless funds.

But it wasn't only his reputation in business, his reputation with women was even more legendary. He was one of the wealthiest playboys this side of Brisbane.

And that was a problem.

Jared dragged himself to the edge of the pool and watched the eastern sky's pearl-grey dawn lighten. He and Sophie hadn't discussed exclusivity. Well, of course they hadn't. Why would they? A couple of weeks of fun, nothing to get serious or heavy about.

Brett Cameron wasn't Sophie's type, Jared assured himself. *And how the hell would he know that?* And even if he wasn't, every woman with a pulse was Cameron's type. Or so the rumours went.

Frowning, Jared padded to a tower of white shelves and helped himself to a towel, rubbed it over his head and face. Brett seemed a nice enough guy and Jared respected his business acumen, but where women were concerned...well, he was just glad he didn't have a daughter living in Noosa. A PA in Surfers Paradise was enough of a worry.

Deliberately, he shook it off and turned his thoughts to the present, swiping his body while he considered whether to let Sophie sleep or wake her. That feeling of desperation, of not being in control, washed through him once more.

No. He wasn't going to allow himself to be led down that path. Not by Sophie Buchanan, not by anyone. He tossed the towel over a lounger. After so many years of being there for his sisters, particularly Lissa, lust and good times were his due. He wasn't ready for anything more.

But... He paused on his way to the shower. He'd make something of the time they had left so that when they went their separate ways they'd both have something to remember.

CHAPTER ELEVEN

Was that wonderful smell hot coffee? Sophie surfaced from sleep just enough to reach for Jared with her eyes still closed. To feel that hot male body next to her and make sure it wasn't a dream this time. But the sheets were cool and she realised she was alone. When she opened her eyes the sun was streaming through the window and sparkling on the surface of the pool outside.

She checked the time and bolted upright. Cripes, she'd slept in. They had a meeting in just over half an hour. Why had Jared not woken her? If she didn't know better she'd have thought he was deliberately leaving her behind, except she also knew he had a firm policy on not allowing pleasure to interfere with business. He'd expect his PA to be ready on time, no matter what her personal circumstances. Pam could attest to that. So was it some kind of test?

She scrambled out of bed and dragged the sheet around her like a toga since her clothes were in another bedroom and she was not going to wander the corridor naked. He was probably busy with last-minute details and just expected her to be ready…yikes…any minute now. Clutching the sheet, she made a dash to her room, grabbed her toiletries and flew into the shower.

Ten minutes later, a record by any woman's standards, she figured, dressed, minimum make-up, hair knotted severely beneath its clasp to mask its untamed nature since she'd not had time to wash it, she walked smartly into the kitchen area as if she weren't half an hour later than she ought to be.

She started to greet him, then stopped, suddenly self-conscious. What did you say to a new lover you'd had sex with all night long? A man who'd seen almost every inch of her body up close and personal. This was her second time at facing him after sex and she really needed to get used to it, but still, a flush rose up her neck. She was hardly an expert on such etiquette. *Just call me Ms Naïvety.*

He was sitting at a polished wooden table, the only furniture in the room that wasn't white, frowning over something on his laptop, but he looked up as she came to a stop by the coffee maker.

The residual heat she saw in his eyes was enough to light her fire all over again. But that was the only remnant of last night's passion and it flickered and died as he said, 'Good morning, Sophie.'

She thought of the impatient growl when he'd murmured her name against her breast last night. When he'd come deep inside her in the early hours. A contrast to this morning's briskly delivered greeting. And in the harsher, more demanding light of day it wasn't her lover she saw, but her boss. He was dressed for their upcoming appointments, his suit jacket on the sofa nearby. Freshly showered and shaved, he looked a picture of urban success and sophistication.

'Good morning.' She ran a finger inside the waistband of her slimline skirt and adjusted it, tucked a wayward strand of hair behind her ear and hoped she scrubbed up as well as he.

That she could be as sophisticated about last night as he.

Because he didn't mention it. Not a word, not even a hint, for goodness' sake… How awkward. No wonder they said office affairs were mistakes. She turned away, poured herself a mug of coffee and had only taken the first sip when Jared informed her they were leaving in five.

Fine. Be a pain in the proverbial. 'Okay.' She set her mug on the bench with a sharp *chink.* 'I'll get my stuff.'

She was tempted, so tempted, to demand he tell her what his problem was, but they had no time to spare and she didn't want to get into something they might have to stop in the middle of, which in turn could make the situation even more awkward.

Later, *after hours,* they were going to have a conversation about this. What did he think—that she was going to jump his bones in front of the client? That she didn't know what the word *professional* meant?

Or that he'd changed his mind and one night was enough.

An iron band tightened around her stomach. *Please, not that.* She knew they only had a short time but she wasn't ready to let him go yet. She wanted more. She needed to get him out of her system before she left Australia.

Jared turned the car radio's volume up and scowled at the road in front of them as they covered the few minutes it took to drive to their destination. He hadn't given Sophie time to eat breakfast. He should've woken her. His idea to go to the meeting without his PA was unprofessional. His usual clarity of mind was this morning a jumble of confusion. She was getting to him in ways that weren't supposed to happen. Making him indecisive. Making him look a complete incompetent.

Cameron met them at the front of the building. With his dark surfer-streaked gold hair and ocean-blue eyes, even Jared could see why women would find him attractive. He introduced Sophie.

'Welcome to Noosa, Sophie.' He shook her hand. 'You're a new member of Jared's team?'

'Just filling in for Pam for a few days.' She looked about her, took out a small pad and pen in favour of high tech. 'You have a lovely position here. Great potential.'

'I reckon so. I want Jared's opinion on it.'

Jared nodded. 'Okay, let's take a look around outside first and get a feel for the place.'

Perched on the hillside with breathtaking views of the beach and ocean, it had definite potential. Jared noted that Sophie returned their host's casual charm with a smile and professional courtesy as they inspected the premises. Jotting notes, asking pertinent questions of the two of them. If she found Cameron irresistible, she showed absolutely no sign.

On the other hand, neither did she show any sign that she found Jared even the tiniest bit irresistible. Busy with her notes, she barely acknowledged him at all, unless it was to clarify something, and then she did so with politeness and professionalism.

As it bloody well should be. Exactly what he expected, no, *demanded* of his PA. Why the hell should this time be any different?

Downstairs in a makeshift office, she set up her laptop on a small desk and worked on her own while Jared and Brett discussed the proposal and possible contractors.

Over coffee, she asked a question of Cameron. He leaned over to study her screen and met her eyes as he spoke. Sophie seemed to be riveted to her chair, those big amber eyes of hers looking up at him.

And Jared felt something uneasy and unfamiliar scratch across his skin and bury itself in his solar plexus like a hot blunt knife. The scrape and burn of possessiveness.

'What's your opinion, Jared?'

Jared blinked, aware they were both watching him and expecting some sort of reply. Sophie raised her eyebrows at him.

'Jared was only talking about that yesterday on the way up,' she said smoothly. 'Didn't you say you preferred to use local labour where possible?'

'Yes,' he replied. *What's your problem?* her expression said. He wished to hell he knew. *Thank you,* was his wordless reply. He shifted his gaze to his client. 'Did you have someone in mind...?'

When they were leaving, Cameron turned to Sophie and said, 'If you're looking for work and want something more permanent, my organisation has a vacancy at present. I'm sure you'd fill it more than adequately.'

His organisation? Not bloody likely, Jared thought. If she decided to stay, she'd be staying at Sanderson's.

Did she hesitate? He wasn't sure, but his breath caught in his chest. Then she smiled up at the other man. 'Thanks, but I'm going overseas soon.' Jared's relief, and a certain smugness, was short-lived.

'When you return...' Cameron pulled out a business card '...the offer will still be valid.' He wrote something on the back then handed it to her, trademark blue eyes twinkling. 'If circumstances change...'

Jared frowned. Was that an invitation in his tone? Was it business? Was it social? Was it pertinent to the message on the card? Damn it, from his position opposite Sophie he couldn't see what the guy had written.

Sophie glanced at the writing, smiled, nodded then tucked it into her purse. And then they were shaking hands. Smiles all round...

Paranoia. Jared clenched his fingers then very deliberately relaxed them. He extended his hand the moment Cameron relinquished Sophie's. 'Brett. Thank you for thinking of Sanderson's. You can expect our written proposal by next Wednesday.'

Cameron nodded, his grip firm. 'Look forward to it.'

Sophie wandered the Noosa Marina with Jared late that afternoon. Lots of cool blue—blue sails, blue paint, blue sky. There was a casual holiday atmosphere with tourists and locals alike eating at the variety of local cafés on the wharf, strolling the decking, poking around the one-of-a-kind stores from high-end fashion to fishing tackle.

Jared had suggested it as a good place to unwind after a

day's work and he was right. Trouble was, Sophie noticed, he never seemed to completely switch off. Not healthy.

The strong smell of the water pervaded the aroma of fresh-cooked seafood and the exotic fragrances emanating from the local day-spa shop. She rubbed a slight stiffness at the base of her skull as they passed the open door.

'Did I work you too hard today?'

She dropped her hand from her neck, shook her head. 'But I'd kill for one of those day-spa pampering packages.'

'According to Crystal, they're heaven-sent.'

'Actually I've never had one.' Sophie shrugged. 'The money never seems to stretch that far. But it's definitely on my to-do list.'

'Good idea.'

'Yes.' She glanced at him. 'They're good for men too, you know.'

His response was a mere rumble that sounded suspiciously like disagreement. Typical macho man.

There was a band playing in one of the restaurants; the wooden decking vibrated with the sounds of countless feet. A plethora of boats bobbed on the water; ferries and cruising restaurants all jostling for space in the popular marina, their gentle putter and the sound of water washing against their hulls filling the air.

Jared slowed as they approached a small cruiser tied up at the jetty, its paintwork gleaming red-gold in the late afternoon sun. A sunset dinner cruise by the looks of it, Sophie thought, admiring the little white-cloth-covered tables on board.

'You like sunsets and tonight looks like we might be in for a good one. How would you like to see it over the water tonight?'

'I'd love to. But if you're thinking this boat, it doesn't look like it's ready to sail for a while. There's no one else here. And you probably have to book.'

'Let's see.' Jared walked to the gangway where one of the

crew, dressed in whites, was laying out cutlery on one of the tables.

He looked up as they approached. 'Good evening.'

'Good evening.' Jared nodded to him. 'I made a booking earlier.'

The guy smiled. 'Mr Sanderson?'

'Yes.' Jared turned to Sophie. 'Feeling hungry yet?'

Her stomach fluttered but it wasn't with hunger. He'd remembered a throwaway comment she'd made last week about sunsets. Macho *and* romantic was Jared Sanderson. And she had the perfect dress to wear—a soft floaty sea/tea green that she'd popped in her bag at the last moment...back at their house. Right now her navy skirt and cream blouse were limp with a day's wear and humidity. 'Now?'

'Why not?'

'I'm in my work gear...and I've been in it all day. I'm hardly dressed for eating out.'

His gaze smouldered down her body like slow-moving lava. She'd never get used to that look and how it made her feel. Desired, dreamy, distracted.

Hot.

'Relax, Ms Buchanan, it's just you and me and a couple of crew. And you look as fresh as you did at ten o'clock.' He held out his hand to her, palm up. 'What do you say, is it all aboard?'

'And anchors away.' She had to smile because who could resist that roguish grin? Those scorching eyes? She laid her palm on his.

A cool breeze drifted across the river. They stood on the tiny deck upstairs and drank pink champagne from tall crystal flutes. She discovered a wild hibiscus flower in syrup at the bottom and enjoyed its delicious raspberry and rhubarb flavour on her tongue almost as much as she enjoyed the kiss Jared gave her the moment they were alone.

The aroma of roasting garlic and other herbs whetted their

appetites as they watched a gold-rimmed orange fireball sink below the bruised horizon. Within seconds the jagged slices of black and gold glinting on the water faded to a muted charcoal.

Moments later they returned to their table below, where a basket of steaming rolls awaited them.

'That was beautiful,' Sophie murmured. 'There's nothing quite like a tropical sun sliding into the water.'

'And you want to leave it all behind for cold, grey London smog.'

'It's not all smog.' She allowed the waiter to lay a napkin across her lap and admitted, 'But I am going to miss the tropics.'

'So what's at the top of your London to-do list?'

'All the traditional must-see places. But especially the Victoria Memorial in front of Buckingham Palace. I had a painting of it when I was a little girl. It was so whimsical and caught my imagination. You've been to London, I suppose.'

'No. Not yet. Don't even have a passport.'

'Oh?' Then she remembered he'd been guardian to his sisters his entire adult life, had focused on responsibility rather than his own pleasures, and nodded. 'You'll have to visit sometime.'

His eyes lingered on hers. 'Maybe I will.'

Confusion stole through her and she turned away and said, 'I can't wait to see that statue with its gold and marble and magical winged beings. And Queen Victoria in the midst of it all. I'll stand there and know that I've finally achieved my goal.'

She reached for her topped-up glass and took a liberal gulp while she studied the thin strip of land between water and fading aquamarine sky. The conical and distinctive volcanic shape of the distant Glasshouse Mountains on the horizon.

For the first time since she'd met Jared, she questioned her motivation for leaving. Did she have to leave everyone she knew and travel to the other side of the world for a change in scenery?

No. But she focused on what her head was telling her, not what her heart and emotions were saying. She wanted this trip. She'd wanted it for as long as she could remember. If she didn't go, she'd regret it.

And she wasn't going to change anything for a man. Not even a man she was falling for. Especially not for a man she was falling for. Going to the UK was the *best* thing she could do. For herself. And for Jared.

The main course arrived. Sophie chose salmon fillets on a bed of mashed potato with coriander, ginger and lime dressing, served with asparagus spears. Jared enjoyed a rare fillet steak with mushroom sauce and a selection of vegetables. It was a magnificent feast after the simple budget meals she'd been living on.

They ate for several minutes without talking. Just listening to the boat's motor, the swish of water against the hull.

'What about the people?' Jared said, scraping his fork over the bottom of his plate.

'People?'

'You said you'd miss the tropical climate.'

'Oh, yes, I'll miss the people too. I've got friends here.' She slid the last mouthful of salmon between her lips while she watched Jared and found she couldn't read his eyes now, at all. No matter how gorgeous he was or how much he was coming to mean to her... For the first time, she wavered. Then she pushed it away and said, 'But I'm not changing my mind.'

He watched her a moment, then set his cutlery on his empty plate, pushed it aside and leaned close so that his eyes reflected hers in the flickering candlelight. 'In that case we'll have to make the most of the time we have left.' His tone was low, rough and full of promise. And hypnotic. Like his gaze.

Everything around them seemed to fade out until all she was aware of was his intensity. From his eyes with their dark-rimmed irises that seemed to draw her into their depths, to the electric, almost mesmerising touch of his hand as it stroked her knuckles.

Drowning. 'Yes. Yes, we will.'

Her answer seemed to shake off the dreamy well they found themselves in and the look he gave her could only be interpreted as sinful determination. 'We'll return to the marina,' he said, gesturing the waiter hovering nearby over. 'Is that okay with you?'

'Very okay.'

There was still time to eat the dessert—fresh mango vanilla ice cream on an individual pavlova base—and enjoy a coffee before the boat pulled up alongside its berth.

Jared had plans for the rest of the evening. On the outside he maintained the cool, calm business façade he'd worn since this morning, but inside he was a bundle of firelighters ready for that first strike of the match. The way he'd been all day. The way he'd been every day since Sophie Buchanan had walked into his office.

He couldn't wait to feel her soft, summer-scented flesh against his again. Soon, very soon, he'd be burying himself inside her hot slippery centre. Easing the ache. Satisfying his need. Again and again, over and over, until he'd sated this all-consuming lust...

Because that was all it was. Wasn't it?

He tightened his grip on the wheel as they drove back to the house. That was all he'd allow it to be. She was leaving for London. But he hoped she'd remember this evening fondly and think of him.

The garage door rolled up, he slid into the parking spot, killed the engine and they both climbed out. He rounded the car, took her hand. 'There's something I want to show you before we go inside.' He led her to an enclosed garden at the side of the house, where a patch of velvety lawn bordered a garden of tea roses and the air was heavy with the scent of rich earth and the river.

And watched her jaw drop, her eyes widen in the soft light. It warmed him all the way through.

Sophie stared, unable to believe her eyes. A quilted throw lay on the lawn. A bottle of champagne chilled in a silver ice bucket alongside a cute terracotta pot crammed with cream roses. The scene was lit by a couple of Moroccan lamps, their intricate filigree silhouetted against the candle's warm glow. 'What's all this?'

'Jared Sanderson, at your service.' She turned her gaze on him and he smiled at her. 'You wanted to make love under the stars? Well, here we are.' He glanced up, waved a hand. 'Complete privacy under the Southern Cross at moonrise. Couldn't have asked for a better night.'

Oh. It looked like something out of a movie and her heart rolled over in her chest. 'But how?' she whispered. 'When…?'

'Magic. Aided by a little modern technology called a phone.' Jared stepped to her, turned her in his arms. The lamp glow sheened her skin. Her feminine fragrance drifted to his nostrils. He wanted slow and dreamy, but the sight of her, almost ethereal in the glow, nearly undid him. He tugged her down with him onto the quilt.

And while he popped the cork and poured the fizzy liquid into two crystal glasses, she gathered the roses to her nose. 'And chocolates…' She set the blooms down to grab the box, rip off the cellophane and pluck one out. 'This is like a dream.'

'So it is.' He felt the smile touch his lips, then his heart, as he offered her a glass, raised his own and clinked it to hers. 'To dreams.'

'To dreams.' She raised the crystal flute, took a sip, then lifted a chocolate to his lips. 'Share.'

He bit off half and his mouth flooded with caramel while she popped the remainder into her mouth and their gazes meshed and held. Even as she slid slowly down onto the quilt.

'Tonight I want to watch you come.' He saw her eyes widen, darken and for a few erratic heartbeats he gazed down at the vision sprawled beneath him. Her skin was flushed, as if she had a fever, a fever that put blooming roses in her cheeks and an extra spark in her eyes.

Then she was reaching for him and he followed her down and she had her hands in his hair, her fingertips scoring his scalp. And that spark in her eyes was a luminous topaz as she wrapped her hands behind his head and yanked him closer and murmured, 'So what are we waiting for?' against his lips.

His mouth dropped onto hers and his tongue plunged inside to savour her soft, full lips, her rich, dark drugging taste, so potent he felt light-headed with it.

Deliberately, he slowed his movements, cruising a hand over her knee, her outer thigh, then the tender inside of her leg and up...to find the barrier over her feminine hot spot already damp. For him. The knowledge vibrated through his body.

He lifted his mouth to trace a path over her jaw, to nibble his way down her neck, over her breast. To push her bra out of the way and roll her nipple between his lips. To taste its salty sweetness on his tongue and hear her suck in a sharp breath between her teeth while her restless fingers plucked at his hair and shoulders.

He could feel her heart galloping against his fingers and he wondered if she could hear his own. Because he'd never known it to beat this way before. This strange achy, urgent way that made him feel as if he were being pulled in opposite directions.

Shaking the confusing feeling away, he slid his fingers around her torso and unsnapped her bra. 'Let's lose the clothes.'

'Yes.'

He tugged her up onto her feet so that they stood toe to toe.

He stripped off his shirt, tossed it behind him while he watched her slip out of her blouse. Pull off her bra. Shimmy skirt and panties over her hips and down those amazingly long legs.

His blood pulsed through his body, throbbed in his erection, pounded low and insistent in his ears. She left him spellbound. He forgot to draw breath. Forgot to move until she reached out, undid his trousers with quick fingers and shoved them to his ankles. His boxers next. He stepped out of them, kicked them away. Then he realised the rest of her had followed her hands to the floor and was crouched in front of him.

She looked up and met his eyes and the message he read there... If he hadn't been transfixed to the spot, he swore he'd have stumbled. Then she reached out, her fingertips tracing his calves ever so gently, drawing circles on the backs of his knees, over his thighs...

Then, by God... Her face, her lips, a murmur away from his aching erection. He could feel her breath, a sweet torture on his burning flesh. His legs quivered. He fisted his hands in her hair as much for support as to stop her. Because if she touched him there, now, he'd explode... And as tempting as that was, it just wouldn't be fair.

'Sophie...' His hands still in her hair, he dragged her up against him until they were eye to eye. 'Later,' was all he said as he tumbled her back onto the quilt.

CHAPTER TWELVE

'I NEVER want to move again.' Sophie was tucked against Jared's shoulder in the main bedroom now, watching the play of light from the pool's reflection on the ceiling.

'Not even for ice cream?'

'Nope. I'm perfectly satisfied just as I am. You bought ice cream?'

'Yup.'

'Hmm.' They'd made love outside under the Southern Cross, then inside on top of the white silk quilt cover. They'd taken a shower and he'd seduced her again under the warm fragrant spray. She was well and truly satisfied. She didn't want to think about tomorrow, or next week. Or next month.

'But, oh, ye of great stamina,' she murmured, making an effort to lift one finger, slide its nail over a hard pectoral muscle and feel him shiver. 'If you're so inclined, I wouldn't object to you feeding me ice cream.'

'Not in the bedroom. You have to eat it in the kitchen—'

'Pfft. You sound just like—' *A father.* 'A big brother. A big, bossy brother.' Then because an image of him playing the daddy role threw her thoughts into disarray, she said, 'Do you treat all your girlfriends like they're kids?'

'I was going to say you have to eat it in the kitchen *naked.* Blackberry ripple? Your dream fantasy? Okay,' he continued when she pressed her lips together and didn't respond. He rolled onto his side and studied her curiously. 'All my girlfriends?'

Sophie felt her skin heat and wished the words unsaid. 'Pam

said you attend staff functions with a different girl every time, so I just assumed…'

Still watching her, he raised his brows as if it had never occurred to him that his trusted PA liked to gossip. 'Pam's got it wrong.'

Who did Sophie believe? Could she ever trust a man's word again? 'So you don't attend functions with a different girl each time?'

'Yes. No. Probably. Hell, I don't remember. It's not important enough.' He blew out an impatient breath and rolled onto his back once more. 'I'm no Casanova, Sophie, if that's what you think. I haven't got the time for it.'

She regretted her words. Even as a lover, she had no rights where he was concerned. Their relationship was temporary. She'd be gone soon and he'd be a memory.

'You've never had someone special? Someone you might have dated more than once?'

His answer was a while coming. 'Bianca. But she was a long time ago.'

'Tell me about her.'

'Why? She's in the past.'

'I told you about Glen. Were you in love with her?'

'In love?' Flicking her a glance, he said the words as if they were in a foreign language. 'We were too different,' he said at last.

Sophie wanted to know what had made him decide Bianca wasn't right for him. What was Jared's ideal woman and what kind of partner would he want on a permanent basis? 'Why were you attracted to her? How were you different? What made you change your mind?'

He looked at her again, eyes glittering in the dimness, and she was glad of the shadows. 'So many questions, Sophie?'

'I'm just curious.' She shrugged beneath his scrutiny as if it didn't matter. As if she didn't care. 'I like to understand people, that's all. No big deal.'

'Just curious, eh?'

She heard that familiar pumped male ego in his lazy tone. He scratched his chest with his free hand and she wanted to hit him.

She watched his profile as he stuck his arm beneath his head and looked up at the ceiling. 'We were the same in lots of ways. We both loved the outdoors and enjoyed the same activities. But when it came right down to it, she didn't want a kid interrupting the life she'd already mapped out for the two of us. And I couldn't live with that.'

The way he coupled himself with the faceless woman made Sophie's stomach clench. But the reason his relationship with Bianca hadn't worked out was the same reason he'd never want long term with Sophie.

No kids wasn't an option for Jared.

The back of Sophie's throat, her eyes, burned with the sting of unshed tears. Low in her belly the eternal aching emptiness unfurled, then twisted in on itself. She didn't have what a man—any man—wanted in a wife. She didn't have what it took to be the woman Jared would eventually marry. And he would marry down the track a bit, she knew. If what Pam said was true, he might be Playboy of the Gold Coast right now, but he was the marrying kind, a family guy.

It wouldn't be her he'd settle down with. Because she could never give him the babies she knew would be a non-negotiable part of any commitment.

Desperate to change the mood, to put some space between them, she sat up, reached for her plain cotton dressing gown with the pink polka dots on the wicker chair by the bed. 'Tell you what, I've changed my mind. I've decided I *can* move after all, and I want ice cream. In the kitchen. *Not* naked.'

Right now she couldn't be naked and be with him at the same time. Pulling on her dressing gown and hugging it around her like a security blanket, she headed down the hallway, her feet silent on the marble tiles. If he made a move on her any time soon she'd probably lose what little composure she had left, and she would *not* allow him to see that.

She set a couple of bowls on the counter top, pulled the tub of ice cream from the freezer. She'd just had a timely reminder that her life's path lay in a different direction from his.

A path she'd chosen. A path she'd wanted for a long time. She was jetting thousands of kilometres across the world. Independent. Living her dream.

Strange how it suddenly didn't sound half as exciting as it had a few days ago.

'Okay, not naked.'

At the sound of Jared's voice, Sophie turned to see him not naked too. He wore his boxers and a serious expression that asked too many hard questions. About the way she'd escaped from their bed so quickly.

Lose the angst fast, Sophie. She dipped her finger in the ice cream and licked its cold creamy-tart taste. 'It's good.'

'It's blackberry.' His eyes had that familiar wicked glint.

'I noticed.' She dipped her finger in again, held the blob to Jared's lips. *Keep things bright.*

They watched each other as he sucked it off her fingertip, but he was attuned enough to her mood to say, 'Let's sit somewhere comfortable and you can tell me what you think of this place.'

Changing the topic to something neutral, switching the focus away from her. She was surprised how sensitive he was to her emotions. Maybe because he was surrounded by females. Growing up with two sisters, a female dog and now a niece, he probably knew women better than she did herself.

They stretched out on the sofa, their legs close, their feet on the coffee table in front of them and their bowls of ice cream on their stomachs.

'You've bought yourself a new home in Surfers to renovate, Pam told me.'

'Yes, but I'm in no hurry. That's why we're staying here. I like some of the ideas and I wanted a close-up inspection.'

'So what do you like about it?' Sophie asked, sucking on her spoon.

'The pool outside the bedroom, for starters. I can sleep, swim, then breakfast in one fluid sequence.'

'It's a very dangerous idea with young children around,' she pointed out.

He turned to her, his eyes probing hers before saying, 'I don't have any children.'

Not yet. 'What about Arabella? When she comes to visit? In a year she'll probably be walking and getting up to no end of mischief.'

He frowned, tapping his spoon pensively against his bowl. 'Good point. I hadn't thought of that. Thank you.'

'Other than that, though, the pool's a splendid idea.'

'Any other thoughts on the place?'

'I like that it's so light and airy you feel as if you're outdoors. And the open-air kitchen that's not really a kitchen but more of an island.'

'Speaking of feeling as if you're outdoors…' he reached for her bowl, set it on the coffee table with his '…there's an architectural wonder in the master bedroom I haven't shown you yet.'

And a wonder it was indeed.

Long after Jared had fallen asleep, Sophie was still staring up at the field of stars visible through the massive circular window. With a flick of a switch it could be cleverly concealed by a ceiling panel in the form of a rosette. Amongst the snowy pillows it was like lying on top of a cloud and watching the night drift past. Like magic.

And hadn't these last few days been magic? she thought on a sigh. One magic moment after another with the man of her dreams. Literally.

The man she'd fallen in love with.

Yes. She'd fallen in love with Jared, and perhaps it was the most magic thing of all that she could allow herself that luxury.

But magic wasn't real; it was an illusion and it didn't last. And Sophie knew, with a heart that was already breaking apart, that very soon the magic would end.

'I've got another job for you, if you'd like it,' Jared told Sophie late the next afternoon. They'd arrived back at the office after lunch and were going over some work that had accumulated in their absence. Pam would be back on board on Monday and Jared knew Sophie could do with the extra money.

She looked up from the folder she was studying. 'What kind of work?'

'I promised Melissa an eighteenth birthday party. I've been too busy to make a time with her to organise it. If you could meet with her, make and oversee the arrangements, I'll continue paying you what you're making now until the night of the party. You probably have more idea what she wants than I do anyway.'

Her expression brightened, but then a little frown creased her brow. 'When were you planning it for? I'm leaving in a couple of weeks, remember.'

He remembered. And the knowledge was like a grass seed in his sock. A minor but constant niggle. If he'd been a less focused man he might have said to hell with the paperwork and spent what was left of the afternoon in Sophie's bed. He really was in danger of turning into an indulgent and irresponsible idiot.

He reached for a business card, jotted Melissa's contact details on the back. 'It'll fit in well, then. It's two weekends from now.'

'Two weeks on my current pay? To organise a party? That's… generous…thank you.'

'You're helping me out, so thank *you*.' He slid the card across the desk. 'I'll leave it to you to contact Melissa. I've already set up a credit card. It'll be available Monday, spend whatever you need.'

'Okay… It sounds like fun.' She shifted forward on her chair. 'I'll just sort these and make sure everything's ready for your efficient PA's return before I leave.'

'She'll appreciate it.' All business, he noted as Sophie stood, shuffled the folders on his desk into a neat little pile. He and Sophie worked well as a team. Understood each other. Respected each other. They could be professional when required.

And he could have her naked on his desk in five seconds flat.

His imagination slammed into overdrive and its very lack of that professionalism was its own appeal. His body tightened. Blood thickened and throbbed in his groin. It was five-thirty on a Friday afternoon. Those employees who hadn't yet left for their weekend were drinking up a storm in the staff lounge—he could hear the laughter and clink of glass, the muted hum of a middle-of-the-road CD.

No one was going to come looking for workaholic Jared.

He stood too, stepped around to the side of his desk. *Lock the door, close the blinds. For once, do what no one expects of Jared Sanderson.* 'Sophie…' He could barely recognise his own husky voice. But he heard the possessive tone and the promise…

And he saw barely veiled humour flit across her expression as she backed up and crossed the room in record time. 'In your dreams, Mr Sanderson.' She poked her head around the door a few seconds later with a seductive sparkle in her eyes. 'My place, thirty minutes. Don't keep me waiting.'

He grinned, warnings to self about the dangers of indulgence and irresponsibility where Sophie was concerned already forgotten. 'I'll be there with wine.'

Still grinning, he returned to his chair. His lover and his

PA rolled into one generous, intelligent, talented package. He'd never have thought of his PA in that way. Then again, he'd never had a PA quite like Sophie. And it worked. With Sophie it worked.

They'd come into the office this afternoon as professionals, as equals. They'd been able to put aside the fact that they'd spent the past couple of nights bonking each other senseless. Difficult. Very difficult.

Shaking his head, he forced his attention back to work. What the hell, he decided, slapping his folder shut. He deserved an early finish.

The weekend flew by as quickly as their stay in Noosa had. Except that for the first time in as long as he could remember, Jared allowed no interruptions from the office to impinge on their time together. No emails, no text messages, no phone calls.

They walked touristy shopping malls and drank coffee, wandered the beach and watched surfers ride waves, took a leisurely drive and a picnic basket into the Hinterland where the air was cool and green.

He showed her some of the developments he'd overseen up and down the Gold Coast. The new apartment block in Broad Beach that he intended renovating and living in someday. He took her home to his place where she and Lissa got along as if they were best friends rather than recent acquaintances.

But he didn't stay the nights with her. In the early hours he left her warm comfort and went home. He knew his sister wasn't fooled, but it wasn't so much about Melissa as about himself. This way it was easier to remember that this…whatever it was that he had with Sophie wasn't serious. It was temporary. A fling with a rapidly approaching use-by date.

Just a fling, Sophie reminded herself as she woke up alone at seven a.m. She hadn't asked him to stay the night when he'd rolled out of bed and gone home around two a.m. for the last three mornings. *Because it was just a fling.* She touched a fingertip to the dent in the pillow where he'd lain. No point in getting used to waking up beside him. Cocooned in their shared musky warmth. Seeing his eyes darken with desire when he turned his head on the pillow and saw her watching.

Shaking it away, she dragged herself out of bed and pointed herself in the direction of the bathroom. She focused her thoughts on this morning. No doubt he was already at work and she was meeting Melissa and Enzo at Enzo's restaurant to plan Melissa's birthday.

Enzo was waiting when she arrived. At this hour, the restaurant was closed to the public, but they sat at a table where a couple of floor-to-ceiling windows were thrown open to the salty sting of beach air. Early sunshine spilled onto the table and the aroma of croissants and coffee stirred her appetite.

While they waited for Melissa, Enzo poured coffee. 'So you're planning Melissa's party?'

'Yes.' She took a sip of the strong black brew. 'I know Jared would've preferred some fancy-schmancy event planner but Pam's back this week so Jared asked me if I'd like the job. Very kind of him since he knows I could do with the extra money. I'm going overseas.' She mentally frowned at the distinct lack of enthusiasm she heard in her last words. Of course she wanted to go overseas. She did.

Enzo nodded. 'Jared is a very kind man.'

'You've known him a long time?'

'He worked for Rico and Luigi a long time ago in the fish shop. I was fourteen at the time. Jared wanted to show he could support his sisters, bring in some money and study all at once.'

'That sounds like Jared. Who's Luigi? Another brother?'

Enzo shook his head. 'Rico loved him like a brother but he was, in fact, Rico's business partner. But Luigi was an evil man. My brother trusted Luigi but he fiddled the books, then absconded with all their money. Bankrupted Rico, put my restaurant into financial difficulties while I was trying to bail my brother out.'

She shook her head. 'That's horrible.'

'Jared came to our rescue. He was a rich man by then. Set Rico up in new premises. Gave us both financial backing. We owe him a great debt.'

'He's a pretty special guy.'

'He likes you. I can tell. Did you say you were going overseas?'

'Very soon.'

'Maybe you should reconsider. You don't want to let a good man like that get away.'

She felt a twitch of irritation between her shoulder blades but Enzo was a typical family-oriented Italian and she needed to remember that for Jared, too, family was everything. She pasted on a smile. 'I'm not trying to catch a guy, Enzo.'

His brows shot up. 'No? What about babies? A little Jared? Or a little Soph—'

'No.' She cut him off. The images he was conjuring jabbed at her heart. 'I'm—ah, Melissa's arrived.'

Enzo turned. 'Good morning, Melissa.'

'Good morning.' Melissa exchanged a quick sisterly kiss with Enzo then sat, smoothing her flyaway red hair behind her ears. 'I'm late. Sorry.' She beamed at Sophie. 'This is so exciting getting you to help organise things. Perhaps we should let Enzo carry on with his own work while we come up with a few ideas first?'

'Good idea.'

'I'll let you two get on with it.' He poured Melissa a coffee. 'Give me a call when you're ready.'

'Mmm, smells heavenly. Thanks, Enzo. I have a few suggestions…' Melissa pulled out a notebook.

Sophie switched on her laptop. 'That's a good start.' She

could see a variety of quick and clever sketches as Melissa flipped through for the page she was looking for.

'Got it,' Melissa said finally, and reached into her bag for a pen. 'Ready.'

'Okay.' Sophie's fingers hovered over the keyboard. 'What kind of party were you thinking of?'

CHAPTER THIRTEEN

THE rest of the week passed in a flash for Sophie. She and Melissa had come up with plenty of ideas for Sophie to chase up, and, being virtually last minute, the invitations had to be printed and sent pronto. She wondered why Jared had left it so late—if it had been an idea he'd had on the spur of the moment or whether he'd been too busy and forgotten.

The evenings were spent together in her apartment, but sometimes if he finished work early they went out for dinner or caught a movie. He surprised her one night at a club where she discovered he was a pretty cool dancer.

One thing didn't change. They couldn't keep their hands off each other. Sometimes it was in a rush of heat and energy, at other times the mood was slow and lazy. Always both familiar and sparkling new. Always exciting.

She let her fun, flirtatious side fly and kept her darker emotions firmly bolted down. There'd be a time when she'd have to take them out and confront them, and that time loomed like a storm on the horizon.

The phone rang late on Saturday afternoon. According to Jared, Crystal and Ian were taking a well-deserved break and were having dinner out, Jared's treat. He was babysitting Arabella for a few hours and would see Sophie around eleven p.m.

Sophie was relieved that he hadn't asked her to join him at Crystal's place. She didn't want the ordeal of seeing baby Arabella again. Last night she and Jared had been to a concert in Brisbane and hadn't arrived home till after midnight. She'd spent the day sorting through stuff and packing and they had no definite plans for this evening.

So when the buzzer sounded around seven while Sophie was ironing, she was unprepared for the sight of Jared and baby Arabella at her front door.

He smiled at Sophie, and with Arabella tucked up against him, her tiny face over his heart, Sophie's own heart felt as if it were being squeezed in a vice. That was Sophie's favourite place too.

Stupid to be jealous of a baby. To be jealous of Jared because it was all so easy for him, so natural, so inevitable that he'd probably have his own baby in a few years and she'd *never have the chance*. Stupid to be so jealous she wanted to lash out at him for her own inadequacies. *Stupid, stupid, stupid.*

She bit her lip. She was *not* going to cry. Not in front of Jared. Never in front of Jared. He held a baby capsule in his free hand. Sophie did not offer to help. 'What are you doing here?'

'I couldn't get her to settle,' was his excuse. 'I thought a drive might help.'

Arabella's eyes were closed, the eyelids so fragile they were almost transparent. Sophie wanted to reach out and touch the silky, sweet-smelling skin. To snatch her away and cuddle her against her own breast. Over her own heart. 'She looks just fine to me.'

Looking away, Sophie walked back to her ironing task, leaving Jared to put the capsule down so that he could close the door.

'She is. *Now*,' he said, bringing baby and carrier to the sofa. 'The car's motion put her to sleep.'

'Great.' She smoothed a blouse over the ironing board. 'So what's the problem?'

'But she woke the moment I stopped,' he went on. 'So I've been walking up and down your street for the past fifteen minutes. She's just dropped off again but I've got a sneaky feeling she's going to wake up the moment I put her in her capsule and I only have one bottle of milk left.'

'Then don't.' *Please don't.* She didn't want to have to notice her. A newborn's cry set off emotions she didn't want to deal with. Especially not with Jared watching on.

'I have to, Sophie, so I can get her stuff out of the car. Unless you want to hold her?'

She picked up the iron, swiped it over the garment in front of her. 'Try putting her in her capsule first.'

'Didn't think so,' he murmured, almost to himself. He peeled Arabella off him with the greatest care and laid her in her carrier. She snuffled but didn't wake. 'I'll get her gear. Be back in a jiff.' Then he was gone.

And in the perverse way of things, Arabella woke at that moment with a snorting noise that quickly turned to hiccuping sobs and finally one piercing wail.

Sophie told herself the baby was perfectly safe, that the sound was normal baby noise. That Jared would be back any moment. She closed her eyes as another howl rent the air and tried to resist but...oh, it was like...telling your heart to stop beating.

When Sophie turned, the little face was scrunched up and red, her tiny fists were waving in the air. And, oh... It seemed... it seemed Sophie's legs had a will of their own.

She knelt beside the sofa, reached out a finger. Her heart thumped fast against her ribs. Everything inside her yearned. Just one touch... One touch of that petal skin... So smooth, so silky.

The moment Sophie stroked a finger down the infant's cheek, all noise ceased instantly and Arabella stared at her with barely focused eyes. For a beat out of time Sophie froze. Then she caressed her again. Leaned closer to smell that baby scent of powder and milk, to curve her palm over the soft fuzzy scalp.

And forgot she didn't go near babies.

'Hush little baby, don't you cry…' She sang the lyrics so quietly she barely heard herself. But Arabella heard. And she seemed entranced, her tiny mouth open, her eyes…Sophie swore they knew her.

No. She bit her lip to stop the tears. Why was fate so cruel? To give her such a gift and at the same time to take her ability to have babies away? It wasn't fair.

Yet she was still a woman, she reminded herself. Jared had shown her that. For the first time in five years he'd made her feel like a woman, feminine and desired and cherished.

But as she gazed down at the infant, the doubt demons perched on her shoulder. Would he still feel the same way if he knew? To be rejected again, to see the man she'd fallen in love with look at her as less…she didn't think she'd ever get over it.

Jared came to a halt inside the doorway. Sophie was leaning towards the baby capsule, her hand fisted against her mouth and a moment's alarm slid through him. 'Sophie?'

She whirled to him, eyes wide and panicked before she blanked the emotion and said, 'She seems to be settled now.'

He hadn't seen her touch the infant but he could've sworn he'd witnessed…something.

And in that blinding moment of clarity he'd seen his future flash before him.

A future that included Sophie. A home. And kids.

Home and kids? He wasn't near ready for any of that and shook his head to clear it. 'Sophie, wh—'

'I'm sorry to run out on you.' She glanced at her watch, then yanked the iron's cord from the wall socket and picked up a little black blouse from the ironing board. 'But I wasn't expecting you yet. I'm meeting friends for a drink this evening since you weren't coming by till eleven. Feel free to stay here for a while though…'

As long as you and the baby are gone when I get back. He

read those words in her expression as clear as glass, in the lack of eye contact, her jerky movements. 'You didn't say you were going out.'

'I'm not meeting a guy, if that's what you're thinking.'

'No,' he said carefully, 'that's not what I'm thinking.'

She held the blouse up and inspected it. 'I wasn't aware we had to account to each other for every moment of our time.'

No strings. Wasn't that the exact kind of relationship he wanted? *Damn it.* 'Is that what you think this is about, Sophie?'

'Jared.' Her fists tightened on the garment she held and now her eyes found his. Locked on his and pleaded with him. 'Let's just enjoy our last few days?' Her appeal was like a tangible presence in the room with them. 'Please?'

'Okay,' he said finally, the remnants of his vision of a future he'd never imagined fluttering like petals on the periphery of his consciousness. Hitching the baby bag onto his shoulder, he picked up the carry basket with its now cooing passenger. What choice did he have with an infant in his care for the next few hours? 'Go and enjoy your evening. I'll be back at eleven.'

As he turned to pull the door shut he saw her shoulders slump and her eyes held a puzzle he wished to hell he understood.

Twenty-three minutes past two. He should be doing what Sophie had asked and making the most of the rest of the night with her. Instead, he wandered the night-darkened esplanade, the eternal *thump-boom* of the surf in his ears, his thoughts going around in circles and coming back to what Sophie had said when he'd left earlier.

Ten days. Why let her obvious hang-ups with kids come between them and a good time? Live and love to the max, enjoy what they had while they had it. Wasn't that all that mattered in their 'short-term relationship'? That was obviously what mattered to Sophie.

And it was exactly what he'd told himself he wanted. She

wasn't looking for more either. So it was just about perfect, right?

Right. He turned back, following the sandy path back to his car. He ignored the hollow feeling in his gut as he slid onto the leather seat.

But he didn't switch the ignition on. Instead, he slammed his fists on the steering wheel. *No.* Not *right.* Nothing about this was right. Just good times?

The hell it was.

He stared through the windscreen but he wasn't looking at the ocean view. He was seeing Sophie leaning over the baby. Moreover, he wasn't seeing himself as only his sisters' guardian, he was seeing himself as a father in the truest sense of the word.

He shook his head. Wrong decade. Sophie wasn't the woman for him long term, she was all about adventure and discovering new places. As was her right, he told himself, and after what she'd been through, she deserved it. Who was he to interfere with her dreams and plans? Nor was this trip she was embarking on the end of the world. A few months. A year tops and she'd be back. He could almost guarantee it.

Over the week Sophie had brought sunshine and summer and sparkle to what he was only now realising had become an exceedingly dull existence.

He'd made love to her in the sea and watched the sense of humour spark in her eyes, made love to her in the centre of a macadamia plantation and watched the green reflected in the amber. He'd laughed more. Because he'd found more to laugh about with Sophie to share it with.

And every now and then he'd remember she was leaving and a shadow would steal over the sun.

He forked frustrated fingers through his hair. For the second time in his life he'd fallen for a woman. And this time he'd fallen hard. And these feelings he had were nothing like those he'd had for Bianca.

These feelings ran deep. So deep they touched his soul and he didn't know if he'd ever be free of them. And powerful enough to rock his world to its very foundation. It was nothing like he'd ever experienced—dangerously so.

Despite his deepening feelings, he wasn't prepared to compromise what he believed in or how he wanted to live his life for someone else's whims and fancies and ideals. Bianca hadn't fitted into the world he'd created for himself and his sisters, so Bianca was history. Simple.

With her outlook on life so different from his own, Sophie didn't fit into his world either. But something didn't gel and he couldn't put his finger on what it was. Whatever it was, it was far from simple.

Sunday morning. Sophie woke to daybreak's murky light stealing over her window sill, although she couldn't remember falling asleep. The last time she'd checked the time it had been ten past four. She'd resisted trying to contact Jared. He'd come when he was ready, and if he didn't… She had no one to blame but herself.

He hadn't come.

Sitting on the edge of her bed, she dragged on her dressing gown. Her eyes felt swollen and gritty, her nose was still blocked from her crying jag hours ago and there was an empty ache in her chest that wouldn't go away.

She had no idea whether it was over with Jared, why he hadn't turned up last night or what he was thinking. But rather than sitting around like a misery guts and moping about it, she had packing to do. The furniture belonged to the apartment but she needed to sort what she was taking with her, and toss or store the rest.

She could ring Jared…and apologise. She headed for the kitchen. She'd seen the disappointment in his eyes when she'd mentioned keeping tabs on one another. No, he'd come on his own terms or not at all.

She'd just made a pot of tea when he turned up. Leaning on the door frame with his darkly stubbled jaw, furrowed hair and bloodshot eyes, he looked as ragged and sleep-deprived as she felt.

He was just about the most beautiful sight she'd ever seen.

She stood back to let him enter. He smelled of the beach, cool morning air and impossible dreams. He closed the door behind him and they stared at each other for a long moment.

She couldn't read his expression but maybe she saw something that gave her hope? Courage? 'I missed you.' She hadn't meant to say them but the words tumbled out.

He didn't answer. Just wrapped one large hand around the back of her neck, hauled her face up to his and kissed her. Hard. Possessively and with a kind of angry passion.

She felt his strength in the rigid arm that supported her, in his rock-hard body as she melted against him. Perhaps some of that strength would flow into her...

But no. He released her with such speed and vehemence she almost stumbled. 'We need to cool it.' He shoved his hands in the back pockets of his jeans and shook his head, then watched the window where the pale sun slid through a smudge of grey. 'This has got way too intense and I sure as hell don't need it right now. Neither do you.'

He regretted that kiss and the loss of control. The knowledge was both painful and poignant for Sophie. But it was for the best and he was right, they needed to put some distance between them. In one week the man she loved would be a world-away-distant memory.

She wouldn't cancel her trip; she needed it, now more than ever. She wouldn't try to convince him that they could be more than short term. She wouldn't lay open her vulnerable heart and tell him the things she wanted to tell him—that she not only wanted to be his lover but his wife, the mother of those children he so obviously wanted and expected of a marriage...

She couldn't give him those children and she couldn't risk

seeing the light in his eyes dull to disappointment when she told him.

She should back off now, tell him it had been fun then pack up and go to Brisbane for the last week until her flight left from there, and never see him again.

But with the party next weekend, she couldn't let Melissa or Jared down now and Jared had paid her up front to do the job.

She'd never been a quitter, she told herself, ignoring the little voice saying, *Except where Jared's concerned.* And the thought of never seeing him again was too painful, what with him standing within touching distance, larger than life and twice as thrilling. Twice as precious.

'So what are you trying to say?' she asked his back. She didn't want to know. She had to know. Better to know now...

For the second time, he didn't answer her. Turning around, he didn't give her time to read his expression, just swept her into his arms and carried her towards the bedroom like an impatient man claiming what belonged to him...

They didn't talk at all, they made love. Tumultuous love-making of the deep and dark and desperate kind that satisfied the flesh but resolved nothing.

Jared didn't give her time to refuse or argue or demand. He wanted her now—all of her—heart, body and mind—all, and with an urgency he'd never known.

And she gave him everything. He felt it flow from her like a fast-flowing stream. Momentarily sweeping away those earlier doubts and questions on a tide of emotion he struggled to contain.

After, he held her trapped within his arms, breathing in the musky scent of their own creation. Revelled in the silken rain of ebony hair that cascaded over his shoulder and down his chest. His words had dried up like cockles in the sun. He couldn't remember a single one. One look at her when she'd opened the door all mussed and flushed and sleepy and all he could think was, *Home*. All he knew was that he wanted her. In every way. Whatever the cost. Whatever the sacrifice, whatever the risk.

But how would she respond if he opened his heart and told her? Would she be willing to make that sacrifice too, and take that risk with him? Was he even ready to find out?

CHAPTER FOURTEEN

ON THE following Saturday night Sophie put the finishing touches to her make-up and stood back to check her reflection. She'd chosen a sapphire-blue dress that left one shoulder bare and had an asymmetric hemline. But tonight wasn't about her, it was Melissa's big night.

The past week had been hectic. She'd stored what she wasn't taking. The rest spilled out of two open suitcases on her living-room floor.

The time had also given Sophie an opportunity to get better acquainted with Melissa. She was a complex girl but she obviously adored her big brother. It was just that, according to Lissa, she was feeling suffocated.

Sophie understood Melissa wanted to test her independence. Having a protective brother, while a wonderful thing, could prove stifling—or so Sophie imagined, thinking of her own long-lost sibling. Lissa wanted her own place and she'd said Jared needed his privacy too.

Sophie agreed. She added a pair of silver drop earrings to complete her look. But Melissa knew Sophie was leaving so why the conspiratorial smile when she'd mentioned his need for space? Did she think she and Jared were something more?

Did she maybe think Sophie was coming back sooner rather than later? Sophie stared at her eyes in the mirror. *No regrets, remember.*

She and Lissa had come to an arrangement. Lissa was taking over Sophie's apartment. The landlord was satisfied. Jared had accepted the inevitability with only minor reservations. Everyone was happy…except Sophie.

Oh, she *was* happy. She told herself so every day and smiled at her reflection to prove it. Who wouldn't be, with the trip of a lifetime so close she could almost smell it?

Because there was Jared.

Her smile slipped away, her heart contracted and a brief mist clouded her vision. Jared, with that adorable crease in his cheek and something deep in his eyes that told her he had secrets he wasn't going to share with her.

She was leaving and she knew he cared for her more than a little. His sister was moving out after she left and he'd be on his own for the first time. A man who loved having his family close and enjoyed companionship. Sophie wondered how he'd deal with that.

And he'd given her a most precious gift, a gift he wasn't even aware he'd given: her acceptance of self, belief in herself. So after consulting Melissa, and with Crystal's okay, Sophie had arranged a surprise she hoped he'd recognise for what it was and enjoy.

Even with Melissa planning to live independently, Jared was still very much his youngest sister's protector. Sophie remembered a conversation she'd had with Melissa.

'I guess that's because you're the baby,' Sophie had said. 'When your father died, Jared wanted to make sure you—'

'No.' Melissa shook her head. 'My father wanted nothing to do with me. I'm not his biological daughter. Our mum had an affair. He discovered it after she died. I was only a few weeks old, so I don't remember her.

'But I remember my father's coldness towards me and my bad behaviour as a result and getting attention for all the wrong reasons. I was alone, I was different, I was an outsider. I had no biological parents and only a half brother and sister and they had each other.'

Sophie touched Melissa's hand, sad that she couldn't see the blessing she'd been given in Jared. 'But, Melissa...'

'I know.' Melissa flapped a hand. 'I'm so lucky. Even as a four-year-old I remember Jared standing up to his father and copping a beating to protect me.'

'Beating?'

'Oh, yeah.'

Which sounded to Sophie as if it had happened more than once.

Melissa didn't want to hurt Jared's feelings by appearing ungrateful and moving out and leaving him all on his lonesome but she needed to do her own thing. She and Crystal were also very concerned about his work-life balance.

Yes, there were women, but not often and he never dated the same one more than a couple of times. He needed a woman who could light his fire, Melissa had said. And she'd looked at Sophie when she'd said it. A woman he could settle down with and make a family of his own.

Melissa worried he wasn't looking because he still felt that responsibility for his baby sister who was no longer a baby, but that he might see things differently if she wasn't around...

The apartment solution was a good one, Sophie thought, on the short cab journey to Enzo's. Jared had organised a taxi for Sophie ahead of time so she could ensure everything was organised and he was bringing Lissa. A place of her own would give Melissa independence, she'd be ten minutes away from Jared, and Pam lived in the same complex if she needed help.

And Jared could move on with his life.

And Sophie was *not* going to think about that tonight. She'd be much too busy making sure everyone else had a good time.

Jared shuffled Sophie around the makeshift dance floor to one of the local band's recent hits. The rhythm was essentially fast but they moved to their own beat—much slower and out of time if anybody cared enough to look.

The restaurant's sliding doors had been removed and the dance floor set up outside. Coloured lanterns danced on their strings in the gentle ocean breeze, the scents of kerosene torches and salty air and fried garlic assaulted the senses.

'You did a brilliant job getting it together on such short notice,' Jared said against her ear. 'You've worked practically non-stop and I appreciate it. Thank you.'

Sophie looked over his elegantly clad shoulder. Pam was in the corner having an up-close and serious conversation with some hotshot Sophie recognised from the office. Crystal and Ian had left earlier with Arabella, but the guest of honour was laughing up a storm with some of her friends by the remains of the birthday cake inside. 'You're very welcome and I'm grateful for the opportunity.'

Melissa had wanted the occasion to be a formal affair. All the guys looked gorgeous in suits despite the warm evening and the girls, glad of an excuse to tart themselves up for a change in what was normally a casual lifestyle, wore semi-formal dresses and plenty of bling.

Every one seemed to be having a good time. Sophie had enjoyed a champagne to celebrate the cake cutting. And Jared, as usual, looked irresistible in his dark suit and classy silver tie.

He must have noticed her smiling—or was she drooling?— because he tilted her face up to his, placed a slow melting kiss on her lips that promised all kinds of anticipated delights and murmured against her mouth, 'I think we can leave now.'

Oh, and she wanted that promise fulfilled. 'But it's only ten-thirty and the party's my responsibility. I need to—'

'Please the man who paid you,' he murmured again.

He slid one large finger beneath the strap on her right shoulder and drew a sensuous circle there. 'Ah…' She shivered at the little thrill of anticipation that trickled all the way down to her toes, but she had a job to do. 'But I...Lissa—'

'Will thank you very much for all you've done. Then she'll say goodnight and tell us to enjoy the rest of the evening.'

The way he said that, the way his eyes darkened, the way his finger slid lower, beneath the fabric of her dress and towards the top of her bra... That promise again... And the trickle became a torrent.

'These young things don't want us oldies hanging around.' He was already withdrawing his finger to take her hand and lead her towards Melissa to say their goodbyes.

Sophie laughed. 'You talk as if we're over the hill.'

'We are to them. Come on.'

And she knew why he was insisting they leave early. It was their last night together. Tomorrow afternoon she was flying to Sydney to catch her international flight scheduled for Monday morning.

Jared drove her home. Except...they didn't seem to be headed in that direction. 'Where are we going?'

'Wait and see.' Apartment buildings and luxury hotels twinkled with a million lights as they drove a short distance, then Jared pulled to a stop under the portico of a well-known five-star hotel.

'We're staying here?' She stared up at the gold and marble and glass.

'I thought we might.' His desire-darkened eyes burned into hers.

'All night.' They hadn't spent the night together since Noosa. She'd hated that, but now, with only this night left, maybe it was a very unwise idea. Maybe the most dangerous idea she could think of.

And far too seductive to refuse.

He seduced her further with the gentle brush of a fingertip over her lips. 'All night. We even have a late checkout in the morning.'

'But I didn't bring—'

He leaned across the centre console and nuzzled the underside of her jaw. 'Believe me, you won't need a thing.' When he straightened again, her pulse was already leaping in anticipation.

'But tomorrow morning…'

'Got it sorted…' He pulled a small bag from behind his seat and set it on her lap. 'Pam packed a few things. She hoped you wouldn't mind her using her spare key for your apartment without your permission.'

'Oh, Pamela, Pamela…you're in on this too?' She pressed her hands to her flushed cheeks. They'd organised this behind her back. Pam hadn't breathed a word at the party. Not a look. Not even a glimmer.

'Okay?'

She nodded, struggling not to feel overwhelmed. 'Okay.'

A woman met them in the lobby. She wore a baby-pink shirt, smelled of sandalwood and exuded serenity. She smiled a somewhat conspiratorial welcome at Jared, then turned her smile on Sophie. 'Good evening, Sophie.'

'Good evening.' When the woman indicated she should follow her, Sophie looked to Jared. 'What's happening?'

'A thank-you for your effort on Lissa's behalf, and mine, these past couple of weeks. You wanted a day-spa package. You've got a night-spa one instead.'

'Oh, I…'

'I'll be waiting when you're done. Thanks for this, Aimee. I owe you one.' He nodded to the woman, then kissed Sophie lightly on the cheek. 'Enjoy.'

And Sophie spent the next hour and a half in the hotel's Wellness centre being treated like a celebrity by two—yes, *two*—therapists. The popular Goddess facial. A de-stress and aromatherapy massage. Chakra balancing. Mineral salt scrub and manicure.

She was pampered within an inch of her life.

When she was done Aimee gave her a luxuriously soft towelling robe embroidered with the hotel's logo to put on and showed her to a private elevator that led to a penthouse suite. She should be tired but she'd never felt more alive.

When Sophie had stepped inside the lift, Aimee pressed the button and smiled. 'Enjoy your evening.'

'Oh, I will.' *I will.* Wow, she didn't need an elevator, she was already floating.

But she left her stomach behind as the lift shot skyward. When the doors slid open again Jared was waiting in a matching robe. The warm golden glow of candlelight greeted her. Too many to count. Squat, thin, tall, a rainbow of colours, they were scattered over every available surface. 'Oh, my…Jared… this is…too much.'

'I told you before, there's never too much of a good thing.' He moved in for a long knee-weakening kiss. 'Mmm. You smell divine,' he murmured moments later.

'I *feel* divine.' She threw her arms around his neck. 'And my chakras are in perfect balance.'

'Are they now?' He sniffed her jaw. 'Jasmine?'

'And geranium and rose, with a whiff of citrus.' She licked his lips. 'Mmm. And you've been eating chocolate berries.'

'Strawberries, actually. Want one?'

'In a minute.' She lingered over the taste a moment longer, then moved to the wide panoramic window where a table held a bottle of celebratory bubbly and two glasses. Surfers Paradise nightlife sprawled below them like fairyland.

The view was as seductive as the man behind her. She caught his reflection in the darkened glass pane as he moved towards her. Tonight's whole experience was an aphrodisiac.

Watching his eyes in the glass, she poured two glasses of the wine but left them on the table and murmured a seductive, 'You know I'm naked under this robe.'

Large, firm hands reached out and squeezed her shoulders. 'I was counting on it,' he murmured back, his deep voice rumbling down her spine as he tugged the robe's belt open and drew the fabric off her shoulders. He kissed one shoulder then the other, pulled the robe completely away.

She heard the soft swish of air as he stripped off his own and then he turned her in his arms. He reached for the glasses, handed her one. 'To fantasies…whatever form they take.'

She raised her glass. 'To fantasies.' She took a sip. 'You've made mine come true, you know. I…I don't know how to…I can't—'

'Shh.' Jared put a finger against her lips. 'Not now.' He took their glasses, set them down on the table.

Jared didn't take his eyes off her as he carried her to the bed. This luxury suite might have been a dingy motel room on the edge of the Pacific Highway out of Ballina for all Jared knew, or even cared.

Their last night.

Their last time.

She rose up on her knees in the centre of the bed and he joined her, taking it slow as if they could make time stand still while the candlelight flickered and danced. Neither spoke but neither felt the necessity because everything was in their eyes as they watched each other. Their emotions, their desires, their awareness of the inverted hourglass.

They lay down together. It was different tonight. He felt it in the way she touched him, as if memorising the imprint of his skin against hers.

He was making his own memories. His lips lingered at her neck so he might recall the taste of her skin tomorrow, when she was gone. A week from now. A year.

He moved on top of her and, bracing himself on his elbows, stared down. Hair an ebony fan on the pillow, her own unique scent beneath the jasmine…just a shimmer of it in the air. Her eyes drenched with passion…and more.

Through fighting it, he almost surrendered to the inevitable. Was this the time to tell her that his feelings for her went deeper than they had for any woman he'd known? To ask her to consider something on a more permanent basis? Or tell her he'd meet her in a month for a weekend of loving in Paris before bringing her home to live with him.

He leaned down and kissed her. She moaned and moved beneath him as he slid inside her, her hands caressing his cheeks. Perhaps this was where she might tell him she'd changed her mind about going. Or that she'd be back in a month because she couldn't stand to be without him. She might ask him to take a break from work, to fly over and meet her for a romantic weekend in Paris or Rome, then surprise him by accompanying him back to Australia. To his bed, his home, his life.

And that would be the emotion of the night talking. But in the clear light of day...

Sophie's hands were cold. It was a clear Gold Coast day but she clamped them together to ease the chill while she waited beside her luggage. Her gaze roamed over the apartment she'd called home for the past four years. The plumped cushions, the cheery mugs on the kitchen bench. The first place she'd ever felt comfortable in. Safe in. Melissa would love it. Jared would no doubt come by and check on his sister...*Jared.*

Last night... Two fat tears welled up and spilled down her cheeks. When she was ready, when she was strong enough, brave enough, she'd write it all down. The man, the memories. She'd start a book of memoirs instead of a dream diary—she didn't need that crutch any more. Jared had taught her self-acceptance, given her back her self-esteem.

She just couldn't be the woman he needed.

He'd dropped her off after a quick lunch in the hotel's bistro and was coming by any moment now to take her to the airport. But he wouldn't be taking her—she'd booked a cab. No lingering farewells. A swift clean break.

She jumped at his familiar knock, checked her watch

then, inhaling a deep breath, walked to the door and pulled it open.

Their eyes met. The way they had the first time he'd come to her door. Same heart-stopping response. He'd always be *it* for her. She dredged up a smile. 'You're early.'

He didn't smile back, just stood there a moment, then rubbed a hand over his jaw. 'I wanted to talk to you before we leave for the airport.'

He closed the door, tangled her fingers with his to lead her to the couch. 'It might be easier if we sit down.'

Perched on the edge, she watched his eyes change, the way they did when he was deep in thought. Or deep inside her…

Her whole body went rigid—with fear, with hope, with fear again. Her heart wept in her chest. She would have clenched her fingers together again or pulled them away but he had a firm hold on both hands. She shook her head. 'I think we—'

'Sophie.' He looked down at their joined hands, then up to her eyes again. 'I realise my timing's all wrong, and maybe you don't want to hear this, but I can't let you leave without telling you.'

Her breath hitched and he paused, just looking at her like… like…

'I know you need to tick this trip off your list of life's goals,' he said, 'and if you don't you'll regret it. I will never intentionally tread on your dreams, Sophie, or try to stifle your life in any way, but I was thinking, *hoping*, that we might—'

'Stop.' She tugged her hands from his and pushed at him. 'Wait.' He was heading in a direction she couldn't go and her heart was already breaking. 'I need to tell *you* something first.'

Needing distance and at least some modicum of control, she stood. Not wanting to read what she'd see in those jade-green eyes, she needed to look somewhere else, anywhere but at his face. She dropped her chin, stared at the floor. 'I can't have children, Jared.' Her words choked in her throat and in the stunned silence she heard his indrawn breath. 'So whatever you were about to say, don't.'

She was aware of the muted traffic hum and small bird chatter outside the window. The refrigerator's noisy drone kicked in.

'Sophie…honey…' he began, finally. 'I…'

Closing her eyes, she shook her head. 'No. I don't want to hear it.'

'Okay. I need a minute here.' His voice was tight, as if he was having trouble breathing.

She knew. He was having trouble breathing because he was *deciding on the best way to extricate himself from the knot he'd been about to tie around his own throat.*

'I should have told you.' She opened her eyes, this time daring to look up, past compressed lips and into that maelstrom in his eyes. *Or maybe I shouldn't have told you at all.*

And now to tell him the whole truth and nothing but the truth. 'I fell in love with you, Jared. Your loyalty, your sense of humour, your perceptiveness, your integrity. You've given me the most precious of gifts. You valued me as an employee, desired me as a lover, you respect me as a woman. You've given me strength and a new belief in myself, but I can't give you what you want most.'

Jared stared at her while an iron fist pummelled his chest. 'Let me be the judge of that.' His words slashed the air, harsh and deep, like the shock carving a canyon through his body. 'I'll be the one who decides what I want.'

'Don't you see?' she said softly. 'I'm saving you from having to make that decision.' The sound of a car's horn drew her attention to the window. 'I have to go—I have a cab waiting.'

'But…hang on just a damn minute here.' He crossed to her in quick strides, caught her arm. 'I'm taking you to the airport. We arranged it.'

Again she lifted her hand to his chest. 'No. Please, no. I hate emotional airport goodbyes. It's better this way.'

'So you're…what…just dropping this bomb on me and leaving? Without giving me a chance to discuss this with you?'

'There's nothing to say. It's just the way it is.'

'The *hell* it is.' He slammed a fist against his thigh. He felt as if he were sinking in quicksand. He needed time but he didn't have it.

The buzzer sounded and she walked to the door, opened it. 'Good afternoon, just these cases,' she told the cabbie, indicating the two rolling suitcases beside her.

She swung a large bag over her shoulder, then placed her key on the kitchen bench. 'You'll need this to lock up.'

So caught up in the whirlwind tearing through his mind, he almost forgot, withdrawing a brown-paper package from his jacket pocket. 'Parting gift. Don't open it till you're on your way tomorrow.' He crossed the few steps between them, tucked it into her carry-all.

'Oh…thank you…' Her eyes welled with moisture. 'I left something for you too. With Melissa. She's at home with it, waiting for you right now.' She leaned close and whispered, 'Goodbye, Jared,' then kissed him softly.

Her lips clung to his for the longest time. Not long enough. Not nearly long enough.

And then she was gone.

A short time later he was staring down at the skinny black and white dog in Melissa's arms, a new red collar around his scrawny neck. 'What's the mutt doing here?' he demanded. But he couldn't resist scratching behind the silky ears. He'd always been a sucker where animals were concerned. 'Looks like he could do with a good feed.'

'This is Angus and he's from the pound. He's a year old so you don't have to worry about the puppy thing. He's fully house-trained and vaccinated and needs a loving home.' She held him out. 'He's yours.'

'Mine? I don't want a dog. What would I do with a dog?'

'He's Sophie's gift to you,' she said softly.

He frowned, stepping away, denying the choked feeling clawing up his throat. She'd given him a dog. 'What in hell was she thinking?' he muttered. 'You need to spend time with them, walk them, train them.' *Love them.*

That was what she'd been thinking.

'Sophie's thoughts exactly,' Lissa said. 'He'll be a companion now that you're on your own. You'll need to come home from work earlier—a good thing, Jared. Sophie understood that. She left food, bedding, toys…and a letter.'

He reached for the envelope in Lissa's hand.

Dear Jared,

Angus means 'unique choice', and that's what he is—the moment I saw him at the kennels, my search for a suitable companion for you was over. You said you didn't have time for pets but now you'll make the time. And in return, I promise that Angus will give you absolute loyalty and unconditional love.

Sophie.

CHAPTER FIFTEEN

BARELY over her jet lag, Sophie walked into a job in a London pub on her fourth day. Waiting tables wasn't her preferred choice but the position included meals and dormitory-style accommodation and it suited her fine for now.

It kept her hands busy and her mind occupied, she reminded herself three weeks later as she climbed the narrow staircase to the room she shared with two Aussies and an American from Philadelphia. Dwelling on Jared and what she'd left behind was a waste of energy and was a downer on what was supposed to be the best year of her life.

While she showered she reminded herself that even if he'd asked her to cancel her plans and stay with him she'd have said no. Which he wouldn't have, she thought, remembering his promise not to tread on her dreams. It was finally her turn and she'd worked long and hard for it.

Under different circumstances she might have told the man she loved she'd come back and asked him if he'd wait. But these weren't ordinary circumstances and this was no ordinary man. This was Jared, who loved kids, wanted a family and had already broken up with one woman because she didn't want children cluttering up their lives. In fact he'd been openly frank about it.

Her room mates had gone clubbing after their shifts but she'd told them she was too tired. She slipped into long flannel pants and a T-shirt and climbed into bed. It had become a nightly ritual to deal with her emails first. Another to tell herself she didn't expect Jared to contact her. And he didn't.

But every night she got that same fluttering anticipation in her belly when she opened her inbox, and the same dragging sensation when she didn't see his name. She'd had a couple of emails from Pam, but nothing about the office and Jared and how he was doing. Same with his sister. Melissa loved her new living arrangements, Angus was putting on weight and growing more handsome by the day. But no mention of his new owner.

Tonight was no different and she closed her laptop refusing to be disappointed. She was going to compose another entry in her new book of dreams instead. She caressed the silk-brocade-covered notebook. Jared's farewell package. He'd written on the first page:

Sophie,
For your dreams. May they all come true.
Always, Jared.

She'd spent the long-haul flight crying and staring out of the window and wondering what he was doing. What *she* was doing.

She'd unwrapped it somewhere over China and could almost hear him tell her, 'They'll be safer on paper...' And she could still see him smile that sexy smile that said he shared the joke.

Except now she wrote daydreams. Castles-in-the-air dreams. Where she and Jared and their offspring played happy families for ever after.

Impossible dreams that could never come true.

'Pam,' Jared boomed from his office at four o'clock one after-noon. 'The reports on those soil samples for Surfers' Retreat and Spa should've been back Monday. Get on the phone and give them a blast, I—'

'Calm down.' Pam popped her head into Jared's office and added in a lower but no less aggravated voice, 'You're frightening Mimi, not to mention little Angus there.'

He looked down at the bundle of black and white fur in the basket. Angus whimpered while two black eyes stared up at him. He didn't approve of dogs in the office, but this afternoon it had been unavoidable.

'It's okay, boy. Go back to your puppy-dog dreams. Liss'll be here to pick you up any minute now.' And didn't the mutt look spiffy with his new doggy trim and shampoo?

Shaking her head, Pam watched him like an exasperated parent complaining over her unruly child. 'I left a hard copy on your desk on Monday afternoon.'

Jared ran his hands down his cheeks and muttered, 'Where the hell is it now, then?' When Pam popped back out again, he muttered some more choice phrases she wouldn't want to hear.

He stared at his desk. Or what he could see of it. He'd sort it tonight when Pam went home. It would give him something to do. He leaned back in his chair and scowled.

Maybe he wouldn't sort it at all. He should take Angus for a walk on the beach. He'd left the little guy with Melissa too many times to count and it wasn't fair on the dog. Or Liss—she wasn't supposed to have pets in her apartment and was growing tired of splitting her time between her new home and his.

Sophie's idea wasn't working.

Sophie.

It had been over three weeks since she'd left. Three fiercely frustrating weeks where he lay in bed at night and remembered how Sophie had looked on their last evening together. How she'd felt beside him—smooth and sexy and silky.

Three long lean weeks where he didn't sleep, couldn't eat. Where he clocked up a ridiculous number of hours in the office and still his workload increased—no surprise there because his efficiency was decreasing.

He yanked open the filing cabinet beside his desk. Maybe he'd filed that report himself without reading it. Nope. He slammed the drawer shut again.

Sophie.

She'd smelled like summer and he found himself breathing deeply, as if he might conjure up the fragrance.

He hadn't contacted her but he knew she'd arrived safely because Pam had informed him. That had been a damn difficult day. It could only get better, right?

Wrong.

She'd left him. *Them.* There wasn't a *them*, he reminded himself. He'd had his chance to tell her how he felt. Days. Weeks, even. He'd always known she was leaving, she'd always been open about her plans.

She'd been honest about everything, except, it seemed, what mattered most.

She loved him.

She'd told him she loved him in the same breath she'd told him she couldn't have children. His silence had hurt her, he knew. But how was a man supposed to get his head around that bomb two minutes before she left for the other side of the world?

His open palm connected solidly with his desk. The registered packet that he'd signed for earlier today slipped a bit and caught his eye. He reached for it. The compact book slid out, he flipped to the first page and studied his photo. He'd never had a passport. Never needed one.

Pam appeared in the doorway and she didn't look happy. 'Impeccable timing,' he told her, leaning back in his chair, hands braced on the edge of his desk. 'Shut the door, I want to talk to you.'

'Good, because I have a few things to say to you too.' In a firm but businesslike manner she closed the door and sat down opposite him. Shoved a hand through her unruly brown locks. 'Does the word "resignation" mean anything to you?'

He barked out a humourless laugh. Then stared at her. She hadn't moved. Her mouth was flat, her eyes steady on his. 'You're serious.' Straightening, he rolled his chair nearer and placed his hands on the desk.

'Maybe I am. If you don't sort yourself out, I won't be the only one requesting that form.'

A strange feeling slid through him and his heart thumped hard in his chest.

'Excuses, stalling, evading,' she went on. 'They've never cut it with you, Jared, and they won't cut it with me. You're my friend as well as my boss, and Sophie's as close as a sister.'

She ran out of breath but he was the one who sat back as if he'd just run a marathon. He slid the legal document across the desk. 'So what do you say to this, then? How would you like to try out the boss's chair for a while?'

She met his eyes. 'Fine by me, but I'll need a raise.'

'You got it.'

She nodded, a smile chasing away the worry lines. 'That's the Jared I know.' Rising, she kissed him on the cheek and closed the door softly behind her on her way out.

He sat there and made lists, contacted clients, postponed projects while the sky turned from blue to apricot rose to aqua. He was still there when lavender had long turned indigo and a shimmering gold staircase on the sea pointed the way to a full moon rising.

Then he picked up the phone and called Liss. 'I know it's an imposition but I was wondering if you could stay over at the house for a bit and look after Angus. I'm taking a trip.'

When Sophie clicked into her inbox after her late shift a couple of nights later she saw the email she'd hoped for, waited for, dreaded. Her hands stilled on the keyboard, her breath hitched and everything, everything seemed to stop. Why now after all these weeks?

She blinked to make sure she hadn't imagined it, but there it was. 'Jared Sanderson' in bold black print. Flagged as high priority with a document with the enigmatic title of 'rustymagpie' attached.

Torn between elation and despair, she chewed on her lip while one finger trembled above the delete key. She could kill it with one click of a button. Any contact would jab at the still-raw wound in her heart and set her back by weeks.

Just this unopened email had the power to hurt simply by its very existence. Because she loved him and she'd opened her heart and told him everything and he'd rejected her. It could only be rejection, because he'd made no attempt to contact her. Nor did she expect him to. She'd not been honest with him until too late. She'd wanted him close as long as she could have him. Selfish. Thoughtless. No better than Bianca.

But like a chocoholic craving her next double-dipped dark-chocolate rum truffle, she clicked on his name. There was no message in the body of the email. She opened the attachment.

A rainbow of watercolours bled onto the screen as the file loaded. There was music, soft and sweet and low, a song about Sophie's presence still lingering there and not leaving him alone...

She knuckled moisture away from her eyes. Oh, he sure knew how to make her tear up. She should have deleted it. And yet...and yet...why would he do this?

The music finished and words scrolled onto the screen in a romantically flowing script:

Last night I had a dream. It was Tuesday morning. Ten o'clock—I remember because somewhere I heard a clock chime the hour. And I was standing at the Victoria Memorial in front of Buckingham Palace. Waiting for you. Charcoal clouds sagged, their underbellies like Spanish moss above the sculptured marble statues and Victory's gold wings. But still it was a magical place, just like you said.

And I made a wish. And in the way of dreams, the clouds dissolved and then the whole world was shining and golden and I turned and you were walking towards me with such a smile that I could barely breathe…

Sophie's breath caught. Now she was the one who could barely breathe. She concentrated on drawing air in, filling her lungs as far as she could. Letting it out slowly.

Tomorrow was Tuesday…

The realisation smacked her upright. No. No, no, no. She slammed the machine shut. Slid it to the bottom of her bed. *Not* possible. Jared was *not* in London and he was definitely *not* going to be waiting for her in front of the Victoria Memorial tomorrow morning. Never gonna happen. Lies. All lies, designed to make her…what?

She wanted to cry and scream and pull her hair out. *And dare to hope?* The best she could do was to drag the thin quilt over her head and pretend she'd never read it.

But of course she couldn't sleep. And she couldn't pretend. She sniffed under the cover of darkness and tried to sift through her jumbled thoughts and emotions. At ten o'clock tomorrow morning she was going to make sure she was sightseeing at Windsor Castle or Oxford or somewhere well away from Buckingham Palace.

Except…that was the coward's way out and if he really was here…he was here to see her…and what was that telling her? Had he really left his business and come all this way around the world *just to see her*?

You didn't come all the way around the world just to *see* someone. Her heart throbbed harder. Not ordinary people anyway.

Maybe it was just an email after all. To tell her…what…? Little shivers rippled up and down her body. What if…?

Jared stopped pacing a groove around the Victoria Memorial to check his watch for the third time in two minutes. If she didn't turn up soon he was going to wear a rut in the pavement.

He fisted his hands in the pockets of his coat. *Positive thoughts.* He was a positive kind of guy, wasn't he? Tourists swirled around him, snapping photos, enjoying London's brisk morning. It smelled of autumn and fresh-turned earth from the garden beds nearby. A couple of kids chased up and down the shallow steps.

Had she even read his email? he wondered for the millionth time. Maybe she didn't check daily… Maybe she hadn't understood the message.

Maybe she'd simply deleted it unread.

She'd be here.

And as if those words had conjured her up, there she was. Walking towards the memorial, her hands in the pockets of a rust-coloured coat. She wore black boots and a cream beret on her dark hair. Looking at her was like looking at a cream cupcake when you've been on a life-long diet.

When she passed the Buckingham Palace gates she caught sight of him and their gazes collided. Fused. He had to breathe in deep because suddenly he'd forgotten how. She appeared to falter, then picked up the pace again. Moving swiftly.

He moved too, dodging a group of noisy schoolkids on an excursion and for a moment he lost sight of her behind a tall robust man but then, there she was, smiling at him and he could smell her familiar fragrance before he could reach out and cup her face between his hands and lose himself in those dewy amber eyes.

He hauled her face to his before she could answer and kissed her. Tasted her unique sweet caramel flavour, heard her murmured sigh against his mouth. And all he knew was that he never wanted to let her go again. He drew back a little to see her better, stroking her cheeks before he took her hands and held them against his chest.

'Jared.' A shadowed expression crossed her face and her smile faded a little and he knew he'd put those shadows there.

'How long have you been here?' she asked, obviously expecting him to loosen her hands. 'In London, I mean.'

He didn't let her go. 'Just over twenty-four hours.'

'I got your email...' With a rueful grimace, she shook her head. 'Of course I did or I wouldn't be here...'

An awkward silence suddenly enveloped them. 'Let's go somewhere nearby where we can talk,' he suggested.

'St James's Park,' she said, indicating the way. Already a local, he thought, and, still holding one trembling hand, he accompanied her along the footpath.

They had a somewhat stilted conversation while they walked along Pall Mall. Her job was busy, she loved London. She'd seen the Tower and Westminster Abbey and been to Brighton on her day off last week. Melissa was enjoying her new apartment but staying at the house to babysit Angus. And yes, the mutt was gaining weight. A real personality, no doubt about that.

But all he could think was how right her hand felt in his, how he'd missed her, how much he wanted her in his life.

They passed through some beautiful ornate gates and, because the ground was damp, chose a wooden bench facing the lake. Autumn was busy here, painting a glorious palette of red and brown and gold amongst the green. A weeping willow on the little island in the lake reflected in the water. Even the air smelled different.

Sophie breathed in the scents of autumn and Jared. As long as she lived, she'd never forget this moment. They sat at an angle facing one another. He'd lost a few kilos. Fatigue shadowed his green eyes but there was emotion there too. And nerves, she thought, like her. She waited for him to speak first.

'Sophie.' He paused, then took both her hands and looked into her eyes. 'First off, I love you, Sophie. I'll always love you.'

She blinked up at him. Just for a moment her heart glowed and the whole world glowed with the wonder of it. A huge ball of emotion lodged in her throat.

'And knowing that you feel the same way, I have a question. The most important question I'll ever ask. Sophie Buchanan... will you marry me?' He squeezed her hands, his green-eyed gaze so tender and true she felt as if she'd been sliced through the heart, because it couldn't happen—not with them. She'd told him why.

'No.'

Something flitted across his gaze but he jogged their joined hands gently on his knees just once. Then he leaned in, pressed a quick but tender kiss on her lips. 'You told me you loved me—have you changed your mind already?'

'I... No.'

'Well, I sure as hell can't think of a single solitary reason why two people who love each other shouldn't get married.'

'You know why. Kids, Jared. You want kids. You...you told me you broke up with Bianca because she didn't want children.'

'Ah, Sophie, Sophie, is that what you thought?' He shook his head, pressed a kiss to her brow. 'I broke up with Bianca because she didn't want *Melissa* as part of the marriage deal. She expected me to shunt her off to her big sister after we got married and I wouldn't do it. That's entirely different, honey.'

'Oh...' It was, it was. Sophie's heart started to gallop.

'Now, is there any other reason?' he said. 'Because if there's not I'm going to ask you to marry me again.'

'You didn't try to stop me leaving, you didn't tell me you loved me when I left.'

'Because I was fighting my feelings. Afraid of how I felt. And I knew how much you wanted this trip, Sophie. I wouldn't dream of trying to stop you. After what you told me I needed time to think. I asked myself if I wanted those kids without you, and the answer is no. Never. You are my life, Sophie.'

She could no longer hold those carefully banked tears back and they spilled over and down her cheeks. 'I know how much you love kids, what a great father you'd make...'

Barely a pause, hardly a flicker in his eye. But there was something steely in the determined jut of his jaw. 'Sophie. *We* can't have children. We, plural. Shared. The two of us. Together. I'll say it again—*we* can't have children.'

Her tears spilled faster. He'd known, yet still he'd come all the way across the world for her. Because he loved her. He wanted to marry her.

'Tell me about it,' he begged her softly. 'Did you lose a baby? Is that why you didn't want anything to do with Arabella?'

She sniffed away her tears. 'I'd always wanted children. Glen wanted children almost as badly as me. But I'd always had problems in that area. When I didn't fall pregnant they ran tests. The doctors told me it was unlikely I'd ever conceive even with surgery, I had too much scarred tissue. And I was only twenty-one.

'Then a miracle happened. I was pregnant.' She looked down at her hands, remembering the heartache. 'It was an ectopic pregnancy. After...I only had one tube left and my chances were halved. Practically zero.'

She was conscious of Jared's hand over hers, his quiet empathy. 'Go on,' he murmured.

'Glen didn't see why he should miss out on being a father just because I was only half a woman—'

'Hang on, *half a woman*? He said that?'

She nodded and felt a tremor run from his hand to hers. 'So he set out to find a woman who could give him what I couldn't. He didn't consider being married to me to be an impediment.

Apparently he worked his way through quite a few lovers before he hit the jackpot.'

'Bastard.' The word slid out between clenched teeth.

'I think so.'

'Did you look at other alternatives? IVF, for instance?'

She shook her head. 'Why would Glen want to pay all that money with no guarantees? A divorce is faster and cheaper. And far easier to go out and find someone more fertile to father his offspring.'

'I'm not like Glen.' He seemed to choke on the man's name.

She looked into his eyes. 'I know you're not like him. But I've seen you with Arabella and I know how good you are with babies. You'd want your own children...'

He shook his head. 'Sophie, maybe under present circumstances we can't have our own children, but we haven't really given it a go yet, have we? You talked about your miracle—what makes you think two miracles can't happen? In the meantime we can look into those alternatives. And if all else fails, we can foster or adopt. There are always kids in need of loving homes. You have to remember, you're not alone in this. We're a team. All you have to do is say you'll marry me.'

'You mean that.' She breathed the wonder of it. 'You really mean it.'

'Don't look so surprised, honey.' Smiling at her, he stroked her hair. 'Of course I do, with all my heart and soul and everything that I have.'

'I love you too, and I don't want to be without you but it's taken me years to get here...I...haven't finished yet.'

'That's okay. I've taken leave. I've never taken leave so I reckon I deserve it. And I've got a nice suite for the two of us in a top hotel with a view of the Thames a ten-minute walk from your place of work. That is if you still want to work... Or would you rather travel the UK and Europe in style? With me.'

'Oh…' A whole new world was opening up to her. A world with Jared by her side…

'You don't have to be alone any more, Sophie. Let me be a part of your decisions. Let's make those plans together. Paris, Rome, Florence…wherever you want to go. As long as we go home together when we're done.'

Home. And she realised that was what she wanted, more than anything. To have this man—the man she loved—sharing her life. The good times…and the bad. She could still maintain her independence. She knew Jared would support her one hundred per cent in whatever she chose to do.

She looked up into his eyes warm with love. 'Yes,' she murmured, then louder, clearer, firmer, 'Yes. I'll marry you.'

The visitors to St James's Park might have looked on in amusement as he let out a joyous whoop then rose, hauling her up with him. 'Right answer,' he murmured, before laying his mouth against hers. Then, lips locked, he managed to twirl her around three times before setting her down.

He grabbed her hand once more and they began retracing their steps back to the Mall. 'Do you think you can get the evening off?'

'We have the afternoon…'

EPILOGUE

Two years later

SOPHIE smiled as she glanced out of the kitchen window while she stirred the gravy for their traditional lamb roast dinner. She loved lazy Sunday afternoons when all the family was here. Lissa and Jared were playing ball with a chubby little Arabella and a much larger Goldie while Angus chased and barked joyously between their feet. Crystal and Ian watched on under the shade of an umbrella.

They'd been back in Australia for twenty-two months now. It hadn't taken Sophie long to decide to give up the job in favour of being with Jared. They'd completed a whirlwind tour of the UK, France and Italy but in the end they'd just wanted to get home and become husband and wife and Jared couldn't neglect his business commitments any longer.

They were living in a beautifully renovated house with a large garden where Arabella could play when she visited, which was at least twice a week. Jared had given up his idea of condo living in favour of a more family-friendly home. Space to grow…

And miracles did happen twice. It had taken time, pain and a few disappointments, but now…Sophie touched her slightly rounded belly as she watched Jared pick up his squealing niece and toss her into the air. The modern miracle of IVF had given her a second chance. Given *them* a second chance.

At that moment Jared glanced at the window and she waved.

She saw him set Arabella down by Lissa and walk towards the back door. Twenty seconds later he was right there behind her, their linked hands resting over their unborn child. Already sixteen weeks along and everything was fine.

Sophie had never felt healthier in her life.

'What say we tell them the good news now?' he murmured against her ear. 'I don't think I can wait till after lunch.'

'Me neither.' She smiled. She was doing a lot of that these days. She checked the oven, untied her apron. 'Let's get this celebration started.'

He took her hands and lifted them to his lips, murmuring, 'Have I told you today how much I love you?'

'In so many ways,' she murmured back, kissing their joined hands.

And together they walked out into the sunshine.

Discover more romance at

www.millsandboon.co.uk

- ❤ WIN great prizes in our exclusive competitions
- ❤ BUY new titles before they hit the shops
- ❤ BROWSE new books and REVIEW your favourites
- ❤ SAVE on new books with the Mills & Boon® Bookclub™
- ❤ DISCOVER new authors

PLUS, to chat about your favourite reads, get the latest news and find special offers:

- Find us on facebook.com/millsandboon
- Follow us on twitter.com/millsandboonuk
- ❤ Sign up to our newsletter at millsandboon.co.uk

EB_SD

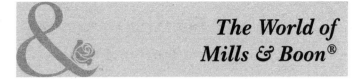

The World of Mills & Boon®

There's a Mills & Boon® series that's perfect for you. We publish ten series and, with new titles every month, you never have to wait long for your favourite to come along.

By Request

Relive the romance with the best of the best
12 stories every month

™

Experience the ultimate rush of falling in love
12 new stories every month

Desire™

Passionate and dramatic love stories
6 new stories every month

n o c t u r n e™

An exhilarating underworld of dark desires
Up to 3 new stories every month

What will you treat yourself to next?

INTRIGUE... *A seductive combination of danger and desire...*
6 new stories every month

Awaken the romance of the past...
6 new stories every month

The ultimate in romantic medical drama
6 new stories every month

MODERN™ *Power, passion and irresistible temptation*
8 new stories every month

MODERN **tempted**™ *True love and temptation!*
4 new stories every month